W9-BUF-169

Catch and Release

Catch and Release

Stories *by* **Lawrence Block**

Subterranean Press 2013

Design direction by Max Phillips.
www.maxphillips.net

First Edition

ISBN
978-1-59606-571-0

Subterranean Press
PO Box 190106
Burton, MI 48519

The name "Hard Case Crime" and the Hard Case Crime logo
are trademarks of Winterfall LLC. Hard Case Crime books
are selected and edited by Charles Ardai.

www.subterraneanpress.com
www.hardcasecrime.com

CONTENTS

A BURGLAR'S-EYE VIEW OF GREED

S O I WALKED OVER to Barnegat Books on East Eleventh Street for a word with my favorite bookseller, Bernie Rhodenbarr. He was behind the counter with his nose in a book while his cat lay in the window, soaking up the sun. The store's sole customer was a young woman with multiple piercings who was reading a biography of St. Sebastian.

"I understand the used-book business is hot these days," I said. "You must be making money hand over fist."

He gave me a look. "Every now and then," he said, "somebody actually buys a book. It's a good thing I don't have to depend on this place to keep body and soul together."

He doesn't have to pay rent, either, having bought the building with the profits from his other career as the last of the gentleman burglars. Seriously, I told him, lots of people were making big bucks selling books on the Internet. Couldn't he do the same?

"I could," he agreed. "I could list my entire stock on Ebay and spend my time wrapping books and shlepping them to the Post Office. I could close the store, because who needs a retail outlet when you've got a computer and a modem? But I didn't open this store to get rich. I opened it so I could have a bookstore, and have fun running it, and occasionally meet girls. See, I'm not greedy."

"But you steal," I pointed out.

He frowned, and nodded toward St. Sebastian's biggest fan. "Not to get rich," he said. "Only enough to get by. I don't want to get rich, see, because it would turn me into a greedy pig."

"You're saying the rich are greedy?"

7

"They don't necessarily start out that way," he said, "but that's how it seems to work. Look at all the CEOs with their eight-figure salaries. The more you pay them, the more they want, and when the company goes down the tubes they float down on their golden parachute and look for another corporation to sink. Or look at baseball."

"Baseball?"

"America's pastime," he said. "The players used to have off-season jobs so they could make ends meet. The owners were always rich guys, but they were in it for the sport. They didn't expect to make money."

"And?"

"And now the players average something like two million dollars a year, and the owners have watched their investments increase in value by a factor of five or ten, and everybody's rich, so everybody's greedy. And that's why we're going to have a strike this fall. Because they're all pigs, and all they want is more."

"In other words," I said, "success turns men to swine."

"And women," he said. "Success is an equal-opportunity corrupter. And it seems to be inevitable nowadays. Nobody's happy just running a business and making a living. Everybody wants to grow the business, and either franchise it or sell it to a huge corporation. Luckily, I'm safe. Nobody's aching to franchise Barnegat Books, and no multinational corporation's trying to buy me out."

"So you'll go on selling books."

"Every now and then," he said, as the young woman put St. Sebastian back on the shelf and walked away empty-handed. "I'll tell you, it's a good thing I'm a thief. It keeps me honest."

A CHANCE TO GET EVEN

A LITTLE AFTER MIDNIGHT, Gordon Benning, a balding gastroenterologist with a perpetually dyspeptic expression on his long face, announced as he dealt the cards that his next deal would be his final hand. Several players indicated their agreement, and one, a CPA with a propensity for stating the obvious, said, "So this is the last round."

And so it was. Richard Krale (Dick to his friends, Richard to his wife, who reserved the diminutive for a specific portion of her husband) would have preferred it otherwise. He wished the game could go on for another three hours, so that he might recoup his losses, or that it had ended three hours earlier, when he'd been briefly ahead. Now he had, what? Six, seven hands to get even?

The game was dealer's choice, and ninety percent of the time the choice was seven-card stud. The dealer anted a buck for the table, the limit was five dollars, ten dollars on the last card. (The same betting rules applied in five-card stud. In draw poker, the bet was five dollars before the draw, ten dollars after.)

Krale was the host, as well as being the evening's big loser. In the latter capacity more than the former, he suggested doubling the betting limits for the final round. That was all right with Mark Taggert, who had a mountain of chips in front of him, but the other players shook their heads dismissively, and that was that. It was by no means unusual for someone, generally the biggest loser, to make this suggestion; it was always voted down.

And that was just as well for Krale, as it turned out, because his luck was no better in the last round than it had been for the preceding three hours. It was worse, if anything, because desperation led him to play hands he'd have been well advised to fold at their onset, and to stay to the end in hands where he should have cut his losses. When Benning dealt the last hand of the evening, Krale chased flush and straight possibilities, backed into two pair, queens over fives, tried to buy the pot with a raise, and lost to Taggert's three sixes.

"Hey, the night's a pup," he said. "No reason to quit now."

No one even bothered to respond. They were all counting their chips and figuring out what they had coming, and in turn they announced their totals and waited for Krale to pay them. He'd set aside the cash they'd all bought in with, and when that was gone he still had two players to pay off—Norm McLeod, who had $120 coming, and Taggert, who'd had a very good last round.

He dug out his wallet, counted out five twenties and a pair of tens, and paid McLeod, who looked almost apologetic as he pocketed the money. Taggert, who looked not at all apologetic, announced that the chips in front of him came to $538.

"Stick around," Krale said. "I'll have to write you a check."

THE OTHERS left, and Krale shook their hands and wished them well. Then he took his time finding his checkbook.

"Some run of cards," he said.

"You caught a lot of second-best hands," Taggert said. "Nothing much you can do when that happens but wait for the cards to turn."

"They never did."

"There's always next week."

"I hate to wait that long," Krale said. He'd uncapped the pen but had not as yet touched it to the check. "You in a rush to get home?"

"You want to play some more?"

"I wouldn't mind."

"Heads up, you mean? Just the two of us?"

Krale made a show of looking to his left and right, then at Taggert. "I don't see anybody else here," he said, "so I guess we're stuck with each other."

Taggert thought about it. "I'll just keep these chips, then."

"Right. And I'll help myself from the bank." He did so, stacking the chips in front of him, giving himself a bigger bankroll than Taggert's. That would help psychologically, he told himself. The player with fewer chips was at a disadvantage, doomed to play with a loser's mentality. This way he could feel like a winner, and it was only a matter of time before he'd be one.

Taggert didn't seem awed by Krale's chips. He rearranged his own stacks, and for some reason the new arrangement made it look to Krale as though there were more of them.

"Same rules?"

Krale nodded. "Except we can forget about the three-raise limit," he said. "Since there's just the two of us."

"Makes sense."

"How about a drink before we get started?"

"Good idea," Taggert said.

Krale went to the bar and poured a brandy for each of them. They sat with their drinks, and he suggested they cut for deal, and then his wife walked into the room. She said, "Hi, hon. I hope it went—" and stopped in midsentence when she realized her husband had company.

"Hello, Tina."

"Mark," she said. "I'm sorry, I wouldn't have come in if I'd known you were still here."

"What's the matter, don't you love me anymore?"

She grinned. "I know better than to interrupt you boys. Poker's a serious matter."

"Oh, it's not all that serious," Taggert said. "We just pretend it's serious so that we can keep up our interest in it. Like war or business."

"I see."

"Mark's the big winner," Krale said, "and he's giving me a chance to win some of my money back."

"You'll probably win it all back," Taggert said, "and then some."

"Not unless the cards turn."

"They always do, sooner or later."

"Well," Tina Krale said. "Is it all right if I wish you both good luck?"

When she left the room, Taggert's eyes lingered on her retreating form. This did not go unnoticed by Krale.

• • •

THEY CUT cards to determine who'd deal the first hand, and Krale was high.

"Look at that," Taggert said. "The cards are turning already."

But his tone was ironic, and it was clear to Krale that he didn't believe it. Taggert expected to go on winning for as long as Krale sat across the table form him. As though it wasn't a matter of luck, or cards, or the breaks of the game. As though it was all predetermined by the character of the players, and winners won while losers lost, and he was a winner as sure as Krale was a loser.

A loser with a big house and a going business and money in the bank. A loser with a beautiful wife.

But a loser all the same.

The big house was mortgaged to the rafters. The money in the bank came to less than the outstanding bills. The going business…well, it was going, all right. Going broke, going to hell in a handbasket, going, barring a miracle, out of business. Going, going, gone.

And the beautiful wife?

Krale took a deep breath and dealt the cards.

HALF A dozen rounds in, Taggert dealt and Krale looked at a deuce and six to go with the ten he had showing. Different suits, of course. "Check," he said, and Taggert shook his head.

"Oh, right," Krale said. They'd changed the rules to avoid hands that got checked to excess, and whoever was high had to make a first-round bet. "Bet," he said, unnecessarily, and tossed a chip into the pot.

His next card paired the six. This time he was entitled to check, and did, but Taggert bet, and the pair of sixes kept him in the hand. He kept having enough to call, and the ten he caught on the river gave him two pair, and he knew his tens up were beat but called the last bet anyway, because he had so much in the pot already, and Taggert had kings up and won the hand.

He gathered up the cards, shuffled them. "Maybe we should raise the stakes," he suggested.

"Sure," Taggert said. "What do you say we make the raise retroactive?"

"Very funny."

"I've got a better idea, Dick. Why don't we call it a night?"

"I thought you were going to give me a chance to get even."

"At this rate, that'll take a while."

"So we'll raise the stakes."

"To what?"

"We've been playing five and ten. Let's up it to ten-twenty."

"Fine with me," Taggert said.

AT FIRST he thought raising the stakes was the charm. He won three small pots in a row, got out of a fourth hand with an early fold, and then, after staying in too long with an unmade hand, caught the king of hearts for a flush while Taggert, who'd held three queens all the way, failed to catch his full house. He bet the hand, too, and pulled in a handsome pot.

"Well played," Taggert said. Krale glowed, even though he knew he hadn't really played the hand well. He shouldn't have stayed long enough to catch that king, and he'd had no business betting into Taggert at the end. He'd been lucky, lucky to catch the king, lucky that Taggert hadn't filled.

But wasn't that as good as playing smart? In fact, wasn't it better? Because it meant that the cards were turning, that his luck was returning, and that he could get even and then some. Wouldn't it be nice if the evening ended with Taggert writing a check to him instead of the other way around?

Taggert yawned. Because he was tired? Or because he wanted to appear tired, so he'd have an excuse to end the game?

"Hang on a sec," Krale said.

He left without an explanation and came back a few minutes later with a glass of brandy for each of them. "A little pick-me-up," he said. "And how do you take your coffee? Tina's making a fresh pot."

"I don't like to drink coffee after dinner," Taggert said. "It screws up my sleeping."

"I find they smooth one another out," Krale said. "The coffee and the brandy. Keeps you awake while you're at the table, then lets you sleep like a baby when you get home."

"And in the morning?"

"You wake up bright-eyed and bushy-tailed and ready to do battle."

Taggert raised an eyebrow. "You've made a study of this," he said.

13

"Personal observation," he said, "along with an exhaustive study of the available literature." He raised his glass, and Taggert, after a moment, raised his.

YOU HAD to expect the occasional setback. You couldn't sit there and win every hand. But this one hurt.

He'd started with nines rolled up, two down and one up, trip nines, gorgeous cards. And he'd nursed them along, played them just right, while Taggert got enough of a diamond flush to keep him in the hand. And on sixth street Krale stopped caring about Taggert's diamonds, because he caught a pair for the five he had showing, which gave him a full house, so who cared if Taggert had his flush?

With the river cards dealt, he bet and Taggert raised, which made him very happy, and he raised back and so did Taggert, and now he wasn't all that happy. Taggert had four diamonds showing, and there was no way he could have a straight flush, not with the five and nine of diamonds in Krale's hand, but neither was there any way Taggert could make that second raise with nothing better than a flush.

So Krale called, and Taggert turned over a pair of tens that matched one of his diamonds and an eight that matched another, giving him tens full, which, alas, beat Krale's nines full.

He sat there, trying to catch his breath, watching Taggert pull in the pot, and that was when Tina came in with the coffee.

"And I made sandwiches," she said. "I figured you boys must have worked up an appetite by now."

APPETITE? IF there was one thing Krale didn't have, besides the fourth nine, it was an appetite. He felt a hollowness in his middle, but had no urge whatsoever to try to fill it. He didn't want the coffee, either, and as for the brandy, well, he'd already swallowed it, and all he could hope was that it would stay down.

He excused himself, and as he left the room he heard Tina asking Taggert if something was wrong. He didn't catch Taggert's reply.

Nines full, carefully nursed along, with every bet calculated to get the maximum amount of money in the pot. Everything was perfect about that hand except the outcome.

He tried to look at the bright side, but there didn't seem to be one. At least he hadn't raised one more time. He could have been stubborn enough to throw another twenty dollars in the pot, in which case Taggert would certainly have bumped him again. So, yes, he'd managed to save forty dollars, but was that a bright side? Glimpsing it, would one be well advised to pop on a pair of sunglasses?

Krale didn't think so.

He went to the bathroom, the one in the back of the house off the master bedroom, so that they wouldn't hear him gagging. He decided he might feel better if he threw up, but as it turned out he couldn't throw up, nor did he feel better.

On the way back, he stopped in the den and opened the upper left hand drawer of his desk. It was the one with the lock, although the key had been misplaced years ago. So it was never locked, but still it was the natural place to keep a gun, and that's where Krale kept his .38-calibre revolver. He took it out, held it in one hand and then the other, swung out the cylinder to make sure that all its chambers were loaded, closed the cylinder again, and held the gun to his temple, then put the barrel in his mouth.

And how would it play?

They'd hear the shot. They'd run in, see him. And then?

It'd almost be worth it if he could see the expressions on their faces. Tina, who typically looked as if she was trying not to look disappointed, would show some other, more forceful emotion on her beautiful face. And Taggert's habitual poker face would almost certainly lose its composure, if only for a moment.

But he wouldn't get to see it. He'd be dead, with his brains spattered on one wall or another, depending which way he faced when he pulled the trigger. And he wouldn't know whether they laughed or cried.

So what was the point? Well, he'd be out of it. There was that. The pain, which might be quite bad for a moment there, would stop, once and for all. But was that reason enough to do it?

You can kill yourself, he thought. Or you can go back to the table and take that sonofabitch for everything he's got.

He returned the gun to the drawer. On his way to the table, he found himself wondering if he'd made the right choice.

• • •

HE BEGAN winning.

It wasn't terribly dramatic. Most of the pots were small ones, and he couldn't get any real momentum, but he was gaining ground, inching along, taking two steps forward and one back.

"Slow going," he said, when Taggert folded after receiving his second up card. "Maybe we should raise the stakes."

"Oh?"

"Make it twenty-five and fifty," he suggested.

Taggert frowned. "Let me think about it," he said, and reached for the cards. "I'm not sure how much longer I want to play."

"Come on," Krale said. "The night is young."

"Well, I'm not, and it's past my bedtime. And the trouble with a two-handed game is you're always either dealing or shuffling. It's a pain in the ass, passing the cards back and forth all night long."

He opened his mouth to protest, but knew that Taggert was right. "What we need," he said, "is a house dealer."

"Yeah, right," Taggert said. "Why not wish for a full range of casino perks while you're at it?"

"I'm serious," Krale said. He got to his feet, called out, "Tina!"

"WE'LL STICK to seven-card stud," he said. "That's what we've been playing anyway, nine hands out of ten. Tina, you know how to deal stud, don't you? Two down cards, four up cards, one down card."

"What about the ante? We've been playing dealer ante, and if we don't take turns dealing—"

"What do we need with an ante?" Krale said. "Remember, the high hand's compelled to bet the first round, and that's enough to get the pot started. Tina deals the blue cards, and while we play the hand she shuffles the red cards. You don't mind, do you?"

"It might even be fun," she said.

"And while we're at it," Krale said, "we can up the stakes to twenty-five and fifty."

Taggert shook his head.

"Twenty-forty? If you insist, although I'd just as soon boost it a little bit higher."

"I was thinking we could make the first bet five dollars," Taggert said.

"Five dollars!"

"And make the betting pot limit. That way you don't bleed away too much on hands that fizzle out on fourth street, and the big hands are really big."

"Pot limit," Krale said. "Well, hell, why not?"

HE FOUND out the answer to that question when his three jacks ran headlong into a small straight. He'd been moving up nicely, banking a string of small pots, and the straight killed him.

He sat there, working to maintain his composure while Taggert pulled in the pot. Midway through the task of stacking them, he picked up a blue chip and tossed it to Tina.

"One thing I learned in Atlantic City," he said. "A pot like that, you damn well tip the dealer."

She picked up the chip, looked at it.

"It's a joke," Krale said. "Give it back."

"It's not a joke," Taggert said. "You keep it, Teen."

Teen?

"Well, thanks," she said, and grinned, and tucked the chip into her cleavage.

And all at once Krale didn't mind losing.

THE CARDS didn't favor either of them, not really. The hands tended to average out. Krale sat there and played what Tina dealt him, and he won his share of hands, pulled in his share of pots.

But two hands killed him. Two moves, really. In one hand, he limped along with four small spades, filled his flush on sixth street, and called a big bet because Taggert needed the case nine for a full house, that was his only out, and Krale just didn't believe he had it.

Wrong.

A little while later, he just flat knew Taggert had a busted flush, and no backup pair for his pair of aces. The aces were enough to beat Krale's jacks, but how could Taggert call a big bet if all he had was aces?

Wrong again. Right about the unsupported aces, but the sonofabitch called all the same, and aces beat jacks, the way they always do.

17

Beaten, Krale didn't curse his luck, or the cards, or Taggert. What he did do was note the expression on Taggert's face, and the one on Tina's, and the look that passed between them.

"Kills me," he announced. "How you made that call…well, I guess that's poker."

"Maybe it's time to call it a night."

"Maybe," Krale said, and found that he could read Taggert now as if the man had subtitles etched on his forehead. Because Taggert didn't want to quit. He'd wanted to earlier, but not now.

Nice.

"All I want," Krale said, "is a chance to get even."

"Seems reasonable."

"But I'm running out of money to play with. If I had to write you a check for what I owe you right this minute, I'd have to do some fancy footwork to keep it from bouncing."

"I hate to take a marker," Taggert said, "but in this case—"

"I hate to give one. Here's my thought. I'm going to stake myself to a thousand dollars worth of chips. If I win, I win. And if I lose the lot…"

He had their attention.

"…then you can take Tina in the bedroom," he said, "and play dealer's choice for as long as you want."

"You know, if I thought you were serious—"

"Oh, he's serious," Tina said.

"Really? Dick, don't you figure Tina has some say in the matter?"

"Tina wouldn't mind."

"Is that true, Teen?"

Teen.

"You sonofabitch," she said to Krale. "No," she said to Taggert. "No, Mark, I wouldn't mind."

AT FIRST they took turns picking up small pots. The cards were uninteresting, and the hands generally ended with the second up card, but Krale could feel the game's level of intensity rise in spite of the cards.

Fifteen or twenty minutes in, Tina dealt Krale a pair of tens in the hole and a seven on board. Taggert's face card was a queen; he bet and Krale called.

On the next round, Krale paired his seven while Taggert picked up a king. Krale bet, Taggert called.

Krale caught a ten on fifth street, filling his hand, while Taggert paired his king and made a medium-size bet. He had kings and queens, Krale decided, and didn't want to chase Krale out of the pot. Krale thought it over and called.

Taggert's next card was a queen. Two pair on board, and Krale read him for a boat.

His own card was a ten, giving him two pair showing.

"Maybe you're not full yet," Taggert said, and bet into him.

Maybe you're not full yet. Like it mattered to Taggert, who clearly was full himself, with a boat that would swamp tens full or sevens full or anything Krale might have.

Krale just called.

And Tina dealt the river cards. Krale looked at his, for form's sake, and it was a queen, which meant that Taggert couldn't have four of them. He could still have four kings, though.

Taggert made a show of looking at his river card, squeezing it out between his other two down cards. Nothing showed on his face. He sat there considering, and pushed chips into the pot.

"Here's your chance to double up," he said. "My bet's whatever you've got in front of you."

"Oh, what the hell," Krale said. "Let's get this over with." And he shoved his chips to the middle of the table. "I call, Mark. What have you got?"

Big surprise—Taggert showed a king and a queen, giving him the full house Krale had read him for all along.

"Kings full," Krale said. He felt the blood in his veins, felt energy pulsing through his body. He noted the way Taggert was trying not to look at Tina, and the way Tina was allowing herself to look at Taggert. And then he turned over one of the two tens he had in the hole.

"Tens full," he announced. "I just didn't believe you had it, Mark." He dropped his other two hole cards face-down on the table, mixed them in with the pack Tina had been dealing from.

He stood up. "That's it," he said. "Enjoy yourself, kids. You deserve it."

• • •

HE POURED himself a brandy, and held the glass to the light while he listened to their footsteps on the staircase.

Now they're at the top of the stairs, he thought. *Now they're in the bedroom, our bedroom. Now he's kissing her, now he's got his hand on her ass, now she's pressing herself into him the way she does.*

He sipped the brandy.

Suppose Taggert had caught a fourth king. Then he could have shown the fourth ten, and he'd still be sipping brandy and they'd still be up in the bedroom.

He thought about them up there, and he took another small sip of brandy.

Better this way, he decided. Better that he'd had the winning hand and refrained from showing it. This way he had a secret, and he liked that.

Noble of him. Self-sacrificing.

He finished the brandy, went to his desk, opened the upper lefthand drawer, took out the gun. Assured himself once again that all the chambers were loaded.

Another brandy?

No, he didn't need it.

He was quiet on the stairs, avoiding the one that creaked. Not that they'd be likely to hear him, not that they'd be paying attention to anything but each other.

He walked the length of the hall. They hadn't bother to close the door. He saw their clothes, scattered here and there, and then he saw them, looking for all the world like internet porn.

He approached to within ten feet of the bed. He was within Tina's peripheral vision, and he could tell when she registered his presence. She froze, and then so did Taggert.

"Nice," Krale said.

They looked at him, and saw his face, his poker face, and then they saw the gun.

God, the looks on their faces!

"I had four tens," Krale said. "So you both lose."

A VISION IN WHITE

THE GAME CHANGED OVER time. Technology made change inevitable: racquets were larger and lighter and stronger, and even shoes got a little better every few years. And human technology had much the same effect; each generation of tennis players was taller and rangier than the one before it, and players improved on genetics by getting stronger through weight training and more durable through nutrition. So of course the game changed. It had to change.

But the players still—with rare exception—wore the traditional white clothing, and that was one thing he hoped would never change. Oh, some of them sported logos, and maybe that was inevitable, too, with all the money the corporations were throwing around. And you saw colored stripes on some of the white shirts and shorts, and periodically the self-appointed Brat of the Year would turn up in plaid shorts and a scarlet top, but by and large white prevailed.

And he liked it that way. For the women, especially. He didn't really care what the men wore, and, truth to tell, found it difficult to work up much enthusiasm for the men's game. Service played too great a role, and the top players scored too many aces. It was the long drawn-out points that most engaged him, with both players drawing on unsuspected reserves of strength and tenacity to reach impossible balls and make impossible returns. That was tennis, not a handful of 120-mile-an-hour serves and a round of applause.

And there was something about a girl dressed entirely in white, shifting her weight nervously as she waited for her opponent to serve, bouncing the ball before her own serve. Something pure and innocent and remarkably courageous, something that touched your heart as you watched, and wasn't that what spectator sports were about? Yes, you admired the technique, you applauded the skill, but it was an emotional response of the viewer to some quality in the participant that made the game genuinely engaging, and even important.

Interesting how some of them engaged you and others did not.

The one who grunted, for example. Grunted like a little pig every time she hit the ball. Maybe she couldn't help it, maybe it was some Eastern breathing technique that added energy to her stroke. He didn't care. All he knew was that it put him right off Miss Piglet. Whenever he watched her play, he rooted for her opponent.

With others it was something subtler. The stance, the walk, the attitude. One responded or one didn't.

And, of course, the game the woman played was paramount. Not just the raw ability but the heart, the soul, the inner strength that enabled one player to reach and return shots that drew no more than a futile wave from another.

He sat in his chair, drew on his cigarette, watched the television set.

This one, this Miranda DiStefano. Sixteen years old, her blond hair hanging in a ponytail, her face a perfect oval, her nose the slightest bit retroussé. She had a slight overbite, and one close-up revealed braces on her teeth.

How charming…

He'd seen her before, and now he watched her play a match she was not likely to win, a quarterfinal that pitted her with one of the sisters who seemed to win everything these days. He liked both sisters well enough, respected them as the dominant players of their generation, but they didn't engage him the way Miranda did. She didn't have to win, he just wanted to watch her play, and do the best she could.

A vision in white. Perfectly delightful and charming. He wished only the best for her.

THERE WERE sports you could see better on television. Boxing, certainly. Even if you sat at ringside, you didn't get nearly as good a view of the action as the TV camera provided. Football was a toss-up; at home you had the benefit of good close-up camera work and instant replay, while

22

from a good stadium seat you could watch a play develop and see the whole of a pass pattern. Basketball was better in person, and hockey (if you could endure it at all) was only worth watching in person; on TV, you could never find the bloody puck.

TV covered tennis reasonably well, but it was much better in person. The court was small enough so that, from a halfway decent seat, you were assured a good view of the whole of it. And, of course, watching in person had other benefits that it shared with other sports. There were no commercials, no team of announcers droning on and on, and, most important, it was exciting in a way that televised sport could never be. You were there, you were watching, it was happening right before your eyes, and your excitement was magnified by the presence of hundreds or thousands of other similarly excited fans.

He'd been here for the entire tournament, and was glad he'd come. He'd managed to see some superb tennis (as well as some that was a good deal less than superb) and he'd made a point of watching all of Miranda DiStefano's matches. The blond   ches in straight sets, and he'd
                                        onents quite handily. In the
                                        -faulted to lose the first set
                                        through the second set. But
                                        ithin, and broke back, and
                                        ntest; Miranda, buoyed by
                                        l you could see the will to
                                        Croatian girl who was five
                                        arms and shoulders that
                                        testosterone.
                                        ared to see it!
              the quarterfinals, and it looked as though she was going to beat the bigger, taller girl on the opposite side of the net. A strong player, he thought, but lacking finesse. All power and speed, but no subtlety.

A lesbian, from the look of her. He hadn't heard or read anything to that effect, but you could tell. Not that he had anything against them. They were as ubiquitous in women's sports as were their male counterparts in ballet and the design trades. If they played good tennis, he could certainly admire their game.

23

But he wouldn't leave his house to watch a lesbian, let alone travel a few hundred miles.

He watched, his heart singing in his chest, as Miranda worked the ball back and forth, chasing her opponent from one side of the court to the other, running the legs off the bigger girl. Running her ragged, crushing her, beating her.

He was there two days later, cheering her on in the semifinals. Her opponent was one of the sisters, and Miranda gave her a good fight, but the outcome was never in doubt. He applauded enthusiastically every time she won a point, cheered a couple of difficult returns she managed, and took her eventual loss in good grace—as did Miranda, skipping up to the net to congratulate the girl who beat her.

A good sport, too. The girl was one in a million.

HE KNEW better than to write to her.

Oh, the impulse was there, no question about it. Sometimes he found himself composing letters in his head, but that was all right. You could write anything to anybody in the privacy of your own mind. It was when you put your thoughts on paper and entrusted them to the mails that things could go wrong.

Because there were a lot of lunatics out there. An attractive young woman could find herself an unwitting magnet for the aberrant and the delusional, and a letter from a devoted fan could seem as fraught with potential danger as one threatening the life of the president. There was a difference, you wouldn't get in trouble writing a fan letter, but the effect on its recipient might be even greater. The president of the United States would never see your letter, a secretary would open it and hand it over to the FBI, but a young tennis player, especially a relative novice who probably didn't get all that much fan mail, might well open it and read it herself.

And might take it the wrong way. Whatever you said, however you phrased it, she might read something unintended into it. Might begin to wonder if perhaps this enthusiastic fan might be a little too enthusiastic, and if this admiration for her athletic ability might cloak a disturbing obsession.

And what, really, was the point in a fan letter? To reward the recipient for the pleasure her performance had brought him? Hardly, if such a letter were more likely to provoke anxiety than to hearten. What kind of a reward was that?

No, it was the writer's own ego that a fan letter supported. It was an attempt to create a relationship with a stranger, and the only fit relationship for two such people was distant and anonymous. She played tennis, and sparkled on the court. He watched, rapt with enjoyment, and she didn't even know he existed. Which was as it should be.

In the letters he wrote in the privacy of his own mind, sometimes he was a wee bit suggestive, a trifle risqué. Sometimes he thought of things that would bring a blush to that pretty face.

But he never wrote them down, not a sentence, not a word. So where was the harm in that?

HER GAME was off.

Last month she'd played in the French Open, and the television coverage had been frustrating; he'd only been able to see one of her matches, and highlights of others. She didn't make the quarterfinals this time, went out in the third round, beaten in a third-set tiebreaker by an unseeded player she should have swept in straight sets.

Something was missing. Some spark, some inner fire.

And now she was back in the States, playing in the women-only Virago tournament in Indianapolis, and he'd driven almost a thousand miles to watch her play, and she wasn't playing well. At game point in the opening set, the girl double-faulted. You just didn't do that. When the serve had to be in or you lost the set, you made sure you got that serve in. You just did it.

He watched, heartsick, as his Miranda lost point after point to a girl who wasn't fit to carry her racquet. Watched her run after balls she should have gotten to, watched her make unforced errors, watched her beat herself. Well, she had to, didn't she? Her opponent couldn't beat her. She could only beat herself.

And she did.

Toward the end, he tried to inspire her through sheer force of will. He narrowed his gaze, stared hard at her, willed her to look at him, to meet his eyes. And she just wouldn't do it. She looked everywhere but at him, and a fat lot of good it did her.

Then she did look over at him, and her eyes met his and drew away. She was ashamed, he realized, ashamed of her performance, ashamed of herself. She couldn't meet his eyes.

Nor could she turn the tide. The other girl beat her, and she was out of the tournament. He'd driven a thousand miles, and for what?

HE WROTE her a letter.

I don't know what you think you're doing, he wrote, *but the net result—no pun intended—is to sabotage not merely a career but a life.*

He went on to the end, read the thing over, and decided he didn't like the parenthetical *no pun intended* bit. He copied the letter over, dropping it and changing *net* to *overall.* Then he signed it: *A Man Who Cares.*

He left it on his desk, and the next day he rewrote it, and added some personal advice. *Stay away from the lesbians,* he counseled her. *They're only after one thing. The same goes for boys. You could never be happy with someone your own age.* He read it over, copied it with a word changed here and there, and signed it: *The Man Who Loves You.*

The following night he read the letter, went to bed, and got up, unable to sleep. He went to his desk and redrafted the letter one more time, adding some material that he supposed some might regard as overly frank, even pornographic. *The Man For Whom You Were Destined.* The phrase struck him as stilted, but he let it stand, and below it, with a flourish, he signed his name. He destroyed all the other drafts and went to bed.

In the morning he read the letter, sighed, shook his head, and burned it in the fireplace. The words, he thought, would go up the chimney and up into the sky, and, in the form of pure energy, would find their way to the intended recipient.

HER NEXT tournament was in a city less than a hundred miles from his residence.

He thought about going, decided against it because he didn't want the disappointment. He'd developed a feeling for her, he'd invested emotionally in the girl, and she wasn't worth it. Better to stay home and cut his losses.

Better to avoid her on television as well. He wouldn't tune in to the coverage until she was eliminated. Which, given the massive deterioration of her game, would probably come in the first or second round. Then, once she was out of it, he could sit back and watch the sport he loved.

But, perversely, she sailed through the opening rounds. He read the sports pages every morning, and noted the results of her matches. One reporter commented on the renewed determination she was showing, and the inner reserves upon which she seemed able to draw.

There's a sparkle in her eye, too, he added, *that hints at an off-court relationship.*

He was not surprised.

She won in the quarterfinals, won again in the semis. He didn't watch, although the pull toward the television set was almost irresistible.

If she reached the finals, he promised himself, then he would watch.

She got there, and didn't have to contend with either of the formidable sisters; one had skipped the tournament with a sore heel tendon, while the other lost in the semis to Ana Dravic, the Croatian lesbian he'd watched Miranda lose to in a quarterfinal match when she was still his Miranda, pure and innocent, glowing with promise. Now Miranda would play Dravic again, for the tournament, and could she win? Would she win?

She lost the first set 4-6, won the second in a fierce tiebreaker. She was on serve in the first game of the third and final set, won that, and then broke Dravic's serve to lead two games to none.

And then her game fell apart.

She double-faulted, made unforced errors. She never won another game, and, when she trotted up to the net to congratulate the hulking Croatian, the TV commentators were at a loss to explain what had happened to her game.

But he knew. He looked at her hand as she clasped Dravic's larger hand, caught the expression on her face. And then, when she turned and looked into the camera, looked straight at *him*, he knew that she knew, too.

HER NEXT tournament was in California. It took him four days to drive there.

He went to one early-round match, watched her win handily. Her tennis was purposeful, efficient, but now it left him cold. There was no heart and soul in it. It had changed, even as she had changed.

At one point, she turned and looked him right in the eye. Her thoughts were as clear as if she'd spoken them aloud, ads if she'd shouted them into his ear. *There! What are you going to do about it?*

He didn't go to any more of the matches, hers or anyone else's. He stayed in his cheap motel, smoked cigarettes, watched the television set.

When he smoked, he removed the white cotton glove from the hand that held the cigarette. Otherwise, he kept the gloves on while he was alone in his room.

And periodically he emptied his ashtray into the toilet and flushed the cigarette butts.

He was ready. He knew where she was staying, had driven there twice and scouted the place. He had a gun, if he needed it. It was untraceable, he'd bought it for cash at a gun show from a man with a beard and a beer belly and a lot to say on the subject of government regulation. He had a knife, equally impossible to trace. He had his hands, and flexed them now, imagining them encircling her throat.

And there was nothing to connect him to her. He'd never sent a letter, never met her face to face, never given another human being the slightest hint of the way he and she were bonded. He'd always driven to the tournaments he'd attended, always paid cash at the motels where he stayed, always registered under a different false name. Never made a phone call from his room, never left a fingerprint, not even so much as a DNA-bearing cigarette butt.

He would stalk her, and he would get to her when she was alone, and he would do what he'd come to do, what he had to do. And the world would never know why she'd died, or who had killed her.

He was confident of that. And why shouldn't he be? After all, they'd never found out about any of the others.

CATCH AND RELEASE

WHEN YOU SPENT ENOUGH time fishing, you got so you knew the waters. You had certain spots that had worked for you over the years, and you went to them at certain times of the day in certain seasons of the year. You chose the tackle appropriate to the circumstances, picked the right bait or lure, and tried your luck.

If they weren't biting, you moved on. Picked another spot.

HE WAS cruising the Interstate, staying in the right-hand lane, keeping the big SUV a steady five miles an hour below the speed limit. As he passed each exit, he let up on the gas pedal while he kept an eye out for hitchhikers. There was a string of four exits where they were apt to queue up, college students looking to thumb their way home, or to another campus, or wherever they felt a need to go. There were so many of them, and they were always going someplace, and it hardly mattered where or why.

He drove north, passed four exits, took the fifth, crossed over and got on the southbound entrance ramp. Four more exits, then off again and on again and he was once more heading north.

Taking his time.

There were hitchhikers at each exit, but his foot never touched the brake pedal. It would hover there, but he always saw something that made him drive on. There were plenty of girls out there today, some of them especially alluring in tight jeans and braless T-shirts, but they all seemed to have boys or other girls as companions. The only solitary hitchhikers he saw were male. And he was not interested in boys. He wanted a girl, a girl all by herself.

• • •

LUKE, 5:5. *Lord, we fished all night and caught nothing.*

Sometimes you could drive all day, and the only reason you'd have to stop was to fill the gas tank. But the true fisherman could fish all night and catch nothing and not regard the time as ill-spent. A true fisherman was patient, and while he waited he gave his mind over to the recollection of other days at the water's edge. He'd let himself remember in detail how a particular quarry had risen to the bait and taken the hook. And put up a game fight.

And sizzled in the pan.

WHEN HE stopped for her, she picked up her backpack and trotted up to the car. He rolled down the window and asked her where she was headed, and she hesitated long enough to have a look at him and decide he was okay. She named a town fifty or sixty miles up the road.

"No problem," he said. "I can just about take you to your front door."

She tossed her pack in the back, then got in front beside him. Closed the door, fastened her seat belt.

She said something about how grateful she was, and he said something appropriate, and he joined the stream of cars heading north. What, he wondered, had she seen in that quick appraising glance? What was it that had assured her he was all right?

His face was an unmemorable one. The features were regular and average and, well, ordinary. Nothing stuck out.

Once, years ago, he'd grown a mustache. He had thought it might give his face some character, but all it did was look out of place. What was it doing there on his lip? He kept it there, waiting to get used to it, and one day he realized that wasn't going to happen, and shaved it off.

And went back to his forgettable face. Unremarkable, unthreatening. Safe.

"A FISHERMAN," she said. "My dad likes to go fishing. Once, twice a year he'll go away for the weekend with a couple of his buddies and come back with an ice chest full of fish. And my mom gets stuck with cleaning them, and for a week the house totally smells of fish."

"Well, that's a problem I'm spared," he told her. "I'm what they call a catch-and-release fisherman."

"You don't come home with a full ice chest?"

"I don't even have an ice chest. Oh, I used to. But what I found over time was that it was the sport I enjoyed, and it was a lot simpler and easier if the game ended with the fish removed from the hook and slipped gently back into the water."

She was silent for a moment. Then she asked if he thought they enjoyed it.

"The fish? Now that's an interesting question. It's hard to know what a fish does or doesn't enjoy, or even if the word *enjoy* can be applied to a fish. You could make the case that a fish fighting for its life gets to be intensely alive in a way it otherwise doesn't, but is that good or bad from the fish's point of view?" He smiled. "When they swim away," he said, "I get the sense that they're glad to be alive. But I may just be trying to put myself in their position. I can't really know what it's like for them."

"I guess not."

"One thing I can't help but wonder," he said, "is if they learn anything from the experience. Are they warier the next time around? Or will they take the hook just as readily for the next fisherman who comes along?"

She thought about it. "I guess they're just fish," she said.

"Well now," he said. "I guess they are."

SHE WAS a pretty thing. A business major, she told him, taking most of her elective courses in English, because she'd always like to read. Her hair was brown with auburn highlights, and she had a good figure, with large breasts and wide hips. Built for childbearing, he thought, and she'd bear three or four of them, and she'd gain weight with each pregnancy and never quite manage to lose all of it. And her face, already a little chubby, would broaden and turn bovine, and the sparkle would fade out of her eyes.

There was a time when he'd have been inclined to spare her all that.

"REALLY," SHE said, "you could have just dropped me at the exit. I mean, this is taking you way out of your way."

"Less so than you'd think. Is that your street coming up?"

"Uh-huh. If you want to drop me at the corner—"

But he drove her to the door of her suburban house. He waited while she retrieved her backpack, then let her get halfway up the path to her door before he called her back.

"You know," he said, "I was going to ask you something earlier, but I didn't want to upset you."

"Oh?"

"Aren't you nervous hitching rides with strangers? Don't you think it's dangerous?"

"Oh," she said. "Well, you know, everybody does it."

"I see."

"And I've always been okay so far."

"A young woman alone—"

"Well, I usually team up with somebody. A boy, or at least another girl. But this time, well…"

"You figured you'd take a chance."

She flashed a smile. "It worked out okay, didn't it?"

He was silent for a moment, but held her with his eyes. Then he said, "Remember the fish we were talking about?"

"The fish?"

"How it feels when it slips back into the water. And whether it learns anything from the experience."

"I don't understand."

"Not everyone is a catch-and-release fisherman," he said. "That's probably something you ought to keep in mind."

She was still standing there, looking puzzled, while he put the SUV in gear and pulled away.

HE DROVE home, feeling fulfilled. He had never moved from the house he was born in, and it had been his alone ever since his mother's death ten years ago.

He checked the mail, which yielded half a dozen envelopes with checks in them. He had a mail-order business, selling fishing lures, and he spent the better part of an hour preparing the checks for deposit and packing the orders for shipment. He'd make more money if he put his business online and let people pay with credit cards, but he didn't need much money, and he found it easier to let things remain as they were. He ran the same ads every month in the same magazines, and his old customers reordered, and enough new customers turned up to keep him going.

He cooked some pasta, heated some meat sauce, chopped some lettuce for a salad, drizzled a little olive oil over it. He ate at the kitchen table, washed the dishes, watched the TV news. When it ended he left the picture on but muted the sound, and thought about the girl.

Now, though, he gave himself over to the fantasy she inspired. A lonely road. A piece of tape across her mouth. A struggle ending with her arms broken.

Stripping her. Piercing each of her openings in turn. Giving her physical pain to keep her terror company.

And finishing her with a knife. No, with his hands, strangling her. No, better yet, with his forearm across her throat, and his weight pressing down, throttling her.

Ah, the joy of it, the thrill of it, the sweet release of it. And now it was almost as real to him as if it had happened.

But it hadn't happened. He'd left her at her door, untouched, with only a hint of what might have been. And, because it hadn't happened, there was no ice chest full of fish to clean—no body to dispose of, no evidence to get rid of, not even that feeling of regret that had undercut his pleasure on so many otherwise perfect occasions.

Catch and release. That was the ticket, catch and release.

THE ROADHOUSE had a name, Toddle Inn, but nobody ever called it anything but Roy's, after the man who'd owned it for close to fifty years until his liver quit on him.

That was something he would probably never have to worry about, as he'd never been much of a drinker. Tonight, three days after he'd dropped the young hitchhiker at her door, he'd had the impulse to go bar-hopping, and Roy's was his fourth stop. He'd ordered a beer at the first place and drank two sips of it, left the second bar without ordering anything, and drank most of the Coke he ordered at bar number three.

Roy's had beer on draft, and he stood at the bar and ordered a glass of it. There was an English song he'd heard once, of which he recalled only one verse:

The man who buys a pint of beer
Gets half a pint of water;
The only thing the landlord's got
That's any good's his daughter.

The beer was watery, to be sure, but it didn't matter because he didn't care about beer, good or bad. But the bar held something to interest him, the very thing he'd come out for.

She was two stools away from him, and she was drinking something in a stemmed glass, with an orange slice in it. At first glance she looked like the hitchhiker, or like her older sister, the one who'd gone wrong. Her blouse was a size too small, and she'd tried to cope by unbuttoning an extra button. The lipstick was smeared on her full-lipped mouth, and her nail polish was chipped.

She picked up her drink and was surprised to find that she'd finished it. She shook her head, as if wondering how to contend with this unanticipated development, and while she was working it out he lifted a hand to catch the barman's eye, then pointed at the girl's empty glass.

She waited until the fresh drink was in front of her, then picked it up and turned toward her benefactor. "Thank you," she said, "You're a gentleman."

He closed the distance between them. "And a fisherman," he said.

SOMETIMES IT didn't matter what you had on your hook. Sometimes it wasn't even necessary to wet a line. Sometimes all you had to do was sit there and they'd jump right into the boat.

She'd had several drinks before the one he'd bought her, and she didn't really need the two others he bought her after that. But she thought she did, and he didn't mind spending the money or sitting there while she drank them.

Her name, she told him repeatedly, was Marni. He was in no danger of forgetting that fact, nor did she seem to be in any danger of remembering his name, which she kept asking him over and over. He'd said it was Jack—it wasn't—and she kept apologizing for her inability to retain that information. "I'm Marni," she'd say on each occasion. "With an I," she added, more often than not.

34

He found himself remembering a woman he'd picked up years ago in a bar with much the same ambience. She'd been a very different sort of a drunk, although she'd been punishing the Harvey Wallbangers as industriously as Marni was knocking back the Gandy Dancers. She'd grown quieter and quieter, and her eyes went glassy, and by the time he'd driven them to the place he'd selected in advance, she was out cold. He'd had some very interesting plans for her, and here she was, the next thing to comatose, and wholly incapable of knowing what was being done to her.

So he'd let himself imagine that she was dead, and took her that way, and kept waiting for her to wake up, but she didn't. And it was exciting, more exciting than he'd have guessed, but at the end he held himself back.

And paused for a moment to consider the situation, and then very deliberately broke her neck. And then took her again, imagining that she was only sleeping.

And that was good, too.

"AT LEAST I got the house," she was saying. "My ex took the kids away from me, can you imagine that? Got some lawyer saying I was an unfit mother. Can you imagine that?"

The house her ex-husband had let her keep certainly looked like a drunk lived in it. It wasn't filthy, just remarkably untidy. She grabbed him by the hand and led him up a flight of stairs and into her bedroom, which was no neater than the rest of the place, then turned and threw herself into his arms.

He disengaged, and she seemed puzzled. He asked if there was anything in the house to drink, and she said there was beer in the fridge, and there might be some vodka in the freezer. He said he'd be right back.

He gave her five minutes, and when he returned with a can of Rolling Rock and a half-pint of vodka, she was sprawled naked on her back, snoring. He set the beer can and the vodka bottle on the bedside table, and drew the blanket to cover her.

"Catch and release," he said, and left her there.

FISHING WAS not just a metaphor. A couple of days later he walked out his front door into a cool autumn morning. The sky was overcast, the humidity lower than it had been. The breeze was out of the west.

It was just the day for it. He got his gear together, made his choices, and drove to the bank of a creek that was always good on this kind of day. He fished the spot for an hour, and by the time he left he had hooked and landed three trout. Each had put up a good fight, and as he released them he might have observed that they'd earned their freedom, that each deserved another chance at life.

But what did that mean, really? Could a fish be said to earn or deserve anything? Could anyone? And did a desperate effort to remain alive somehow entitle one to live?

Consider the humble flounder. He was salt-water fish, a bottom fish, and when you hooked him he rarely did much more than flop around a little while you reeled him in. Did this make him the trout's moral inferior? Did he have less right to live because of his genetically prescribed behavior?

He stopped on the way home, had a hamburger and a side of well-done fries. Drank a cup of coffee. Read the paper.

Back home, he cleaned and sorted his tackle and put everything away where it belonged.

THAT NIGHT it rained, and did so off and on for the next three days. He stayed close to home, watched a little television.

Nights, he'd lean back in his recliner and close his eyes, letting himself remember. Once, a few months back, he'd tried to count. He'd been doing this for years, long before his mother died, and in the early years his appetite had been ravenous. It was, he sometimes thought, a miracle he hadn't been caught. Back then he'd left DNA all over the place, along with God knew what else in the way of trace evidence.

Somehow he'd gotten away with it. If they'd ever picked him up, if he'd ever attracted the slightest bit of official attention, he was sure he'd have caved immediately. He'd have told them everything, confessed to everything. They wouldn't have needed trace evidence, let alone DNA. All they'd have needed was a cell to lock him into and a key to throw away.

So there had been many, but he'd ranged far and wide and little of what he did ran to pattern. He'd read about other men who had very specific tastes, in essence always hunting the same woman and killing her in the same fashion. If anything, he'd deliberately sought variety, not for precautionary reasons but because it was indeed the spice of life—or death, as you prefer. *When I have to choose between two evils*, Mae West had said, *I pick the one I haven't tried yet*. Made sense to him.

And after he'd changed, after he had in fact become a catch-and-release fisherman, there'd been a point when it seemed to him as though he'd had a divine hand keeping him safe all those years. Who was to say that there was not a purpose to it all, and a guiding force running the universe? He'd been spared so that he could—do what? Catch and release?

It hadn't taken him long to decide that was nonsense. He'd killed all those girls because he'd wanted to—or needed to, whatever. And he'd stopped killing because he no longer needed or wanted to kill, was in fact better served by, well, catching and releasing.

So how many had there been? The simple answer was that he did not know, and had no way of knowing. He had never taken trophies, never kept souvenirs. He had memories, but it had become virtually impossible to distinguish between recollections of actual events and recollections of fantasies. One memory was as real as another, whether it had happened or not. And, really, what difference did it make?

He thought of that serial killer they'd caught in Texas, the idiot who kept finding new killings to confess to and leading the authorities to more unmarked graves. Except some of the victims turned out to have been killed when he was in custody in another state. Was he conning them, for some inexplicable reason? Or was he simply remembering—vividly, and in detail—acts he had not in actuality committed?

HE DIDN'T mind the rain. His had been a solitary childhood, and he'd grown into a solitary adult. He had never had friends, and had never felt the need. Sometimes he liked the illusion of society, and at such times he would go to a bar or restaurant, or walk in a shopping mall, or sit in a movie theater, simply to be among strangers. But most of the time his own company was company enough.

One rainy afternoon he picked a book from the shelf. It was *The Compleat Angler*, by Izaak Walton, and he'd read it through countless times and flipped through it many times more. He always seemed to find something worth thinking about between its covers.

God never did make a more calm, quiet, innocent recreation than angling,
he read. The line resonated with him, as it always did, and he decided the
only change he could make would be to the final word of it. He preferred
fishing to angling, fisherman to angler. Stephen Leacock, after all, had
observed that angling was the name given to fishing by people who
couldn't fish.

On the first clear day he made a grocery list and went to the mall. He
pushed a cart up one aisle and down the next, picking up eggs and bacon
and pasta and canned sauce, and he was weighing the merits of two brands
of laundry detergent when he saw the woman.

He hadn't been looking for her, hadn't been looking for anyone. The
only thing on his mind was detergent and fabric softener, and then he
looked up and there she was.

She was beautiful, not young-pretty like the hitchhiker or slutty-
available like Marni the barfly, but genuinely beautiful. She could have
been an actress or a model, though he somehow knew she wasn't.

Long dark hair, long legs, a figure that was at once athletic and
womanly. An oval face, a strong nose, high cheekbones. But it wasn't
her beauty he found himself responding to. It was something else, some
indefinable quality that suddenly rendered the Tide and the Downy,
indeed all the contents of his shopping cart, entirely unimportant.

She was wearing slacks and an unbuttoned long-sleeved canvas shirt
over a pale blue T-shirt, and there was nothing terribly provocative about
her outfit, but it scarcely mattered what she wore. He saw that she had
a long shopping list she consulted, and only a few items already in her
cart. He had time, he decided, time enough to wheel his cart to the bank
of cashiers and pay cash for his groceries. That was better than simply
walking away from the cart. People tended to remember you when you
did that.

He loaded the bags of groceries back into his cart, and on the way to
his SUV he turned periodically for a look at the entrance. He stowed the
bags in back, got behind the wheel and found a good spot to wait for her.

He sat there patiently with the motor idling. He wasn't paying
attention to the time, was scarcely conscious of its passage, but felt he'd be
comfortable waiting forever for the doors to slide open and the woman to
emerge. The impatient man was not meant for fishing, and indeed waiting,

patient passive waiting, was part of the pleasure of the pastime. If you got a bite every time your hook broke the water's surface, if you hauled up one fish after another, why, where was the joy? Might as well drag a net. Hell, might as well toss a grenade into a trout stream and scoop up what floated to the surface.

Ah. There she was.

"I'M A fisherman," he said.

These were not the first words he spoke to her. Those were, "Let me give you a hand." He'd pulled up behind her just as she was about to put her groceries into the trunk of her car, and hopped out and offered his help. She smiled, and was about to thank him, but she never had the chance. He had a flashlight in one hand, three C batteries in a hard rubber case, and he took her by the shoulder and swung her around and hit her hard on the back of the head. He caught her as she fell, eased her down gently.

In no time at all she was propped up in the passenger seat of his SUV, and her groceries were in her trunk and the lid slammed shut. She was out cold, and for a moment he thought he might have struck too hard a blow, but he checked and found she had a pulse. He used duct tape on her wrists and ankles and across her mouth, fastened her seat belt, and drove off with her.

And, as patiently as he'd waited for her to emerge from the supermarket, he waited for her to return to consciousness. *I'm a fisherman*, he thought, and waited for the chance to say the words. He kept his eyes on the road ahead, but from time to time he shot her a glance, and her appearance never changed. Her eyes were shut, her muscles slack.

Then, not long after he'd turned onto a secondary road, he sensed that she was awake. He looked at her, and she looked the same, but he could somehow detect a change. He gave her another moment to listen to the silence, and then he spoke, told her that he was a fisherman.

No reaction from her. But he was certain she'd heard him.

"A catch-and-release fisherman," he said. "Not everybody knows what that means. See, I enjoy fishing. It does something for me that nothing else has ever done. Call it a sport or a pastime, as you prefer, but it's what I do and what I've always done."

He thought about that. What he'd always done? Well, just about. Some of his earliest childhood memories involved fishing with a bamboo pole and baiting his hook with worms he'd dug himself in the backyard. And some of his earliest and most enduring adult memories involved fishing of another sort.

"Now I wasn't always a catch-and-release fisherman," he said. "Way I saw it back in the day, why would a man go to all the trouble of catching a fish and then just throw it back? Way it looked to me, you catch something, you kill it. You kill something, you eat it. Pretty clear cut, wouldn't you say?"

Wouldn't you say? But she wouldn't say anything, couldn't say anything, not with the duct tape over her mouth. He saw, though, that she'd given up the pretense of unconsciousness. Her eye were open now, although he couldn't see what expression they may have held.

"What happened," he said, "is I lost the taste for it. The killing and all. Most people, they think of fishing, and they somehow manage not to think about killing. They seem to think the fish comes out of the water, gulps for air a couple of times, and then obligingly gives up the ghost. Maybe he flops around a little first, but that's all there is to it. But, see, it's not like that. A fish can live longer out of water than you'd think. What you have to do, you gaff it. Hit it in the head with a club. It's quick and easy, but you can't get around the fact that you're killing it."

He went on, telling her how you were spared the chore of killing when you released your catch. And the other unpleasant chores, the gutting, the scaling, the disposal of offal.

He turned from a blacktop road to a dirt road. He hadn't been down this road in quite a while, but it was as he remembered it, a quiet path through the woods that led to a spot he'd always liked. He quit talking now, letting her think about what he'd said, letting her figure out what to make of it, and he didn't speak again until he'd parked the car in a copse of trees, where it couldn't be seen from the road.

"I have to tell you," he said, unfastening her seat belt, wrestling her out of the car. "I enjoy life a lot more as a catch-and-release fisherman. It's got all the pleasure of fishing without the downside, you know?"

He arranged her on the ground on her back. He went back for a tire iron, and smashed both her kneecaps before untaping her ankles, but left the tape on her wrists and across her mouth.

He cut her clothing off her. Then he took off his own clothes and folded them neatly. Adam and Eve in the garden, he thought. Naked and unashamed. *Lord, we fished all night and caught nothing.*

He fell on her.

BACK HOME, he loaded his clothes into the washing machine, then drew a bath for himself. But he didn't get into the tub right away. He had her scent on him, and found himself in no hurry to wash it off. Better to be able to breathe it in while he relived the experience, all of it, from the first sight of her in the supermarket to the snapped-twig sound of her neck when he broke it.

And he remembered as well the first time he'd departed from the catch-and-release pattern. It had been less impulsive that time, he'd thought long and hard about it, and when the right girl turned up—young, blonde, a cheerleader type, with a turned-up nose and a beauty mark on one cheek—when she turned up, he was ready.

Afterward he'd been upset with himself. Was he regressing? Had he been untrue to the code he'd adopted? But it hadn't taken him long to get past those thoughts, and this time he felt nothing but calm satisfaction.

He was still a catch-and-release fisherman. He probably always would be. But, for God's sake, that didn't make him a vegetarian, did it?

Hell, no. A man still had to have a square meal now and then.

CLEAN SLATE

TOLEDO. WHAT DID SHE know about Toledo?

Like, Holy Toledo. The original city, in Spain, was famous for fine swords, and the newspaper here in Ohio called itself The Toledo Blade. That was a better name than the Mud Hens, which was what they called the baseball team.

And here she was in Toledo.

There was a Starbucks just across the street from the building where he had his office, and she settled in at a window table a little before five. She thought she might be in for a long wait. In New York, young associates at law firms typically worked until midnight and took lunch and dinner at their desks. Was it the same in Toledo?

Well, the cappuccino was the same. She sipped hers, making it last, and was about to go to the counter for another when she saw him.

But was it him? He was tall and slender, wearing a dark suit and a tie, clutching a briefcase, walking with purpose. His hair when she'd known him was long and shaggy, a match for the jeans and tee shirt that was his usual costume, and now it was cut to match the suit and the briefcase. And he wore glasses now, and they gave him a serious, studious look. He hadn't worn them then, and he'd certainly never looked studious.

But it was Douglas. No question, it was him.

She rose from her chair, hit the door, quickened her pace to catch up with him at the corner. She said, "Doug? Douglas Pratter?"

He turned, and she caught the puzzlement in his eyes. She helped him out. "It's Kit," she said. "Katherine Tolliver." She smiled softly. "A voice from the past. Well, a whole person from the past, actually."

"My God," he said, "It's really you."

"I was having a cup of coffee," she said, "and looking out the window and wishing I knew somebody in this town, and when I saw you I thought you were a mirage. Or that you were just somebody who looked the way Doug Pratter might look eight years later."

"Is that how long it's been?"

"Just about. I was fifteen and I'm twenty-three now. You were two years older."

"Still am. That much hasn't changed."

"And your family picked up and moved right in the middle of your junior year of high school."

"My dad got a job he couldn't say no to. He was going to send for us at the end of the term, but my mother wouldn't hear of it. We'd all be too lonely is what she said. It took me years before I realized she just didn't trust him on his own."

"Was he not to be trusted?"

"I don't know about that, but the marriage failed two years later anyway. He went a little nuts and wound up in California. He got it in his head that he wanted to be a surfer."

"Seriously? Well, good for him, I guess."

"Not all that good for him. He drowned."

"I'm sorry."

"Who knows? Maybe that's what he wanted, whether he knew it or not. Mom's still alive and well."

"In Toledo?"

"Bowling Green."

"*That's* it. I knew you'd moved to Ohio, and I couldn't remember the city, and I didn't think it was Toledo. Bowling Green."

"I've always thought of it as a color. Lime green, forest green, and bowling green."

"Same old Doug."

"You think? I wear a suit and go to an office. Christ, I wear glasses."

"And a wedding ring." And, before he could tell her about his wife and kiddies and adorable suburban house, she said, "But you've got to get home, and I've got plans of my own. I want to catch up, though. Have you got any time tomorrow?"

• • •

IT'S KIT. Katherine Tolliver.

Just saying her name had taken her back in time. She hadn't been Kit or Katherine or Tolliver in years. Names were like clothes, she'd put them on and wear them for a while and then let them go. The analogy only went so far, because you could wash clothes when you'd soiled them, but there was no dry cleaner for a name that had outlived its usefulness.

Katherine "Kit" Tolliver. That wasn't the name on the ID she was carrying, or the one she'd signed on the motel register. Once she'd identified herself to Doug Pratter, she'd become the person she'd proclaimed herself to be. She was Kit again—and, at the same time, she wasn't.

Interesting, the whole business.

Back in her motel room, she surfed her way around the TV channels, then switched off the set and took a shower. Afterward she spent a few minutes studying her nude body and wondering how it would look to him. She was a little fuller in the breasts than she'd been eight years before, a little rounder in the butt, a little closer to ripeness overall. She had always been confident of her attractiveness, but she couldn't help wondering what she might look like to those eyes that had seen her years ago.

Of course, he hadn't needed glasses back in the day.

She had read somewhere that a man who has once had a particular woman somehow assumes he can have her again. She didn't know how true this might be, but it seemed to her that something similar applied to women. A woman who had once been with a particular man was ordained to doubt her ability to attract him a second time. And so she felt a little of that uncertainty, but willed herself to dismiss it.

He was married, and might well be in love with his wife. He was busy establishing himself in his profession, and settling into an orderly existence. Why would he want a meaningless fling with an old girlfriend, who'd had to say her name before he could even place her?

She smiled. *Lunch*, he'd said. *We'll have lunch tomorrow.*

FUNNY HOW it started.

She was in Kansas City, sitting at a table with six or seven others, a mix of men and women in their twenties. And one of the men mentioned a woman she didn't know, though she seemed to be known to most if not all of the others. And one of the women said, "That slut."

And the next thing she knew, the putative slut was forgotten while the whole table turned to the question of just what constituted sluttiness. Was it a matter of attitude? Of specific behavior? Was one born to slutdom, or was the status acquired?

Was it solely a female province? Could you have male sluts?

That got nipped in the bud. "A man can take sex too casually," one of the men asserted, "and he can consequently be an asshole, and deserving of a certain measure of contempt. But as far as I'm concerned, the word *slut* is gender-linked. Nobody with a Y chromosome can qualify as a genuine slut."

And, finally, was there a numerical cutoff? Could an equation be drawn up? Did a certain number of partners within a certain number of years make one a slut?

"Suppose," one woman suggested, "suppose once a month you go out after work and have a couple—"

"A couple of men?"

"A couple of drinks, you idiot, and you start flirting, and one things leads to another, and you drag somebody home with you."

"Once a month?"

"It could happen."

"So that's twelve men in a year."

"When you put it that way," the woman allowed, "it seems like a lot."

"It's also a hundred and twenty partners in ten years."

"Except you wouldn't keep it up for that long, because sooner or later one of those hookups would take."

"And you'd get married and live happily ever after?"

"Or at least live together more or less monogamously for a year or two, which would cut down on the frequency of hookups, wouldn't it?"

Throughout all of this, she barely said a word. Why bother? The conversation buzzed along quite well without her, and she was free to sit back and listen, and to wonder just what place she occupied in what someone had already labeled "the saint-slut continuum."

"With cats," one of the men said, "it's nice and clear-cut."

"Cats can be sluts?"

He shook his head. "With women and cats. A woman has one cat, or even two or three cats, she's an animal lover. Four or more cats and she's a demented cat lady."

"That's how it works?"

"That's exactly how it works. With sluts, it looks to be more complicated."

Another thing that complicated it, someone said, was if the woman in question had a significant other, whether husband or boyfriend. If she didn't, and she hooked up half a dozen times a year, well, she certainly wasn't a slut. If she was married and still fit in that many hookups on the side, well, that changed things, didn't it?

"Let's get personal," one of the men said to one of the women. "How many partners have you had?"

"Me?"

"Well?"

"You mean in the past year?"

"Or lifetime. You decide."

"If I'm going to answer a question like that," she said, "I think we definitely need another round of drinks."

The drinks came, and the conversation slid into a game of truth, though it seemed to Jennifer—these people knew her as Jennifer, a name she seemed to have picked up again, after having left it behind months ago in New York—it seemed to her that the actual veracity of the responses was moot.

And then it was her turn.

"Well, Jen? How many?"

Would she ever see any of these people again? Probably not. Kansas City was all right, but she was about ready for a change of venue. So it really didn't matter what she said.

And what she said was, "Well, it depends. How do you decide what counts?"

"What do you mean? Like blow jobs don't count?"

"That's what Clinton said, remember?"

"As far as I'm concerned, blow jobs count."

"And hand jobs?"

"They don't count," one man said, and there seemed to be general agreement on that point. "Not that there's anything wrong with them," he added.

"So what's your criterion here, exactly? Something has to be inside of something?"

"As far as the nature of the act," one man said, "I think it has to be subjective. It counts if you think it counts. So, Jen? What's your count?"

"Suppose you passed out, and you know something happened, but you don't remember any of it?"

"Same answer. It counts if you think it counts."

The conversation kept going, but she was detached from it now, thinking, remembering, working it out in her mind. How many men, if gathered around a table or a campfire, could compare notes and tell each other about her? That, she thought, was the real criterion, not what part of her anatomy had been in contact with what portion of his. Who could tell stories? Who could bear witness?

And, when the table quieted down again, she said, "Five."

"Five? That's all? Just five?"

"Five."

SHE HAD arranged to meet Douglas Pratter at noon in the lobby of a downtown hotel not far from his office. She arrived early and sat where she could watch the entrance. He was five minutes early himself, and she saw him stop to remove his glasses, polishing their lenses with a breast-pocket handkerchief. Then he put them on again and stood there, his eyes scanning the room.

She got to her feet, and now he caught sight of her, and she saw him smile. He'd always had a winning smile, optimistic and confident. Years ago, it had been one of the things she liked most about him.

She walked to meet him. Yesterday she'd been wearing a dark gray pants suit; today she'd paired the jacket with a matching skirt. The effect was still business attire, but softer, more feminine. More accessible.

"I hope you don't mind a ride," he told her. "There are places we could walk to, but they're crowded and noisy and no place to have a conversation. Plus they rush you, and I don't want to be in a hurry. Unless you've got an early afternoon appointment?"

She shook her head. "I had a full morning," she said, "and there's a cocktail party this evening that I'm supposed to go to, but until then I'm free as the breeze."

"Then we can take our time. We've probably got a lot to talk about."

As they crossed the lobby, she took his arm.

THE FELLOW'S name in Kansas City was Lucas. She'd taken note of him early on, and his eyes had shown a certain degree of interest in her, but his interest mounted when she told the group how many sexual partners she'd had. It was he who'd said, "Five? That's all? Just five?" When she'd confirmed her count, his eyes grabbed hers and held on.

And now he'd taken her to another bar, the lounge of the Hotel Phillips, a nice quiet place where they could really get to know each other. Just the two of them.

The lighting was soft, the décor soothing. A pianist played show tunes unobtrusively, and a waitress with an indeterminate accent took their order and brought their drinks. They touched glasses, sipped, and he said, "Five."

"That really did it for you," she said. "What, is it your lucky number?"

"Actually," he said, "my lucky number is six."

"I see."

"You were never married."

"No."

"Never lived with anybody."

"Only my parents."

"You don't still live with them?"

"No."

"You live alone?"

"I have a roommate."

"A woman, you mean."

"Right."

"Uh, the two of you aren't..."

"We have separate beds," she said, "in separate rooms, and we live separate lives."

"Right. Were you ever, uh, in a convent or anything?"

She gave him a look.

"Because you're remarkably attractive, you walk into a room and you light it up, and I can imagine the number of guys who must hit on you on a daily basis. And you're how old? Twenty-one, twenty-two?"

"Twenty-three."

"And you've only been with five guys? What, were you a late bloomer?"

"I wouldn't say so."

"I'm sorry, I'm pressing and I shouldn't. It's just that, well, I can't help being fascinated. But the last thing I want is to make you uncomfortable."

The conversation wasn't making her uncomfortable. It was merely boring her. Was there any reason to prolong it? Was there any reason not to cut to the chase?

She'd already slipped one foot out of its shoe, and now she raised it and rested it on his lap, massaging his groin with the ball of her foot. The expression on his face was worth the price of admission all by itself.

"My turn to ask questions," she said. "Do you live with your parents?"

"You're kidding, right? Of course not."

"Do you have a roommate?"

"Not since college, and that was a while ago."

"So" she said. "What are we waiting for?"

THE RESTAURANT Doug had chosen was on Detroit Avenue, just north of I-75. Walking across the parking lot, she noted a motel two doors down and another across the street.

Inside, it was dark and quiet, and the décor reminded her of the cocktail lounge where Lucas had taken her. She had a sudden memory of her foot in his lap, and the expression on his face. Further memories followed, but she let them glide on by. The present moment was a nice one, and she wanted to live in it while it was at hand.

She asked for a dry Rob Roy, and Doug hesitated, then ordered the same for himself. The cuisine on offer was Italian, and he started to order the scampi, then caught himself and selected a small steak instead. Scampi, she thought, was full of garlic, and he wanted to make sure he didn't have it on his breath.

The conversation started in the present, but she quickly steered it back to the past, where it properly belonged. "You always wanted to be a lawyer," she remembered.

"Right, I was going to be a criminal lawyer, a courtroom whiz. The defender of the innocent. So here I am doing corporate work, and if I ever see the inside of a courtroom, that means I've done something wrong."

"I guess it's hard to make a living with a criminal practice."

"You can do okay," he said, "but you spend your life with the scum of the earth, and you do everything you can to keep them from getting what they damn well deserve. Of course I didn't know any of that when I was seventeen and starry-eyed over *To Kill a Mockingbird*."

"You were my first boyfriend."

"You were my first real girlfriend."

She thought, Oh? And how many unreal ones were there? And what made her real by comparison? Because she'd slept with him?

Had he been a virgin the first time they had sex? She hadn't given the matter much thought at the time, and had been too intent upon her own role in the proceedings to be aware of his experience or lack thereof. It hadn't really mattered then, and she couldn't see that it mattered now.

And, she'd just told him, he'd been her first boyfriend. No need to qualify that; he'd truly been her first boyfriend, real or otherwise.

But she hadn't been a virgin. She'd crossed that barrier two years earlier, a month or so after her thirteenth birthday, and had had sex in one form or another perhaps a hundred times before she hooked up with Doug.

Not with a boyfriend, however. I mean, your father couldn't be your boyfriend, could he?

LUCAS LIVED alone in a large L-shaped studio apartment on the top floor of a new building. "I'm the first tenant the place has ever had," he told her. "I've never lived in something brand spanking new before. It's like I've taken the apartment's virginity."

"Now you can take mine."

"Not quite. But this is better. Remember, I told you my lucky number."

"Six."

"There you go."

And just when, she wondered, had six become his lucky number? When she'd acknowledged five partners? Probably, but never mind. It was a good enough line, and one he was no doubt feeling proud of right about now, because it had worked, hadn't it?

As if he'd had any chance of failing...

He made drinks, and they kissed, and she was pleased but not surprised to note that the requisite chemistry was there. And, keeping it company, there was that delicious surge of anticipatory excitement that was always present on such occasions. It was at once sexual and non-sexual, and she felt it even when the chemistry was not present, even when the sexual act was destined to be perfunctory at best, and at worst distasteful. Even then she'd feel that rush, that urgent excitement, but it was greatly increased when she knew the sex was going to be good.

He excused himself and went to the bathroom, and she opened her purse and found the little unlabeled vial she kept in the change compartment. She looked at it and at the drink he'd left on the table, but in the end she left the vial in her purse, left his drink untouched.

As it turned out, it wouldn't have mattered. When he emerged from the bathroom he reached not for his drink but for her instead, and it was as good as she'd known it would be, inventive and eager and passionate, and finally they fell away from each other, spent and sated.

"Wow," he said.

"That's the right word for it."

"You think? It's the best I can come up with, and yet it somehow seems inadequate. You're—"

"What?"

"Amazing. I have to say this, I can't help it. It's almost impossible to believe you've had so little experience."

"Because I'm clearly jaded?"

"No, just because you're so good at it. And in a way that's the complete opposite of jaded. I swear to God this is the last time I'll ask you, but were you telling the truth? Have you really only been with five men?"

She nodded.

"Well," he said, "now it's six, isn't it?"

"Your lucky number, right?"

"Luckier than ever," he said.

"Lucky for me, too."

She was glad she hadn't put anything in his drink, because after a brief rest they made love again, and that wouldn't have happened otherwise.

"Still six," he told her afterward, "unless you figure I ought to get extra credit."

She said something, her voice soft and soothing, and he said something, and that went on until he stopped responding. She lay beside him, in that familiar but ever-new combination of afterglow and anticipation, and then finally she slipped out of bed, and a little while later she let herself out of his apartment.

All by herself in the descending elevator, she said out loud, "Five."

A SECOND round of Rob Roys arrived before their entrees. Then the waiter brought her fish and his steak, along with a glass of red wine for him and white for her. She'd only had half of her second Rob Roy, and she barely touched her wine.

"So you're in New York," he said. "You went there straight from college?"

She brought him up to date, keeping the responses vague for fear of contradicting herself. The story she told was all fabrication; she'd never even been to college, and her job résumé was a spotty mélange of waitressing and office temp work. She didn't have a career, and she worked only when she had to.

If she needed money—and she didn't need much, she didn't live high—well, there were other ways to get it beside work.

But today she was Connie Corporate, with a job history to match her clothes, and yes, she'd gone to Penn State and then tacked on a Wharton MBA, and ever since she'd been in New York, and she couldn't really talk about what had brought her to Toledo, or even on whose behalf she was traveling, because it was all hush-hush for the time being, and she was sworn to secrecy.

"Not that there's a really big deal to be secretive about," she said, "but, you know, I try to do what they tell me."

"Like a good little soldier."

"Exactly," she said, and beamed across the table at him.

"YOU'RE MY little soldier," her father had told her. "A trooper, a little warrior."

In the accounts she sometimes found herself reading, the father (or the stepfather, or the uncle, or the mother's boyfriend, or even the next-door neighbor) was a drunk and a brute, a bloody-minded savage, forcing himself upon the child who was his helpless and unwilling partner. She would get angry, reading those case histories. She would hate the male responsible for the incest, would sympathize with the young female victim, and her blood would surge in her veins with the desire to even the score, to exact a cruel but just vengeance. Her mind supplied scenarios—castration, mutilation, disembowelment, all of them brutal and heartless, all richly deserved.

But her own experience was quite unlike what she read.

Some of her earliest memories were of sitting on her father's lap, his hands touching her, patting her, petting her. Sometimes he was with her at bath time, making sure she soaped and rinsed herself thoroughly. Sometimes he tucked her in at night, and sat by the side of the bed stroking her hair until she fell asleep.

Was his touch ever inappropriate? Looking back, she thought that it probably was, but she'd never been aware of it at the time. She knew that she loved her daddy and he loved her, and that there was a bond between them that excluded her mother. But it never consciously occurred to her that there was anything wrong about it.

He would put her to bed and tuck her in. One night a dream woke her, and without opening her eyes she realized that he was in bed with her. She felt his hand on her shoulder and slipped back beneath the cover of sleep.

She learned to feign sleep. She'd lie awake, and at last her door would ease open and he'd be in her room, and he'd stand there while she pretended to be asleep, then get into bed with her. He'd hold her and pet her, and his presence would somehow give her permission to fall genuinely asleep.

Then, when she was thirteen, when her body had begun to change, there was a night when he came to her bed and slipped beneath the covers. "It's all right," he murmured. "I know you're awake." And he held her and touched her and kissed her.

The holding and touching and kissing was different that night, and she recognized it as such immediately, and somehow knew that it would be a secret, that she could never tell anybody. And yet no enormous barriers were crossed that night. He was very gentle with her, always gentle, and his seduction of her was infinitely gradual. She had since read how the Plains Indians took wild horses and domesticated them, not by breaking their spirit but by slowly, slowly winning them over, and the description resonated with her immediately, because that was precisely how her father had turned her from a child who sat so innocently on his lap into an eager and spirited sexual partner.

He never broke her spirit. What he did was awaken it.

He came to her every night for months, and by the time he took her virginity she had long since lost her innocence, because he had schooled her quite thoroughly in the sexual arts. There was no pain on the night he led her across the last divide. She had been well prepared, and was entirely ready.

Away from her bed, they were the same as they'd always been.

"Nothing can show," he'd explained. "No one would understand the way you and I love each other. So we must not let them know. If your mother knew—"

He hadn't needed to finish that sentence.

"Someday," he'd told her, "you and I will get in the car, and we'll drive to some city where no one knows us. We'll both be older then, and the difference in our ages won't be that remarkable, especially when we've tacked on a few years to you and shaved them off of me. And we'll live together, and we'll get married, and no one will be the wiser."

She tried to imagine that. Sometimes it seemed like something that could actually happen, something that would indeed come about in the course of time. And other times it seemed like a story an adult might tell a child, right up there with Santa Claus and the Tooth Fairy.

"But for now," he'd said more than once, "for now we have to be soldiers. You're my little soldier, aren't you? Aren't you?"

"I GET to New York now and then," Doug Pratter said.

"I suppose you and your wife fly in," she said. "Stay at a nice hotel, see a couple of shows."

"She doesn't like to fly."

"Well, who does? What they make you go through these days, all in the name of security. And it just keeps getting worse, doesn't it? First they started giving you plastic utensils with your in-flight meal, because there's nothing as dangerous as a terrorist with a metal fork. Then they stopped giving you a meal altogether, so you couldn't complain about the plastic utensils."

"It's pretty bad, isn't it? But it's a short flight. I don't mind it that much. I just open up a book, and the next thing I know I'm in New York."

"By yourself."

"On business," he said. "Not that frequently, but every once in a while. Actually, I could get there more often, if I had a reason to go."

"Oh?"

"But lately I've been turning down chances," he said, his eyes avoiding hers now. "Because, see, when my business is done for the day I don't know what to do with myself. It would be different if I knew anybody there, but I don't."

"You know me," she said.

"That's right," he agreed, his eyes finding hers again. "That's right. I do, don't I?"

OVER THE years, she'd read a lot about incest. She didn't think her interest was compulsive, or morbidly obsessive, and in fact it seemed to her as if it would be more pathological if she were not interested in reading about it.

One case imprinted itself strongly upon her. A man had three daughters, and he had sexual relations with two of them. He was not the artful Daughter Whisperer that her own father had been, but a good deal closer to the Drunken Brute end of the spectrum. A widower, he told the two older daughters that it was their duty to take their mother's place. They felt it was wrong, but they also felt it was something they had to do, and so they did it.

And, predictably enough, they were both psychologically scarred by the experience. Almost every incest victim seemed to be, one way or the other.

But it was their younger sister who wound up being the most damaged of the three. Because Daddy never touched her, she figured there was something wrong with her. Was she ugly? Was she insufficiently feminine? Was there something disgusting about her?

Jeepers, what was the matter with her, anyway? Why didn't he want her?

AFTER THE dishes were cleared, Doug suggested a brandy. "I don't think so," she said. "I don't usually drink this much early in the day."

"Actually, neither do I. I guess there's something about the occasion that feels like a celebration."

56

"I know what you mean."

"Some coffee? Because I'm in no hurry for this to end."

She agreed that coffee sounded like a good idea. And it was pretty good coffee, and a fitting conclusion to a pretty good meal. Better than a person might expect to find on the outskirts of Toledo.

How did he know the place? Did he come here with his wife? She somehow doubted it. Had he brought other women here? She doubted that as well. Maybe it was something he'd picked up at the office water cooler. *So I took her to this Eye-tie place on Detroit Avenue, and then we just popped into the Comfort Inn down the block, and I mean to tell you that girl was good to go.*

Something like that.

"I don't want to go back to the office," he was saying. "All these years, and then you walk back into my life, and I'm not ready for you to walk out of it again."

You were the one who walked, she thought. Clear to Bowling Green.

But what she said was, "We could go to my hotel room, but a downtown hotel right in the middle of the city—"

"Actually," he said, "there's a nice place right across the street."

"Oh?"

"A Holiday Inn, actually."

"Do you think they'd have a room at this hour?"

He managed to look embarrassed and pleased with himself, all at the same time. "As a matter of fact," he said, "I have a reservation."

SHE WAS four months shy of her eighteenth birthday when everything changed.

What she came to realize, although she hadn't been consciously aware of it at the time, was that things had already been changing for some time. Her father came a little less frequently to her bed, sometimes telling her he was tired from a hard day's work, sometimes explaining that he had to stay up late with work he'd brought home, sometimes not bothering with an explanation of any sort.

Then one afternoon he invited her to come for a ride. Sometimes rides in the family car would end at a motel, and she thought that was what he planned on this occasion. In anticipation, no sooner had he backed the car out of the driveway than she'd dropped her hand into his lap, stroking him, awaiting his response.

He pushed her hand away.

She wondered why, but didn't say anything, and he didn't say anything, either, not for ten minutes of suburban streets. Then abruptly he pulled into a strip mall, parked opposite a shuttered bowling alley, and said, "You're my little soldier, aren't you?"

She nodded.

"And that's what you'll always be. But we have to stop. You're a grown woman, you have to be able to lead your own life, I can't go on like this…"

She scarcely listened. The words washed over her like a stream, a babbling stream, and what came through to her was not so much the words he spoke but what seemed to underlie those words: *I don't want you anymore.*

After he'd stopped talking, and after she'd waited long enough to know he wasn't going to say anything else, and because she knew he was awaiting her response, she said, "Okay."

"I love you, you know."

"I know."

"You've never said anything to anyone, have you?"

"No."

"Of course you haven't. You're a soldier, and I've always known I could count on you."

On the way back, he asked her if she'd like to stop for ice cream. She just shook her head, and he drove the rest of the way home.

She got out of the car and went up to her room. She sprawled on her bed, turning the pages of a book without registering their contents. After a few minutes she stopped trying to read and sat up, her eyes focused on a spot on one wall where the wallpaper was misaligned.

She found herself thinking of Doug, her first real boyfriend. She'd never told her father about Doug; of course he knew that they were spending time together, but she'd kept their intimacy a secret. And of course she'd never said a word about what she and her father had been doing, not to Doug or to anybody else.

The two relationships were worlds apart in her mind. But now they had something in common, because they had both ended. Doug's family had moved to Ohio, and their exchange of letters had trickled out. And her father didn't want to have sex with her anymore.

Something really bad was going to happen. She just knew it.

A FEW days later, she went to her friend Rosemary's house after school. Rosemary, who lived just a few blocks away on Covington, had three brothers and two sisters, and anybody who was still there at dinner time was always invited to stay.

She accepted gratefully. She could have gone home, but she just didn't want to, and she still didn't want to a few hours later. "I wish I could just stay here overnight," she told Rosemary. "My parents are acting weird."

"Hang on, I'll ask my mom."

She had to call home and get permission. "No one's answering," she said. "Maybe they went out. If you want I'll go home."

"You'll stay right here," Rosemary's mother said. "You'll call right before bedtime, and if there's still no answer, well, if they're not home, they won't miss you, will they?"

Rosemary had twin beds, and fell asleep instantly in her own. Kit, a few feet away, had this thought that Rosemary's father would let himself into the room, and into her bed, but of course this didn't happen, and the next thing she knew she was asleep.

In the morning she went home, and the first thing she did was call Rosemary's house, hysterical. Rosemary's mother calmed her down, and then she was able to call 911 to report the deaths of her parents. Rosemary's mother came over to be with her, and shortly after that the police came, and it became pretty clear what had happened. Her father had killed her mother and then turned the gun on himself.

"You sensed that something was wrong," Rosemary's mother said. "That's why it was so easy to get you to stay for dinner, and why you wanted to sleep over."

"They were fighting," she said, "and there was something different about it. Not just a normal argument. God, it's my fault, isn't it? I should have been able to do something. The least I could have done was to say something."

Everybody told her that was nonsense.

• • •

AFTER SHE'D left Lucas's brand-new high-floor apartment, she returned to her own older less imposing sublet, where she brewed a pot of coffee and sat up at the kitchen table with a pad and paper. She wrote down the numbers one though five in descending order, and after each she wrote a name, or as much of the name as she knew. Sometimes she added an identifying phrase or two. The list began with 5, and the first entry read as follows:

Said his name was Sid. Pasty complexion, gap between top incisors. Met in Philadelphia at bar on Race Street (?), went to his hotel, don't remember name of it. Gone when I woke up.

Hmmm. Sid might be hard to find. How would she even know where to start looking for him?

At the bottom of the list, her entry was simpler and more specific. *Douglas Pratter. Last known address Bowling Green. Lawyer? Google him?*

She booted up her laptop.

THEIR ROOM in the Detroit Avenue Holiday Inn was on the third floor in the rear. With the drapes drawn and the door locked, with their clothes hastily discarded and the bedclothes as hastily tossed aside, it seemed to her for at least a few minutes that she was fifteen years old again, and in bed with her first boyfriend. She tasted a familiar sweetness in his kisses, a familiar raw urgency in his ardor.

But the illusion didn't last. And then it was just lovemaking, at which each of them had a commendable proficiency. He went down on her this time, which was something he'd never done when they were teenage sweethearts, and the first thought that came to her was that he had turned into her father, because her father had done that all the time.

Afterward, after a fairly long shared silence, he said, "I can't tell you how many times I've wondered."

"What it would be like to be together again?"

"Well, sure, but more than that. What life would have been like if I'd never moved away in the first place. What would have become of the two of us, if we'd had the chance to let things find their way."

"Probably the same as most high school lovers. We'd have stayed together for awhile, and then we'd have broken up and gone separate ways."

"Maybe."

"Or I'd have gotten pregnant, and you'd have married me, and we'd be divorced by now."

"Maybe."

"Or we'd still be together, and bored to death with each other, and you'd be in a motel fucking somebody new."

"God, how'd you get so cynical?"

"You're right, I got off on the wrong foot there. How about this? If your father hadn't moved you all to Bowling Green, you and I would have stayed together, and our feeling for each other would have grown from teenage hormonal infatuation to the profound mature love it was always destined to be. You'd have gone off to college, and as soon as I finished high school I'd have enrolled there myself, and when you finished law school I'd have my undergraduate degree, and I'd be your secretary and office manager when you set up your own law practice. By then we'd have gotten married, and by now we'd have one child with a second on the way, and we would remain unwavering in our love for one another, and as passionate as ever." She gazed wide-eyed at him. "Better?"

His expression was hard to read, and he appeared to be on the point of saying something, but she turned toward him and ran a hand over his flank, and the prospect of a further adventure in adultery trumped whatever he might have wanted to say. Whatever it was, she thought, it would keep.

"I'D BETTER get going," he said, and rose from the bed, and rummaged through the clothes he'd tossed on the chair.

She said, "Doug? Don't you think you might want to take a shower first?"

"Oh, Jesus. Yeah, I guess I better, huh?"

He'd known where to take her to lunch, knew to make a room reservation ahead of time, but he evidently didn't know enough to shower away her spoor before returning to home and hearth. So perhaps this sort of adventure was not the usual thing for him. Oh, she was fairly certain he tried to get lucky on business trips—those oh-so-lonely New York visits he'd mentioned, for instance—but you didn't have to shower after that sort of interlude, because you were going back to your own hotel room, not to your unsuspecting wife.

She started to get dressed. There was no one waiting for her, and her own shower could wait until she was back at her own motel. But she changed her mind about dressing, and was still naked when he emerged from the shower, a towel wrapped around his middle.

"Here," she said, handing him a glass of water. "Drink this."

"What is it?"

"Water."

"I'm not thirsty."

"Just drink it, will you?"

He shrugged, drank it. He went and picked up his undershorts, and kept losing his balance when he tried stepping into them. She took his arm and led him over to the bed, and he sat down and told her he didn't feel so good. She took the undershorts away from him and got him to lie down on the bed, and she watched him struggling to keep a grip on consciousness.

She put a pillow over his face, and she sat on it. She felt him trying to move beneath her, and she watched his hands make feeble clawing motions at the bedsheet, and observed the muscles working in his lower legs. Then he was still, and she stayed where she was for a few minutes, and an involuntary tremor, a very subtle one, went through her hindquarters.

And what was that, pray tell? Could have been her coming, could have been him going. Hard to tell, and did it really matter?

When she got up, well, duh, he was dead. No surprise there. She put her clothes on, cleaned up all traces of her presence, and transferred all of the cash from his wallet to her purse. A few hundred dollars in tens and twenties, plus an emergency hundred-dollar bill tucked away behind his driver's license. She might have missed it, but she'd learned years ago that you had to give a man's wallet a thorough search.

Not that the money was ever the point. But they couldn't take it with them and it had to go somewhere, so it might as well go to her. Right?

HOW IT happened: That final morning, shortly after she left for school, her father and mother had argued, and her father had gone for the handgun he kept in a locked desk drawer and shot her mother dead. He left the house and went to his office, saying nothing to anyone, although a coworker did say that he'd seemed troubled. And sometime during the afternoon he returned home, where his wife's body remained undiscovered. The gun was still there (unless he'd been carrying it around with him during the intervening hours) and he put the barrel in his mouth and blew his brains out.

Except that wasn't really how it happened, it was how the police figured it out. What did in fact happen, of course, is that she got the handgun from the drawer before she left for school, and went into the kitchen where her mother was loading the dishwasher.

She said, "You knew, right? You had to know. I mean, how could you miss it?"

"I don't know what you're talking about," her mother said, but her eyes said otherwise.

"That he was fucking me," she said. "You know, Daddy? Your husband?"

"How can you say that word?"

How indeed? So she shot her mother before she left for school, and called her father on his cell as soon as she got home from school, summoning him on account of an unspecified emergency. He came right home, and by then she would have liked to change her mind, but how could she with her mother dead on the kitchen floor? So she shot him and arranged the evidence appropriately, and then she went over to Rosemary's.

Di dah di dah di dah.

YOU COULD see Doug's car from the motel room window. He'd parked in the back and they'd come up the back stairs, never going anywhere near the front desk. So no one had seen her, and no one saw her now as she went to his car, unlocked it with his key, and drove it downtown.

She'd have preferred to leave it there, but her own rental was parked near the Crowne Plaza, so she had to get downtown to reclaim it. You couldn't stand on the corner and hail a cab, not in Toledo, and she didn't want to call one. So she drove to within a few blocks of the lot where she'd stowed her Honda, parked his Volvo at an expired meter, and used the hanky with which he'd cleaned his glasses to wipe away any fingerprints she might have left behind.

She redeemed her car and headed for her own motel. Halfway there, she realized she had no real need to go there. She'd packed that morning and left no traces of herself in her room. She hadn't checked out, electing to keep her options open, so she could go there now with no problem, but for what? Just to take a shower?

She sniffed herself. She could use a shower, no question, but she wasn't so rank that people would draw away from her. And she kind of liked the faint trace of his smell coming off her flesh.

And the sooner she got to the airport, the sooner she'd be out of Toledo.

SHE MANAGED to catch a 4:18 flight that was scheduled to stop in Cincinnati, on its way to Denver. She'd stay in Denver for a while, until she'd decided where she wanted to go next.

She hadn't had a reservation, or even a set destination, and she took the flight because it was there to be taken. The leg from Toledo to Cincinnati was more than half empty, and she had a row of seats to herself, but she was stuck in a middle seat from Cincinnati to Denver, wedged between a fat lady who looked to be scared stiff of something, possibly the flight itself, and a man who tapped away at his laptop and invaded her space with his elbows.

Not the most pleasant travel experience she'd ever had, but nothing she couldn't live through. She closed her eyes, let her thoughts turn inward.

AFTER HER parents were buried and the estate settled, after she'd finished the high school year and collected her diploma, after a realtor had listed her house and, after commission and closing costs, netted her a few thousand over and above the outstanding first and second mortgages, she'd stuffed what she could into one of her father's suitcases and boarded a bus.

She'd never gone back. And, until her brief but gratifying reunion with Douglas Pratter, Esq., she'd never been Katherine Tolliver again.

On the tram to Baggage Claim, a businessman from Wichita told her how much simpler it had been getting in and out of Denver before they built Denver International Airport. "Not that Stapleton was all that wonderful," he said, "but it was a quick cheap cab ride from the Brown Palace. It wasn't stuck out in the middle of a few thousand square miles of prairie."

It was funny he should mention the Brown, she said, because that's where she was staying. So of course he suggested she share his cab, and when they reached the hotel and she offered to pay half, well, he wouldn't hear of it. "My company pays," he said, "and if you really want to thank me, why don't you let the old firm buy you dinner?"

Tempting, but she begged off, said she'd eaten a big lunch, said all she wanted to do was get to sleep. "If you change your mind," he said, "just ring my room. If I'm not there, you'll find me in the bar."

She didn't have a reservation, but they had a room for her, and she sank into an armchair with a glass of water from the tap. The Brown Palace had its own artesian well, and took great pride in their water, so how could she turn it down?

"Just drink it," she'd told Doug, and he'd done what she told him. It was funny, people usually did.

"Five," she'd told Lucas, who'd been so eager to be number six. But he'd only managed it for a matter of minutes, because the list was composed of men who could sit around that mythical table and tell each other how they'd had her, and you had to be alive to do that. So Lucas had dropped off the list when she'd chosen a knife from his kitchen and slipped it right between his ribs and into his heart. He fell off her list without even opening his eyes.

After her parents died, she didn't sleep with anyone until she'd graduated and left home for good. Then she got a waitress job, and the manager took her out drinking after work one night, got her drunk, and performed something that might have been date rape; she didn't remember it that clearly, so it was hard to say.

When she saw him at work the next night he gave her a wink and a pat on the behind, and something came into her mind, and that night she got him to take her for a ride and park on the golf course, where she took him by surprise and beat his brains out with a tire iron.

There, she'd thought. Now it was as if the rape—if that's what it was, and did it really matter what it was? Whatever it was, it was as if it had never happened.

A week or so later, in another city, she quite deliberately picked up a man in a bar, went home with him, had sex with him, killed him, robbed him, and left him there. And that set the pattern.

Four times the pattern had been broken, and those four men had joined Doug Pratter on her list. Two of them, Sid from Philadelphia and

Peter from Wall Street, had escaped because she drank too much. Sid was gone when she woke up. Peter was there, and in the mood for morning sex, after which she'd laced his bottle of vodka with the little crystals she'd meant to put in his drink the night before.

She'd gone away from there wondering how it would play out, figuring she'd know when she read about it in the papers. But if there'd been a story it escaped her attention, so she didn't really know whether Peter deserved a place on her list.

It wouldn't be hard to find out, and if he was still on the list, well, she could deal with it. It would be a lot harder to find Sid, because all she knew about him was his first name, and that might well have been improvised for the occasion. And she'd met him in Philadelphia, but he was already registered at a hotel, so that meant he was probably from someplace other than Philadelphia, and that meant the only place she knew to look was the one place where she could be fairly certain he didn't live.

She knew the first and last names of the two other men on her list. Graham Weider was a Chicagoan she'd met in New York; he'd taken her to lunch and to bed, then jumped up and hurried her out of there, claiming an urgent appointment and arranging to meet her later. But he'd never turned up, and the desk at his hotel told her he'd checked out.

So he was lucky, and Alvin Kirkaby was lucky in another way. He was an infantry corporal on leave before they shipped him off to Iraq, and if she'd realized that she wouldn't have picked him up in the first place, and she wasn't sure what kept her from doing to him as she did to the other men who entered her life. Pity? Patriotism? Both seemed unlikely, and when she thought about it later she decided it was simply because he was a soldier. That gave them something in common, because weren't they both military types? Wasn't she her father's little soldier?

Maybe he'd been killed over there. She supposed she could find out. And then she could decide what she wanted to do about it.

Graham Weider, though, couldn't claim combatant status, unless you considered him a corporate warrior. And while his name might not be unique, neither was it by any means common. And it was almost certainly his real name, too, because they'd known it at the front desk. Graham Weider, from Chicago. It would be easy enough to find him, when she got around to it.

Of them all, Sid would be the real challenge. She sat there going over what little she knew about him and how she might go about playing detective. Then she treated herself to another half-glass of Brown Palace water and flavored it with a miniature of Johnnie Walker from the minibar. She sat down with the drink and shook her head, amused by her own behavior. She was dawdling, postponing her shower, as if she couldn't bear to wash away the traces of Doug's lovemaking.

But she was tired, and she certainly didn't want to wake up the next morning with his smell still on her. She undressed and stood for a long time in the shower, and when she got out of it she stood for a moment alongside the tub and watched the water go down the drain.

Four, she thought. Why, before you knew it, she'd be a virgin all over again.

DOLLY'S TRASH AND TREASURES

"MRS. SAUGERTIES?"
A nod.

"That would be Dorothy Saugerties? And did I pronounce that correctly? Like the Hudson River town?"

Another nod.

"Well, Mrs. Saugerties, I'm Baird Lewis, and this is my colleague, Rita Raschman. We're with Child Protective Services."

No response.

"One of your neighbors called to express concern over the living conditions here, and how they might impact upon your children."

"Haven't got any."

"I beg your pardon? According to our records, you have four children, three girls and a boy, and—"

"Haven't got neighbors. This here's mine, from the road back to the creek. Then there's state land on that side. Nearest neighbors would be a quarter mile from here."

"Well, one of them—"

"Might be more like a half mile. If it matters."

"Baird, may I? Mrs. Saugerties, you do have four children, don't you?"

"Did."

"They're not living here now?"

"Not anymore. Tricia, Calder, Maxine, and Little Debby. Moved away and left me here."

"When was this, Mrs. Saugerties?"

"Hard for me to keep track of time."

"I see."

"He moved out, see, and—"

"That would be your son, Calder?"

"My husband. It got so he couldn't take it, you know, so he moved out."

"Does he live nearby?"

"Don't know where he took himself off to. But he left, and then the children."

"They just left?"

"Here one day and gone the next."

"But how could—"

"Rita, if I may? Mrs. Saugerties, let me make sure I have the names right. Patricia, Calder, Maxine, and Deborah, is that right?"

"Tricia."

"That's her actual name? Good, Tricia."

"And not Deborah. Little Debby."

"Debby."

"*Little* Debby. Like the cakes."

"Like—?"

"The cakes."

"It's a brand of cupcake, Baird. You can find them next to the Twinkies."

"My life is ever the richer for knowing that, Rita. They just left, Mrs. Saugerties?"

"Might be they went with their father."

"I was wondering if that might be a possibility."

"Because, see, they just hated it here, same as he did. On account of there's no room in the house anymore. On account of my stuff."

"Your stuff. I can't help noticing there's a pile of trash on either side of the porch glider. Is that the sort of stuff you mean?"

"Ain't trash. 'Smy stuff."

"I see."

"I like to have things, and then I like to keep 'em. Other people, they don't care for it."

"Like your husband."

"And the children. Their rooms filled up, along with everything else, and there was no place for them to play. But you know, there's the whole yard. It's our property clear back to the creek."

"Yes. Do you suppose I could use your bathroom, Mrs. Saugerties?"

"Don't work."

"I see. Well, let me just go in and get myself a glass of water."

"That don't work either. Oh, I guess he didn't hear me. He wasn't really supposed to go into the house."

"I'm sure Baird won't disturb anything, Mrs. Saugerties."

"It's just such a mess, you know. No room for a body to get around. And the animals mess in the house. I don't know why I can't keep up with their messes."

"Animals?"

"Well, dogs and cats."

"How many do you have?"

"I don't know. There's different ones, and they come and they go."

"Like the children."

"Except all *they* did was go. I wish they'd come back, but I don't think they will."

"Well—"

"And there was a raccoon. Besides the dogs and cats, I mean. But I ain't seen him in I don't know how long. They don't belong in a house anyhow, you know. Raccoons, I mean. They'll make a godawful mess."

"I'm sure that's true. Baird, are you all right?"

"Yes, of course."

"You look like you saw a raccoon."

"I look like what?"

"I just said—"

"Never mind. I have *never* seen the like."

"I can imagine."

"No, Rita, I don't think you can. How anyone can live like this is quite beyond me. No children, so we can wash *our* hands of it, and I'll tell you, right now mine could use washing. We'll refer it, of course. And I don't envy the poor bastards at APS who draw this one. Mrs. Saugerties? I think we'll be going now. Uh, some other people may be in touch. They'll be able to give you a good deal of assistance."

HELP? DON'T want help.

Got all I need, right here where I am. Got my stuff right where I can put my hands on it. A whole house full of my things, and the cellar and attic, too.

Oh, I know this is no way to live. I'm not crazy. I'm not stupid, either. I don't talk much. Better if you don't. What's it they say? A fish'd never get hisself caught if he just kept his mouth shut.

That's unless they come with a net.

"MRS. SAUGERTIES? How do you do, ma'am? My name is Thelma Weider and this is my associate, John Ruddy. And may I call you Dorothy?"

"I guess."

"Dorothy, John and I are with Adult Protective Services of Lantenango County, and we're here to provide you with some assistance, and—"

"Don't need it."

"Well, I believe you'll find—"

"Who're them two?"

"The tall gentleman is Mark, and his partner is Clayton. They're with the Sheriff's Office, and they've come along on the chance that they might be needed, but I'm sure we'll be able to work this out without bringing them into it. Now before we go inside—"

"Not going inside."

"Ah. Dorothy, I believe I see bedding and a pillow on the porch glider. Is that where you've been sleeping?"

"Nice sleeping in the fresh air."

"I'm sure it was comfortable this summer, but it's autumn now, isn't it? The trees are starting to drop their leaves. The nights are getting cold."

"Ain't too bad."

"And winter's coming, and then it will be *really* cold."

"Got lots of blankets."

"But you've got a big house. What do you have, four or five bedrooms?"

"About."

"And you're all by yourself here."

"With my stuff."

"Yes, I've heard about your stuff. Rooms filled almost to the ceiling, isn't that what Baird and Rita told us?"

"What Thelma's getting at, Dorothy, is that we could help you be a lot more comfortable."

"Dolly."

"I'm sorry, do you want a doll? I don't—"

"What to call me. Dolly. Not Dorothy, nobody calls me Dorothy."

"Ah, I see. Dolly, why don't we go inside and have a look around your house? Maybe you can point out some of your most treasured things for us."

"No."

"I'm afraid we have a warrant, Dolly, that empowers us to enter and search the premises, and Mark and Clayton are here to guarantee your compliance. So I'm going in. Would you like to come with me, or would you prefer to stay out here with Thelma?"

IT'S EMBARRASSING, having people go through your house and look at your things. Knowing they're judging you, feeling the thoughts they're thinking as sure as if they were saying them out loud.

What a pig, what a slob, how could a woman let herself go this way, how could she let her house get away from her like this? Blah blah blah. All this junk, all this rubbish, why would anyone want to live with these broken dolls and old newspapers? And look at the plates, the food still encrusted on them, rotting there. Blah blah blah. And the smell, who could stay in a house with such a smell in every room? Blah blah blah.

Someday I might read the newspapers. There's plenty of interesting articles in them, if I ever get around to it. No reason not to hang onto them for when the time comes. Same with the books and magazines. I don't read much these days, but it's something I might get back to, and when I do the books will be there for me, and the magazines, and the newspapers.

And yes, a lot of the dolls are broken, but they could be fixed. Why, there's doll hospitals that do nothing but repair broken dolls, because they recognize the importance of preserving treasured memories. Even as they are, the dolls and other toys bring back memories. I bought the Raggedy Ann for Tricia, the Storybook dolls for Maxine. And there were Barbies, so many of them, that I bought for all three of the girls. And Chatty Cathy, how Little Debby loved that doll! Of course the voice is gone, and there's no string to pull, but Cathy's still there, and if you pick her up and look at her you can almost hear her little voice again, almost hear Little Debby parroting the phrases right back at her.

And some of my stuff is worth money. All those Jim Beam decanters, they're scattered all over the house, but they're here somewhere, and a few of them are genuinely rare, and worth good money to a collector. The Colorado Centennial

73

one? *You think that's easy to find? Or cheap to buy when you do find it? Walter was a Scotch drinker, but he was a good enough sport to switch to bourbon when they came out with those decanters, and in a sense they never cost me a cent, because he had to drink something and he said it might as well be bourbon. And didn't he say he'd got to prefer Jim Beam to the Cutty Sark he used to drink?*

What's he drinking nowadays, wherever he is? Did he go back to Scotch? Or did he stay with Jim Beam?

What's it they say? One man's trash is another man's treasure. Just 'cause it's trash to you don't make it wrong for me to cherish it. But it's all empty bottles as far as these two are concerned, John and Thelma, all empty Pepsi cans and beer bottles.

Trash and treasures. If I ever opened a shop, that's what I'd call it. Dolly's Trash & Treasures. Which is which? Well, that's up to you, isn't it?

And then there's the bottle caps, and don't ask me how many of those I've got. I decided I could make earrings for the girls, they'd be cute and cost next to nothing, so I started saving bottle caps, and I bought a box of the posts you mount the caps on, and got the right kind of quick-setting glue, and no, I haven't actually made any earrings yet, but who's to say I won't one of these days? With the girls run off there's not much point in making earrings now, but who's to say they won't come back?

Nehi Orange, that was always Little Debby's favorite. And somewhere I know I've got a pair of orange bottle caps set aside, and wouldn't they make perfect earrings for Little Debby?

"I'M JUST not getting through to her. What do we have to do, throw her in the back of the Sheriff's car and haul her off to the nuthouse?"

"John!"

"I know, I didn't mean to use the word. I find this stressful, I admit it. I'm sorry."

"John, let me try. Dolly, at this point you only have two choices, and—"

"Dorothy."

"I thought you said people call you Dolly."

"My *friends* call me Dolly."

"Ouch. I gather you don't think we're your friends."

"If you were my friends you wouldn't be trying to force me out of my own house and home."

"Oh, I love it. A home? It's a home to vermin and unidentifiable rodents, not to a human being."

"John—"

"And it won't even be a house much longer either, with the structural damage you've got going on there."

"John, this isn't helping."

"Sorry."

"If you could just allow me to—"

"I know, I know. I won't say anything more."

"Now Dolly, as I was saying, you've got two choices, and you're the one who has to make the decision. The first possibility is that you allow us to relocate you to a really beautiful county facility for assisted living."

"A nuthouse."

"No, Dolly, and if John used that expression it was a mistake."

"A loony bin."

"Not at all. The people are perfectly nice and the staff is wonderful. My own mother is there, as it happens, and she's truly happy. Would I let my mother go there if it wasn't a good place?"

"My children moved away and left me all alone, but at least they never put me in a loony bin."

"Oh, Christ."

"John! The other choice you have, Dolly, is to allow us to clean your house. We'll get a crew in here to clean it top to bottom."

"And throw out all my things."

"A lot of what you've got here is trash, Dolly. We know that and you know that. Old newspapers, empty pizza boxes, paper plates with food on them—"

"I guess some of it's trash."

"See? If it wasn't such an overwhelming chore, you'd throw out a lot of it yourself."

"There's times I've wanted to. But I wouldn't even know where to start."

"Well, that's where we'll be able to help you. We'll bring in a full crew of trained professionals who've been through all this more times than you could imagine. They'll know where to start and they'll be able to see it through to the finish."

"It sort of got away from me, you know. It wasn't like this when I moved in."

"I'm sure it wasn't."

"And I didn't set out to make it like this. But, you know, I like things, and I don't want to part with my memories. And throwing out useful things is wasteful."

"Well, that's true, isn't it?"

"And if these men start throwing away all of my good things—"

"Dolly, you'll be here the whole time. The things you want to keep, you just say so, and they'll be put in boxes to be saved. Or if it's too tiring, we can make some of the decisions for you. And before you know it you'll have a clean house, a home you can take pride in."

"It's not so bad the way it is. And I have some wonderful things here."

"Oh, Christ."

"John—"

"I mean, it's my house. I'm the only one here. Why can't you all just leave me be?"

"Dolly, let me explain it one more time…"

ALL THESE people. There must be twenty men, all dressed alike with royal blue shirts and navy blue slacks. Their first names are embroidered in gold braid on their shirt pockets. The only names I've managed to read are Harry and Ben. I keep reading those two names over and over, Harry and Ben, Harry and Ben. Maybe there are ten Harrys and ten Bens, or maybe I just keep seeing the same two young men over and over. They all look the same anyway, with those white masks covering their noses and mouths. Like the air in here would kill them.

Going through my things. Picking up a Little Debby cake box or a book with the cover missing, holding it out, rolling their eyes. They don't think I notice what they're doing.

They'll throw out some things I'd like to keep. I know that. I do what I can, I tell them no, I want to save this, put it in a box to be saved. And sometimes the woman talks me out of saving it, or else she agrees and they put it in a box, but how do I know what will happen to all those boxes? If I let them, they'd take everything I own and cart it to the landfill.

When your house is clean again, the woman tells me, you'll have a much richer life. Richer without things than with them? You'll have space, she says. And who knows? Maybe your children will come back, when they have a decent clean place to live, when they can have their own rooms again.

It would be so nice to believe that. And maybe it's true. Maybe Calder will come back, and Tricia, and Maxine. And Little Debby. Oh what I'd give to see my Little Debby again!

"I DON'T believe this."

"You've never had a case like this before?"

"Never anything like this. I mean, I read about the Collyer brothers, but I thought they were the only people in the world who ever lived like this."

"It's more common than anyone realizes, John. I've heard estimates that one percent of the population has a problem with compulsive hoarding."

"That sounds crazy. That'd be what, three million people?"

"I know. The thing is, most of the time it's invisible. The people seem completely normal until you get inside their homes."

"Not our Dolly. Spend thirty seconds with her and you know you're dealing with a fruitcake."

"John!"

"She can't hear me, she's in the kitchen explaining why an empty Peter Pan peanut butter jar is a priceless treasure. See, it's glass, and nowadays they make them out of plastic, so who'd be crazy enough to throw it out?"

"I know."

"And the rotten peanut butter at the bottom just adds to the value. Proves it's authentic. Plus it gives the ants something to eat."

"Oh, dear. But there are people who are almost as far gone as Dolly and you wouldn't know it. There was a woman in Swedish Haven, and she was always immaculately groomed and clean about her person, and she walked to and from her place of business every day—"

"She had a place of business?"

"A shop, actually. She sold notions and bric-a-brac and, oh, local souvenirs. The shop was neat as a pin."

"And I bet she sold pins, too."

"And doilies and place mats. Until one day the shop never opened, and when her doorbell and phone went unanswered someone broke into her house and found her there. A stroke or a heart attack, whatever it was, but dead or alive she was in better shape than her house. It turned out she could have been a Collyer sister."

"Don't tell me it was like this."

"It wasn't filthy, and everything was in a semblance of order. But she never threw anything out, and the newspapers were packed in orderly stacks until they reached clear to the ceiling, and so were old clothes and everything else you could think of. Including empty jars, peanut butter and otherwise. She soaked off the labels and scrubbed the jars clean, but she kept them all, along with just about everything else that came into her hands."

"Good grief."

"I don't know that you can call it a disease, but it's certainly a disorder. I understand the FBI profilers divide serial killers into organized and disorganized, and I suppose you could distinguish between Dolly and the woman in Swedish Haven in much the same way, and—"

"John? Thelma? Excuse me, but there's something you ought to see."

"What is it, Arnie?"

"Well, it's a cat."

"There've been a few of them running around. What's so special about this one?"

"Well, for one thing, it's running days ended a while ago. A couple of years, would be my guess. Come on, you're not gonna believe this."

I WONDERED whatever happened to that cat. It was a gray tabby, and I can remember the sound it made when it purred. Although I guess all cats make the same sound, pretty much. It's a comfort, hearing them make that sound, which I guess is part of the reason I always liked having animals in the house.

I thought it probably wandered off. They come and they go. But something must have happened to this one, and then it just turned up again.

"IT'S LIKE an archaeological dig. You go down another stratum and you're in another year."

"And if it's a truly productive site, sooner or later you unearth a dead cat."

"Did you hear what she said? She always wondered what happened to that cat. You know what it looked like?"

"A cartoon cat."

"Exactly! Like Wiley Coyote when he falls off a cliff and flattens out on the pavement. Or like Tom when Jerry outsmarts him—"

"Which is all the time."

"—and he gets run over by a steamroller. Then he picks himself up, fills out again, and gets back into the game."

"Without having learned his lesson. But I'm afraid this cat's not going to fill out again."

"No."

"I wonder how it died. And when."

"I hope you're not going to order an autopsy."

"No, hardly that, but they didn't come across it until they'd moved a whole mountain of junk. It must have been there for years."

"Unless it dug its way under there and died."

"Why would it do something like that?"

"Maybe it knew it was dying, and how else could it make sure it got buried? You know what else I was wondering? I was just—oh, hang on a minute. Arnie, is there a problem?"

"A problem? It's all of it a problem, isn't it? The thing is, well, I don't know if you need to know this, or if you even *want* to know it, but the boys just found another cat."

IT WAS the little calico.

Except I should say she. All calico cats are female. It's genetic, and you'll never find a male one. How many people know that?

They think I'm stupid and ignorant, but I'm not. There are a lot of things I know that most people probably don't. All white cats with blue eyes are deaf. Born that way. Genetic.

How do I know? Well, I sure didn't learn it in school. There's a book about cats, a very good book, and there's a chapter in it about genetics. One gene decides if a cat is Siamese or not.

I've got the book here somewhere. Unless one of them threw it out, one of these geniuses with his name on his shirt so he won't forget who he is.

That calico cat, she was always Little Debby's favorite. Of course all of the children liked all of the animals, that's the way they were brought up, but that calico, Little Debby was crazy about her.

"THAT WOMAN in Swedish Haven?"

"She was remarkable. The way the inner and outer lives were at such utter variance."

"Right, but here's my question. How many cats did she have?"

"Not a one."

"Seriously? I thought they all had a house full of cats."

"She didn't have any, living or dead. Unless you count china cats."

"She had those?"

"Oh, plenty of them. She collected them. And patterned glass, and travel books, and postcards and matchbooks. All of them carefully organized and neatly displayed, except that there was such a profusion of clutter that you couldn't really see any of the displays. But they were all there, and all in apple-pie order."

"Your organized lunatic, as opposed to your disorganized lunatic."

"Except they're not lunatics, or at least not all of them. Something goes wrong in their wiring, or maybe it's a way to come to terms with a horrible childhood, or—"

"Oh, shit, everybody had a bad childhood."

"Well, I have to say nobody molested me, or locked me in the closet for a week at a time. While some of the cases we get—"

"All right, point taken. Mine wasn't that bad, either. I used to say I had as miserable a childhood as the next braggart, but it was way short of being that kind of nightmare."

"I just hope there aren't any more dead animals. Because the good news is that we're making real progress here."

"Well, give the dead cats some credit."

"What do you mean, John?"

"Ever since the first one turned up, she hasn't been kicking up a fuss. Haven't you noticed? Instead of putting up a fight every time somebody wants to throw out the 1972 *World Almanac*, she stays locked into her own private world and leaves the men alone. It makes a big difference."

"Maybe she's resigned herself to it."

"And maybe she figured she knows where the county landfill is, and she can just drive down there and retrieve her treasures after we're gone."

"Oh, God, don't even say that."

"Plus who knows what other treasures she might find while she's there, and—Arnie, what is it? And please don't tell me dead cats come in threes."

"No, John, I think it's worse than that. Arnie, you're white as a sheet. It's bad, isn't it?"

"Yeah."

"Arnie, what is it?"

"Eddie and that other fellow, I can't think of his name right now—"

"Never mind his name."

"I don't know why I can't think of it. But it don't matter for now. The two of them, they was in the basement, which is no judgment calls involved, you know, because it's all water-damaged and all gotta be thrown out, and they were in, I don't know, the root cellar or the fruit cellar, or maybe it was the coal cellar back in the day."

"And?"

"You just better come downstairs. You better come see for yourselves."

ONE LOOK and I knew who I was looking at. I recognized her right off. Her T-shirt was faded, it used to be yellow and now it's more of a gray, but you can still make out Minnie Mouse's picture on it, and that meant it was Little Debby. It was one of her favorite shirts, she plain loved Minnie Mouse.

But I'd have known anyway, because of the size. She was the youngest, and small for her age on top of that, so it for sure wasn't Tricia or Maxine. Plus her red hair was a dead giveaway. Nobody else had hair that color. I guess she got it from her father, not that he was a redhead but his mother was. And nobody on my side of the family had red hair.

Not that I know just how that works in people. Cat genetics, there's something I know a little about, but I think it's more complicated in human beings.

I'll tell you something, I think I knew it was Little Debby before I even set eyes on her. I just got this powerful feeling on the way down the cellar stairs. I couldn't guess when was the last time I went anywhere near the cellar, but on the staircase, well, I had this feeling.

So I guess she didn't run off after all. I guess it couldn't have been so bad here at home, I guess she liked it well enough to stay.

A mother's not supposed to play favorites, but she was my favorite, Little Debby. It's funny, I don't know how to explain this, but I have to say it: I'm sort of glad she's here.

I wonder what else will turn up.

HOW FAR
A ONE-ACT STAGE PLAY

SCENE: A restaurant in Hoboken, New Jersey. BILLY CUTLER is at a table for two, reading a thick hardcover novel. DOROTHY MORGAN enters, looks around the room, unsure if this is the man she's supposed to meet. She goes offstage and returns accompanied by a WAITER, who steers her toward Billy's table. Billy looks up, and closes his book and stands as she approaches.

> BILLY
> Billy Cutler. And you're Dorothy Morgan, and you could probably use a drink. What would you like?

> DOROTHY
> I don't know. What are you having?

> BILLY
> Well, night like this, minute I sat down I ordered a martini, straight up and dry as a bone. And I'm about ready for another.

> DOROTHY
> Martini's are in, aren't they?

> BILLY
> Far as I'm concerned, they were never out.

DOROTHY

I'll have one.

BILLY

Joe?

(The waiter withdraws)

It's treacherous out there. The main roads, the Jersey Turnpike and the Garden State, they get these chain collisions where fifty or a hundred cars slam into each other. Used to be a lawyer's dream before no-fault came in. I hope you didn't drive.

DOROTHY

No, I took the PATH train. And then a cab.

BILLY

Much better off.

DOROTHY

Well, I've been to Hoboken before. In fact we looked at houses here about a year and a half ago.

BILLY

You bought anything then, you'd be way ahead now. Prices are through the roof.

DOROTHY

We decided to stay in Manhattan.

BILLY

And you knew to take the PATH train. Well, I drove, and the fog's terrible, no question, but I took my time and I didn't have any trouble. Matter of fact, I couldn't remember if we said seven or seven-thirty, so I made sure I was here by seven.

DOROTHY

Then I kept you waiting. I wrote down seven-thirty, but—

BILLY

I figured it was probably seven-thirty. I also figured I'd rather do the waiting myself than keep you waiting. Anyway, I had a book to read, and I ordered a drink, and what more does a man need? Ah, here we go.

(The waiter appears with two drinks on a tray. She takes a sip, relaxes visibly.)

DOROTHY

That was just what I needed.

BILLY

Well, there's nothing like a martini, and they make a good one here. Matter of fact, it's a pretty decent restaurant altogether. They serve a good steak, a strip sirloin.

DOROTHY

Also coming back in style, along with the martini.

BILLY

So? You want to be right up with the latest trends? Should I order us a couple of steaks?

DOROTHY

Oh, I don't think so. I really shouldn't stay that long.

BILLY

Whatever you say.

DOROTHY

I just thought we'd have a drink and—

BILLY

And handle what we have to handle.

DOROTHY

That's right.

BILLY

Sure. That'll be fine.

DOROTHY

(She picks up her drink, sips it, looking for a way
back into the conversation.)
Even without the fog, I'd have come by train and taxi. I
don't have a car.

BILLY

No car? Didn't Tommy say you had a weekend place up
near him? You can't go back and forth on the bus.

DOROTHY

It's his car.

BILLY

His car. Oh, the fella's.

DOROTHY

Howard Bellamy's. His car, his weekend place in the
country. His loft on Greene Street, as far as that goes.

BILLY

But you're not still living there.

DOROTHY

No, of course not. And I don't have any of my stuff at
the house in the country. And I gave back my set of car
keys. All my keys, the car and both houses. I kept my old

apartment on West Tenth Street all this time. I didn't even sublet it because I figured I might need it in a hurry. And I was right, wasn't I?

BILLY
What's your beef with him exactly, if you don't mind me asking?

DOROTHY
My beef. I never had one, as far as I was concerned. We lived together three years, and the first two weren't too bad. Trust me, it was never Romeo and Juliet, but it was all right. And then the third year was bad, and it was time to bail out.
(She reaches for her drink, surprised to note it's empty.)
He says I owe him ten thousand dollars.

BILLY
Ten large.

DOROTHY
He says.

BILLY
Do you?

DOROTHY
(shakes her head no)
But he's got a piece of paper. A note I signed.

BILLY
For ten thousand dollars.

DOROTHY
Right.

BILLY

Like he loaned you the money.

DOROTHY

Right. But he didn't. Oh, he's got the paper I signed, and he's got a canceled check made out to me and deposited to my account. But it wasn't a loan. He gave me the money and I used it to pay for a cruise the two of us took.

BILLY

Where? The Caribbean?

DOROTHY

The Far East. We flew to Singapore and cruised down to Bali.

BILLY

That sounds pretty exotic.

DOROTHY

I guess it was. This was while things were still good between us, or as good as they ever were.

BILLY

This paper you signed.

DOROTHY

Something with taxes. So he could write it off, don't ask me how. Look, all the time we lived together I paid my own way. We split expenses right down the middle. The cruise was something else, it was on him. If he wanted me to sign a piece of paper so the government would pick up part of the tab—

BILLY

Why not?

DOROTHY

Exactly. And now he says it's a debt, and I should pay it, and I got a letter from his lawyer. Can you believe it? A letter from a lawyer?

BILLY

He's not going to sue you.

DOROTHY

Who knows? That's what the lawyer letter says he's going to do.

BILLY

The minute he goes into court and you start testifying about a tax dodge—

DOROTHY

But how can I, if I was a party to it?

BILLY

Still, the idea of him suing you after you were living with him. Usually it's the other way around, isn't it? They got a word for it.

DOROTHY

Palimony.

BILLY

That's it, palimony. You're not trying for any, are you?

DOROTHY

Are you kidding? I said I paid my own way.

BILLY

That's right, you did say that.

DOROTHY

I paid my own way before I met him, the son of a bitch, and I paid my own way while I was with him, and I'll go on paying my own way now that I'm rid of him. The last time I took money from a man was when my Uncle Ralph lent me busfare to New York when I was eighteen years old. He didn't call it a loan, and he sure as hell didn't give me a piece of paper to sign, but I paid him back all the same. I saved up the money and sent him a money order. I didn't even have a bank account. I got a money order at the post office and sent it to him.

BILLY

That's when you came here? When you were eighteen?

DOROTHY

Fresh out of high school. And I've been on my own ever since, and paying my own way. I would have paid my own way to Singapore, as far as that goes, but that wasn't the deal. It was supposed to be a present. And he wants me to pay my way and his way, he wants the whole ten thousand plus interest, and—

BILLY

He's looking to charge you interest?

DOROTHY

Well, the note I signed. Ten thousand dollars plus interest at the rate of eight percent per annum.

BILLY

Interest.

DOROTHY

He's pissed off that I wanted to end the relationship. That's what this is all about.

90

BILLY
I figured.

DOROTHY
And what *I* figured is if a couple of the right sort of people
had a talk with him, maybe he would change his mind.

BILLY
And that's what brings you here.
> (She nods. She's toying with her empty glass.
> He points to it, raises his eyebrows. She nods, he
> raises a hand, catches the offstage waiter's eye,
> signals for another round.)

DOROTHY
(pause)
I didn't know who to call, and then I thought of Tommy,
and he said maybe he knew somebody.

BILLY
And here you are.

DOROTHY
And here I am, and—
> (He holds up a hand, cutting her off, and the
> waiter appears, and they're silent until he has
> served their drinks and withdrawn.)

BILLY
A couple of the boys could talk to him.

DOROTHY
That would be great. What would it cost me?

BILLY
Five hundred dollars would do it.

DOROTHY

Well, that sounds good to me.

BILLY

The thing is, when you say talk, it'll have to be more than talk. You want to make an impression, situation like this, the implication is either he goes along with it or something physical is going to happen. Now, if you want to give that impression, you have to get physical at the beginning.

DOROTHY

So he knows you mean it?

BILLY

So he's scared. Because otherwise what he gets is angry. Not right away, but later. Two tough-looking guys push him against a wall and tell him what he's gotta do, that scares him, but then they don't get physical and he goes home, and he starts to think about it, and he gets angry.

DOROTHY

I can see how that might happen.

BILLY

But if he gets knocked around a little the first time, enough so he's gonna feel it for the next four, five days, he's too scared to get angry. That's what you want.

DOROTHY

Okay.

BILLY

(Sips his drink, looks at her over the brim)
There's things I need to know about the guy.

DOROTHY

Like?

BILLY

Like what kind of shape is he in.

DOROTHY

He could stand to lose twenty pounds, but other than that he's okay.

BILLY

No heart condition, nothing like that?

DOROTHY

No.

BILLY

He work out?

DOROTHY

He belongs to a gym, and he went four times a week for the first month after he joined, and now if he gets there twice a month it's a lot.

BILLY

Like everybody. That's how the gyms stay in business. If all their paid-up members showed up, you couldn't get in the door.

DOROTHY

You work out.

BILLY

Well, yeah. Weights, mostly, a few times a week. I got in the habit. I won't tell you where I got in the habit.

DOROTHY

And I won't ask, but I could probably guess.

BILLY

(grinning)

You probably could.

(back to business)

Martial arts. He ever get into any of that?

DOROTHY

No.

BILLY

You're sure? Not lately, but maybe before the two of you started keeping company?

DOROTHY

He never said. And he would, it's the kind of thing he'd brag about.

BILLY

Does he carry?

DOROTHY

Carry?

BILLY

A gun.

DOROTHY

God, no.

BILLY

You know this for a fact?

DOROTHY

He doesn't even own a gun.

BILLY

Same question. Do you know this for a fact?

DOROTHY

Well, how would you know something like that for a fact? I mean, you could know for a fact that a person *did* own a gun, but how would you know that he didn't? I can say this much—I lived with him for three years and there was never anything I saw or heard that gave me the slightest reason to think he might own a gun. Until you asked the question just now it never entered my mind, and my guess is it never entered *his* mind, either.

BILLY

You'd be surprised how many people own guns.

DOROTHY

I probably would.

BILLY

Sometimes it feels like half the country walks around strapped. There's more carrying than there are carry permits. A guy doesn't have a permit, he's likely to keep it to himself that he's carrying, or that he even owns a gun in the first place.

DOROTHY

I'm pretty sure he doesn't own a gun, let alone carry one.

BILLY

And you're probably right, but the thing is you never know. What you got to prepare for is he *might* have a gun, and he *might* be carrying it.

(he waits while she takes this in and nods)
So here's what I've got to ask you. What you got to ask
yourself, and come up with the answer. How far are you
prepared for this to go?

DOROTHY

I'm not sure what you mean.

BILLY

We already said it's gonna be physical. Manhandling
him, and a couple of shots he'll feel for the better part of
a week. Work the rib cage, say.

DOROTHY

All right.

BILLY

Well, that's great, if that's how it goes. But you got to
recognize it could go farther.

DOROTHY

What do you mean?

BILLY

I mean you can't necessarily decide where it stops. I don't
know if you ever heard the expression, but it's like, uh,
having relations with a gorilla. You don't stop when you
decide. You stop when the gorilla decides.

DOROTHY

I never heard that before. It's cute, and I sort of get the
point, or maybe I don't. Is Howard Bellamy the gorilla?

BILLY

He's not the gorilla. The violence is the gorilla.

DOROTHY

Oh.

BILLY

You start something, you don't know where it goes. Does he fight back? If he does, then it goes a little farther than you planned. Does he keep coming back for more? As long as he keeps coming back for it, you got to keep dishing it out. You got no choice.

DOROTHY

I see.

BILLY

Plus there's the human factor. The boys themselves, they don't have an emotional stake. So you figure they're cool and professional about it.

DOROTHY

That's what I figured.

BILLY

But it's only true up to a point, because they're human, you know? So they start out making themselves angry with the guy, they tell themselves how he's a lowlife piece of garbage, so it's easier for them to shove him around. Part of it's an act but part of it's not, and say he mouths off, or fights back and gets in a good lick. Now they're really angry, and maybe they do more damage than they intended to.

DOROTHY

I can see how that could happen.

BILLY

So it could go farther than anybody had in mind. He could wind up in the hospital.

DOROTHY

You mean like broken bones?

BILLY

Or worse. Like a ruptured spleen, which I've known of cases. Or as far as that goes there's people who've died from a bare-knuckle punch in the stomach.

DOROTHY

I saw a movie where that happened.

BILLY

Well, I saw a movie where a guy spreads his arms and flies, but dying from a punch in the stomach, they didn't just make that up for the movies. It can happen.

DOROTHY

Now you've got me thinking.

BILLY

Well, it's something you got to think about. Because you have to be prepared for this to go all the way, and by all the way I mean all the way. It probably won't, ninety-five times out of a hundred it won't.

DOROTHY

But it could.

BILLY

Right. It could.

DOROTHY

Jesus. He's a son of a bitch, but I don't want him dead. I want to be done with the son of a bitch. I don't want him on my conscience for the rest of my life.

BILLY

That's what I figured.

DOROTHY

But I don't want to pay him ten thousand dollars either, the son of a bitch. This is getting complicated, isn't it?

BILLY

(getting to his feet)

Let me excuse myself for a minute, and you think about it, and we'll talk some more.

> (He goes to the men's room. She takes a small sip from her half-empty glass, sets it down, picks up his book, examines it, puts it back. He comes back.)

DOROTHY

Well, I thought about it.

BILLY

And?

DOROTHY

I think you just talked yourself out of five hundred dollars.

BILLY

That's what I figured.

DOROTHY

Because I certainly don't want him dead, and I don't even want him in the hospital. I have to admit I like the idea of him being scared, really scared bad. And hurt a little. But that's just because I'm angry.

BILLY

Anybody'd be angry.

DOROTHY

But when I get past the anger, all I really want is for him to forget this crap about ten thousand dollars. For Christ's sake, that's all the money I've got in the world. I don't want to give it to him.

BILLY

Maybe you don't have to.

DOROTHY

What do you mean?

BILLY

I don't think it's about money. Not for him. It's about sticking it to you for dumping him, or whatever. So it's an emotional thing and it's easy for you to buy into it. But say it was a business thing. You're right and he's wrong, but it's more trouble than it's worth to fight it out. So what you do is settle.

DOROTHY

Settle?

BILLY

You always paid your own way, so it wouldn't be out of the question for you to pay half the cost of the cruise, would it?

DOROTHY

No, but—

BILLY

But it was supposed to be a present, from him to you. But forget that for the time being. You could pay half.
(beat)

Still, that's too much. What you do is offer him two thousand dollars. I have a feeling he'll take it.

DOROTHY
God, I can't even talk to him. How am I going to offer him anything?

BILLY
You'll have someone else make the offer.

DOROTHY
You mean like a lawyer?

BILLY
Then you owe the lawyer. No, I was thinking I could do it.

DOROTHY
Are you serious?

BILLY
I wouldn't have said it if I wasn't. I think if I was to make the offer he'd accept it. I wouldn't be threatening him, but there's a way to do it so a guy feels threatened.

DOROTHY
(sizing him up)
He'd feel threatened, all right.

BILLY
I'll have your check with me, two thousand dollars, payable to him. My guess is he'll take it, and if he does you won't hear any more from him on the subject of the ten grand.

DOROTHY
So I'm out of it for two thousand. And five hundred for you?

BILLY

I wouldn't charge you anything.

DOROTHY

Why not?

BILLY

All I'd be doing is having a conversation with a guy. I don't charge for conversations. I'm not a lawyer, I'm just a guy owns a couple of parking lots.

DOROTHY

And reads thick novels by young Indian writers.

BILLY

Oh, this? You read it?
            (she shakes her head no)
It's hard to keep the names straight, especially when you're not sure how to pronounce them in the first place. And it's like if you ask this guy what time it is he tells you how to make a watch. Or maybe a sun dial. But it's pretty interesting.

DOROTHY

I never thought you'd be a reader.

BILLY

Billy Parking Lots. Guy who knows guys and can get things done. That's probably all Tommy said about me.

DOROTHY

Just about.

BILLY

Maybe that's all I am. Reading, well, it's an edge I got on just about everybody I know. It opens other worlds. I don't live in those worlds, but I get to visit them.

DOROTHY

And you just got in the habit of reading? The way you got in the habit of working out?

BILLY

(laughs)

No, reading's something I've done since I was a kid. I didn't have to go away to get in that particular habit.

DOROTHY

I was wondering about that.

BILLY

Anyway, it's hard to read there, harder than people think. It's noisy all the time.

DOROTHY

Really? I didn't realize. I always figured that's when I'd get to read *War and Peace*, when I got sent to prison. But if it's noisy, then the hell with it. I'm not going.

BILLY

You're something else.

DOROTHY

Me?

BILLY

Yeah, you. The way you look, of course, but beyond the looks. The only word I can think of is *class*, but that's a word that's mostly used by people that haven't got any themselves. Which is probably true enough.

DOROTHY

The hell with that. After the conversation we just had? Talking me out of doing something I could have regretted all my life, *and* figuring out how to get that son of a bitch off my back for two thousand dollars? I'd call that class.

BILLY

Well, you're seeing me at my best.

DOROTHY

And you're seeing me at my worst, or close to it. Looking to hire a guy to beat up an ex-boyfriend. That's class, all right.

BILLY

That's not what I see.

DOROTHY

Oh?

BILLY

I see a woman who won't let herself be pushed around. And if I can find a way that helps you get where you want to be, then I'm glad to do it. But when all's said and done, you're a lady. And I'm a wiseguy.

DOROTHY

I don't know what you mean.

BILLY

Yes, you do.

DOROTHY

Yes, I guess I do.

BILLY

Drink up. I'll run you back to the city.

DOROTHY

You don't have to do that. I can take the PATH train.

BILLY

I've got to go into the city anyway. It's not out of my way to take you wherever you're going.

DOROTHY

If you're sure.

BILLY

I'm sure. Or here's another idea. We both have to eat, and I told you they serve a good steak here. Let me buy you dinner, and then I'll run you home.

DOROTHY

Dinner.

BILLY

A shrimp cocktail, a salad, a steak, a baked potato—

DOROTHY

You're tempting me.

BILLY

So let yourself be tempted. It's just a meal.

DOROTHY

No. It's more than a meal.

BILLY

It's more than that if you want it to be. Or it's just a meal, if that's what you want.

DOROTHY

But you can't know how far it might go. We're back to that again, aren't we? Like what you said about the gorilla, and you stop when the gorilla wants to stop.

BILLY

I guess I'm the gorilla, huh?

DOROTHY

You said the violence was the gorilla. Well, in this case it's not violence, but it's not you or me, either. It's what's going on between us, and it's already going on, isn't it?

BILLY

You tell me.

DOROTHY

(looks down at her hands, then up at him)
A person has to eat.

BILLY

You said it.

DOROTHY

And it's still foggy outside.

BILLY

Like pea soup. And who knows? There's a good chance the fog'll lift by the time we've had our meal.

DOROTHY

I wouldn't be a bit surprised. You know something? I think it's lifting already.

CURTAIN

MICK BALLOU LOOKS AT THE BLANK SCREEN

"AT FIRST," MICK BALLOU said, "I thought the same as everyone else in the country. I thought the fucking cable went out."

We were at Grogan's, the Hell's Kitchen saloon he owns and frequents, and he was talking about the final episode of *The Sopranos*, which ended abruptly with the screen going blank and staying that way for ten or fifteen seconds.

"And then I thought, well, they couldn't think of an ending. But Kristin recalled the time Tony and Bobby were talking of death, and what it would be like, and that you wouldn't even know it when it happened to you. So that was the ending, then. Tony dies, and doesn't even know it."

It was late on a weekday night, and the closemouthed bartender had already shooed the last of the customers out of the place and put the chairs up on the tables, where they'd be out of the way when someone else mopped the floor in the morning. I'd been out late myself, speaking at an AA meeting in Marine Park, then stopping for coffee on the way home. Elaine met me with a message: Mick had called, and could I meet him around two?

There was a time when most of our evenings started around that time, with him drinking twelve-year-old Jameson while I kept him company with coffee or Coke or water. We'd go until dawn, and then he'd drag me down to St. Bernard's on West 14th Street for the butchers' mass. Nowadays our evenings started and ended earlier, and there weren't enough butchers in the gentrified Meat Market district to fill out a mass, and anyway St. Bernard's itself had given up the ghost, and was now Our Lady of Guadalupe.

And we were older, Mick and I. We got tired and went home to bed. And now he'd summoned me to discuss the ending of a television series.

He said, "What do you think happens?"

"You're not talking about tv."

He shook his head. "Life. Or the end of it. Is that what it is? A blank screen?"

I talked about near death experiences, all of them remarkably similar, with the consciousness hovering in midair and being invited to go to the light, then making the decision to return to the body. "But there's not a lot of eyewitness testimony," I said, "from the ones who go to the light."

He thought about it, nodded.

"You're a Catholic," I said. "Doesn't the Church tell you what happens?"

"There's things I take their word for," he said, "and things I don't. Kristin thinks you meet your loved ones on the other side. But of course she'd want to think that."

Kristin Hollander had lost her parents in a brutal home invasion, and had met Mick in its aftermath, when I sent him to her house to keep her safe. They'd grown friendly since.

"She has this set that puts you in mind of a movie screen," he said. "We watched the show together and sat around for hours talking about it." He drank whiskey. "There are some I'd not mind seeing again. My brother Dennis, for one. But after a few words about old times, what would we talk about for the rest of eternity?"

I wondered where this was going. He'd called me out in the middle of the night, and I had a feeling he wanted to tell me something, and I was afraid to ask what it was.

And so we drifted into a shared silence, not uncommon during our late evenings together. I was searching for a way to break it, but it was Mick who spoke first.

"There's a favor I have to ask you," he said.

"I DREADED hearing it," I told Elaine. "I just knew he was going to tell me he was dying."

"But he's not."

"He wants me to stand up for him. He's getting married. To Kristin."

"I figured that's why he wanted to meet you. So he could tell you. You didn't see it coming?"

"I thought they were just friends."

She gave me a look.

"He's forty years older than she is," I said, "and spent those years tearing up the West Side. No, I didn't see it coming."

"You never noticed the way she looks at him? Or the way he looks at her?"

"I knew they enjoyed each other's company," I said, "but—"

"Oy," she said. "Some detective."

ONE LAST NIGHT AT GROGAN'S

WE HAD DINNER AT Paris Green, a few blocks south of our apartment on Ninth Avenue. I ordered the sweetbreads, and wondered not for the first time why they were called that, being neither sweet nor bread. Elaine pointed out that Google could clear that up for us in no more than thirty seconds. More like two hours, I told her, by the time I'd run out of other fascinating things to click on.

The fish of the day was Alaskan halibut, and that's what she chose. After many years as a vegetarian, she'd been persuaded by a nutritionist to regard fish as a vegetable. At first she worried it would be the culinary equivalent of a gateway drug, and in no time at all she'd be cracking beef bones and sucking out the marrow. So far she hadn't progressed past fish a couple of times a week.

It was around eight when Gary showed us to our table, and maybe an hour later when we said no to dessert and yes to espresso. It's rare for her to have coffee, especially late in the day, and my surprise must have shown in my face. "It could be a long night," she said. "I figure I'd better be awake for it."

"I can see how much you're looking forward to it."

"About as much as you are. It's got to be like a wake without a corpse. Except last night would have been the wake, so what's this? The burial?"

"I guess."

"I always thought the Irish wake made a lot of sense. Pour down the booze until you can think of something good to say about the deceased. My people cover the mirrors, sit around on hard wooden benches, and stuff themselves with food. I wonder what it was like last night."

"I'm sure he'll tell us."

We finished our coffee, and I signaled our waitress for the check. Gary brought it himself. How many years had we known him? How many years had we been coming here a couple of times a month?

It seemed to me that neither he nor the restaurant had changed. He always looked as though something reminded him of a joke, and the light in his blue eyes hadn't dimmed any. But his beard, still hanging from his long jaw like an oriole's nest, showed some gray now, and his age showed at the corners of his eyes. And it was a night to notice such things.

"I didn't see you last night," he said. "Of course I didn't go over until we closed up shop here. You'd probably headed for home by then."

"That would be—"

"The big fella's place. You're friends, aren't you? Or have I got it wrong, as I so often do?"

"We're close friends," I said. "I didn't realize you knew him that well."

"I don't, not really. But he's part of the neighborhood, isn't he? I doubt I've been in Grogan's a dozen times in as many years, but I made sure I got there last night."

"Paying your respects," Elaine suggested.

"And watching my neighbors take advantage of the open bar. A sight guaranteed to raise or lower your opinion of the human race, depending where it was to begin with. And, you know, being present for the end of an era, and isn't that the most overused phrase at our command? Every time a sitcom's canceled, someone proclaims it the end of an era."

"And once in a while it is," she said.

"You're thinking of *Seinfeld*."

"Well, yeah."

"An exception," he said, "that proves the rule. As is the shuttering of Grogan's Open House. A fixture in the local landscape, and soon enough the building will be gone and no one will remember what used to be there. Our town, forever reinventing itself. I heard they made the owner such a good offer that he was willing to risk Mr. B's wrath for selling the building out from under him. And I also heard that Mick owned the building, no matter whose name might be on the deed."

"You hear lots of things," I said.

"You do," he agreed. "I'm pleased to report that the era of hearing things is still going strong."

FOR LONGER than I've known him, my friend Mick Ballou has been the proprietor of Grogan's Open House, a Hell's Kitchen saloon at the southeast corner of Tenth Avenue and Fiftieth Street. The place began as a hangout for the neighborhood hoodlums, or at least that segment thereof who pledged some sort of undefined allegiance to the man himself. In recent years it has attained a certain degree of raffish respectability, even as the neighborhood has gentrified around it. The new people who've moved into refurbished tenements or new high-rise condos like to stop in for a draft Guinness and point out what may or may not be bulletholes in the walls.

Mick has always tended to hire Irish lads as bartenders, most of them fresh transplants from Belfast or Derry or Strabane, but a Northern Ireland accent never kept a new man from learning how to make a Wild Mustang or a Novarian Sunset. The new crowd liked bellying up to the bar next to old neighborhood regulars, and a man who'd worked half a century as a subway motorman would be transformed in the telling into a desperate character with blood on his hands. The old fellows didn't mind; they were just trying to make a glass of beer last until the next pension check arrived.

"Don't come on the Friday," Mick had told me. "'Twill be our last night, with the whole of the West Side sure to come out for it. An open bar until the taps run dry, and there'll even be a bit of food."

"And everybody's welcome but me?"

"You would be welcome enough," he said, "but you would hate it, as I expect to hate it myself. I won't have Kristin there, and wouldn't be there my own self had I any choice in the matter. Come on the Saturday, and bring herself."

"Friday's your last night," I said.

"It is. And the following night there'll be none but the four of us. And haven't our best nights always been after closing time?"

WE WALKED down Ninth and over Fiftieth, where the last of the Street Fair vendors were dismantling their booths. "Like nomads in Central Asia," Elaine said. "Packing their yurts and heading for richer grazing."

113

"A few years back their flocks would have gone hungry here," I said, "or been prey for the local wolves. Now they sell T-shirts and Gap knockoffs and Vietnamese sandwiches, and the block association spends the fees installing security cameras and planting more ginkgo trees."

"And look at the ornamental light posts," she said. "Like the ones we saw in Paris."

Grogan's came into view as we neared Tenth Avenue. The tavern occupied the ground floor, with three levels of rental units above it. All the apartment windows facing the street had big white X's on them, indicating that the building was scheduled for demolition. No light showed behind the X's, and Grogan's looked to be dark as well. I wondered if perhaps Mick had changed his mind and gone home, and then I saw one light glowing dimly through the front door's little window.

We hesitated at the curb, although there were no cars coming, and Elaine responded to my unvoiced thought. "We have to," she said.

KRISTIN UNLOCKED the door for us. A light glowed softly in a leaded glass shade hanging over a table way in the back. There were four chairs grouped around the table, the only chairs in the room that hadn't been put up on top of other tables. Mick wasn't at the table, and I didn't see him anywhere else, either.

"I'm glad you're here," she said. "So's himself." She rolled her eyes. "'So's himself.' Listen to me, will you? He's in the office, he'll be out in a minute. And now that you're here—"

She arranged a cardboard CLOSED sign so that it covered the window. "Double duty," she said. "Tells them we're closed and keeps them from seeing there's a light on."

"All the world sees you as a Jewish-American Princess," said the former Elaine Mardell. "Yet it's clear you were born to be an Irish saloonkeeper."

"A wee village pub in Donegal," Kristin said. "On the wind-swept shores of Lough Swilly. That's our favorite fantasy. The funny thing is I think I could actually enjoy it well enough. And so could he, for three weeks tops. Then he'd want to put a match to the adorable thatched roof and come home."

She led us to the table. Her drink was iced tea, and we said that sounded good to us, too. Mick's bottle of twelve-year-old Jameson was on the table, along with a glass and a little water pitcher. The Jameson bottle is clear glass, so I could note the color of its contents. I still like the color of good whiskey. Or of bad whiskey, for that matter, because the color doesn't say anything about the quality. All it tells you is that you've got a thirst for it.

Before Kristin was back with our iced tea, Mick had emerged from the office in back, a paper bag in hand. "I had the devil's own time finding a bag to put this in," he said, "as if it would have been a hardship to tuck it under your arm and carry it unwrapped through the streets. We've no place for it in the house, and himself made the mistake of admiring it."

I knew what it was before Elaine got it out of the bag, a 9x12 framed Irish landscape.

"It's Conor Pass in the Dingle peninsula," Kristin said. "It really looks like that, too. I think it's the most beautiful place I've ever been."

"It's a hand-colored steel engraving," Elaine said. "There was no color printing at the time, so there were people who added color one at a time by hand. There's a lost art for you, but then so's steel engraving."

"The few arts not yet lost," Mick said, "have their heads on the chopping block, waiting for technology to lop them off." His hand moved first to the bottle, then to the water pitcher, then back to the bottle; he picked it up and poured a small measure of good Cork whiskey into his glass.

"Quite the affair last night," he said.

"I was going to ask."

"Oh, it was a right hooley. They paid their twenty dollars at the door and for that they got to drink until the well ran dry. 'Twas for the help, you know. I had four men working, and they got to divide just over eight thousand dollars."

"Not bad for a night's work."

"Well, it was a long night, and that crowd kept them hopping. But they had their tips on top of that, and the tips are decent when the drinks are free." He'd had his glass in his hand, and now he took the smallest sip from it. "I stood at the door taking the money, and being asked the same fucking questions all night long. 'Wasn't it terrible that the greedy landlord sold the building out from under me?'"

Kristin laid a hand on his arm. "When all along," she said, "the man himself was the greedy landlord."

"I was the best landlord that ever lived," he said. "Three floors above me packed full with rent-controlled tenants, and the heat bill for the building was higher than its rent roll, and I never even bothered putting in for what rent increases the law allowed me."

"A saint," Elaine said.

"I was that. If the Creator were half the landlord I was, Adam and Eve would never have left Eden. My lot would be late with the rent, they might not pay for months on end, and I gave them no trouble. If there's one thing that'll save me a bit of time in Purgatory, it's how I treated my tenants. And then, as a final sweetener, I gave each of them fifty thousand dollars to move."

I said that was generous.

"I could well afford it. Don't ask what Rosenstein got them to pay for the building."

"I won't."

"I'll tell you anyway. Twenty-one million dollars."

"A nice round sum."

"The sum," he said, "was to be twenty million, which is rounder if not so nice, and then Rosenstein went back to them and said his client was fond of the old English system, and preferred guineas to pounds. Are you familiar with guineas?"

"You don't mean Italians."

"A guinea was a gold coin," he said, "back when they had such an article, and it was the nearest thing to a pound sterling, but with twenty-one shillings instead of twenty. So a price in guineas is five percent higher than the same in pounds. I suspect the notion died out when decimal currency came in, but there was a time when your carriage trade liked prices in guineas. Rosenstein told me he didn't really expect this to work, but that it wouldn't be outrageous enough to kill the deal altogether, and we could always back off and take the twenty. But they paid us in guineas after all."

"And that small lagniappe paid off your tenants."

"It did." He put his glass down. "You'd have thought they'd won the Powerball, and in a sense they had. Of course there was one wee fucker, fourth floor rear on the left, who thought there might be a toy or two left in Santa's sack. 'Oh, I don't know, Mr. Ballou, and where am I gonna move to, and how'll I find something decent that I can afford, and all the expenses of relocation.'"

I could see the shadow of a smile on Kristin's face.

"I looked at him," Mick said, "and did I settle a hand on his shoulder? No, I don't believe I did. I just held him with my eyes, and I lowered my voice, and I said I knew he'd be able to move, and move quickly, as it would be unsafe for him and his loved ones to be in the presence of men whose job it was to knock things down and blow them up. And in the end his was the first apartment vacated. Can you imagine?"

Kristin clasped her hands, looking like Lois Lane. "My hero," she said.

IT'S NOT impossible to take me by surprise, but I can't think of anything that did so more utterly than Mick's announcement of his upcoming marriage to Kristin. It was at Grogan's that I learned of it, after some preliminary speculation on what happens after you die. I'd been bracing myself for bad news when he asked me to be his best man.

Elaine swears she saw it coming, and can't imagine how I didn't.

Kristin came into our lives when her parents left theirs, the victims of a particularly horrible home invasion. The madman who orchestrated it wasn't finished; he wanted her and the house and the money, and it didn't stop him when I spiked his first try. He came back a few years later, and didn't miss by much.

I got Mick to babysit her, confident that no one would get past him. They sat in the kitchen of her brownstone. They drank coffee and played cribbage. I suppose they talked, though I couldn't guess what they talked about.

That's the same house in which she discovered her parents' bodies. She went on living there, because she is far tougher at the core than you'd think, and she lives there now as my friend's wife, and if they're as unlikely a couple as Beauty and the Beast, you lose sight of the disparity after a few minutes in their company. He's a big man, hard and forbidding as an Easter Island monolith, and she looks to be a frail and slender slip of a girl. He's forty years her senior. She's a child of privilege, while he's a Hell's Kitchen hoodlum who's killed grown men with his hands.

And she settles her hand on his arm, and beams while he tells his stories.

• • •

THERE WAS a silence, with an unasked question hovering. Elaine broke the one and asked the other. Did he regret the sale?

"No," he said, and shook his head. "Why should I? I could run it a thousand years and not take twenty million dollars out of it. And if it's a neighborhood institution, and enough people felt they had to say so last night, well, it's one the neighborhood's well off without."

"There's history here," I said.

"There is, and most of it misfortunate. Crimes planned, oaths sworn and broken. You were here on the worst night of all."

"I was remembering it just now."

"How could you not? Two men in the doorway, spraying bullets as if they were watering the flowers. One tosses a bomb, and I can see the arc of it now, and the flash before the sound of it, like lightning before thunder."

The room went still again, until Mick got to his feet. "We need music," he announced. "They were supposed to come this afternoon for the Wurlitzer, the truck from St. Vincent de Paul. The creature's not old enough to be valuable or new enough to be truly useful, but they said they'd find a home for it. If they get here tomorrow or Monday they're welcome to it, assuming I'm here to let them in. On Tuesday the building changes hands, and what's in it belongs to the new owner, and most likely goes into a landfill along with the bricks and floorboards. You haven't any use for it, have you? Or a two-ton Mosler safe? I didn't think so. What would you like to hear?"

Elaine and I shrugged. Kristin said, "Something sad."

"Something sad, is it?"

"Something mournful and Irish."

"Ah," he said. "Sure, that's easily arranged."

I REMEMBERED an evening some years earlier. Elaine and I on our way out of the Met at Lincoln Center, the last strains of *La Bohème* still resounding. Elaine in a mood, restless. "She always fucking dies. I don't want to go home. Can we hear more music? Something sad, it's fine if it's sad. It can break my fucking heart if it wants. Just so nobody dies."

We hit a couple of clubs, wound up downtown at Small's, and by the time we got out of there the sun was up. And her mood had lifted.

Irish songs on the ground floor of a Hell's Kitchen tenement may be a far cry from jazz in a Village basement, but it served the same purpose, drawing us down into the mood as a means of easing us through it. I don't remember exactly what Mick selected, but there were Clancy Boys and Dubliners cuts, and some ballads of the 1798 Rising, including a rendition of *Boolavogue* with a clear tenor voice backed by a piper's keening.

That was the last record to play, and it would have been a hard one to follow. I was put in mind of the Chesterton poem, and trying to remember just how it went when Elaine read my mind and quoted it:

For the great Gaels of Ireland
Are the men that God made mad,
For all their wars are merry,
And all their songs are sad.

"I wonder," Mick said. "Is it just the Irish? Or are we all of us like that, deep in our hearts?" He got to his feet, picked up his bottle and glass. "That's enough whiskey. Is it iced tea you're all drinking? I'll fetch us another pitcher." And to Kristin: "No, don't get up. 'Tis my establishment still. I'll provide the service."

HE SAID, "Will I miss it? The short answer is it's a bar like any other, and I've lost my taste for them, even my own."

"And the long answer?"

He gave it some thought. "I expect I will," he said. "The years pile up, you know. The sheer weight of them has an effect. I wasn't always on the premises, but the place was always here for me." He filled his glass with iced tea, sipped it as if it were whiskey. "The room is full of ghosts tonight. Can you feel it?"

We all nodded.

"And not just the shades of those who died that one bad night. Others as well, whose deaths were somewhere else altogether. Just now I looked over at the bar and saw a little old man in a cloth cap, perched on a stool and nursing a beer. I pointed him out to you once, but you wouldn't remember."

But I did. "Ex-IRA," I said. "If it's the fellow I'm thinking of."

"It is. One of Tom Barry's lads in West Cork he was, and that lot shed enough blood to redden Bantry Bay. When his regular local closed he brought his custom here, and drank a beer or two seven nights a week.

And then one night he wasn't here, and then the word came that he was gone. No man lives forever, not even a wee cutthroat from Kenmare."

He pronounced it Ken-mahr. There's a Kenmare Street a few blocks long in NoLita, which is the tag realtors have fastened on a few square blocks north of Little Italy. A Tammany hack called Big Tim Sullivan managed to name it for his mother's home town in County Kerry, but he couldn't make people pronounce it in the Irish fashion. Ken-mair's what they say, if indeed they say the name at all; the residents nowadays are mostly Chinese.

"Andy Buckley," he said. "You remember Andy."

That didn't require an answer. I could hardly have forgotten Andy Buckley.

"He was here on that bad night. Got us into the car and away, the two of us."

"I remember."

"As good behind the wheel of a car as any man I've ever known. And as good with darts. He'd scarcely seem to be paying attention, and with a flick of his wrist he'd put the little feathered creature just where he wanted it."

"He made it look effortless."

"He did. You know, when I had them put this place back together again, I bought a new dartboard and had it installed in the usual place on the back wall. And I found I didn't like seeing it there, and I took it down." He took a deep breath, held it, let it out. "I had no choice," he said.

Andy Buckley had betrayed Mick, his employer and friend. Sold him out, set him up. And I'd been there on a lonely road upstate when Mick took Andy's head in his own big hands and broke his neck.

You remember Andy, he'd said.

"No fucking choice," he said, "and yet it never sat easy with me. Or why would I have had them replace the dartboard? And why would I have taken it down?"

"IF THEY hadn't come round with their offer," he said, "I'd never have closed Grogan's. It never would have occurred to me. But the time's right, you know."

Kristin nodded, and I sensed they'd discussed this point before. Elaine asked what was so right about the timing.

"My life's changed," he said. "In many ways, beyond the miracle that an angel came down from heaven to be my bride."

"How he does go on," Kristin said.

"My business interests," he said, "are all legitimate. The few wide boys I had working for me have moved on, and if they're still doing criminal deeds they're doing them at someone else's behest. I'm a silent partner in several enterprises, and I may have come by my interest by canceling a debt or doing someone an illegal favor, but the businesses themselves are lawful and so is my participation."

"And Grogan's is an anomaly?" Elaine frowned. "I don't see how, exactly. It's evolved like the rest of your life, and it's more a yuppie watering hole than a hangout for hoodlums."

He shook his head. "No, that's not the point. In the bar business there's no end of men looking to cheat you. Suppliers billing you for undelivered goods, bartenders making themselves your silent partners, hard men practicing extortion and calling it advertising or charity. But I always had a pass, you know, because they knew to be afraid of me. Who'd try to get over on a man with my reputation? Who'd dare to steal from me, or cheat me, or put pressure on me?"

"Whoever did would be taking his life in his hands."

"Once," he said. "Once that was true. Now the lion's old and toothless and wants only to lie by the fire. And sooner or later some lad would make his move, and I'd have to do something about it, something I'd not care to do, something I'm past doing. No, I'm well out of the game." He sighed. "Will I miss it? There's parts of the old life I miss, and it's no shame to admit it. I wouldn't care to have it back, but there's times when I miss it." His eyes found mine. "And you? Is it not the same for you?"

"I wouldn't want it back."

"Not for anything. But do you miss it? The drink, and all that went with it?"

"Yes," I said. "There are times I do."

IT WAS late when we left. Mick turned off the one light, locked up, proclaiming the latter a waste of time. "If anyone wants to come in and take something, what does it matter? None of it's mine anymore."

He had his car, the big silver Cadillac, and dropped us off. Nobody had much to say beyond a few pleasantries as we got out of the car, and the silence held while Elaine and I crossed the Parc Vendome's lobby and ascended in the elevator. She had her key out and let us in, and we checked Voice Mail and email, and she found a coffee cup I'd left beside the computer and returned it to the kitchen.

We tried the Conor Pass engraving in a few spots—in a hallway, in the front room—and decided to defer the decision of where to hang it. Elaine felt it wanted to be seen at close range, so we left it for now, propped against the base of a lamp on the drum-top table.

The little tasks one does, all of them performed in a companionable silence.

And then she said "It wasn't so bad."

"No. It was a good evening, actually."

"I love the two of them so much. Individually and together."

"I know."

"And he's much better off without the place. He'll be fine, don't you think?"

"I think so."

"But it really is, isn't it? The end of an era."

"Like *Seinfeld*?"

She shook her head. "Not quite," she said. "There won't be any reruns."

PART OF THE JOB

"WALTERS HAS GONE OVER," Jondahl said. He was cleaning his glasses with a specially impregnated tissue. "His was a very sensitive position, you know. He had access to his department's most important plan. Took a copy of it and ran with it." He crumpled the tissue, studied the lenses, put the glasses on and looked across his desk at me. "Now he'll peddle it to the highest bidder."

"It's important?"

"Vital. Walters thinks he's clear. He's not. Security's had an eye on him for months, waiting for something like this. He's been followed, went to ground in a cheap hotel. The hotel's under surveillance." Jondahl looked at me, his glance apologetic. "You have to get to him before the competition does. You see that, of course."

"We want the plan back, I suppose."

"More than that. Walters was in a sensitive spot, I told you that. The plan is on paper. It's in his head as well. He could hurt us."

"So I have to hurt him first."

Jondahl grunted. He passed me an airline ticket folder. "Your flight's in three hours. Don't suppose you'll want to pack much. You can return as soon as you've made contact."

"Good word for it."

"Well. You know the game, of course. Walters knew the rules too, you might keep that in mind. He knew the risks, evidently felt the rewards justify them. Money, glory, whatever he wants. Whatever such people think they want. Well. You'll recover the plan, you'll deal with Walters, you'll return as soon as possible. It's your job."

"Grand job."

He looked at me. "Somebody has to do it. I don't say it's fun, but it needs doing. Most people barely know we exist, but—"

"They sleep better at night because we do our job."

"Well," he said.

I went back to my flat and packed a bag. I knew Walters, a nervous young man with brooding eyes and a high forehead. I had played chess with him several times, and once we had had lunch together. I wondered what made that sort of man decide to go over.

A taxi took me to the airport. I carried my one bag onto the plane. The flight was smooth and generally uneventful. The stewardess declined my dinner invitation, then sent me wistful looks suggesting that she might change her mind if I asked her again. I didn't.

The plane touched down a half hour after sunset. I lugged my bag into the terminal building and dropped a dime in the telephone slot. I dialed and the phone was answered on the third ring. I said, "Marriage has many pains."

"Celibacy has no pleasures."

"Marvellous," I said.

"We've made a reservation for you at his hotel. His room is 412. He's not in it at the moment. He's at dinner. We have two men on him. He didn't meet anyone for dinner."

"Good."

"We believe he has someone coming to see him tomorrow morning. Perhaps earlier."

I hung up and checked to see if they had returned my dime by mistake. They did once, years ago, and ever since I've looked for them to repeat this error. I took a taxi to Walters' hotel. It was seedy. The lobby carpet was threadbare and all the furniture prewar. I signed in at the desk. The clerk punched a bell, and we waited in silence until a bellhop finally appeared. He escorted me to a room on the second floor. I had no change. I gave him a dollar and watched him gape at it. After he went away I put my clothes in the dresser, slipped the gun in one pocket and the ice pick in another. Then I walked past the elevator and climbed two flights of stairs and found 412. I knocked, and no one came.

The lock was laughable. I slipped the bolt with a strip of celluloid, let myself in. I gave the room a toss. The plan didn't turn up, and I gave up and parked myself in a chair. I might have looked more carefully but didn't care to make a mess. Jondahl would want this one to look like natural causes. If it was just a question of recovering the plan I would have tossed the room thoroughly and been gone before Walters returned, but since a confrontation was inevitable I decided to save myself the work and worry and let Walters find it for me.

Evidently he liked a leisurely dinner. I sat in the chair for half an hour before I heard his footsteps in the hall, then his key in the lock. I moved to the side of the door, and when he came through it I put the gun in the small of his back. He gasped, and I kicked the door shut and bolted it. I said, "Hello Walters. The plan, if you don't mind."

"My God." He looked at me, his mouth trembling. "Please. I never thought—"

"You never thought you'd be caught. No one ever does. I want the plan, then I'll be going. That's all."

"I could cut you in."

"The plan, Walters."

"I'd give you half. One hell of a lot of money, all of it cash, and no one would have to know you took it."

"I'm loyal. I don't bite the hand that feeds me."

"Loyal!" He looked again at the gun, then at me again. "Loyal. My God, you're not human."

"If that's an insult, it's the sort I can live with. The plan, and then I don't care what you do."

He may not have believed me. But there wasn't much else to believe. It turned out that the plan was still in his suitcase, tucked between the lining and the frame. I looked it over, and it was what I was after.

"What's that?"

"Where?"

I pointed, and he looked, and I hit him back of the ear, just hard enough to knock him out and not hard enough to leave a bruise that would make anybody wonder. He fell face downward. I rolled him over and stuck the icepick into a nostril and on into the brain. A heart attack, or, if they checked more carefully, a brain hemmorhage.

The body remained undiscovered when I checked out early the next morning. I had breakfast on the plane. When I tossed the report on Jondahl's desk he glanced at it, smiled at me. "And the contact?"

"Clean and neat."

"Excellent. A good job."

"Oh?"

My face bothered him. "You did well," he said. "Take the rest of the week off."

"I intend to."

"Good. Get some sunshine, catch up on your sleep. This was just part of the job, you know that. You know what this—" he tapped the sheaf of papers "—would mean to our competitors."

"Yes."

"A detailed report of our fall merchandising program. Advertising, promotion, packaging, distribution, price structure. Everything." He smiled at me. "I'm recommending a bonus for you. You've got a fine future. General Household Products is a grateful employer."

"And I'm a loyal employee," I said. I went outside to get some fresh air.

THE STORY ABOUT THE STORY...

> ...is arguably better than the story itself. Here's an introduction
> I wrote to accompany "Part of the Job" when it appeared—
> finally!—in *Alfred Hitchcock's Mystery Magazine*:

IN MAY OF 2011 I was in Orange, California, signing copies of *A Drop of the Hard Stuff* at Book Carnival. Lynn Munroe, the dealer/collector with a vast knowledge of midcentury genre fiction and erotica, turned up with a couple of rarities for me to sign. And he showed me a copy of the December 1967 issue of a magazine called *Dapper*. "There's a story of yours in here," he said.

Oh?

I looked at the story, and it had my name on it. I didn't recognize the title, and I knew I'd never had a story in *Dapper*. Far as I could remember, I'd never even laid eyes on a copy of the magazine.

I gave "Part of the Job" a very quick scanning, and it didn't ring any kind of a bell. At the same time, I didn't spot any sentences that I could swear I hadn't written. (Sometimes, you know, you can tell. Back in the early 1960s, I wrote pseudonymous erotic novels for publishers like Midwood and Nightstand under names like Sheldon Lord and Andrew Shaw, and I also licensed those pen names to ghostwriters. I've lately been reissuing some of those works as ebooks—for as surely as rock breaks scissors and paper covers rock, so does avarice trump almost everything. But I'll only bring out those books I wrote myself, and I rarely have to look at more than a page or two to see my own hand at work, or be certain of its absence.)

"Well, it could be mine," I told Lynn. "I have absolutely no recollection of it, but at the same time I can't rule it out."

"I bought two copies," he said magnanimously, "and one's for you. I figured you didn't have the magazine, or you would have included the story in *One Night Stands & Lost Weekends.*"

That was a collection of my earliest work, and "Part of the Job" would have fit in perfectly—if it was mine and if I'd had a clue it existed.

I read the story that night in my hotel room. By the time I'd finished, I was willing to acknowledge the story as my own work. There was not a line in it I couldn't have written, and there were phrases and sentences that sounded to me like my own voice. Moreover, I saw the ending coming—in a way that suggested I had had a hand in devising it.

But how could I have so utterly forgotten it?

I KNOW when I must have written the story. It would have been in late 1962 or early 1963, when I was living on Ebling Avenue in Tonawanda. I'd been writing stories for the crime magazines since 1957, when I'd made my first sale ("You Can't Lose") to *Manhunt.* Sometime in '62 I managed to sell a story to *AHMM*, and that encouraged me to write several more with that market in mind. Some of them sold. One that did not, I'm reasonably certain, was "Part of the Job."

It is, as you'll see, not a terribly complicated story. I'm sure the basic idea occurred to me, and once it did I sat down and wrote it. Since then I've learned to live with an idea for a little while, giving the subconscious a chance to develop it, but back then I would take the idea straight to the typewriter and stand up an hour or two later with a finished manuscript. Short stories were done of an evening; the daytime hours were devoted to the production of twenty or more pages of a novel.

So the story wasn't on my mind for very long before it was in the mail to my agent. It would have gone to AHMM—I believe the magazine was edited in Florida back then—and I wouldn't have necessarily been notified that it failed to sell, but after that happened my agent would have sent it somewhere else.

And so on.

And then, in late '63 or early '64, my agent and I split the blanket. I represented myself for a few months, and then got another agent, and moved to Wisconsin to take an editorial job with Western Printing. I was there for a year and a half, wrote some books nights and weekends, and returned to the New York area to resume writing full-time with a new agent.

So what happened to "Part of the Job"? I can only guess that it was on some editor's desk when that first agent returned my unsold manuscripts to me, and that it kept getting sent out even though I was no longer a client. (That particular agent wasn't overly scrupulous about that sort of thing.) And somewhere down the line it went to *Dapper*, which would have been a market of last resort, and someone there bought it. And paid $50 for it, I would guess, which never found its way to me. (The agent in question wasn't overly scrupulous about that, either.) I never learned of the sale, I never got paid for the sale, and but for Lynn Munroe's good work, you wouldn't be reading it today.

It's not much of a story, and I have to say the story about it is better than the story itself. But here's the part I really like: It's appearing now, at long last, in the magazine for which it was originally written. And here's the part I like even better: I'm getting paid for it!

SCENARIOS

THE ROAD VEERED A few degrees as it reached the outskirts of the city, just enough to move the setting sun into his rear-view mirror. It was almost dawn, its bottom rim already touching the horizon, and would have been somewhere between gold and orange if he'd turned to look at it. In his mirror, some accident of optics turned it the color of blood.

There will be blood, he thought. He'd seen the film with that for a title, drawn into the theater by the four uncompromising words. He couldn't remember the town, or if it had been weeks or months ago, but he could summon up the smell of the movie house, popcorn and musty seats and hairspray, could recall the way his seat felt, and its distance from the screen. His memory was quirky that way, and what did it matter, really, when or where he'd seen the film? What did it matter if he'd seen it at all?

Blood? There was greed, he thought, and bitterness, and raw emotion. There was a performance which never let you forget for a moment that you were watching a brilliant actor hard at work. And there was blood, but not all that much of it.

The sun burned blood-red in his rear-view, and he bared his teeth and grinned at it. He could feel the energy in his body, the tingling sensation in his hands and feet, a palpable electrical current surging within him. The sun was setting and the night was coming and there would be a moon, and it would be a hunter's moon.

His moon.

There would be a woman. Oh, yes, there would be a woman. And there would be pleasure—his—and there would be pain—hers. There would be both those things, growing ever more intense, rushing side by side to an ending.

There would be death, he thought, and felt the blood surging in his veins, felt a throbbing in his loins. Oh, yes, by all means, there would be death.

There might even be blood. There usually was.

YES. THIS was the place.

It was the third bar he'd walked into, and he stepped up to the rail and ordered his third double vodka of the evening, Absolut, straight up.

As far as he could tell, all vodka was the same. He ordered Absolut because he liked the way it sounded. Once in a liquor store window he saw a vodka that called itself Black Death, and he'd tried ordering that for a while, but nobody ever had it. He didn't suppose it would taste any different.

The bartender was a short-haired blonde with hard blue eyes that took his measure as she poured his drink. She didn't like what she saw, he could tell that much, and under the right circumstances he'd enjoy setting her straight. She had an inch-long scar on her sharp chin, and he let himself imagine giving her some new scars. Breaking some bones. Driving the heel of his hand into her temple, right next to the eye socket. If you did it just right, you got the eye to pop out. If you did it wrong, well, there was nothing to stop you from trying again, was there?

He didn't like her, didn't think she was pretty, wasn't drawn to her. But he was hard already, just thinking of what he could do to her.

But all he did was pick up his glass and drain it. On nights like this the only effect alcohol had on him was to energize him. Instead of taking the edge off, it honed it. The anticipation, the heightened excitement, caused his body to metabolize alcohol differently. It coursed in his veins like amphetamine, but without the overamping, the jitters. Picked him up and straightened him out, all at once, and a pity they couldn't use that in their ads.

The bartender had gone off to make a drink for somebody else. He thought again of the hard look in her eyes and pictured her eye popped out. He put his hand in his pocket and touched the knife. Let her keep her eyes, at least for a while. Cut her eyelids off, put her in front of a mirror, let her watch what happened to her. Cut her lips off, cut her ears off, cut her tits off. Teach her to look at him and size him up, teach her to judge him. Teach her good.

He couldn't pick her up, no chance of that, but he could easily wait for her. Lie in ambush, be there in the shadows when she closed the bar and walked to her car. Next thing she knew she'd be naked, wrists and ankles tied, mouth taped, watching herself in the mirror. Like that, bitch? Happy now?

Then he turned away and saw the girl and forgot the bartender forever.

WHAT OTHER men would see, he supposed, was a pretty woman. Not supermodel looks, not heart-stopping beauty, but an exceptionally attractive oval face framed with lustrous dark brown hair that fell to her shoulders. He saw all that himself, of course, but what he saw most clearly was her utter vulnerability.

She was there for the taking, there to be taken, and it was almost too easy, like shooting tame animals at a game farm. Not that he ever considered letting that dissuade him from scooping her up. Her vulnerability had a powerfully erotic effect on him. He was rock-hard, and knew he'd stay that way until dawn. He'd be able to fuck her all night long, he wouldn't stop until she was dead. And maybe not even then. Maybe he'd throw one more fuck into her afterward, just for luck. What was death, after all, but the ultimate submission?

He watched her, felt the energy flowing, and willed her to look his way. He knew she'd be unable to resist, and sure enough her head turned and her eyes met his. He put everything into his smile, and knew the effect it would have. At moments like this his face turned absolutely radiant, as if lit from within.

She answered with a tentative smile of her own. He walked over to her, and didn't she look like a bird hypnotized by a snake? One hand holding her stemmed glass, the other resting on the bar, as if for support.

"Hi," he said, and dropped his own hand on her free hand. Her hand was small beneath his, small and soft. If he pressed down hard he could break all the bones in her sweet little hand, and he could picture the look in her eyes when he did, but for now his hand rested very lightly upon hers.

"My name's Jerry," he said. "Actually it's Gerald, with a G, but people call me Jerry, with a J."

None of this was true.

YOU KNOW where this is going, don't you? Of course you do. Why, you could probably write the rest of it yourself.

Clearly, there's going to be a twist, a surprise. Otherwise there's no story. Boy meets girl, boy fucks girl, boy kills girl—that's not a story. However dramatically you might present it, however engaging their dialogue, however intense his pleasure and her pain, it just won't work as fiction. We might hang on to the very end, completely caught up in the action, but by the time it was all over we'd hear Peggy Lee singing in the background. "Is that all there is?"

No, that's not all there is. We can do better than that.

For example:

HE DIDN'T need any more vodka. But she poured drinks for both of them, and another would do him no harm. He tossed it back, and had just enough time to register the thought that there was more in it than alcohol. Then the lights went out.

They didn't come back on all at once. Consciousness returned piecemeal. He heard music, something orchestral, harshly atonal. He was seated on some sort of chair, and when he tried to move he found that he couldn't, that he was tied to it, his wrists to its arms, his ankles to its legs. He tried opening his eyes and discovered he was blindfolded. He tried opening his mouth and discovered it was taped.

And then she was touching him, caressing him. Her hands knew their business, and he responded almost in spite of himself, desire shoving fear aside. Her hands, her mouth, and then she was astride him, engulfing him, and God knows it wasn't how he'd planned the evening, but then the evening wasn't over yet, was it? They'd do it her way for now, and later it would be his turn to tie her up, and what a surprise he'd have in store for her!

But for now this was fine, this was more than fine, and she took him right up to the edge and held him there, held him there forever, and then tipped him over the edge.

The climax was shattering, and it sent him away somewhere, and when he came back he was no longer wearing the blindfold. He opened his eyes and she was there, naked, glistening with perspiration, and he would have told her how beautiful she was but his mouth was still taped shut.

"You naughty boy," she was saying. "look what I found in your pocket." And she held out her hand and showed him the knife, worked the catch to free the four-inch blade, turned it to catch the light. "Now tell me, Gerald with a G or Jerry with a J, just what were you planning to do with this?"

But he couldn't tell her anything, not with his mouth taped. He tossed his head, trying to get her to take off the tape, but all that did was make her laugh.

"That was a rhetorical question, sweetie. I know what you had in mind. I knew the minute our eyes met. Why do you think I picked you? I wasn't sure you'd be bringing a knife to the party, but it's not as though I don't have a knife or two of my own."

She turned, put the knife down, turned back to him, and her hand reached out to take hold of him, her soft little hand, the one he'd had thoughts of crushing. She stroked and caressed him, and if he could have spoken he'd have told her she was wasting her time, that he wasn't capable of response. But his flesh had ideas of its own, even as the thought went through his mind.

"Oh, good," she said, using both hands now. "I knew you could do it. But sooner or later, you know, you won't be able to." She bent over, kissed him. "And when that happens," she murmured, "that's when I'll cut it off. But whose knife shall I use, yours or mine? That's another rhetorical question, sweetie. You don't have to answer it."

THAT'S BETTER, isn't it? The only thing wrong with it is the predictability of it. The biter bit, hoisted upon his own petard, and what's the use of a petard if you're not going to be hoisted upon it? He's on the hunt, he finds Little Miss Vulnerability and makes off with her, and in the end he's the vulnerable one, even as she turns out to be Diana, goddess of the hunt. Perhaps this particular Diana makes it a little more interesting than most, but still, we saw it coming. A surprise ending is more satisfactory when the reader as well as the protagonist is taken by surprise.

How's this?

THEY TOOK his car, drove to the dead-end lane he'd scouted earlier. Earlier there had been another car parked at the lane's far end, and he'd crept close enough to identify its occupants as a courting couple. He'd entertained the idea of taking them by surprise, and some day he'd have to do that, but he'd stayed with his original plan, and had had the great good fortune to find this girl, and the other car was gone now and they could be alone together.

He parked, killed the engine. He took her in his arms, kissed her, touched her. He noted with satisfaction the quickening of her breath, the heat of her response.

Good. She was turned on. Time now to show her who was in charge.

He took hold of her shoulders, moved to press her down on the seat. She didn't budge. He put more into it, and she pushed back, and how could such a soft and yielding creature be so strong?

Her lips parted, and he saw her fangs, and got his answer.

NOW THAT might work, if we weren't up to our tits in vampires these days. The undead everywhere, curled up in their coffins, guzzling artificial blood in Louisiana, being the coolest kids in a suburban high school, so many vampires it's clear Buffy never made a dent in their ranks.

So what's left? Werewolves? Cannibals? How many ways can we spin this? And to what end?

Ah, the hell with it. I could go on, but why try to dream up something? Here's what really happened:

HER APARTMENT, her bedroom, her bed. Soft lighting, soft music playing.

Soft.

"Jerry? Is there, you know, something I should do?"

Dematerialize, he thought. *Vanish, in a puff of smoke.*

"No."

"I mean—"

"It's not gonna happen," he said.

"That's okay."

"I think that last vodka put me one toke over the line, you know?"

"Sure."

Dammit dammit dammit dammit...

"But here," he said. "Let's see if we can make the magic happen for you, huh?"

"You don't have to—"

"Please."

He used all his tricks, his mouth on her, a finger in front, a finger in back. It took time, because his own failure held her in check, but he was patient and artful and he found her rhythm and took her all the way. At one point he thought her own excitement might be contagious, but that didn't happen.

"That was wonderful," she assured him, afterward. And offered again to do something to arouse him, but seemed just as glad when he told her he was fine, and it was late, and he really ought to be on his way.

He got out of there as quickly as he could, and on the way to his car his hand dropped to feel the knife in his pocket. Its presence was curiously reassuring.

He drove around, thinking about her, thinking of what he could have done, of what he should have done. He found a place to park and thought of what might have been, if he were in life the man he was in his fantasies. The man who didn't let his knife stay in his pocket. The man who acted, and reacted, and lived as he wanted to live.

The scenario played in his mind. And he responded to it, as he'd been unable to respond to her, and he touched himself, as he had done so many times in the past, and as he'd known he would do from those first moments in the bar.

Afterward, driving home, he thought: Next time I'll do it. Next time for sure.

SEE THE WOMAN

RED LIGHT'S ON, SO I guess that thing's recording. This whole project you've got, this oral history, I'll confess I didn't see the point of it. You running a tape recorder while an old man runs his mouth.

But it stirs things up, doesn't it? The other day—Wednesday, it must have been—all I did was talk for an hour or two, and then I went home and lay down for a nap and slept for fifteen hours. I'm an old man, I got up every three hours to pee, but then I went back to bed and fell right back asleep again. And dreams! Can't recall the last time I dreamed so much.

And then I got up, and my memory was coming up with stuff I never thought of in years. Years! All the way back to when I was a boy growing up in Oklahoma. You know, before the dust, before my old man lost the farm and brought us here. Memories of nothing much. Walking down a farm road watching a garter snake wriggling along in a tractor rut. And me kicking a tin can while I'm walking, just watching the snake, just kicking the can. Del Monte peaches, that's what the can was. Why'd anybody remember that?

Mostly, though, what I kept going over in my mind was something that happened in my first year on the force. If it's all the same to you, that's what I'll talk about today.

Now you know I wasn't but sixteen when the Japs bombed Pearl, and like just about everybody else I was down there the next morning looking to get into it. They sent me home when I told them my age, so I waited two days and went back, and wouldn't you know the same sergeant was behind the desk. This time I told him I was eighteen, and either he didn't remember me from before or he didn't give a damn, and they took me.

I went through basic and shipped out to England, and from there to North Africa, and what happened was they cut me out of the infantry and made an MP out of me. But I don't want to get sidetracked here and tell war stories. I came through it fine and wound up back here in Los Angeles, and I'd been Military Police for better than three years, so after a few months of beer and girls I went down and applied to join the LAPD.

Now what they would do then, and they probably still do it, is when they were done training you they'd partner you up with an older guy. You were partners, you'd ride around together, take turns driving, all of that, but he's the guy with the experience, so he'd more or less in charge. He's showing you the ropes and it's something you can't get from a book or in a classroom.

They put me in a car with Lew Hagner. Now I'd heard of him, because he had a big part in the Zoot Suit riots in '43, and there were plenty of Mexicans who'd have liked to see him dead. And after I was home but before I joined up with the department, there was an incident where he got in a gunfight with three Zoot Suiters or pachucos or whatever you want to call 'em. Mexicans, anyway. He got a scratch, treated and released at Valley General, and they were all dead on arrival. One of them, the wounds were in the back, and the press made some noise about that, but most people wanted to give him a medal.

Lew was fifteen years older'n me, and I was what, twenty-two at the time? An old twenty-two, the way everybody's older after a war, but still. Plus my old man died while I was overseas, and a fifteen year age difference, plus he's there to show me the ropes, well, I'm not about to say he was like a father to me, but you might say I looked up to him.

Anyway, we're two guys in a car. And it's good, and I'm learning things you don't learn any other way. All the feel of the streets, and what might be trouble and what's not. What you had to enforce and what you could let slide. When you had to go by the book, when you didn't even have to open it.

How else are you gonna learn that sort of thing?

A thing he told me early and often was that domestics were the biggest headache I'd ever have. By that I mean domestic disturbances. You just say domestics, you could be talking about somebody's cleaning girl.

A domestic disturbance, he said, you got two people trying to kill each other, and you walk in the door and they've got a united front. It's both of them against you, and they'll go back to killing each other as soon as you're out of the picture, but for now they're a tag team and you're it.

And even when that doesn't happen, Lew said, it's just so fucking frustrating.

I'm sorry, I guess I should watch my language.

NO, THAT'S all right, Charles. Don't worry about anything like that.

WELL, IT'S how he said it. But I'll watch it from here on in. I don't know what you're gonna do with all this stuff, but I might as well keep it clean for you.

But about domestics. You get a man's beating his wife like she's a rug, and the neighbors call it in or she calls us herself, and he's there in his underwear, smelling like a bomb went off in a liquor store. And she's sporting two shiners and a split lip, and that's her tooth on the floor there, and you want to pack this bum off to Folsom or Q, and you're lucky if you even get to haul him in. Because maybe six times out of ten she's hanging onto his arm and telling you it was all a mistake, that she fell down, she's just so clumsy. And the rest of the time you take him in, and he's out the next day because she won't press charges. Oh, officer, it was all a mistake, plus it only happens when he drinks, and he never has a drink except on days ending in a Y.

You get the picture.

Well, we had our share of those. Part of the job, you know? Then one night we get a radio call, "See the woman," and it's an address on South Olive. Don't ask me which block, and anyway that whole part of downtown's completely different nowadays. Whatever house it was, you couldn't find it today. Torn down years ago and something else there now, and no loss, because it wasn't the best part of town.

And Lew says, "Oh, hell, not again."

And on our way over there he tells me about this woman, Mildred's her name, and how her husband beats her like he wants to see how much damage he can do. And she won't press charges. She can always manage to come up with an excuse for him.

"*Oh, he really loves me. Oh, it's my fault, there's things I know I shouldn't do because they make him angry, but I do them anyway. I don't know what's wrong with me.*"

Like that.

"No kids," he said. "Usually you see kids in situations like this. What they all got in common, they got the oldest eyes in the youngest faces."

I knew what he meant. You'd see young troops come back from the front lines and their faces'd still be young. But not their eyes, on account of what they'd seen.

"He had kids and beat up on them, be jail tonight and the pen tomorrow. We wouldn't need her testimony to put him away. But she's the only one here, and she gets everything he hands out, and the stupid bitch keeps coming back for more."

The houses on that block were painted different colors, but they were all the same idea—one story tall, and what we used to call bungalows. Maybe they still call 'em that. I haven't heard the word in a long time, but maybe they still use it.

This one was like its neighbors in that it had concrete where most freestanding houses will have a lawn. That's where we parked. I guess she heard us drive up, because she met us at the door, wearing open-toe bedroom slippers and a housedress with the color washed out of it. Stringy blonde hair, patchy red polish on her toenails. Imagine what she must have looked like, and it was two, three times worse than that.

He was in a chair, passed out, a bottle on his lap. Three Feathers, that was the brand. It's a cheap blended whiskey, or it used to be. No idea if they still make it anymore.

The cap was off the bottle, and there was maybe an inch of whiskey left in it. Funny what you remember.

I forget his name, but it'll come to me.

Lew said, "Millie, you about ready to press charges?"

"Oh, I don't know, Lew." Wringing her hands and not meeting his eyes, so you know all *I don't know* means is *No*. "You all put my Joe in jail and then what am I gonna do?"

Joe, that was his name. Told you it'd come to me.

"Live your life," Lew said. "Find a real man."

"I got a real man, Lew."

"Find one who keeps his hands to himself."

"It's my fault as much as it's his, Lew. I know better than to say the things I say. But I go and get him upset, and he's had a drink or two—"

"Or twenty."

"—and he can't help himself. I'll be okay, Lew."

We got back in the car, on account of there was nothing else for us to do, and the rest of the night Lew never said a word unless he had to. Long silences, and if I tried to start a conversation it didn't go anywhere, so I let it go.

It wasn't two weeks later that we got another call for South Olive. *See the woman.* Lew let out a sigh when he heard the address, and when we got there it was the same story, except this time Joe hadn't reached the point of passing out. He was belligerent, and he ran his mouth a little, and that gave Lew the excuse to smack him upside the head. And all that did, besides shut Joe's mouth, was make her feel the need to stand by her man. I said her name a minute ago and now I can't think of it. Damn, what was that woman's name?

I BELIEVE you said it was Millie.

MILLIE, THAT'S right. A man gets old and things just come and go out of his memory. First I can't think of his name and then I can't think of hers. Joe and Millie, Millie and Joe. "Oh, don't hit him, Lew, don't you dare hit my Joe!" And they're arm in arm, a united front against the damn cops.

We got out of there, didn't even bother to ask about pressing charges. Would have been a waste of breath.

Rest of the night same story. Lew's quiet. We wind up in a greasy spoon a block from Pershing Square, sitting over eggs and home fries and coffee, and out of nowhere he says, "You wouldn't know it, but that's a fine-looking woman underneath it all. Beautiful girl, she used to be. Son of a bitch cost her her looks, along with her spirit."

I asked how he knew her. He was quiet, then pointed out something on the other side of the room. Somebody he recognized. Far as how he knew Millie, I never did get an answer.

There may have been a third time we got called there, or maybe not. Hard to keep everything straight. But then our shift changed, and we were working days, and if there were any calls to see the woman at the Olive Street address, well, we were off duty by the time they came in.

I think there must have been. And looking back I think Lew kept up with it, checked reports. He had an interest that ran deeper than mine.

A month, maybe six weeks, and we rotated back to nights. I liked nights better. You didn't have the traffic, and it was dark, and just being in the car was better at night. The things Lew would find to talk about, and the way a conversation would just twist and turn like an old river. And the silences, too. It was all somehow better at night.

Of course domestics were the downside of working nights. Now you'd have husbands drink any hour of the day, so you could in theory have a domestic disturbance on the stroke of noon, but they mostly happened in the hours right after midnight. And we weren't back on the night shift a full week before we heard the Olive Street address coming over the radio. "Seven-forty-four South Olive, see the woman."

You hear that? I just remembered the street number, it popped right into my head. Now ten minutes from now I may forget my own name, but right now I remember the address.

At least I think that was it. But you know it didn't matter when I couldn't remember it and it doesn't matter now. All torn down now, anyway. I can picture that little house clear as day, for all that I only saw it in the middle of the night, but in a few years when I'm gone there probably won't be a person alive who remembers it.

That's when something's really gone, isn't it? When there's nobody left who remembers it....

UH, CHARLES...

SORRY, I just got distracted there. Hopped a train of thought and disappeared into the distance. That particular night, well, it was the same as the others. Maybe he was passed out that time, maybe he was belligerent or ob—what's the word I want?

OBNOXIOUS?

• • •

142

OBSTREPEROUS. MAYBE he was this or that, maybe he was apologizing all over the place. Whatever it was, at bottom it was the same story. She had some new bruises and he was the one that put 'em there. And over the next couple weeks there were two or three more calls, just variations on the theme. No, she won't press charges. No, it's really her fault, and he's sorry, and they're married, and this is something for them to work out on their own, and she's just sorry we had to waste our time coming all that way, but we can go now, and thank you very much.

"Next time we hear that address," Lew told me in the car, "we acknowledge it, and then we'll go grab a hamburger someplace. Why burn gas chasing out there? Why waste our damn time?"

Then we'd get the call again, and we'd answer it, same as always.

And then one night the call came in, with the usual address. One thing different: "See the husband."

I said, "See the husband? What did she do, beat him up?"

Lew shook his head. He knew what it meant, and by the time we got there I'd pretty much worked it out for myself.

He met us on the front step, standing out there in his underwear, and there were bloodstains on the front of his undershirt. He was bleary-eyed, and he reeked of Three Feathers. It wasn't just on his breath. He was sweating like a pig, and the alcohol was coming out of his pores.

"I'm sorry," he was saying. "I didn't mean it, it was an accident, I don't know what happened, I didn't mean it, I'm sorry."

Same thing, over and over and over.

Lew led him inside, and I was surprised to see how gentle his hands were this time, as if all the anger had faded away, with sadness taking its place. He put the man in an armchair, found a bottle with a little booze still in it, and gave it to him. The man took a drink, then clutched the bottle to his chest, as if to shelter it from the world.

Or to keep us from taking it away from him.

WE DIDN'T see Millie right away, but we checked out the rest of the house, and she was in the bedroom. She was sprawled on the floor next to the bed, blood all over, and her head at an odd angle. Lew knelt down next to her, tried for a pulse, put his lips to her mouth, shook his head.

"Oh, you poor baby," he said. "You were dying by inches and now you're gone for real. Ah, Millie, you couldn't listen, could you? You just couldn't, poor baby. By God, you deserved better than what you got."

He stood up and looked surprised to see me there. Like for a minute there it was just the two of them, and him talking to her, and no one else in their world.

To me he said, "Well, we got the fucker now, Charlie. We get to slam the barn door on him now that the horse is miles away and gone forever. If they don't give him the gas, he'll spend the rest of his life in a cell. The one good thing that comes out of all this is the world's through with him."

We were talking about that, and speculating about his chances of winding up in the gas chamber, and what difference it made one way or the other, and then there was a sound from where she was lying, and we stopped talking and turned to look at her.

And she opened her eyes. She said, "Lew?"

Her eyes closed.

And opened again. "Where's Joe? Is Joe okay?"

Her voice was very faint, her eyes unfocused. Lew drew a breath, let it out. "Jesus," he said. It was somewhere between a curse and a prayer. Then he said, "Charlie, go get on the phone. Call in, get an ambulance out here on the double. Go!"

So I went back to the other room, where Joe was passed out in the chair where Lew had put him. I didn't have a number for a hospital, so I called the operator and gave her the address and told her to arrange for an ambulance.

In the bedroom, Millie looked as though she'd been crying. Tears down her cheeks, along with the blood and all. I told Lew I'd made the call, and he lowered his voice and said he didn't know if she would make it. "She goes in and out," he said. "You'd better wait outside so they'll get the right house. Flag 'em down before they fly right on by."

I was on my way, but I stopped in the front room to look at the husband. He'd slipped off the chair and was sitting on the floor with his head on the chair cushion. I thought to myself that this piece of garbage was one lucky son of a bitch. He was sitting on a one-way ticket to Q, and then she opened her eyes and set him free.

Free to do it all over again.

The front door was open, and I'd hear the siren in plenty of time, so I stayed where I was. And I sort of heard something from the bedroom, or half-heard it, and while I was trying to figure out just what it was, I heard the siren of an ambulance maybe three, four blocks away.

So I went outside and stood on the front step, and I motioned to the ambulance and pointed out where they could park, and then Lew was beside me, hanging his head.

"I think she's gone," he said.

JOE WENT to prison. There was no trial, his court-appointed lawyer had him plead it out, and that way he beat the gas chamber. The sentence was twenty-to-life, and Lew said that wasn't long enough, and swore he'd turn up at the guy's parole hearing and make sure he didn't get out early.

Never happened. Lew and I pretty much lost track of each other, I got transferred to the Hollywood division, but I heard about it when he killed himself. That's not what they called it, they said he was cleaning his gun and had an accident, but that's what they used to say at the time. Funny how so many cops'd have a few drinks and decide they better give their gun a good cleaning.

That must have been around 1955. And it wasn't more than one or two years later that the husband died in prison. It seems to me somebody stuck a knife in him, but I may not be remembering that right. Maybe it was natural causes.

Then again, in a state joint getting a knife stuck in you is pretty much a natural cause.

CHARLES, IS there anything more you want to say?

ALL THESE years I kept this strictly to myself. There were stretches when it was on my mind a lot, and other times I'd go months or years without thinking about it at all.

But I never said a word to anybody.

And maybe I should leave it that way.

Same token, all of these people are gone. I must be the only man alive even remembers any of them. Why do I have to keep their secret?

145

Thing is, I don't even know what I know. Not for certain.

UH, CHARLES—

NO, THIS is what, oral history? What you call it?

Only way to say it is to say it.

When I'm in the living room, what I hear is a snapping sound. Like a twig breaking. It's faint, it's coming from the back of the house, and if I'm outside where I'm supposed to be I most likely don't hear it at all.

And after the twig snaps, there's like a little sigh. Like the air going out of something.

"I think she's gone." That's what he said, and as soon as I heard the words I knew she was gone, and I realized I knew it from the moment I heard the twig snap.

The twig?

Easy to call it that, but I don't remember seeing any twigs in that bedroom.

I DIDN'T say anything, and Lew didn't say anything, and then one night he did. Slow night, quiet night, and we're in the car. I remember he was driving that night.

Out of the blue he says, "There's people in this world who never have a chance."

I knew he was talking about her.

I just sat there, and a minute or two later he says, "Say she pulls through. So he kills her next time, or the time after that. Or the twentieth time after that. You call that a life, Charlie?"

"No."

We caught a red light. More often than not what we'd do is slow down enough to see there was no cross traffic and then coast on through it, but this time he braked to a stop and waited for the light to change.

And while he was waiting he took his hands off the wheel and sat there looking at 'em.

The light went to green and we moved on. Two, three blocks along he said, "This way she's in a better place. And he's where he belongs. You don't know what I'm talking about, do you, Charlie?"

"No," I said. "No idea."

It wasn't that much longer before they moved me to the Hollywood division, which was an interesting place to be in those days. Not that you didn't get domestics there, too, and every other damn thing, but the people were a little different. The same in many ways, but a little different.

Where was I?

UH, THE Hollywood division.

NO, BEFORE that. Never mind, I remember. It was maybe another month I was with Lew, before the move to Hollywood. And he never brought up the subject again, and I for sure never said anything, but there was one thing he kept doing, and it made me glad when they transferred me. I'd have been glad anyway, because the move amounted to a promotion, but it gave me a particular reason to be glad to get out of that particular radio car.

What he would do, he'd go silent and look at his hands. And I couldn't see him do that without picturing those hands taking hold of that woman's head and breaking her neck.

I guess he saw the same thing.

And is that why he sat up late one night, all by himself, and gave his gun a good cleaning? Maybe yes, maybe no. The things he supposedly did during the Zoot Suit riots, far as I know he had no trouble living with them, or the other three Mexicans he killed, and he might have been the same way with this.

Because, you know, it was the only way that woman was gonna get out of it, the mess she was in. Look at it that way and he was doing the humane thing. And it was the perfect opportunity, because her husband already thought she was dead and that he'd killed her. So this way she's out of it, and this way he goes away for it, and that's the end of it.

So would it make Lew kill himself a few years down the line? My guess is it wouldn't. My guess is he was feeling low one night, and he took a long look at his life, not what he'd done but what he had to look forward to.

Stuck the gun in his mouth just to see how it felt.

Here's something else I never told anybody. I been that far myself. I remember the taste of the metal. I remember—now I haven't thought of this in ages, but I remember thinking I had to be careful not to chip a tooth. One trigger pull away from the next world and I'm worried about a chipped tooth.

I never broke any woman's neck, or shot any Mexicans, or did any big things that weighed all that heavy on my mind. But looking at it one way, Lew pulled the trigger and I didn't, and on that score that's all the difference there was between us.

Of course that don't mean I won't go home now and do it. I've still got a gun. I guess I can clean it any time I have a mind to.

SPEAKING OF GREED

THE DOCTOR SHUFFLED THE pack of playing cards seven times, then offered them to the soldier, who sat to his right. The soldier cut them, and the doctor picked up the deck and dealt two cards down and one up to each of the players—the policeman, the priest, the soldier, and himself.

The game was poker, seven-card stud, and the priest, who was high on the board with a queen, opened the betting for a dollar, tossing in a chip to keep the doctor's ante comfortable. The soldier called, as did the doctor and the policeman.

Over by the fireplace, the room's other occupant, an elderly gentleman, dozed in an armchair.

The doctor gave each player a second up-card. The policeman caught a king, the priest a nine in the same suit with his queen, the soldier a jack to go with his ten. The doctor, who'd had a five to start with, caught another five for a pair. That made him high on the board, but he took a look at his hole cards, frowned, and checked his hand. The policeman checked as well, and the priest gave his Roman collar a tug and bet two dollars.

The soldier said, "Two dollars? It's a dollar limit until a pair shows, isn't it?"

"Doctor has a pair," the priest pointed out.

"So he does," the soldier agreed, and flicked a speck of dust off the sleeve of his uniform. "Of course he does, he was high with his fives. Still, it's one of the anomalies of the game, isn't it? Priest gets to bet more, not because his own hand just got stronger, but because his opponent's did. What are you so proud of, Priest? Queens and nines? Four hearts?"

149

"I hope I'm not too proud," the priest said. "Pride's a sin, after all."

"Well, I'm proud enough to call you," the soldier said, as did the doctor and the policeman. The doctor dealt another round, and now the policeman was high with a pair of kings. He too was in uniform, and wordlessly he tossed a pair of chips into the center of the table.

The priest had caught a third heart, the seven. He thought for a long moment before tossing four chips into the pot. "Raise," he said softly.

"Priest, Priest, Priest," said the soldier, checking his own cards. "Have you got your damned flush already? If you had two pair, well, I just caught one of your nines. But if I'm chasing a straight that's doomed to lose to the flush you've already got..." The words trailed off, and the soldier sighed and called. So did the doctor, and the policeman looked at his kings and picked up four chips, as if to raise back, then tossed in two of them and returned the others to his stack.

On the next round, three of the players showed visible improvement. The policeman, who'd had a three with his kings, caught a second three for two pair. The priest added the deuce of hearts and showed a four flush on board. The soldier's straight got longer with the addition of the eight of diamonds. The doctor, who'd had a four with his pair of fives, acquired a ten.

The policeman bet, the priest raised, the soldier grumbled and called. The doctor called without grumbling. The policeman raised back, and everyone called.

"Nice little pot," the doctor said, and gave everyone a down card.

The betting limits were a dollar until a pair showed, then two dollars until the last card, at which time you could bet five dollars. The policeman did just that, tossing a red chip into the pot. The priest picked up a red chip to call, thought about it, picked up a second red chip, and raised five dollars. The soldier said something about throwing good money after bad.

"There's no such thing," the doctor said.

"As good money?"

"As bad money."

"It turns bad," said the soldier, "as soon as I throw it in. I was straight in five and got to watch everybody outdraw me. Now I've got a choice of losing to Policeman's full house or Priest's heart flush, depending on which one's telling the truth. Unless you're both full of crap."

"Always a possibility," the doctor allowed.

"The hell with it," the soldier said, and tossed in a red chip and five white chips. "I call," he said, "with no expectation of profit." The doctor was wearing green scrubs, with a stethoscope peeping out of his pocket. He looked at his cards, looked at everyone else's cards, and called. The policeman raised. The priest looked troubled, but took the third and final raise all the same, and everybody called.

"Full," the policeman said, and turned over a third three. "Threes full of kings," he said, but the priest was shaking his head, even as he turned over his hole cards, two queens and a nine. "Queens full," said the priest.

"Oh, hell," said the soldier. "A full house masquerading as a flush. Not that I have a right to complain—the flush would have beaten me just as handily. Got it on the last card, didn't you, Priest? All that raising, and you went in with two pair and a four flush."

"I had great expectations," the priest admitted.

"The Lord will provide and all that," said the soldier, turning over his up cards. The priest, beaming, reached for the chips.

The doctor cleared his throat, turned over his hole cards. Two of them were fives, matching the pair of fives he'd had on board.

"Four fives," the policeman said reverently. "Beats your boat, Priest."

"So it does," said the priest. "So it does."

"Had them in the first four cards," the doctor said.

"You never bet them."

"I never had to," said the doctor. "You fellows were doing such a nice job of it, I saw no reason to interfere."

And he reached out both hands to gather in the chips.

"GREED," SAID the priest.

The policeman was shuffling the cards, the doctor stacking his chips, the soldier looking off into the middle distance, as if remembering a battle in a long-forgotten war. The priest's utterance stopped them all.

"I beg your pardon," said the doctor. "Just what have I done that's so greedy? Play the hand so as to maximize my gains? That, it seems to me, is how one is intended to play the game."

"If you're not trying to win," said the soldier, "you shouldn't be sitting at the table."

"Maybe Priest feels you were gloating," the policeman suggested. "Salivating over your well-gotten gains."

"Was I doing that?" The doctor shrugged. "I wasn't aware of it. Still, why play if you're not going to relish your triumph?"

The priest, who'd been shaking his head, now held up his hands as if to ward off everyone's remarks. "I uttered a single word," he protested, "and intended no judgment, believe me. Perhaps it was the play of the hand that prompted my train of thought, perhaps it was a reflection on the entire ethos of poker that put it in motion. But, when I spoke the word, I was thinking neither of your own conduct, Doctor, or of our game itself. No, I was contemplating the sin of greed, of avarice."

"Greed is a sin, eh?"

"One of the seven deadly sins."

"And yet," said the soldier, "there was a character in a film who argued famously that greed is good. And isn't the profit motive at the root of much of human progress?"

"A man's reach should exceed his grasp," the policeman said, "but it's the desire for what one can in fact grasp that makes one reach out in the first place. And isn't it natural to want to improve one's circumstances?"

"All the sins are natural," said the priest. "All originate as essential impulses and become sins when they overstretch their bounds. Without sexual desire the human race would die out. Without appetite we'd starve. Without ambition we'd graze like cattle. But when desire becomes lust, or appetite turns to gluttony, or ambition to greed—"

"We sin," the doctor said.

The priest nodded. The policeman gave the cards another shuffle. "You know," he said, "that reminds me of a story."

"Tell it," the others urged, and the policeman put down the deck of cards and sat back in his chair.

MANY YEARS ago (said the policeman) there were two brothers, whom I'll call George and Alan Walker. They came from a family that had had some money and respectability at one time, and their paternal grandfather was a physician, but he was also a drunk, and eventually patients stopped going to him, and he wound up with an office on Railroad Avenue, where he wrote prescriptions for dope addicts. Somewhere along the way his wife ran off, and he started popping pills, and the time came when they didn't combine too well with what he was drinking, and he died.

He had three sons and a daughter, and all but the youngest son drifted away. The one who stayed—call him Jack—married a girl whose family had also come down in the world, and they had two boys, George and Alan.

Jack drank, like his father, but he didn't have a medical degree, and thus he couldn't make a living handing out pills. He wasn't trained for anything, and didn't have any ambition, so he picked up day work when it came his way, and sometimes it was honest and sometimes it wasn't. He got arrested a fair number of times, and he went away and did short time on three or four occasions. When he was home he slapped his wife around some, and was generally free with his hands around the house, but no more than you'd expect from a man like that living a life like that.

Now everybody can point to individuals who grew up in homes like the Walkers' who turned out just fine. Won scholarships, put themselves through college, worked hard, applied themselves, and wound up pillars of the community. No reason it can't happen, and often enough it does, but sometimes it doesn't, and it certainly didn't for George and Alan Walker. They were discipline problems in school and dropped out early, and at first they stole hubcaps off cars, and then they stole cars.

And so on.

Jack Walker had been a criminal himself, in a slipshod amateurish sort of way. The boys followed in his footsteps, but improved on his example. They were professionals from very early on, and you would have to say they were good at it. They weren't Raffles, they weren't Professor Moriarty, they weren't Arnold Zeck, and God knows they weren't Willie Sutton or Al Capone. But they made a living at it and they didn't get caught, and isn't that enough for us to call them successful?

They always worked together, and more often than not they used other people as well. Over the years, they tended to team up with the same three men. I don't know that it would be precisely accurate to call the five of them a gang, but it wouldn't be off by much.

One, Louis Creamer, was a couple of years older than the Walkers— George, I should mention, was himself a year and a half older than his brother Alan. Louis looked like a big dumb galoot, and that's exactly what he was. He loved to eat and he loved to work out with weights in his garage, so he kept getting bigger. It's hard to see how he could have gotten any dumber, but he didn't get any smarter, either. He lived with his mother—nobody knew what happened to the father, if he was ever there in the first place—and when his mother died Louis married the girl he'd been keeping company with since he dropped out of school. He moved her into his mother's house and she cooked him the same huge meals his mother used to cook, and he was happy.

Early on, Louis got work day to day as a bouncer, but the day came when he hit a fellow too hard, and the guy died. A good lawyer probably could have gotten him off, but Louis had a bad one, and he wound up serving a year and a day for involuntary manslaughter. When he got out nobody was in a rush to hire him, and he fell in with the Walkers, who didn't have trouble finding a role for a guy who was big and strong and did what you told him to do.

Eddie O'Day was small and undernourished and as close as I've ever seen to a born thief. He got in trouble shoplifting as a child, and then he stopped getting into trouble, not because he stopped stealing but because he stopped getting caught. He grew up to be a man who would, as they say, steal a hot stove, and he'd have it sold before it cooled off. He was the same age as Alan Walker, and they'd dropped out of school together. Eddie lived alone, and was positively gifted when it came to picking up women. He was neither good-looking nor charming, but he was evidently seductive, and women kept taking him home. But they didn't keep him—his relationships never lasted, which was fine as far as he was concerned.

Mike Dunn was older than the others, and had actually qualified as a schoolteacher. He got unqualified in a hurry when he was caught in bed with one of his students. It was a long ways from pedophilia—he was only twenty-six himself at the time, and the girl was almost sixteen and almost as experienced sexually as he was—but that was the end of his teaching career. He drifted some, and the Walkers used him as a lookout in a drugstore break-in, and found out they liked working with him. He had a good mind, and he wound up doing a lot of the planning. When he wasn't working he was pretty much a loner, living in a rented house on the edge of town, and having affairs with unavailable women—generally the wives or daughters of other men.

The Walkers and their associates had a lot of different ways to make money, together or separately. George and Alan always had some money on the street, loans to people whose only collateral was fear. Louis Creamer did their collection work, and provided security at the card and dice games Eddie O'Day ran. George Walker owned a bar and grill, and sold more booze there than he bought from the wholesalers; he bought from bootleggers and hijacked the occasional truck to make up the difference. We knew a lot of what they were doing, but knowing and making a case aren't necessarily the same thing. We arrested all of them at one time or another, for one thing or another, but we could never make anything stick. That's not all that unusual, you know. They say crime doesn't pay, but they're wrong. Of course it pays. If it didn't pay, the pros would do something else.

And the Walkers were pros. They weren't getting rich, but they were making what you could call a decent living, but for the fact that there was nothing decent about it. They always had food on the table and money under the mattress (if not in the bank), and they didn't have to work too hard or too often. That was what they'd had in mind when they chose a life of crime. So they stayed with it, and why not? It suited them fine. They weren't respectable, but neither was their father, or his father before him. The hell with being respectable. They were doing okay.

The years went by and they kept on doing what they were doing, and doing well at it. Jack Walker drank himself to death, and after the funeral George put his arm around his brother and said, "Well, the old bastard's in the ground. He wasn't much good, but he wasn't so bad, you know?"

"When I was a kid," Alan said, "I wanted to kill him."

"Oh, so did I," George said. "Many's the time I thought about it. But, you know, you grow older and you get over it." And they were indeed growing older, settling into a reasonably comfortable middle age. George was thicker around the middle, while Alan's hair was showing a little gray. They both liked a drink, but it didn't have the hold on them it had had on their father and grandfather. It settled George down, fueled Alan, and didn't seem to do either of them any harm.

And this wouldn't be much of a story, except for the fact that one day they set out to steal some money, and succeeded beyond their wildest dreams.

It was a robbery, and the details have largely faded from memory, but I don't suppose they're terribly important. The tip came from an employee of the targeted firm, whose wife was the sister of a woman Mike Dunn was sleeping with; for a cut of the proceeds, he'd provide details of when to hit the place, along with the security codes and keys that would get them in. Their expectations were considerable. Mike Dunn, who brought in the deal, thought they ought to walk off with a minimum of a hundred thousand dollars. Their tipster was in for a ten percent share, and they'd split the residue in five equal shares, as they always did on jobs of this nature. "Even splits," George Walker had said early on. "You hear about different ways of doing it, something off the top for the guy who brings it in, so much extra for whoever bankrolls the operation. All that does is make it complicated, and gives everybody a reason to come up with a resentment. The minute you're getting a dollar more than me, I'm pissed off. And the funny thing is you're pissed off, too, because whatever you're getting isn't enough. Make the splits even and nobody's got cause to complain. You put out more than I do on the one job, well, it evens out later on, when I put out more'n you do. Meantime, every dollar comes in, each one of us gets twenty cents of it." So they stood to bring in eighteen thousand dollars apiece for a few hours work, which, inflation notwithstanding, was a healthy cut above minimum wage, and better than anybody was paying in the fields and factories. Was it a fortune? No. Wealth beyond the dreams of avarice? Hardly that. But all five of the principals would agree that it was a good night's work.

The job was planned and rehearsed, the schedule fine-tuned. When push came to shove, the pushing and shoving went like clockwork. Everything happened just as it was supposed to, and our five masked heroes wound up in a room with five of the firm's employees, one of them the inside man, the brother-in-law of Mike Dunn's paramour. And it strikes me that we need a name for him, although we won't need it for long. But let's call him Alfie. No need for a last name. Just Alfie will do fine.

Like the others, Alfie was tied up tight, a piece of duct tape across his mouth. Mike Dunn had given him a wink when he tied him, and made sure his bonds weren't tight enough to hurt. He sat there and watched as the five men hauled sacks of money out of the vault.

It was Eddie O'Day who found the bearer bonds.

By then they already knew that it was going to be a much bigger payday than they'd anticipated. A hundred thousand? The cash looked as though it would come to at least three and maybe four or five times that. Half a million? A hundred thousand apiece?

The bearer bonds, all by themselves, totaled two million dollars. They were like cash, but better than cash because, relatively speaking, they didn't weigh anything or take up any space. Pieces of paper, two hundred of them, each worth ten thousand dollars. And they weren't registered to an owner, and were as anonymous as a crumpled dollar bill.

In every man's mind, the numbers changed. The night was going to be worth two and a half million dollars, or half a million apiece. Why, Alfie's share as an informant would come to a quarter of a million dollars all by itself, which was not bad compensation for letting yourself be tied up and gagged for a few hours.

Of course, there was another way of looking at it. Alfie was taking fifty thousand dollars from each of them. He was costing them, right off the top, almost three times as much money as they'd expected to net in the first place.

The little son of a bitch...Alan Walker went over to Alfie and hunkered down next to him. "You did good," he said. "There's lots more money than anybody thought, plus all of these bonds." Alfie struggled with his bonds, and his eyes rolled wildly. Alan asked him if something was the matter, and Mike Dunn came over and took the tape from Alfie's mouth.

"Them," Alfie said.

"Them?"

He rolled his eyes toward his fellow employees. "They'll think I'm involved," he said.

"Well, hell, Alfie," Eddie O'Day said, "you are involved, aren'tcha? You're in for what, ten percent?" Alfie just stared.

"Listen," George Walker told him, "don't worry about those guys. What are they gonna say?"

"Their lips are sealed," his brother pointed out.

"But—" George Walker nodded to Louis Creamer, who drew a pistol and shot one of the bound men in the back of the head. Mike Dunn and Eddie O'Day drew their guns, and more shots rang out. Within seconds the four presumably loyal employees were dead.

"Oh, Jesus," Alfie said.

"Had to be," George Walker told him. "They heard what my brother said to you, right? Besides, the money involved, there's gonna be way too much heat coming down. They didn't see anybody's face, but who knows what they might notice that the masks don't hide? And they heard voices. Better this way, Alfie."

"Ten percent," Eddie O'Day said. "You might walk away with a quarter of a million dollars, Alfie. What are you gonna do with all that dough?" Alfie looked like a man who'd heard the good news and the bad news all at once. He was in line for a fortune, but would he get to spend a dime of it?

"Listen," he said, "you guys better beat me up."

"Beat you up?"

"I think so, and—"

"But you're our little buddy," Louis Creamer said. "Why would we want to do that?"

"If I'm the only one left," Alfie said, "they'll suspect me, won't they?"

"Suspect you?"

"Of being involved."

"Ah," George Walker said. "Never thought of that."

"But if you beat me up…"

"You figure it might throw them off? A couple of bruises on your face and they won't even think of questioning you?"

"Maybe you better wound me," Alfie said.

"Wound you, Alfie?"

"Like a flesh wound, you know? A non-fatal wound."

"Oh, hell," Alan Walker said. "We can do better than that." And he put his gun up against Alfie's forehead and blew his brains out.

"Had to be," George Walker announced, as they cleared the area of any possible traces of their presence. "No way on earth he would have stood up, the kind of heat they'd have put on him. The minute the total goes over a mill, far as I'm concerned, they're all dead, all five of them. The other four because of what they might have picked up, and Alfie because of what we damn well know he knows."

"He was in for a quarter of a mill," Eddie O'Day said. "You look at it one way, old Alfie was a rich man for a minute there."

"You think about it," Louis Creamer said, "what'd he ever do was worth a quarter of a mill?"

"He was taking fifty grand apiece from each of us," Alan Walker said. "If you want to look at it that way."

"It's as good a way as any to look at it," George Walker said.

"Beady little eyes," Eddie O'Day said. "Never liked the little bastard. And he'd have sung like a bird, minute they picked him up." The Walkers had a storage locker that nobody knew about, and that was where they went to count the proceeds of the job. The cash, it turned out, ran to just over $650,000, and another count of the bearer bonds confirmed the figure of two million dollars. That made the total $2,650,000, or $530,000 a man after a five-way split.

"Alfie was richer than we thought," George Walker said. "For a minute there, anyway. Two hundred sixty-five grand."

"If we'd left him alive," his brother said, "the cops would have had our names within twenty-four hours."

"Twenty-four hours? He'da been singing the second they got the tape off his mouth."

Eddie O'Day said, "You got to wonder."

"Wonder what?"

"How much singing he already done." They exchanged glances.

To Mike Dunn, George Walker said, "This dame of yours. Alfie was married to her sister?"

"Right."

"I was a cop, I'd take a look at the families of those five guys. Dead or alive, I'd figure there might have been somebody on the inside, you know?"

"I see what you mean."

"They talk to Alfie's wife, who knows what he let slip?"

"Probably nothing."

"Probably nothing, but who knows? Maybe he thought he was keeping her in the dark, but she puts two and two together, you know?"

"Maybe he talked in his sleep," Louis Creamer suggested.

Mike Dunn thought about it, nodded. "I'll take care of it," he said.

Later that evening, the Walkers were in George's den, drinking scotch and smoking cigars. "You know what I'm thinking," George said.

"The wife's dead," Alan said, "and it draws the cops a picture. Five employees dead, plus the wife of one of them? Right away they know which one was working for us."

159

"So they know which direction to go."

"This woman Mike's been nailing. Sister of Alfie's wife."

"Right."

"They talk to her and what do they get?"

"Probably nothing, far as the job's concerned. Even if Alfie talked to his wife, it's a stretch to think the wife talked to her sister."

Alan nodded. "The sister doesn't know shit about the job," he said. "But there's one thing she knows."

"What's that?"

"She knows she's been sleeping with Mike. Of course that's something she most likely wants kept a secret, on account of she's a married lady."

"But when the cops turn her upside-down and shake her..."

"Leads straight to Mike. And now that I think about it, will they even have to shake her hard? Because if she figures out that it was probably Mike that got her sister and her brother-in-law killed..."

George finished his drink, poured another. "Her name's Alice," he said. "Alice Fuhrmann. Be easy enough, drop in on her, take her out. Where I sit, she looks like a big loose end."

"How's Mike gonna take it?"

"Maybe it'll look like an accident."

"He's no dummy. She has an accident, he'll have a pretty good idea who gave it to her."

"Well, that's another thing," George Walker said. "Take out Alfie's wife and her sister and there's nobody with a story to tell. But I can see the cops finding the connection between Mike and this Alice no matter what, because who knows who she told?"

"He's a good man, Mike."

"Damn good man."

"Kind of a loner, though."

"Looks out for himself." The brothers glanced significantly at each other, and drank their whiskey.

The sixth death recorded in connection with the robbery was that of Alfie's wife. Mike Dunn went to her home, found her alone, and accepted her offer of a cup of coffee. She thought he was coming on to her, and had heard from her sister what a good lover he was, and the idea of having a quickie with her sister's boyfriend was not unappealing. She invited him upstairs, and he didn't know what to do. He knew he couldn't afford to leave physical evidence in her bed or on her body. And could he have sex with a woman and then kill her? The thought sickened him, and, not surprisingly, turned him on a little too. He went upstairs with her. She was wearing a robe, and as they ascended the staircase he ran a hand up under the robe and found she was wearing nothing under it. He was wildly excited, and desperate to avoid acting on his excitement, and when they reached the top of the stairs he took her in his arms. She waited for him to kiss her, and instead he got his hands on her neck and throttled her, his hands tightening convulsively around her throat until the light went out of her eyes. Then he pitched her body down the stairs, walked down them himself, stepped over her corpse and got out of the house.

He was shaking. He wanted to tell somebody but he didn't know whom to tell. He got in his car and drove home, and there was George Walker with a duffle bag.

"I did it," Mike blurted out. "She thought I wanted to fuck her, and you want to hear something sick? I wanted to."

"But you took care of it?"

"She fell down the stairs," Mike said. "Broke her neck."

"Accidents happen," George said, and tapped the duffle bag. "Your share."

"I thought we weren't gonna divvy it for a while."

"That was the plan, yeah."

"Because they might come calling, and if anybody has a lot of money at hand…"

"Right."

"Besides, any of us starts spending, it draws attention. Not that I would, but I'd worry about Eddie."

"If he starts throwing money around…"

"Could draw attention."

"Right."

"Thing is," George explained, "we were thinking maybe you ought to get out of town for a while, Mike. Alfie's dead and his wife's dead, but who knows how far back the cops can trace things? This girlfriend of yours—"

"Jesus, don't remind me. I just killed her sister."

"Well, somebody can take care of that." Mike Dunn's eyes widened, but he didn't say anything.

"If you're out of town for a while," George said, "maybe it's not a bad thing." Not a bad thing at all, Mike thought. Not if somebody was going to take care of Alice Fuhrmann, because the next thing that might occur to them was taking care of Mike Dunn, and he didn't want to be around when that happened. He packed a bag, and George walked him to his car, and took a gun from his pocket and shot him behind the ear just as he was getting behind the wheel.

Within hours Mike Dunn was buried at the bottom of an old well at an abandoned farmhouse six miles north of the city, and his car was part of a fleet of stolen cars on their way to the coast, where they'd be loaded aboard a freighter for shipment overseas. By then Alan Walker had decoyed Alice Fuhrmann to a supermarket parking lot, where he killed her with a homemade garrote and stuffed her into the trunk of her car.

"Mike did the right thing," George told Eddie O'Day and Louis Creamer. "He took out Alfie's widow and his own girlfriend, but he figured it might still come back to him, so I gave him his share and he took off. Half a mill, he can stay gone for a good long time."

"More'n that," Eddie O'Day said. "Five hundred thirty, wasn't it?"

"Well, round numbers."

"Speaking of numbers," Eddie said, "when are we gonna cut up the pie? Because I could use some of mine."

"Soon," George told him.

Five-thirty each for Louis Creamer and Eddie O'Day, $795,000 apiece for the Walkers, George thought, because Louis and Eddie didn't know that Mike Dunn had not gone willingly (though he'd been willing enough to do so) and had not taken his share with him. (George had brought the duffle bag home with him, and stashed it behind the furnace.) So why should Eddie and Louis get a split of Mike's share?

For that matter, George thought, he hadn't yet told his brother what had become of Mike Dunn. He'd never intended to give Mike his share, but he'd filled the duffle bag at the storage facility in case he'd had to change his plans on the spot, and he'd held the money out afterward in case the four of them wound up going to the storage bin together to make the split. As far as Alan knew, Mike and his share had vanished, and why burden the lad with the whole story? Why should Alan have a friend's death on his conscience?

No, George's conscience could carry the weight. And, along with the guilt, shouldn't he have Mike's share for himself? Because he couldn't split it with Alan without telling him where it came from.

Which changed the numbers slightly. $530,000 apiece for Alan, Louis, and Eddie. $1,060,000 for George.

Of course we knew who'd pulled off the robbery. Alfie's wife had indeed suffered a broken neck in the fall, but the medical examination quickly revealed she'd been strangled first. Her sister had disappeared, and soon turned up in the trunk of her car, a loop of wire tightened around her neck. Someone was able to connect the sister to Mike Dunn, and we established that he and his clothes and his car had gone missing. Present or not, Mike Dunn automatically led to Creamer and O'Day and the Walkers—but we'd have been looking at them anyway. Just a matter of rounding up the usual suspects, really.

"Eddie called me," Alan said. "They were talking to him."

"And you, and me," George said. "And Louis. They can suspect all they want, long as they can't prove anything."

"He wants his cut."

"Eddie?"

Alan nodded. "I asked him was he planning on running, and he said no. Just that he'll feel better when he's got his share. Mike got his cut, he said, and why's he different?"

"Mike's case was special."

"Just what I told him. He says he owes money he's got to pay, plus there's some things he wants to buy."

"The cops are talking to him, and what he wants to do is pay some debts and spend some money."

"That's about it."

"And if the answer's no? Then what?"

"He didn't say, but next thing I knew he was mentioning how the cops had been talking to him."

"Subtle bastard. You know, when the cops talk to him a few more times—"

"I don't know how he'll stand up. He's always been a stand-up guy before, but the stakes are a lot higher."

"And you can sort of sense him getting ready to spill it. He's working up a resentment about not getting paid. Other hand, if he does get paid…"

"He throws money around."

They fell silent. Finally George said, "We haven't even talked about Louis."

"No."

"Be convenient if the two of them killed each other, wouldn't it?"

"No more worries about who'll stand up. Down side, we'd have nobody to work with, either."

"Why work?" George grinned. "You and me'd be splitting two million, six fifty."

"Less Mike's share," Alan pointed out.

"Right," George said.

They were planning it, working it out together, because it was not going to be easy to get the drop on Eddie, who was pretty shrewd and probably a little suspicious at this stage. And, while they were figuring it all out, Louis Creamer got in touch to tell them he'd just killed Eddie O'Day.

"He came by my house," Louis said, "and he was acting weird, you know? He said you guys were going to pull a fast one and rat us out to the cops, but how could you do that? And he had this scheme for taking you both out and getting the money, and him and me'd split it. And I could see where he was going. He wanted me for about as long as it would take to take you both down, and then it would be my turn to go. The son of a bitch."

"So what did you do?"

"I just punched him out," Louis said, "and then I took hold of him and broke his fucking neck. Now I got him lying in a heap in my living room, and I don't know what to do with him."

"We'll help," said George.

They went to Louis's house, and there was Eddie in a heap on the floor. "Look at this," George said, holding up a gun. "He was packing."

"Yeah, well, he was out cold before he could get it out of his pocket."

"You did good, Louis," George said, pressing the gun into Eddie's dead hand and carefully fitting his index finger around the trigger. "Real good," he said, and pointed the gun at Louis, and put three shots in his chest.

"Amazing," Alan said. "They really did kill each other. Well, you said it would be convenient."

"One of them would have cut a deal. In fact Eddie did try to cut a deal, with Louis."

"But Louis stood up."

"For how long?"

"That was nice, taking him out with Eddie's gun. They'll find nitrate particles in his hand and know he fired the shot. But how'd he get killed?"

"We're not the cops," George said. "Let them worry about it."

We didn't worry much. We looked at who was still standing, and we brought in the Walkers and grilled them separately. They had their stories ready and we couldn't shake them, and hadn't really expected to. They'd been through this countless times before, and they knew to keep their mouths shut, and eventually we sent them home. A week later they were at George's house, in George's basement den, drinking George's scotch. "We maybe got trouble," Alan said. "The cops in San Diego picked up Mike Dunn."

"That's not good," George said, "but what's he gonna say? They'll throw the dame at him, Alfie's wife, and they got him figured for the sister, too. He'll just stay dummied up about everything if he knows what's good for him."

"Unless they offer him a deal."

"That could be a problem." George admitted.

Alan was looking at him carefully. George could almost hear what was going through Alan's mind, but before he could do anything about it Alan had a gun in his hand and it was pointed at George.

"Now put that away," George said. "What the hell's the matter with you? Just put that away and sit down and drink your drink."

"You're good, Georgie. But I know you too well. I just told you they arrested Mike, and you're not the least bit worried."

"I just said it could be a problem."

"What you almost said," Alan told him, "was it was impossible, but you didn't, you were quick on the uptake. But you knew it was impossible because you knew all along Mike Dunn was where nobody could get at him. Where is he, Georgie?"

"Buried. Nobody's gonna find him."

"What I figured. And what happened to his share? You bury it along with him?"

"I tucked it away. I didn't want the others to know what happened, so Mike's share of the money had to disappear."

"The others are gone, Georgie. It's just you and me, and I don't see you rushing to split the money with your brother."

"Jesus," George said, "is that what this is about? And will you please put the gun down and drink your drink?"

"I'll keep the gun," Alan said, "and I think I'll wait on the drink. Now that Louis and Eddie are out of the picture, you were gonna split Mike's share with me, weren't you?"

"Absolutely."

"Why don't I believe you, brother?"

"Because you're tied up in knots. Because they grilled you downtown, same as they grilled me, and they offered you a deal, same as they offered me a deal, and we're the Walkers, we're not gonna sell each other out, and if you'd relax and drink your fucking drink you'd know that. You want your share of Mike's money? Is that what you want?"

"That's exactly what I want."

"Fine," George said, and led him to the furnace room, where he hoisted the duffle bag. They returned to the den, with Alan holding a gun on his brother all the way. George set down the bag and worked the zipper, and the bag was full of money, all right. Alan's eyes widened at the sight of it.

"Half's yours," George said.

"I figure all of it's mine," Alan said. "You were gonna take it all, so I'm gonna take it all. Fair enough?"

"I don't know about fair," George said, "but you know what? I'm not going to argue. You take it, the whole thing, and we'll split what's in the storage locker. And drink your fucking drink before it evaporates."

"I'll take what's in the locker, too," Alan said, and squeezed the trigger, and kept squeezing until the gun was empty. "Jesus," he said, "I just killed my own brother. I guess I'll take that drink now, Georgie. You talked me into it." And he picked up the glass, drained it, and pitched forward onto his face.

THE ROOM fell silent, but for the crackling of the fire and, after a long moment, a rumbling snore from the fireside.

"A fine story," said the doctor, "though not perhaps equally engrossing to everyone. The club's Oldest Member, it would seem, has managed to sleep through it." They all glanced at the fireplace, and the chair beside it, where the little old man dozed in his oversized armchair.

"Poison, I presume," the doctor went on. "In the whiskey, and of course that was why George was so eager to have his brother take a drink."

"Strychnine, as I recall," said the policeman. "Something fast-acting, in any event."

"It's a splendid story," the priest agreed, "but one question arises. All the principals died, and I don't suppose any of them was considerate enough to write out a narrative before departing. So how are you able to recount it?"

"We reconstructed a good deal," the policeman said. "Mike Dunn's body did turn up, eventually, in the well at the old farmhouse. And of course the death scene in George Walker's den spoke for itself, complete with the duffle bag full of money. I put words in their mouths, and filled in the blanks through inference and imagination, but we're not in a court of law, are we? I thought it would do for a story."

"I meant no criticism, Policeman. I just wondered."

"And I wonder," said the soldier, "just what the story implies, and what it says about greed. They were greedy, of course, all of them. It was greed that led them to commit the initial crime, and greed that got them killing each other off, until there was no one left to spend all that money."

"I suppose the point is whatever one thinks it to be," the policeman said. "They were greedy as all criminals are greedy, wanting what other men have and appropriating it by illegal means. But, you know, they weren't that greedy."

"They shared equally," the doctor remembered.

"And lived well, but well within their means. You could say they were businessmen whose business was illegal. They were profit-motivated, but is the desire for profit tantamount to greed?"

"But they became greedy," the doctor observed. "And the greed altered their behavior. I assume these men had killed before."

"Oh, yes."

"But not wantonly, and they had never before turned on each other."

"No."

"The root of all evil," the priest said, and the others looked at him. "Money," he explained. "There was too much of it. That's the point, isn't it, Policeman? There was too much money."

The policeman nodded. "That's what I always thought," he said. "They had been playing the game for years, but suddenly the stakes had been raised exponentially, and they were in over their heads. The moment the bearer bonds turned up, all the deaths that were to follow were carved in stone." They nodded, and the policeman took up the pack of playing cards. "My deal, isn't it?" He shuffled the pack, shuffled it again.

"I wonder," the soldier said. "I wonder just what greed is."

"I would say it's like pornography," the doctor said. "There was a senator who said he couldn't define it, but he knew it when he saw it."

"If he got an erection, it was pornography?"

"Something like that. But don't we all know what greed is? And yet how easy is it to pin down?"

"It's wanting more than you need," the policeman suggested.

"Ah, but that hardly excludes anyone, does it? Anyone who aspires to more than life on a subsistence level wants more than he absolutely needs."

"Perhaps," the priest proposed, "it's wanting more than you think you deserve."

"Oh, I like that," the doctor said. "It's so wonderfully subjective. If I think I deserve—what was your phrase, Policeman? Something about dreaming of avarice?"

"'Wealth beyond the dreams of avarice.' And it's not my phrase, I'm afraid, but Samuel Johnson's."

"A pity he's not here to enliven this conversation, but we'll have to make do without him. But if I think I deserve to have pots and pots of money, Priest, does that protect me from greed?" The priest frowned, considering the matter.

"I think it's where it leads," the policeman said. "If my desire for more moves me to sinful action, then the desire is greedy. If not, I simply want to better myself, and that's a normal and innocent human desire, and where would we be without it?"

"Somewhere in New Jersey," the doctor said. "Does anyone ever think himself to be greedy? You're greedy, but I just want to make a better life for my family. Isn't that how everyone sees it?"

"They always want it for the family," the policeman agreed. "A man embezzles a million dollars and he explains he was just doing it for his family. As if it's not greed if it's on someone else's behalf."

"I'm reminded of the farmer," said the priest, "who insisted he wasn't at all greedy. He just wanted the land that bordered his own."

The soldier snapped his fingers. "That's it," he said. "That's the essence of greed, that it can never be satisfied. You always want more." He shook his head. "Reminds me of a story," he said.

"Then put down the cards," the doctor said, "and let's hear it."

IN MY occupation (said the soldier) greed rarely plays a predominant role. Who becomes a soldier in order to make himself rich? Oh, there are areas of the world where a military career can indeed lead to wealth. One doesn't think of an eastern warlord, for example, slogging it out with an eye on his pension and a cottage in the Cotswolds or a houseboat in Fort Lauderdale. In the western democracies, though, the activating sin is more apt to be pride. One yearns for promotions, for status, perhaps in some instances for political power. And financial reward often accompanies these prizes, but it's not apt to be an end in itself.

Why do men choose a military career? For the security, I suppose. For self-respect, and the respect of one's fellows. For the satisfaction of being a part of something larger than oneself, and not a money-grubbing soulless corporation but an organization bent on advancing and defending the interests of an entire nation. For many reasons, but rarely out of greed.

Even so, opportunities for profit sometimes arise. And greedy men sometimes find themselves in uniform—especially in time of war, when the draft sweeps up men who would not otherwise choose to clothe themselves in khaki. As often as not, such men make perfectly acceptable soldiers. There was a vogue some years ago for giving young criminals a choice—they could enlist in the armed forces or go to jail. This later went out of fashion, the argument against it being that it would turn the service into a sort of penitentiary without walls, filled with criminal types. But in my experience it often worked rather well. Removed from his home environment, and thrown into a world where greed had little opportunity to find satisfaction, the young man was apt to do just fine. The change might or might not last after his military obligation was over, of course.

But let's get down to cases. At the end of the second world war, Allied soldiers in Europe suddenly found several opportunities for profit. They had access to essential goods that were in short supply among the civilian population, and a black market sprang up instantly in cigarettes, chocolate, and liquor, along with such non-essentials as food and clothing. Some soldiers traded Hershey bars and packs of Camels for a fraulein's sexual favors; others parlayed goods from the PX into a small fortune, buying and selling and trading with dispatch.

There was nothing in Gary Carmody's background to suggest that he would become an illicit entrepreneur at war's end. He grew up on a farm in the Corn Belt and enlisted in the army shortly after Pearl Harbor. He was assigned to the infantry and participated in the invasion of Italy, where he picked up a Purple Heart and a shoulder wound at Salerno. Upon recovery from his injury, he was shipped to England, where in due course he took part in the Normandy invasion, landing at Utah Beach and helping to push the Wehrmacht across France. He earned a second Purple Heart during the German counterattack, along with a Bronze Star. He recuperated at a field hospital—the machine-gun bullet broke a rib, but did no major damage—and he was back in harness marching across the Rhine around the time the Germans surrendered.

Neither the bullets he'd taken nor the revelations of the concentration camps led Gary to a blanket condemnation of the entire German nation. While he thought the Nazis ought to be rounded up and shot, and that shooting was probably too good for the SS, he didn't see anything wrong with the German women. They were at once forthright and feminine, and their accents were a lot more charming than the Nazis in the war movies. He had a couple of dates, and then he met a blue-eyed blonde named Helga, and they hit it off. He brought her presents, of course—it was only fitting, the Germans had nothing and what was the big deal in bringing some chocolate and cigarettes? Back home you'd take flowers or candy, and maybe go out to a restaurant, and nobody thought of it as prostitution. He brought a pair of nylons one day, and she tried them on at once, and one thing led to another. Afterward they lay together in her narrow bed and she reached to stroke the stockings, which they hadn't bothered to remove. She said, "You can get more of these, liebchen?"

"Did they get a run in them already?"

"Gott, I hope not. No, I was thinking. We could make money together."

"With nylons?"

"And cigarettes and chocolate. And other things, if you can get them."

"What other things?"

"Anything. Soap, even."

And so he began trading, with Helga as his partner in and out of bed. She was the daughter of shopkeepers and turned out to be a natural at her new career, knowing instinctively what to buy and what to sell and how to set prices. He was just a farm boy, but he had a farm boy's shrewdness plus the quickness it had taken to survive combat as a foot soldier, and he learned the game in a hurry. As with any extralegal trade, there was always a danger that the person you were dealing with would pull a fast one—or a gun or a knife—and use force or guile to take everything. Gary knew how to make sure that didn't happen.

It was another American soldier who got Gary into the art business. The man was an officer, a captain, but the black market was a great leveler, and the two men had done business together. The captain had a fraulein of his own, and the two couples were drinking together one evening when the captain mentioned that he'd taken something in trade and didn't know what the hell he was going to do with it. "It's a painting," he said. "Ugly little thing. Hang on a minute, I'll show you." He went upstairs and returned with a framed canvas nine inches by twelve inches, showing Salome with the head of John the Baptist. "I know it's from the Bible and all," the captain said, "but it's still fucking unpleasant, and if Salome was really that fat I can't see losing your head over her. This look like five hundred dollars to you, Gary?"

"Is that what you gave for it?"

"Yes and no. I was going back and forth with this droopy-eyed Kraut and we reached a point where we're five hundred dollars apart. And he whips out this thing of beauty. 'All right,' he said. 'I vill hate myself for doing zis, but you haff me over a bushel.' And he goes on to tell me how it's a genuine Von Schtupp or whatever the hell it is, and it's worth a fortune.

"The way he did it, I couldn't come back and say, look, Konrad, keep the picture and gimme a hundred dollars more. I do that and I'm slapping him in the face, and I don't want to rub him the wrong way because Konrad and I do a lot of business. And the fact of the matter is yes, we're five hundred bucks apart, but I could take the deal at his price and I'm still okay with it. So I said yes, it sure is a beautiful picture, which it's not, as anyone can plainly see, and I said I'm sure it was valuable, but what am I gonna do with it? Sell it in Paris, he says. Sell it in London, in New York. So I let him talk me into it, because I wanted the deal to go through but what I didn't want was for him to try palming off more of these beauties on me, because I saw the look in his eye, Gary, and I've got a feeling he's got a shitload of them just waiting for a sucker with a suitcase full of dollars to take them off his hands."

"What are you going to do with it?"

"Well, I don't guess I'll throw darts at it. I could take it home, but what's a better souvenir, a genuine Luger or an ugly picture? And which would you rather spend your old age looking at?"

Gary looked at the painting, and he looked at Helga. He saw something in her eyes, and he also saw something in the canvas. "It's not that ugly," he said. "What do you want for it?"

"You serious?"

"Serious enough to ask, anyway."

"Well, let's see. I've got five hundred in it, and—"

"You've got zero in it. You'd have done the deal for what he offered, without the painting."

"I said that, didn't I? Strategic error, corporal. I'll tell you what, give me a hundred dollars and it's yours."

"Let's split the difference," Gary said. "I'll give you fifty."

"What is it we're splitting? Oh, hell, I don't want to look at it anymore. Give me the fifty and you can hang it over your bed."

They didn't hang it over the bed. Instead Helga hid it under the mattress. "The Nazis looted everything," she told him. "Museums, private collections. Your friend is stupid. It's a beautiful painting, and we can make money on it. And if we can meet his friend Konrad—"

"There's more where this one came from," he finished. "But how do we sell them?"

"You can get to Switzerland, no?"

"Maybe," he said.

The painting, which he sold without ever learning the artist's name— he somehow knew it was not Von Schtupp—brought him Swiss francs worth twenty-eight hundred American dollars. The proceeds bought four paintings from the droopy-eyed Konrad. These were larger canvases, and Gary removed them from their frames and rolled them up and took them to Zurich, returning to Germany this time with almost $7000. And so it went. It wasn't a foolproof business, as he learned when his Zurich customer dismissed a painting as worthless kitsch. But it was a forgiving trade, and most transactions were quite profitable. If he was in doubt he could take goods on consignment, selling in Zurich or Geneva—or, once, in Madrid—and sharing the proceeds with the consignor. But you made more money if you owned what you were selling, and he liked owning it, liked the way it felt. And if there was more risk that way, well, he liked the risk, too.

All his time and energy went into the business. Art was all he bothered with now—there were enough other soldiers making deals in stockings and cigarettes—and he was preoccupied with it, with the buying and selling and, almost as an afterthought, with the paintings themselves. Because it turned out he had a feel for it. He'd seen something in that first painting of Salome, even if he hadn't realized it at the time. He'd responded to the artistry. Before he enlisted, he'd never been to a museum, never seen a painting hanging in a private home, never looked at any art beyond the reproductions in his mother's J. C. Penney calendar. He learned to look at the paintings, as he'd never looked at anything before. The more he liked a painting, the harder it was to part with it. He fell in love with a Goya, and held onto it until something else came along that he liked better. Then he sold the Goya—that was the one he took to Madrid, where he'd heard about a crony of Franco's who wouldn't be put off by the work's dodgy provenance.

It was easier to part with Helga. They'd been good for each other, as lovers and as business partners, but the affair ran its course, and he didn't need or want a partner in his art dealings. He gave her a fair share of their capital and went on by himself.

Nothing lasts forever, not even military service. There came a time for Gary to board a troopship headed back to the States. He thought of staying in Europe—he had a career here, for as long as it could last—but in the end he realized it was time to go home. But what to do with his money? He had run his original stake of cigarettes and nylons up to something like eighty thousand dollars. That was a lot of cash to carry, and it was cash he couldn't explain, so he had to carry it—he couldn't put it in a bank and write himself a check.

But what he could do, and in fact did, was buy a painting and bring that home with him. He chose a Vermeer, a luminous domestic interior, the most beautiful thing he'd ever seen in his life. It hadn't come to him in the usual way; instead, he'd found it in an art gallery in Paris and had been hard pressed to get the snooty owner to cut the price by ten percent. On the troopship, squinting at the painting in his footlocker by what little illumination his flashlight afforded, he decided he must have been out of his mind. He'd had all that cash, and now he was down to what, fifteen thousand dollars? That was a lot of money in 1946, it would buy him a house and get him started in a business, but it was a fifth of what he'd had. Well, maybe he could run it up a little. It would be a week before the ship docked in New York, and there were plenty of men on board with money in their pockets and time on their hands. There were card games and crap games running twenty-four hours a day, and he'd always been pretty good at a poker table.

I suspect you can guess at the rest. Maybe he ran up against some card sharps, or maybe the cards just weren't running his way. He never knew for sure, but what he did know was that he reached New York with nothing in his kick but the five hundred dollars of case money he'd tucked away before he started. Everything else was gone, invested in straights that ran into flushes, flushes that never came in, and bluffs some other guy called. You'd think he'd be desolate, wouldn't you? He thought so himself, and was surprised to discover that he actually felt pretty good. If you looked at it one way, he left Germany with eighty thousand dollars and landed in New York with five hundred. But there was another way to see it, and that was that he had five hundred dollars more than he'd had when he left Iowa in the first place, and he'd been shot twice and lived to tell the tale, and he had a Bronze Star to keep his two Purple Hearts company, and he knew as much about women as anybody in Iowa, and more about art. The money he'd had, well, in a sense it had never been real in the first place, and, as for the paintings he'd trafficked in, well, they hadn't been real either. They'd all of them been stolen, and they had no provenance, and sooner or later they could very well be confiscated and restored to their rightful owners. He figured he'd done just fine.

• • •

"SOLDIER? HAVE you finished?"

The soldier looked up, blinked. "More or less," he said. "Why? Don't you like the story?"

"It's a fine story," the doctor said, "but isn't it unfinished? There's a sense of closure, in that our hero is back where he started. That's if he went back to his family's farm, which I don't believe you mentioned."

"Didn't I? Yes, he returned to the farm."

"And to the girl he left behind him?"

"I don't believe there was a girl he'd left behind," said the soldier, "and if there was, well, she'd been left too far behind to catch up with him."

"That must have been true of the farm as well," the priest offered.

The soldier nodded. "That proved to be the case," he said. "He had, as it were, seen Paree—and Madrid and Geneva and Zurich and Berlin, and no end of other places more stimulating than an Iowa cornfield. He'd spent two days in New York, waiting for his train, and he'd spent much of it at the Metropolitan Museum of Art, and in the galleries on upper Madison Avenue. He stayed in Iowa for as long as he could, and then he packed a bag and returned to New York."

"And?"

"He found a cheap flat, a fifth-floor walkup in Greenwich Village for $22 a month. He made the rounds of the art galleries and auction houses until he found someone who was willing to hire him for $40 a week. And, gradually, he learned the business from the ground up. From the very beginning he saved his money—I don't know how he could have saved much when he earned forty dollars a week, but he managed. Half of it went into a permanent savings account. The other half went into a fund to purchase art.

"Years passed. Although there was often a woman in his life, he never married, never formed a long-term alliance. Nor did he move from his original apartment in the Village. The neighborhood became increasingly desirable, the surrounding rents went up accordingly, but his own rent, frozen by the miracle of rent control, was still under a hundred dollars a month twenty-five years later.

"His capital grew, as did his collection of prints and paintings. The time came when he was able to open a gallery of his own, stocking it with the works he'd amassed. Rather than represent living artists, he dealt in older works, and on more than one occasion he was offered work he recognized from his time in Germany, stolen paintings he'd brokered years ago. Since then they'd acquired provenance and could be openly bought and sold.

"He's in the business today. He could retire, he'll tell you, but then what would he do with himself? He walks with a cane, and on damp days he feels the pain of his second wound, the rib broken by the machine-gun bullet. It's funny, he says, that it never bothered him once it healed, and now it aches again, after all those years. You think you're done with a thing, he'll say philosophically, but perhaps no one is ever done with anything.

"He's respected, successful, and if I told you his name, which is certainly not Gary Carmody, you might very well recognize it. There were rumors over the years that he occasionally dealt in, well, not stolen goods exactly, but works of art with something shady about them, and I don't mean chiaroscuro. But nothing was ever substantiated, and there was never a scandal, and few people even remember what was once said of him."

"And that's the end of the story," the policeman said.

"Well, the man's still alive, and is any story ever entirely over while one lives? But yes, the story is over."

"And what does it all mean?" the priest wondered. "He was a rather ordinary young man, not particularly greedy, until circumstances created a great opportunity for greed to flourish. Greed led him into a marginally criminal existence, at which he seems to have thrived, and then his circumstances changed, and he tried to change with them. But greed led him to try his hand at poker—"

"Even as you and I," murmured the doctor.

"—and he lost everything. But what he retained, acquired through greed, was a love of art and a passion for dealing in it, and as soon as he could he returned to it, and worked and sacrificed to achieve legitimate success."

"Unless those rumors were true," the policeman said.

"It's a fine story," the doctor said, "and well told. But there's something I don't entirely understand."

"Oh?"

"The Vermeer, Soldier. He was working for nothing and living on less. My God, he must have been scraping by on bread and water, and it would have been day-old bread and tap water, too. Why couldn't he sell the Vermeer? That would have set him up in business and kept him living decently until the gallery started paying for itself."

"He fell in love with it," the policeman offered. "How could he sell it? I daresay he still owns it to this day."

"He does," the soldier said. "It hung briefly on the wall of his room in the farmhouse in Iowa, and for years it hung on a nail in that fifth-floor Village walkup. The day he opened his own gallery he hung it above his desk in the gallery office, and it's still there."

"A lucky penny," the doctor said. "'Keep me and you'll never go broke.' And I'd say he's a long way from broke. I haven't priced any Vermeers lately, but I would think his would have to be worth an eight-figure price by now."

"You would think so," the soldier allowed.

"And he wouldn't part with it. Is that greed, clinging so tenaciously to that which, if he would but let it go, might allow him to reach his goals? Or is it some other sin?"

"Like what, Doctor?"

"Oh, pride, perhaps. He defines himself as a man who possesses a Vermeer. And so it hangs on his crumbling wall while he lives like a churchmouse. No, make that like a ruined aristocrat, putting on a black tie every night for dinner, setting the table with Rosenthal china and Waterford crystal, and dining on stone soup. Made, you'll no doubt recall, by simmering a stone in water for half an hour, then adding salt."

"An old family recipe," the policeman said. "But would the painting be worth that much? An eight-figure price—that's quite a range, from ten to a hundred million dollars."

"Ninety-nine," the doctor said.

"I stand corrected. But if it increased in value from fifty thousand dollars to—oh, take the low figure, ten million. If it performed that well, how can you possibly argue that he should have sold it? He may have struggled, but it doesn't seem to have harmed him. Who can say he was wrong to keep it? He's a success now, he's been a success for some years— and he owns a Vermeer."

They fell silent, thinking about it. Then the priest cleared his throat, and all eyes turned toward him.

"I should think," he said, "that at least two of the figures are after the decimal point." He drew a breath, smiled gently. "I suspect Soldier has neglected to tell us everything. It's a forgery, isn't it? That priceless Vermeer." The soldier nodded.

"By Van Meegeren, I would suppose, if it fooled our Mr. Carmody the first time around. That fellow's Vermeers, sold as the fakes that they are, have reached a point where they command decent prices in their own right. I don't suppose this one is worth quite what that young soldier gave for it half a century ago, but it's a long way from valueless."

"A fake," the policeman said. "How did you guess, Priest?"

"The clues were there, weren't they? Why else would his heart sink when he peered at the painting as it reposed in his footlocker? He saw then by flashlight what he hadn't seen in the gallery's more favorable lighting—that he'd squandered all his profits on a canvas that was never in the same room as Vermeer. No wonder he gambled, hoping to recoup his losses. And, given the state of mind he must have been in, no wonder he lost everything."

"An expert in New York confirmed what he already knew," the soldier said. "Could he have sold it anyway? Perhaps, even as the Parisian dealer, knowingly or unknowingly, had sold it to him. But he'd have taken a considerable loss, and would risk blackening his reputation before he even had one. Better, he always felt, to keep the painting, and to hang it where he would see it every day, and never forget the lesson it was there to teach him."

"And what was that lesson, Soldier?"

"That greed can lead to error, with devastating results. Because it was greed that led him to sink the better part of his capital into that worthless Vermeer. It was a bargain, and he should have been suspicious, but the opportunity to get it at that price led him astray. Greed made him want it to be a Vermeer, and so he believed it to be one, and paid the price for his greed."

"And hung it on his wall," the priest said.

"Yes."

"And moved it to his office when he opened his own gallery. So that he could look at it every day while conducting his business. But others would see it as well, wouldn't they? What did he tell them when they asked about it?"

"Only that it was not for sale."

"I don't suppose it harmed his reputation to have it known that this new kid on the block was sufficiently well-fixed to hang a Vermeer on his wall and not even entertain offers for it," the doctor mused. "I'm not so sure he didn't get his money's worth out of it after all."

THEY FELL silent again, and the policeman dealt the cards. The game was seven-card stud, but this time the betting was restrained and the pot small, won at length by the priest with two pair, nines and threes. "If we were playing Baseball," he said, raking in the chips, "with nines and threes wild, I'd have five aces."

"If we were playing tennis," said the doctor, who had held fours and deuces, "it would be your serve. So shut up and deal." The priest gathered the cards, shuffled them. The soldier filled his pipe, scratched a match, held it to the bowl. "Oh, it's your pipe," the doctor said. "I thought the old man over there had treated us to a fart."

"He did," said the soldier. "That's one reason I lit the pipe."

"Two wrongs don't make a right," the doctor declared, and the priest offered the cards and the policeman cut them, and, from the fireside, the four men heard a sound that had become familiar to them over time.

"You see?" said the doctor. "He's done it again. Try to counteract his flatulence with your smoke, and he simply redoubles his efforts."

"He's an old man," the policeman said.

"So? Who among us is not?"

"He's a bit older than we are."

"And isn't he a pretty picture of what the future holds? One day we too can sleep twenty-three hours out of every twenty-four, and fill the happy hours with coughing and snuffling and snoring and, last but alas not least, great rumbling pungent farts. And what's left after that but the grave? Or is there more to come, Priest?"

"I used to wonder," the priest admitted.

"But you no longer doubt?"

"I no longer wonder, knowing that all will be made clear soon enough. But I'm still thinking of greed."

"Deal the cards, and we can do something about it."

"As I understand it," the priest went on, "crimes of greed, crimes with mercenary motives, fluctuate with economic conditions. When and where unemployment is high and need is great, the crime rate goes up. When times are good, it drops."

"That would stand to reason," the soldier said.

"On the other hand," said the priest, "the criminals in Policeman's story fell tragically under the influence of greed not when they lacked money, but when they were awash in it. When there was not so much to be divided, they shared fairly and equally. When the money flooded in, they killed to increase their portion of it."

"It seems paradoxical," the policeman agreed, "but that's just how it was."

"And your corporal-turned-art dealer, Soldier. How does he fit into the need-greed continuum?"

"Opportunity awakened his greed," the soldier said. "Perhaps it was there all along, just waiting until the chance came along to make money on the black market. We could say he was greediest when he bought the fake Vermeer, and again when he realized what he'd done and tried to recoup at the card table."

"A forlorn hope," said the doctor, "in a game like this one, where hours go by before someone deals the cards."

"His money gone," the soldier went on, "he applied himself like a character out of Horatio Alger, but was he any less avaricious for the fact that his actions were now ethical and lawful? He was as ambitious as ever, and there was a pot of gold looming at the end of his rainbow."

"So greed's a constant," said the priest, and took up the deck of cards once again.

"It is and it isn't," the doctor said. "Hell, put down the damned cards. You just reminded me of a story." The priest placed the cards, undealt, upon the table. By the fireside, the old man sighed deeply in his sleep. And the priest and the soldier and the policeman sat up in their chairs, waiting for the doctor to begin.

SOME YEARS ago (said the doctor) I had as a patient a young man who wanted to be a writer. Upon completion of his education he moved to New York, where he took an apartment rather like your art dealer,

Soldier, but lacking a faux-Vermeer on the wall. He placed his typewriter on a rickety card table and began banging out poems and short stories and no end of first chapters that failed to thrive and grow into novels. And he looked for a job, hoping for something that would help him on his way to literary success.

The position he secured was at a literary agency, owned and operated by a fellow I'll call Byron Fielding. That was not his name, but neither was the name he used, which he created precisely as I've created an alias for him, by putting together the surnames of two English writers. Fielding started out as a writer himself, sending stories to magazines while he was still in high school, and getting some of them published. Then World War Two came along, even as it did to Gary Carmody, and Byron Fielding was drafted and, upon completion of basic training, assigned to a non-combat clerical position. It was his literary skills that kept him out of the front lines—not his skill in stringing words together but his ability to type. Most men couldn't do it.

When he got out of the service, young Fielding wrote a few more stories, but he found the business discouraging. There were, he had come to realize, too many people who wanted to be writers. Sometimes it seemed as though everybody wanted to be a writer, including people who could barely read. And when they tried their hand at it, they almost always thought it was good.

Was such monumental self-delusion as easy in other areas of human endeavor? I think not. Every boy wants to be a professional baseball player, but an inability to hit a curveball generally disabuses a person of the fantasy. Untalented artists, trying to draw something, can look at it and see that it didn't come out as they intended. Singers squawk, hear themselves, and find something else to do. But writers write, and look at what they have written, and wonder what's keeping the Nobel Commission fellows from ringing them up.

You shake your heads at this, and call it folly. Byron Fielding called it opportunity, and opened his arms wide.

He set up shop as a literary agent; he would represent authors, placing their work with publishers, overseeing the details of their contracts, and taking ten percent of their earnings for his troubles. This was nothing new; there were quite a few people earning their livings in this fashion—though not a fraction of the number there are today. But how, one wondered, could Byron Fielding hope to establish himself as an agent? He had no contacts. He didn't know any writers—or publishers, or anyone else. What would persuade an established writer to do business with him?

In point of fact, Fielding had no particular interest in established writers, realizing that he had little to offer them. What he wanted was the wannabes, the hopeful hopeless scribblers looking for the one break that would transform a drawer full of form rejection slips into a life of wealth and fame. He rented office space, called himself Byron Fielding, called his company the Byron Fielding Literary Agency, and ran ads in magazines catering to the same hopeful hopeless ones he was counting on to make him rich. "I sell fiction and non-fiction to America's top markets," he announced. "I'd like to sell them your material." And he explained his terms. If you were a professional writer, with several sales to national publishers to your credit, he would represent you at the standard terms of 10% commission. If you were a beginner, he was forced to charge you a reading fee of $1 per thousand words, with a minimum of $5 and a maximum of $25 for book-length manuscripts. If your material was salable, he would rush it out to market on his usual terms. If it could be revised, he'd tell you how to fix it—and not charge you an extra dime for the advice. And if, sadly, it was unsalable, he'd tell you just what was wrong with it, and how to avoid such errors in the future.

The money rolled in.

And so did the stories, and they were terrible. Fielding stacked them, and when each had been in his office for two weeks, so that it would look as though he'd taken his time and given it a careful reading, he returned it with a letter explaining just what was wrong with it. Most of the time what was wrong was the writer's utter lack of talent, but he never said that. Instead he praised the style and found fault with the plot, which somehow was always flawed in ways that revision could not cure. Put this one away, he advised each author, and write another, and send that along as soon as it's finished. With, of course, another reading fee.

The business was profitable from the beginning, with writers incredibly sending in story after story, failing entirely to learn from experience. Fielding thought he'd milk it for as long as it lasted, but a strange thing happened. Skimming through the garbage, he found himself coming across a story now and then that wasn't too bad. "Congratulations!" he wrote the author. "I'm taking this right out to market." It was probably a mistake, he thought, but this way at least he got away with a shorter letter.

And some of the stories sold. And, out of the blue, a professional writer got in touch, wondering if Fielding would represent him on a straight commission basis. By the time my patient, young Gerald Metzner, went to work for him, Byron Fielding was an established agent with over ten years in the business and a string of professional clients whose work he sold to established book and magazine publishers throughout the world.

Fielding had half a dozen people working for him by then. One ran a writing school, with a post office box for an address and no visible connection with Byron Fielding or his agency. The lucky student worked his way through a ten-lesson correspondence course, and upon graduating received a certificate of completion and the suggestion that he might submit his work (with a reading fee) to guess who. Another employee dealt with the professional clients, working up market lists for the material they submitted. Two others—Gerald Metzner was one of them—read the scripts that came in over the transom, the ones accompanied by reading fees. "I can see you are no stranger to your typewriter," he would write to some poor devil who couldn't write an intelligible laundry list. "Although this story has flaws that render it unsalable, I'll be eager to see your next effort. I feel confident that you're on your way." The letter, needless to say, went out over Byron Fielding's signature. As far as the mopes were concerned, Fielding was reading every word himself, and writing every word of his replies. Another employee, also writing over Fielding's mean little scrawl, engaged in personal collaboration with the more desperate clients. For a hundred bucks, the great man himself would purportedly work with them step-by-step, from outline through first draft to final polish. They would be writing their stories hand in hand with Byron Fielding, and when it was finished to his satisfaction he would take it out to market.

The client (or victim, as you prefer) would mail in his money and his outline. The hireling, who had very likely never sold anything himself, and might in fact not ever have written anything, would suggest some arbitrary change. The client would send in the revised outline, and when it was approved he would furnish a first draft. Again the employee would suggest improvements, and again the poor bastard would do as instructed, whereupon he'd be told that the story, a solid professional effort, was on its way to market.

But it remained a sow's ear, however artfully embroidered, and Fielding wouldn't have dreamed of sullying what little reputation he had by showing such tripe to an editor. So the manuscript went into a drawer in the office, and there it remained, while the hapless scribbler was encouraged to get cracking on another story.

The fee business was ethically and morally offensive, and one wondered why Fielding didn't give it up once he could afford to. The personal collaboration racket was worse; it was actionably fraudulent, and a client who learned what was going on could clearly have pressed criminal charges against his conniving collaborator. It's not terribly likely that Fielding could have gone to jail for it, but a determined prosecutor with the wind up could have given him some bad moments. And if there were a writer or two on the jury, he couldn't expect much in the way of mercy.

Fielding hung on to it because he didn't want to give up a dime. He didn't treat his professional clients a great deal better, for in a sense he had only one client, and that client was Byron Fielding. He acted, not in his clients' interests, but in his own. If they coincided, fine. If not, tough.

I could go on, but you get the idea. So did young Metzner, and he wasn't there for long. He worked for Fielding for a year and a half, then resigned to do his own writing. A lot of the agency's pro clients were writing soft-core paperback fiction, and Metzner tried one of his own. When it was done he sent it to Fielding, who sold it for him.

He did a few more, and was making more money than he'd made as an employee, and working his own hours. But it wasn't what he really wanted to write, and he tried a few other things, and wound up out in California, writing for film and television. Fielding referred him to a Hollywood agent, who, out of gratitude and the hope of more business, split commissions on Metzner's sales with Byron Fielding. Thus Fielding made far more money over the years from Gerald Metzner's screenwriting than he had ever made from his prose, and all he had to do for it was cash the checks the Hollywood agent sent him. That was, to his way of thinking, the ideal author-agent relationship, and he had warm feelings for Metzner—or what passed for warm feelings in such a man.

When Metzner had occasion to come to New York, he more often than not dropped in on his agent. He and Fielding would chat for fifteen minutes, and then he could return to Hollywood and tell himself he hadn't entirely lost touch with the world of books and publishing. He had an agent, didn't he? His agent was always happy to see him, wasn't he? And who was to say he wouldn't someday try his hand at another novel?

Years passed, as they so often do. Business again called Gerald Metzner to New York, and he arranged to drop by Fielding's office on a free afternoon. As usual, he waited for a few minutes in the outer office, taking a look at the sea of minions banging away at typewriters. It seemed to him that there were more of them every time he visited, more men sitting at more desks, telling even more of the hopeful hopeless that they had talent in rare abundance, and surely the next story would make the grade, but, sad to say, this story, with its poorly constructed plot, was not the one to bring their dreams to fulfillment. What a story required, you see, was a strong and sympathetic lead character confronted by a problem, and…Di dah di dah di dah.

He broke off his reverie when he was summoned to Fielding's private office. There the agent waited, looking younger than his years, health club-toned and sunlamp-tanned, a broad white-toothed smile on his face. The two men shook hands and took seats on opposite sides of the agent's immaculate desk.

They chatted a bit, about nothing in particular, and then Fielding fixed his eyes on Gerald. "You probably notice that there's something different about me," he said.

"Now that you mention it," Metzner said, "I did notice that." Years of pitching doubtful premises to studio heads and network execs had taught him to think on his feet—or, more accurately, on his behind. What, he wondered, was *different* about the man? Same military haircut, same horn-rimmed glasses. No beard, no mustache. What the hell was Fielding talking about?

"But I'll bet you can't quite put your finger on it."

Well, that was a help. Maybe this would be like soap opera dialogue—you could get through it without a script, just going with the flow.

"You know," he said, "that's it exactly. I sense it, but I can't quite put my finger on it."

"That's because it's abstract, Gerry."

"That would explain it."

"But no less real."

"No less real," he echoed.

Fielding smiled like a shark, but then how else would he smile? "I won't keep you in suspense," he said. "I'll tell you what it is. I've got peace of mind."

"Peace of mind," Metzner marveled.

"Yes, peace of mind." The agent leaned forward. "Gerry," he said, "ever since I opened up for business I've been the toughest, meanest, most miserable sonofabitch who ever lived. I've always wrung every nickel I could out of every deal I touched. I worked sixty, seventy hours a week, and I used the whip on the people who worked for me. And do you know why?"

Metzner shook his head.

"Because I thought I had to," Fielding said. "I really believed I'd be screwed otherwise. I'd run out of money, I'd be out on the street, my family would go hungry. So I couldn't let a penny get away from me. You know, until my lawyers absolutely insisted, I wouldn't even shut down the Personal Collaboration dodge. 'Byron, you're out of your mind,' they told me. 'That's consumer fraud, and you're doing it through the mails. It's a fucking federal offense and you could go to Leavenworth for it, and what the hell do you need it for? Shut it down!' And they were right, and I knew they were right, but they had to tell me a dozen times before I did what they wanted. Because we made good money out of the PC clients, and I thought I needed every cent of it."

"But now you have peace of mind," Metzner prompted.

"I do, Gerry, and you could see it right away, couldn't you? Even if you didn't know what it was you were seeing. Peace of mind, Gerry. It's a wonderful thing, maybe the single most wonderful thing in the world."

Time for the violins to come in, Metzner thought. "How did it happen, Byron?"

"A funny thing," Fielding said. "I sat down with my accountant about eight months ago, the way I always do once a year. To go over things, look at the big picture. And he told me I had more than enough money left to keep me in great shape for as long as I live. 'You could shut down tomorrow,' he said, 'and you could live like a king for another fifty years, and you won't run out of money. You've got all the money you could possibly need, and it's in solid risk-free inflation-resistant investments, and I just wish every client of mine was in such good shape.'"

"That's great," said Metzner, who wished he himself were in such good shape, or within a thousand miles thereof.

"And a feeling came over me," Fielding said, "and I didn't know what the feeling was, because I had never felt anything like it before. It was a relief, but it was a permanent kind of relief, the kind that means you can stay relieved. You're not just out of the woods for the time being. You're all of a sudden in a place where there are no woods. Free and clear—and I realized there was a name for the feeling I had, and it was peace of mind."

"I see."

"Do you, Gerry? I'll tell you, it changed my life. All that pressure, all that anxiety—gone!" He grinned, then straightened up in his chair. "Of course," he said, "on the surface, nothing's all that different. I still hustle every bit as hard as I ever did. I still squeeze every dime I can out of every deal I touch. I still go for the throat, I still hang on like a bulldog, I'm still the most miserable sonofabitch in the business."

"Oh?"

"But now it's not because I *have* to be like that," Fielding exulted. "It's because I *want* to. That's what I love, Gerry. It's who I am. But now, thank God, I've got peace of mind!"

"WHAT A curious story," said the priest. "I'm as hard pressed to put my finger on the point of it as your young man was to recognize Fielding's peace of mind. Fielding seems to be saying that his greed had its roots in his insecurity. I suppose his origins were humble?"

"Lower middle class," the doctor said. "No money in the family, but they were a long way from impoverished. Still, insecurity, like the heart, has reasons that reason knows nothing of. If he's to be believed, Byron Fielding grew up believing he had to grab every dollar he could or he risked ruin, poverty, and death."

"Then he became wealthy," the priest said, "and, more to the point, came to *believe* he was wealthy, and financially secure."

"Fuck-you money," the policeman said, and explained the phrase when the priest raised an eyebrow. "Enough money, Priest, so that the possessor can say 'fuck you' to anyone."

"An enviable state," the priest said. "Or is it? The man attained that state, and his greed, which no longer imprisoned him, still operated as before. It was his identity, part and parcel of his personality. He remained greedy and heartless, not out of compulsion but out of choice, out of a sense of self." He frowned. "Unless we're to take his final remarks *cum grano salis?*" To the puzzled policeman he said, "With a grain of salt, that is to say. You translated fuck-you money for me, so at least I can return the favor. A sort of *quid pro quo*, which in turn means..."

"That one I know, Priest."

"And Fielding was not stretching the truth when he said he was the same vicious bastard he'd always been," the doctor put in. "Peace of mind didn't seem to have mellowed him at all. Did I mention his brother?"

The men shook their heads.

"Fielding had a brother," the doctor said, "and, when it began to appear as though this scam of his might prove profitable, Fielding put his brother to work for him. He made his brother change his name, and picked Arnold Fielding for him, having in mind the poet Matthew Arnold. The brother, whom everyone called Arnie, functioned as a sort of office manager, and was also a sort of mythical beast invoked by Byron in time of need. If, for example, an author came in to cadge an advance, or ask for something else Byron Fielding didn't want to grant, the agent wouldn't simply turn him down. 'Let me ask Arnie,' he would say, and then he'd go into the other office and twiddle his thumbs for a moment, before returning to shake his head sadly at the client. 'Arnie says no,' he'd report. 'If it were up to me it'd be a different story, but Arnie says no.'"

"But he hadn't actually consulted his brother?"

"No, of course not. Well, here's the point. Some years after Gerald Metzner learned about Byron Fielding's peace of mind, Arnie Fielding had a health scare and retired to Florida. He recovered, and in due course found Florida and retirement both bored him to distraction, and he came back to New York. He went to see his brother Byron and told him he had decided to go into business. And what would he do? Well, he said, there was only one business he knew, and that's the one he would pick. He intended to set up shop on his own as a literary agent.

"'The best of luck to you,' Byron Fielding told him. 'What are you going to call yourself?'

"'The Arnold Fielding Literary Agency,' Arnie said.

"Byron shook his head. 'Better not,' he said. 'You use the Fielding name and I'll take you to court. I'll sue you.'

"'You'd sue me? Your own brother?'

"'For every cent you've got,' Byron told him."

The soldier lit his pipe. "He'd sue his own brother," he said, "to prevent him from doing business under the name he had foisted upon him. The man may have achieved peace of mind, Doctor, but I don't think we have to worry that it mellowed him."

"Arnie never did open his own agency," the doctor said. "He died a year or so after that, though not of a broken heart, but from a recurrence of the illness that had sent him into retirement initially. And the old pirate himself, Byron Fielding, only survived him by a couple of years."

"And your young writer?"

"Not so young anymore," said the doctor. "He had a successful career as a screenwriter, until ageism lessened his market value, at which time he returned to novel-writing. But the well-paid Hollywood work had taken its toll, and the novels he wrote all failed."

They were considering that in companionable silence when a log burned through and fell in the fireplace. They turned at the sound, observed the shower of sparks, and heard in answer a powerful discharge of methane from the old man's bowels.

"God, the man can fart!" cried the doctor. "Light up your pipe, Soldier. What I wouldn't give for a cigar!"

"A cigar," said the priest, thoughtfully.

"Sometimes it's only a cigar," the doctor said, "as the good Dr. Freud once told us. But in this instance it would do double duty as an air freshener. Priest, are you going to deal those cards?"

"I was just about to," said the priest, "until you mentioned the cigar."

"What has a cigar, and a purely hypothetical cigar at that, to do with playing a long-delayed hand of poker?"

189

"Nothing," said the priest, "but it has something to do with greed. In a manner of speaking."

"I'm greedy because I'd rather inhale the aroma of good Havana leaf than the wind from that old codger's intestines?"

"No, no, no," said the priest. "It's a story, that's all. Your mention of a cigar put me in mind of a story."

"Tell it," the policeman urged.

"It's a poor story compared to those you all have told," the priest said. "But it has to do with greed."

"And cigars?"

"And cigars, yes. It definitely has to do with cigars."

"Put the cards down," the doctor said, "and tell the story."

THERE WAS a man I used to know (said the priest) whom I'll call Archibald O'Bannion, Archie to his intimates. He started off as a hod carrier on building sites, applied himself diligently learning his trade, and wound up with his own construction business. He was a hard worker and a good businessman, as it turned out, and he did well. He was motivated by the desire for profit, and for the accoutrements of success, but I don't know that I would call him a greedy man. He was a hard bargainer and an intense competitor, certainly, and he liked to win. But greedy? He never struck me that way.

And he was charitable, more than generous in his contributions to the church and to other good causes. It is possible, to be sure, for a man to be at once greedy and generous, to grab with one hand while dispensing with the other. But Archie O'Bannion never struck me as a greedy man. He was a cigar smoker, and he never lit a cigar without offering them around, nor was there anything perfunctory about the offer. When he smoked a cigar, he genuinely wanted you to join him.

He treated himself well, as he could well afford to do. His home was large and imposing, his wardrobe extensive and well chosen, his table rich and varied. In all these areas, his expenditures were consistent with his income and status.

His one indulgence—he thought it an indulgence—was his cigars.

He smoked half a dozen a day, and they weren't William Penn or Hav-a-Tampa, either. They were the finest cigars he could buy. I liked a good cigar myself in those days, though I could rarely afford one, and when Archie would offer me one of his, well, I didn't often turn him down. He was a frequent visitor to the rectory, and I can recall no end of evenings when we sat in pleasantly idle conversation, puffing on cigars he'd provided.

Then the day came when a collection of cigars went on the auction block, and he bought them all.

A cigar smoker's humidor is not entirely unlike an oenophile's wine cellar, and sometimes there is even an aftermarket for its contents. Cigars don't command the prices of rare bottles of wine, and I don't know that they're collected in quite the same way, but when a cigar smoker dies, the contents of his humidor are worth something, especially since Castro came into power in Cuba. With the American embargo in force, Havana cigars were suddenly unobtainable. One could always have them smuggled in through some country that continued to trade with Cuba, but that was expensive and illegal, and, people said, the post-revolution cigars were just not the same. Many of the cigar makers had fled the island nation, and the leaf did not seem to be what it was, and, well, the result was that pre-Castro cigars became intensely desirable.

A cigar is a perishable thing, but properly stored and maintained there's no reason why it cannot last almost forever. In this particular instance, the original owner was a cigar aficionado who began laying in a supply of premium Havanas shortly after Castro took power. Perhaps he anticipated the embargo. Perhaps he feared a new regime would mean diminished quality. Whatever it was, he bought heavily, stored his purchases properly, and then, his treasures barely sampled, he was diagnosed with oral cancer. The lip, the mouth, the palate—I don't know the details, but his doctor told him in no uncertain terms that he had to give up his cigars.

Not everyone can. Sigmund Freud, whom Doctor quoted a few minutes ago, went on smoking while his mouth and jaw rotted around his cigar. But this chap's addiction was not so powerful as his instinct for self-preservation, and so he stopped smoking then and there.

But he held on to his cigars. His several humidors were attractive furnishings as well as being marvels of temperature and humidity control, and he liked the looks of them in his den. He broke the habit entirely, to the point where his eyes would pass over the humidors regularly without his ever registering a conscious thought of their contents, let alone a longing for them. You might think he'd have pressed cigars upon his friends, but he didn't, perhaps out of reluctance to have to stand idly by and breathe in the smoke of a cigar he could not enjoy directly. Or perhaps, as I somehow suspect, he was saving them for some future date when it would be safe for him to enjoy them as they were meant to be enjoyed.

Well, no matter. In the event he did recover from his cancer, and some years passed, and he died of something else. And, since neither his widow nor his daughters smoked cigars, they wound up consigned for sale at auction, and Archie O'Bannion bought them all.

There were two thousand of them, and Archie paid just under sixty thousand dollars for the lot. That included the several humidors, which were by no means valueless, but when all was said and done he'd shelled out upwards of twenty-five dollars a cigar. If he consumed them at his usual rate, a day's smoking would cost him $150. He could afford that, but there was no denying it was an indulgence.

But what troubled him more than the cost was the fact that his stock was virtually irreplaceable. Every cigar he smoked was a cigar he could never smoke again. Two thousand cigars sounded like an extraordinary quantity, but if you smoked six a day starting the first of January, you'd light up the last one after Thanksgiving dinner. They wouldn't last the year.

"It's a damned puzzle," he told me. "What do I do? Smoke one a day? That way they'll last five years and change, but all the while five out of six of the cigars I smoke will be slightly disappointing. Maybe I should smoke 'em all up, one right after the other, and enjoy them while I can. Or maybe I should just let them sit there in their beautiful humidors, remaining moist and youthful while I dry up and age. Then when I drop dead it'll be Mary Katherine's turn to put them up for auction."

I said something banal about the conundrum of having one's cake and eating it, too.

"By God," he said. "That's it, isn't it? Have a cigar, Father."

But, I demurred, surely not one of his Havanas? "You smoke it," he said. "You earned it, Father, and you can damn well smoke it and enjoy it."

And he picked up the phone and called his insurance agent.

Archie, I should mention, had come to regard the insurance industry as a necessary evil. He'd had trouble getting his insurers to pay claims he felt were entirely legitimate, and disliked the way they'd do anything they could to weasel out of their responsibility. So he had no compunctions about what he did now.

He insured his cigars, opting for the top-of-the-line policy, one which provided complete coverage, not even excluding losses resulting from flood, earthquake, or volcanic eruption. He declared their value at the price he had paid for them, paid the first year's premium in advance, and went on with his life.

A little less than a year later, he smoked the last of his premium Havanas. Whereupon he filed a claim against his insurance company, explaining that all two thousand of the cigars were lost in a series of small fires.

You will probably not be surprised that the insurance company refused to pay the claim, dismissing it as frivolous. The cigars, they were quick to inform him, had been consumed in the normal fashion, and said consumption was therefore not a recoverable loss.

Archie took them to court, where the judge agreed that his claim was frivolous, but ordered the company to pay it all the same. The policy, he pointed out, did not exclude fire, and in fact specifically included it as a hazard against which Archie's cigars were covered. Nor did it exclude as unacceptable risk the consumption of the cigars in the usual fashion. "I won," he told me. "They warranted the cigars were insurable, they assumed the risk, and then of course they found something to whine about, the way they always do. But I stuck it to the bastards and I beat 'em in court. I thought they'd drag it out and appeal the judgment, and I was set to fight it all the way, but they caved in. Wrote me a check for the full amount of the policy, and now I can go looking for someone else with pre-Castro Havanas to sell, because I've developed a taste for them, let me tell you. And I've got you to thank, Father, for a remark you made about having your cake and eating it, too, because I smoked my cigars and I'll have 'em, too, just as soon as I find someone who's got 'em for sale. Of course this is a stunt you can only pull once, but once is enough, and I feel pretty good about it. The Havanas are all gone, but these Conquistadores from Honduras aren't bad, so what the hell, Father. Have a cigar!"

"I DON'T know why you were so apologetic about your story, Priest," the soldier said. "I think it's a fine one. I'm a pipe smoker myself, and any dismay one might conceivably feel at watching one's tobacco go up in smoke is more than offset by the satisfaction of improving the pipe itself, as one does with each pipeful one smokes. But pipe tobacco, even very fine pipe tobacco, costs next to nothing compared to premium cigars. I can well understand the man's initial frustration, and ultimate satisfaction."

"An excellent story," the doctor agreed, "but then it would be hard for me not to delight in a story in which an insurance company is hoist on its own petard. The swine have institutionalized greed, and it's nice to see them get one in the eye."

"I wonder," said the policeman.

"I know what you're thinking," the doctor told him. "You're thinking that this fellow Archie committed lawful fraud. You're thinking it was his intention to make the insurance company subsidize his indulgence in costly Cuban tobacco. That's entirely correct, but as far as I'm concerned it's quite beside the point. Lawful fraud is an insurance company's stock in trade, and anyway what's sixty thousand dollars on their corporate balance sheet? I say more power to Archie, and long may he puff away."

"All well and good," the policeman said, "but that's not what I was thinking."

"It's not?"

"Not at all," he told the doctor, and turned to the priest. "There's more to the story, isn't there, Priest?"

The priest smiled. "I was wondering if anyone would think of it," he said. "I rather thought you might, Policeman."

"Think of what?" the soldier wanted to know.

"And what did they do?" the policeman asked. "Did they merely voice the threat? Or did they go all the way and have him arrested?"

"Arrested?" cried the doctor. "For what?"

"Arson," the policeman said. "Didn't he say the cigars were lost in a series of small fires? I suppose they could have charged him with two thousand counts of criminal arson."

"Arson? They were his cigars, weren't they?"

"As I understand it."

"And doesn't a man have the right to smoke his own cigars?"

"Not in a public place," said the policeman. "But yes, in the ordinary course of events, he would have been well within his rights to smoke them. But he had so arranged matters that smoking one of those cigars amounted to intentional destruction of insured property."

"But that's an outrage," the doctor said.

"Is it, Doctor?" The soldier puffed on his pipe. "You liked the story when the insurance company was hoist on its own petard. Now Archie's hoisted even higher on a petard of his own making. Wouldn't you say that makes it a better story?"

"A splendid story," said the doctor, "but no less an outrage for it."

"In point of fact," the policeman said, "Archie could have been charged with arson even in the absence of a claim, the argument being that he forfeited the right to smoke the cigars the moment he insured them. Practically speaking, though, it was pressing the claim that triggered the criminal charge. Did he actually go to jail, Priest? Because that would seem a little excessive."

The priest shook his head. "Charges were dropped," he said, "when the parties reached agreement. Archie gave back the money, and both sides paid their own legal costs. And he got to tell the story on himself, and he was a good fellow, you know, and could see the humor in a situation. He said it was worth it, all things considered, and a real pre-Castro cigar was worth the money, even if you had to pay for it yourself."

The other three nodded at the wisdom of that, and once again the room fell silent. The priest took the deck of cards in hand, looked at the others in turn, and put the cards down undealt. And then, from the fireside, the fifth man present broke the silence.

"GREED," SAID the old man, in a voice like the wind in dry grass. "What a subject for conversation!"

"We've awakened you," said the priest, "and for that let me apologize on everyone's behalf."

"It is I who should apologize," said the old man, "for dozing intermittently during such an illuminating and entertaining conversation. But at my age the line between sleep and wakefulness is a tenuous proposition at best. One is increasingly uncertain whether one is dreaming or awake, and past and present become hopelessly entangled. I close my eyes and lose myself in thought, and all at once I am a boy. I open them and I am an old man."

"Ah," said the doctor, and the others nodded in assent.

"And while I am apologizing," the old man said, "I should add a word of apology for my bowels. I seem to have an endless supply of wind, which in turn grows increasingly malodorous. Still, I'm not incontinent. One grows thankful in the course of time for so many things one took for granted, if indeed one ever considered them at all."

"One keeps thanking God," the priest said, "for increasingly smaller favors."

"Greed," said the old man. "What a greedy young man I was! And what a greedy man I stayed, throughout all the years of my life!"

"No more than anyone, I'm sure," the policeman said.

"I always wanted more," the old man remembered. "My parents were comfortably situated, and furnished me with a decent upbringing and a good education. They hoped I would go into a profession where I might be expected to do some good in the world. Medicine, for example."

"'First, do no harm,'" the doctor murmured.

"But I went into business," said the old man, "because I wanted more money than I could expect to earn from medicine or law or any of the professions. And I stopped at nothing legal to succeed in all my enterprises. I was merciless to competitors, I drove my employees, I squeezed my suppliers, and every decision I made was calculated to maximize my profits."

"That," said the soldier, "seems to be how business is done. Struggling for the highest possible profits, men of business act ultimately for the greatest good of the population at large."

"You probably believe in the tooth fairy, too," the old man said, and cackled. "If I did any good for the rest of the world, it was inadvertent and immaterial. I was trying only to do good for myself, and to amass great wealth. And in that I succeeded. You might not guess it to look at me now, but I became very wealthy."

"And what happened to your riches?"

"What happened to them? Why, nothing happened to them. I won them and I kept them." The old man's bowels rumbled, but he didn't appear to notice. "I lived well," he said, "and I invested wisely and with good fortune. And I bought things."

"What did you buy?" the policeman wondered.

"Things," said the old man. "I bought paintings, and I don't think I was ever taken in by any false Vermeers, like the young man in your story. I bought fine furniture, and a palatial home to keep it in. I bought antique oriental carpets, I bought Roman glass, I bought pre-Columbian sculpture. I bought rare coins, ancient and modern, and I collected postage stamps."

"And cigars?"

"I never cared for them," the old man said, "but if I had I would have bought the best, and I can well appreciate that builder's dilemma. Because I would have wanted to smoke them, but my desire to go on owning them would have been at least as strong."

They waited for him to go on; when he remained silent, the priest spoke up. "I suppose," he said, "that, as with so many desires, the passage of time lessened your desire for more."

"You think so?"

"Well, it would stand to reason that—"

"The vultures thought so," the old man said. "My nephews and nieces, thoughtfully telling me the advantages of making gifts during my lifetime rather than waiting for my estate to be subject to inheritance taxes. Museum curators, hoping I'd give them paintings now, or so arrange things that they'd be given over to them immediately upon my death. Auctioneers, assuring me of the considerable advantages of disposing of my stamps and coins and ancient artifacts while I still had breath in my body. That way, they said, I could have the satisfaction of seeing my collections properly sold, and the pleasure of getting the best possible terms for them.

"I told them I'd rather have the pleasure and satisfaction of continuing ownership. And do you know what they said? Why, they told me the same thing that everybody told me, everybody who was trying to get me to give up something that I treasured. You can guess what they said, can't you?"

It was the doctor who guessed. "You can't take it with you," he said.

"Exactly! Each of the fools said it as if he were repeating the wisdom of the ages. 'You can't take it with you.' And the worst of the lot, the mean little devils from organized charities, armored by the pretense that they were seeking not for themselves but for others, they would sometimes add yet another pearl of wisdom. There are no pockets in a shroud, they would assure me."

"I think that's a line in a song," the soldier said.

"Well, please don't sing it," said the old man. "Can't take it with you! No pockets in a shroud! And the worst of it is that they're quite right, aren't they? Wherever that last long journey leads, a man has to take it alone. He can't bring his French impressionists, his proof Liberty Seated quarters, his Belgian semi-postals. He can't even take along a checkbook. No matter what I have, no matter how greatly I cherish it, I can't take it with me."

"And you realized the truth in that," the priest said.

"Of course I did. I may be a doddering old man, but I'm not a fool."

"And the knowledge changed your life," the priest suggested.

"It did," the old man agreed. "Why do you think I'm here, baking by the fire, souring the air with the gas from within me? Why do you think I cling so resolutely, neither asleep nor awake, to this hollow husk of life?"

"Why?" the doctor asked, after waiting without success for the old man to answer his own question.

"Because," the old man said, "if I can't take it with me, the hell with it. I don't intend to go."

His eyes flashed in triumph, then closed abruptly as he slumped in his chair. The others glanced at one another, alarm showing in their eyes. "A wonderful exit line," the doctor said, "and a leading candidate for the next edition of *Famous Last Words*, but do you suppose the old boy took the opportunity to catch the bus to Elysium?"

"We should call someone," the soldier said. "But whom? A doctor? A policeman? A priest?"

There was a snore, shortly followed by a zestful fart. "Thank heavens," said the doctor, and the others sighed and nodded, and the priest picked up the deck and began to deal out the cards for the next hand.

SPEAKING OF LUST

"**I**DEALT, DIDN'T I?" the soldier said. He looked at his cards, shook his head. "What do you figure I had in mind? I pass."

The policeman, sitting to the dealer's left—East to his South—nodded, closed his eyes, opened them, and announced: "One club."

"Pass," said the doctor.

The priest said, "You bid a club, partner?" And, without waiting for a response, "One heart."

The soldier passed. You could tell he was a soldier, as he wore the dress uniform of a brigadier general in the United States Army.

"A spade," the policeman said. He too was in uniform, down to the revolver on his hip and the handcuffs hanging from his belt.

The doctor, wearing green scrubs, looked as though he might have just emerged from the operating room. He was silent, looking off into the middle distance, until the priest stared at him. "Oh, sorry," he said. "I pass."

"Two spades," said the priest, with a tug at his Roman collar.

"Pass," said the soldier.

"Four spades," the policeman said, and glanced around the table as if to confirm that the bidding was over. The doctor and priest and soldier dutifully passed in turn. The doctor studied his cards, frowned, and led the nine of hearts. The priest laid down his cards—four to the king in the trump suit, five hearts to the ace-jack—and sat back in his chair. The policeman won the trick with the ace of hearts from dummy and set about drawing trump.

Play was rapid and virtually silent. A fire crackled on the hearth, and the clock on the mantel chimed the quarter hour. Smoke drifted to the high ceiling—from the doctor's cigar, the priest's cigarette, the soldier's stubby briar pipe. Books, many of them bound in full leather, filled the shelves on either side of the fireplace, and one lay open in the lap of the room's only other occupant, the old man who sat by the fire. He had been sitting there when the four began their card game, the book open, his eyes closed, and he was there still.

"Four spades bid, five spades made," the policeman said, gathering the final trick. The priest took up his pencil and wrote down the score. The policeman shuffled the cards. The soldier cut them, and the policeman scooped them up and began to deal. He opened the bidding with a diamond, and the doctor doubled. The priest looked at his cards for a long moment.

"Lust," he said.

The others stared at him. "Is that your bid?" his partner said. "Lust?"

The priest stroked his chin. "Did I actually say that?" he said, bemused. "I meant to pass."

"Which made you think of making a pass," the doctor suggested, "and so you spoke as you did."

"Hardly that," the priest said. "I was thinking of lust, but I assure you I entertained no lustful thoughts. I was thinking of lust in the abstract, the sin of lust."

"Lust is a sin, is it?" said the soldier.

"One of the seven cardinal sins," the priest said.

"Lust is desire, isn't it?"

"A form of desire," the priest said. "A perversion of desire, perhaps. Desire raised to sinful proportions."

"But it's a desire all the same," the soldier insisted. "It's not an act, and a sin ought to be an act. Lust may prompt a sinful act, but it's not a sin in and of itself."

"One can sin in the mind," the policeman pointed out. "On the other hand, you can't hang a man for his thoughts."

"Hanging him is one thing," said the doctor. "Sending him to Hell is another."

"The seven deadly sins are all in the mind," the priest explained. "Pride, avarice, jealousy, anger, gluttony, sloth, and lust."

"Quite a menu," the soldier said.

"Sin is error," the priest went on. "A mistake, a tragic mistake, if you will. Out of pride, out of anger, out of gluttony, one commits an action which is sinful, or, if you will, entertains a sinful thought. Thus any sinful act a man might commit can be assigned to one of these seven categories."

"Without a certain amount of lust," the doctor said, "the human race would cease to exist."

"You could make the same argument for the other six sins as well," the priest told him, "because what is any of them but a distortion of a normal and essential human instinct? There is a difference, I submit, between the natural desire of a man for a maid and what we would label as sinful lust."

"What about the desire of a man for a man?" the doctor wondered. "Or a maid for a maid?"

"Or a farmer's son for a sheep?" The priest sat back in his chair. "We call some desires normal, others abnormal, and much depends on who's making the call."

The discussion was a lively one, and ranged far and wide. At length the policeman held up a hand. "If I may," he said. "Priest, you started this. Unintentionally, perhaps, by voicing a thought when you only meant to pass. But you must have had something in mind."

"An altar boy," suggested the doctor. "Or an altered boy."

"Nun of the above," the soldier put in.

"You should show the cloth a measure of respect," the priest said. "But I did have something in mind, as a matter of fact. Something that came to me, though I couldn't tell you why. Rather an interesting incident that took place some years ago. But we're in the middle of a game, aren't we?"

A gentle snore came from the old man dozing beside the fire. The four card players looked at him. Then the policeman and the doctor and the soldier turned their gaze to the priest.

"Tell the story," the policeman said.

SOME YEARS ago (said the priest) I came to know a young couple named William and Carolyn Thompson. I say a young couple because they were slightly younger than I, and I was not quite forty at the time, which now seems to me to be very young indeed. Let's say that he was thirty-six when I met them, and she thirty-eight. I may be off slightly in their ages, but not in the age difference between them. She was just two years the elder.

They were an attractive couple, both of them tall and slender and fair, with not dissimilar facial features—long narrow noses and penetrating blue eyes. I've noticed that couples grow to resemble one another after they've been together a long time, and I suspect this is largely the result of their having each learned facial expressions from the other. The same thing happens on a larger scale, doesn't it? The French, say, shrug and grimace and raise their eyebrows in a certain way, and their faces develop lines accordingly, until a national physiognomy emerges. Have you observed how older persons will look more French, or Italian, or Russian? It's not that the genes thin out in the younger generations. It's that the old have had more time to acquire the characteristic look.

The Thompsons had been married for a decade and a half, long enough, certainly, for this phenomenon to operate. And, spending as much time as they did together (living in a small house in one of the northwestern suburbs, working side by side in their shop) they'd had ample opportunity to mirror one another. Still, the resemblance they bore was more than a matter of shared attitudes and expressions. Why, they looked enough alike to be brother and sister.

As indeed they were.

William and Carolyn attended my church, though not with great regularity. I'd heard their confessions from time to time, and neither of them disclosed anything remarkable. I didn't really get to know them until Bill and I were brought into contact in connection with a community action project. We got accustomed to having a few beers after a meeting, and we became friends.

One afternoon he turned up at the rectory and asked if we could talk. "I don't want to make a formal confession," he said. "I just need to talk to someone, but it has to be confidential. If we just go over to Paddy Mac's and have a beer or two, could our conversation still be bound by the seal of the confessional?"

I told him I didn't see why not, and that I would certainly consider myself to be so bound.

The tavern we went to, a busy place in the evening, was dark and quiet of an afternoon. We sat off by ourselves, and Bill told me his story.

He grew up in another city on the other side of the country. He had an older sister—Carolyn, of course, but that revelation was to come later—and lived with her and his mother and father in a pre-war brick house in one of the older suburbs. He and his sister took after their mother, who was tall and blond. Their father was tall, too, but dark-complected, and heavily built.

His sister taught him to dance, took him shopping, and clued him in on all the things a young boy was supposed to learn. She comforted him, too, when he got a beating from their father. The man was a drinker, he said, and sometimes when he drank Bill would piss him off without knowing what he'd done wrong. Then he'd catch it.

One night when he was thirteen years old he said or did something to upset the man and got a few whacks with a belt as punishment. Afterward, his sister came to his room. He had been crying, and he was a little ashamed of that, too, and she told him he'd had a punishment he hadn't deserved, so now he was going to get a reward. Just as she'd taught him how to dance, now she would teach him how to kiss.

"So you'll know what to do when you're out with a girl," she said.

She sat next to him on his bed and they kissed. They'd kissed each other before, of course, but this was entirely different. Do you know how an unexciting activity may be said to be "like kissing your sister"? This was not like kissing your sister.

Over the next several months, the kissing lessons continued. She always initiated them, coming into his room when he was doing his homework, closing the door, sitting on his bed with him. This was very exciting for him, especially when she let him touch her breasts, first through her clothing, then with his hand inside her blouse. When she would leave his room, finally, he would relieve himself.

He was so occupied one day when, having recently left his room, she returned to it, opening his door without knocking and catching him in the act. He covered himself at once, but she had seen him, and she asked him what he had been doing.

"Nothing," he said.

"You were touching yourself," she said. "Right? But you shouldn't have to do that, Billy."

He said he couldn't help it. He knew it was wrong, but he couldn't help it.

"I'm not saying it's wrong," she said, "but you shouldn't have to do it *yourself.*"

She did it for him. And, from then on, that was how their sessions concluded, with her hand doing what his hand had previously done, and making a far more satisfying job of it. When they hadn't had time together during the day, she would make a point of slipping into his room at night after he'd gone to bed. He would usually pretend to sleep, and without a word she would satisfy him with her hands and return just as silently to her own room.

One night she used her mouth. The next day he asked her if she would do that again, and she said, "Oh, you mean you weren't really sleeping?"

Their play continued, and over time she led him on a veritable Cook's tour of sexuality, which eventually included every act either of them could think of short of actual coition. Their pleasure was hampered only by the fear of discovery, and on more than one occasion they narrowly escaped having a parent walk in on them. Thus they limited themselves to relatively brief encounters, and had to avoid crying out in fulfillment. Quick and quiet, that was the nature of their coupling.

Not surprisingly, they dreamed of being able to spend an entire night together in safety and privacy. The sister raised the subject often, telling him just what she would like to do to him, and what she would have him do to her.

"Maybe when we're older," she said. "When we're both out of the house. Unless you find somebody else by then."

But there would never be anybody else, he assured her. She was the only one he wanted.

What she didn't point out in response, and what he knew without being told, was that what he wanted, what they both wanted, could never be. They were brother and sister. They could never be man and wife.

He couldn't imagine himself with anyone else, couldn't bear the thought of her in someone else's arms. She was his and he was hers. How could he marry another woman, a stranger?

"I thought of becoming a priest," he told me. "If I couldn't have her, then it would be easier if I never had to have anyone. Then the absurdity of the notion struck me. I was in bed with my sister, I was committing all kinds of sins with her, and the fact that I wouldn't be able to go on committing them forever made me think I had a vocation. But I swear it seemed perfectly logical to me at the time."

One day she had an idea. He was still a member of a Boy Scout troop, although he'd become less active. The troop had a camping weekend scheduled. Suppose he signed up for it? And suppose she drove to the encampment and picked him up down the road around the time the troop's bugler blew Taps and turned in for the night? They could go to a motel—she'd take care of booking a room—and they could have a whole night together and get him back to camp before Reveille.

That's what they did. On Friday night, he waited until his tent mate was sleeping, then slipped out and trotted down the road to where she was waiting. It was all set for the following night, she told him. The room was booked, and she'd bought some massage oil and something provocative to wear. She wished they could go there now, but she had to get home. She had an excuse lined up for her absence the following night, but not tonight, and she had to get home.

They got into the back of the car and she brought him off quickly with her lips and fingers. Then he went back to his tent and lay grinning in the darkness, thinking of his tent mate and the other boys, thinking what they were missing.

The following night, Saturday night, he feigned sleep himself so that his tent mate would finally shut up, and then had to lie there listening while the other boy brought himself to lonely fulfillment. Then, when the boy's breathing deepened in sleep, he crept out and hurried to the appointed spot. The car wasn't there waiting for him, and he worried that she wasn't coming, worried that she'd come and gone, worried that something somehow had gone wrong.

Then the car appeared, and minutes later they were at the motel. She had already checked in, signing a false name on the register and paying in cash. She drove straight to the unit, unlocked the door, and led him inside.

She apologized for having been late. "Mama wanted help folding laundry," she said, "and I told her I was expected at Sandy's, and she said Sandy could wait. And then *he* came home, and the two of them started going at it, and that gave me a chance to slip out. Oh, but I don't want to waste time talking. I want to do everything. We don't have to be quiet for once and I want to make noise. I want to make you scream."

They both made noise, although no one screamed. They made love with the tireless enthusiasm of youth, and toward dawn she sighed and swore she couldn't help herself and threw herself astride him and took him deep within herself.

Years later he would recall thinking that this was it, that they'd crossed a line. Up until then they had done everything but, and now they had done it all.

Before the sun was up she dropped him off where she'd picked him up, then headed for her friend's house. "Sandy thinks I'm at a motel with a frat boy," she said. "Little does she know. But she'll let me in, and cover for me."

His tent mate stirred when he returned, wanted to know where he's been. The latrine, he said. The other boy went back to sleep.

He lay there and watched through the tent flap as dawn broke. He was a boy—fourteen now, he'd had a birthday since that first kissing lesson—but he felt like man. *I just got laid*, he told himself. *I fucked my sister.* A man, yes, and a sinner.

He wondered what his punishment would be.

Within hours, he found out.

Shortly after breakfast, after they'd divided into groups for morning activities, a Sheriff's Office car pulled into the camp grounds. A tall man wearing sunglasses got out and talked to the scoutmaster. Then the two men walked to where Billy was sitting, trying to undo a bad knot in the lanyard he was making. It was kid stuff, entwining the plastic lacing to make a lanyard, and pretty tame compared to fucking your sister in a motel room, but if you were going to do it you might as well get it right.

The scoutmaster hunkered down beside him, his red face troubled, the perspiration beading on his large forehead. The Sheriff, or whoever he was, stood up straight as a ramrod. And the scoutmaster explained that there had been some trouble, that Billy was an orphan now, that both of his parents were dead.

Of course he couldn't take it in. He was numb with shock. How could they be dead? He found out gradually, with no one eager to tell him too much too soon. They were shot, he learned, his mother three times, twice in the chest and once in the face, his father once, the bullet entering his open mouth and exiting through the back of his skull. Death for both was virtually instantaneous. They didn't suffer, he was told.

And finally he was told who had done it. His father had come home drunk, and evidently there had been an argument. (He nodded as he took this in, nodded unconsciously, because this was something he already knew. But he wasn't supposed to know it, because who could have told him? He'd been at the camp the whole time.)

The person who told him made nothing of the nod. Maybe it only indicated that this was nothing uncommon, that his father often came home drunk, that his parents often argued.

But this argument had an atypical ending, because Billy's father had concluded it by taking a handgun from his desk drawer and putting three bullets into Billy's mother and, in remorse or anger or God knows what, blowing out his own brains.

The boy knew whose fault it was. It was his, his and his sister's. While they were crossing the last barrier, their father was murdering their mother, then sinning against the Holy Ghost by taking his own life.

As he remembered it, the ensuing days and weeks passed in a blur. While the authorities tried to find a relative who could take them in, Billy and Carolyn went on living in the house where their parents had died. No agreeable relative emerged, and the two were of an inconvenient age, too young to be on their own, too old to be placed in foster care. The officials shuffled papers and forgot about them, and they stayed where they were. Carolyn did the shopping and prepared the meals, Billy cut the grass and raked the lawn and shoveled the walk.

A week after the tragedy, they resumed sleeping together.

"All we've got is each other," she told him. "What happened's not our fault. I'll tell you something, it was going to happen sooner or later, and if we'd been home that night we'd have wound up dead, too. The way he drank, the way he got when he drank? And the way she provoked him? 'Man Kills Wife and Self.' If we had been home, it would have been 'Man Kills Wife, Two Children, and Self.' That's the only difference."

He knew she was right.

All they had was each other, and they loved each other. Socially, they withdrew further into themselves. For a year or two, this was unremarkable, a natural consequence of the family tragedy they had endured. Then, shortly after her eighteenth birthday, she announced that a boy had asked her on a date and she had agreed to go with him.

"People get suspicious. 'What's wrong with her that she never goes out with anybody?' They think I'm pretty, I ought to be interested in boys."

"Let them think you're a lesbian."

"Believe me, some of them already think that. I've had some long looks from a couple members of the sisterhood, and one of them asked me if I'd like to come over and watch the last round of the LPGA at her house. Why would anyone want to watch golf, whether it was men or women playing? And why would I want to go over to her house anyway?"

"I wish you didn't have to go out with some guy," he said.

"You're jealous?"

"I guess so."

"I'm not going to let him do anything, Billy. But I think it makes sense to go out with him. And you're going to have to start going out with girls."

"Or they'll think I'm a fag?"

"Or a retard."

"I don't care what they think," he said, but of course he did. Later he told her he wished they could be where nobody knew anything about them.

"I've been thinking about that," she said.

They put the house on the market and sold it, rented an apartment in a college town a few hundred miles away. She'd been given her mother's maiden name as a middle name, and now she dropped her surname, and they lived together as William Thompson and Carolyn Peyton. She built up a collection of identification in that name, and enrolled at the college, and a year later so did he. The money from the house, supplemented by their earnings from part-time jobs, covered their tuition and expenses, and they had both always been good students. He took an accelerated program and they graduated together, four years after they'd sold the house.

Neither had made a single close friend during those four years. Neither had gone out on a date, or shown any interest in a member of the opposite sex. All they wanted was to be together, and they were confident their feelings were not going to change.

They got married. "We could just say we were married," she told him. "When does anyone ask to see a marriage license? And I already feel married to you. More than married to you. But I want to do it all the same."

"And have kids?"

"A baby with two heads," she said. "That's what you get if you sleep with your brother. Remember how kids used to think that? I've done some research, and it doesn't necessarily work out that way. There's a chance, though, that there might be something abnormal about the child."

"I don't really want kids, anyway."

"Neither do I," she said, "but that might change, for one or both of us. If it does—"

"We could take our chances," he said. "Or adopt."

"But for now," she said, "all I want is you."

And so they got married, and Carolyn Peyton legally changed her name again, back to Carolyn Peyton Thompson. And, as man and wife, they moved to the city where I came to know them. They went into business together, made a success of it, bought a house, and, well, lived happily ever after. They postponed the decision about children until they realized it had resolved itself; they were a complete unit now, they had been a complete unit from that first kissing lesson, and a child would be an unwelcome extra presence in their home.

Legally married, they came to feel less as though they had something to hide. So they were more inclined to make friends, more prepared to play an active role in the life of the community. They were, in everybody's eyes, a decent and charming couple, attractive and personable and very much in love. And you could see at a glance that they belonged together. Why, they even looked alike. If you didn't know better, you'd take them for brother and sister.

"AND THAT'S it?" said the soldier.

The priest nodded. "More or less," he said.

"More or less," echoed the doctor. "Is it more or is it less? Never mind. Lust, eh? Well, I suppose it was lust that got them started, but it sounds to me more like a love story than one of unbridled sexual passion. It's not lust that keeps two people together for—what did you say? A decade and a half? No, that's how long they were married. He was thirteen when she gave him his first kissing lesson and thirty-six or so when he told you about it, so that's twenty-three years. If there's some kind of lust that lasts for twenty-three years, I'd like a case of it sent to my quarters."

"And I'm not sure where the sin comes in," the soldier said. "Unless the incest itself is the sin, and I suppose your church might call it that, but I don't know that I would. Whom did they harm? And where's the dissolute life to which sin's presumed to lead? They became model citizens, from the sound of things. They had a secret, but what couple doesn't have a few secrets, and who's to say they do them any harm?"

A snore came from the old man seated by the fire.

"My sentiments exactly," said the doctor. "What I can't figure out is why the fellow had that conversation with you. Incidentally, is it all right for you to recount it to us? You told him you'd consider yourself bound by the seal of the confessional."

"As you three don't know the people involved," the priest said, "and as I've changed their names, I don't feel I've violated a confidence. The Church might see it differently, but I've long since ceased to be bound by what the Church thinks. My own conscience is clear on this subject, if on few others." He turned to the policeman. "You haven't said anything," he said.

"It's a good story," the policeman said. "There's one question that occurs to me, though, but you may not know the answer."

"Ask it."

"I was wondering," the policeman said, "whether anybody ever gave that girl a paraffin test."

The priest smiled.

ON THE eve of their wedding (the priest continued) Carolyn cooked an elaborate dinner. Afterward they sat with cups of strong coffee, and she said she had something to tell him, something she was afraid to tell him. "If you're going to marry me," she said, "you should know this."

From the time she was eleven years old, she said, their father had taken to coming into her room while she was sleeping. He initiated a pattern of sexual abuse which progressed gradually from inappropriate touches and caresses while she slept, or feigned sleep, to acts which required her to be awake and an active participant. For the last three years of the man's life, the repertoire included sexual intercourse, and the man did not use a condom. She lived in fear that he would make her pregnant, but he managed on each occasion to withdraw in time, depositing his sticky gift on her belly.

Toward the end, though, he seemed to be considering impregnating her, and more than once said he wondered what kind of a mommy she'd make.

She hated him, and wanted to kill him. She hated her mother as well. Early on she had told the woman that he was coming to her room, that he was touching her. The woman refused to take it in. He's your father, she was told. He loves you. You're imagining things.

And so, on that Saturday night, while her father sat in front of the television set in a drunken slack-jawed stupor, she got the handgun from the drawer where he kept it, thrust the barrel into his open mouth, and pulled the trigger. When her mother came in to see what had happened, she leveled the gun and shot the woman three times. Then she wiped her own fingerprints from the gun, placed it in her father's dead hand, and curled his fingers around it.

Then she went off to meet her brother, and arrived just a few minutes late. And, having just committed a double murder, and sure she'd be found out and sent to prison, she blotted it all from her mind and gave herself over to a last night of joy and consummation with her beloved brother.

But of course she was never found out. The murder-suicide scene she'd staged was good enough to pass muster, and no one ever took a good hard look at her alibi. Her friend, Sandy, kept her secret; it wouldn't do to let out that Carolyn had been out cavorting with a boyfriend, nor would Sandy's parents be comfortable with the knowledge that their daughter had facilitated such deception. So why not keep that little secret? Carolyn surely had enough tragedy in her life, with her father having killed her mother and himself. She didn't need to have her sex life exposed to public scrutiny.

Nor did Billy's alibi get much attention. He crawled into his tent after taps and crawled out of it at reveille. Case closed.

And so, on the eve of his wedding, William Thompson learned for the first time that his father was not a murderer and that his sister was.

The following day they were married.

"AND LIVED happily ever after," said the doctor. "A curious business, incest. More common, it turns out, than we used to think. No end of fathers, it turns out, lurch into their daughters' beds. And they're not always hillbillies or immigrants or welfare cases, either. It happens, as they say, in the best of families. As for brothers and sisters, well, what's that but a childhood game carried to its logical conclusion?"

"Playing doctor," the soldier said.

"Quite so. It must happen often, and who'd ever report it? If the two are close in age, if there's no force or intimidation involved, where's the abuse? It may be forbidden, they may be transgressors, but what's the harm?"

"I wonder how often they actually marry," the policeman said.

"Not too often," the doctor said. "I can't imagine marrying my sister, but then I can't imagine fucking her, either. Truth to tell, I can't imagine *anyone* fucking her."

"If you had a better-looking sister..."

"Then it might be a different story," the doctor allowed. "Speaking of stories, that's a good one, Priest. How did it turn out?"

"I don't know that it did," the priest said. "Two years or so after our conversation, Carolyn gave birth to a daughter. I christened the child, and she certainly looked like her parents, for all that you can tell when they're that small."

"So they rolled the dice," the soldier said. "Although I suppose someone else might have been the father. Artificial insemination and all that."

"Or else they'd have been swimming in the shallow end of the gene pool," said the doctor, "and that's dangerous, but not always disastrous. On the one hand you've got the Jukes and the Kallikaks, those horrible examples they tell you about in high school biology class, and on the other hand you've got all the crowned heads of Europe."

"When we have more time," the policeman said, "you can tell me which is worse. Any more to the story, Priest?"

The priest shook his head. "I was transferred shortly thereafter," he said, "and lost track of them. I hope things turned out well for them. I liked them."

"And I like your story," the policeman said. "Lust. I could tell a story about lust."

The others sat back, waiting.

I'M NOT much of a storyteller (said the policeman) and I don't know much about sin. Not that I'm free from it myself, but that I was not trained to think in those terms. My frame of reference is the law, the criminal code specifically. I can tell you whether or not an act is lawful, and, if it's not, I can correctly label it a violation or a misdemeanor or a felony.

And even then my classification will not apply universally, but only in the jurisdiction where I lived and worked.

Determining what is or is not a criminal act is difficult enough. Determining whether or not an act is sinful, well, I wouldn't want to touch that with a stick.

Lust...

When I was still a young man, I was partnered with an older man named—well, let me choose a name for him, as the priest chose a name for his young couple. And I ought to be able to come up with something a little more distinctive and imaginative than William Thompson, don't you think? Michael Walbeck, that's what we'll call my partner. Michael J. Walbeck, and the J stands for John. No, make it Jonathan. Michael Jonathan Walbeck, and everybody called him Mike, except for his mother, who still called him Mickey, and his wife, who called him Michael.

She was a beauty, his wife. Her hair was a heap of black curls that spilled down over her shoulders, and her face was heart-shaped, with dark almond-shaped eyes and a lush mouth. Walbeck was jealous of her. He'd call her eight or ten times a day, just to make sure he knew where she was. As far as I knew, Marie never gave him cause for jealousy, outside of always looking like she just hopped out of bed, and like she was ready at a moment's notice to hop back in again. But he didn't need cause. He was just a jealous man.

Meanwhile, he was running around on her. Here he was, talking about how he'd kill her if he ever caught her with another guy, and how he'd kill the guy, too, and at the same time he always had something going on the side, and sometimes more than one thing.

You've heard of guys who go through life following their own dick, and that was Walbeck. He said himself that he'd screw a snake if somebody would hold its head, and I'm not entirely certain he was exaggerating. He'd roust hookers and let them off in return for a quick blow job—it's safe to say he wasn't the first cop who thought of that one—but his real specialty was the wives and girlfriends of criminals.

That's a little harder than getting a hooker to go down on you, but not by much. The first time I saw Mike in action, we had busted a guy who was cooking crank in his double-wide out on the edge of town. That's methamphetamine, also known as speed, and it's about as tricky to make as chili con carne. And cooking it's a felony in fifty states, and we had this poor bastard dead to rights. His rights were what Mike was reading him, as a matter of fact, but he stopped in midsentence when he got a look at Cheryl.

I don't know if she was his wife or his girlfriend, and I don't remember her name, so for all I know it could have been Cheryl. Doesn't matter. She was a blowsy girl, and in a few years she'd be a real porker, but now she was in her early twenties and she looked hot and sluttish. She had a wrapper on, I remember, and it needed laundering, and you could pretty much tell she wasn't wearing anything under it.

"Nice looking girl," Walbeck told the mope. "You know, I wonder if there's a way we can work something out."

The guy got it before it touched the ground. "You see anything you like," he said, "it's yours."

"She's got to do us both," Walbeck said. "Me and my partner here."

"You got it."

"Eddie—" the girl said, whining.

"Shut up," he told her. "Like you're gonna miss it?"

"She's got some shape on her," Walbeck said. "She does us both, including we get to fuck her in the ass."

"No way," the girl said.

"I said shut up," Eddie said. "You do that, I get to keep the stuff."

"The crank."

"The crank and the money both. You don't confiscate nothing, and I walk, and for that you can fuck her anywhere you want. Cut a hole in her chest and fuck her in the heart, all I care."

"Eddie!"

"Deal," Walbeck said. He asked me if I wanted to go first. I shook my head and waited outside with Eddie, who professed not to care what was going on inside the trailer. I noticed, though, that he lit one cigarette off the butt of another, and smoked as if he wanted to burn up the whole cigarette in one furious drag.

"He's a prick," he said. "That partner of yours." I said something to the effect that nobody'd forced him to go for the deal. "Oh, it's a good deal," he said. "Don't get me wrong. She ain't gonna miss another slice off the loaf, and who gives a shit about her anyway? But he's still a prick."

Walbeck was in there long enough for Eddie to smoke three cigarettes, and he was zipping his pants as he came down the trailer steps.

"Nice," he said, grinning. "I can see why you keep her around. You're up, partner."

You pass in a situation like that, you make trouble in your partnership. Like if you bend the rules for a storekeeper on your beat, let his suppliers park illegally when they're making their deliveries, and he slips you a few bucks out of gratitude. If one partner takes it and the other won't accept his cut, how are they going to get along?

So I managed a grin of my own and went up the steps and into the trailer. I wasn't really in the mood, so I figured I'd just sit around long enough for the guy outside to suck down a few more cigarettes while Walbeck broke his balls some more. But I figured without the woman. I got one look at her, sitting on the edge of the bed with her soiled wrapper hanging open in front, her face and attitude showing vulnerability and sluttishness in equal proportion, and just like that I wanted her. My head thought I ought to be above such things, but my dick had a mind of its own.

She gave me a sad smile and took off the wrapper, and that settled that. I got out of my clothes, and she looked at me and her face clouded. "Jesus," she said, "you're about twice as big as your friend. I hope you don't want to stick it the same place he did."

I told her the conventional route would do.

"You're nice," she said. "Go slow so I can really get into it, and you'll be glad you did."

Afterward, we stopped at a pay phone and Walbeck called his house. He talked to his wife, but that wasn't enough reassurance, and he insisted we take a run past his house to see if there was a strange car in the driveway. There wasn't, but two doors down on the other side of the street he spotted a car he didn't recognize, and right away he called a guy he knew at DMV and ran the plate. The car was registered to a man named Shoenstahl, with a residence listed across town, but there was a family on Walbeck's street with the same name, so it was probably a relative, and not some bastard nailing Walbeck's wife.

"You can't trust them," he told me. "Look at that choice specimen of trailer trash we were just with. Once you get past the surface, they're all like that."

I could have put in for a transfer, but Walbeck wasn't the worst partner in the world. The tail-chasing and the jealousy weren't endearing traits,

215

but in other respects he was a fairly decent cop, and not as much of a pain in the ass to be harnessed with as some of them. I got used to him, and then he took the whole thing to another level when he met a woman I'll call Joanie.

I was with him when he first caught sight of her. It was at a basketball game. Someone had given him tickets and he invited me to come along. I didn't much like to hang out with Walbeck, I got enough of him on the job, but I like basketball and these were good seats. A few minutes into the first period he elbowed me and pointed. "The redhead," he said, "Third row up and on the aisle."

"What about her?"

"I gotta have her," he said.

She was a striking woman, with a lush body and strong facial features. Flaming red hair, and that pale skin redheads have, the ones that don't have freckles. I admired her myself, but it wasn't a matter of admiration with Walbeck. He took one look at her and decided he had to have her.

"If I don't get to fuck her," he said, "I'll fucking die."

She was sitting alone, with an empty seat next to her, and he was on the point of going over and taking the empty seat and hitting on her, when her companion turned up—her husband, although we didn't find that out until later. He was a tall man with a mustache and a sport jacket that looked like it was made from a horse blanket, and he was carrying a tray with a couple of hot dogs and a couple of beers. He sat down next to the redhead, and before he sat down he looked over in our general direction.

"He looks wrong," I said, meaning he looked like a lawbreaker. Hard to say what makes a guy look right or wrong, but a cop gets so he knows. Unconsciously he's adding up a whole batch of signs and mannerisms, and he knows.

"He damn well ought to look wrong," Mike Walbeck said. "That's Harv Jellin. He's got a sheet, he's done state time. Now how in the hell does a skell like Harv Jellin get a broad like that?"

I shrugged and turned my attention back to the game, but Walbeck was lost for the evening, his attention taken up entirely by the redhead and the man beside her. "You know what I wonder?" he said. "I wonder just what Harv Jellin was doing two weeks ago Saturday."

"Two weeks ago—"

"Two weeks ago Saturday," he said, "which was the night a couple of mopes knocked off the Cutler warehouse. All of a sudden I like Harv for that one. I like him a whole lot."

God knows we didn't have anything like a lead in the warehouse robbery, and there was plenty of pressure to solve it, because the perps had left a body behind—the night watchman, dead from a single blow to the head. Within a few days we'd made an arrest, picking up a three-time loser named O'Regan.

"We know you were just along to keep Harv Jellin company," Walbeck told him. "He's the one who set up the job and he's definitely the one hit the watchman over the head. You'd never do a thing like that, would you? Hit an old guy over the head, crack his skull like an eggshell."

"I wasn't even there," O'Regan said.

"We got you dead to rights," Walbeck said, "and the only question is what kind of time you do. You roll over on your pal Jellin and you get the minimum. You hold out and you're in the joint the rest of your life."

"I hardly know Jellin," the mope said.

"Then you don't owe him a thing, do you? And he's your Get Out Of Jail Free card, so you better remember how well you know him."

"It's coming back to me," O'Regan said.

Between O'Regan's testimony and some artfully manufactured and planted evidence, Harvey Jellin didn't stand a chance. His lawyer convinced him to plead to robbery and manslaughter, arguing that otherwise a murder conviction was a foregone conclusion.

When you enter a guilty plea, you have to stand up in court and say what happened. I was there, and you could see how it infuriated Jellin to have to perjure himself in order to dodge a life sentence. "I only hit him once," he said of the dead watchman, "and I never meant to hurt him."

He got ten-to-twenty. The watchman's daughter told a reporter that was far too lenient, but it didn't seem all that lenient to me, given that the sonofabitch hadn't done anything.

Not that I wasted tears on him. Jellin had done plenty of other things we hadn't been able to hang on him, and it was common knowledge that he'd killed a man in a bar fight, and probably one or two others as well.

He went off to serve his time, and Walbeck got busy putting the moves on Joanie.

The wives of convicted felons are easy game, same as recent widows. They're made to order for cops, and Walbeck wasn't the first police officer to move in on a woman after sending her husband to the joint. He might have had a harder time if the redhead had known he'd framed Jellin, but she didn't have a clue. Jellin had protested all along that he was being framed, or at least until he'd taken the plea, but criminals say that all the time, in and out of prison.

It took Walbeck a while, but he got her. And then he was stuck, because he couldn't get enough of her.

"She's in my blood," he said. "The woman's a fucking virus."

I'd never seen him like this before. It stopped him from chasing tail, because Joanie Jellin got all his attention. He didn't turn down what came along—I don't think he was capable of turning anything down in that department—but he quit seeking it out. And he spent every spare moment he could with the redhead.

The prison that housed her husband has an enlightened administration, and prisoners with good conduct privileges were able to receive monthly conjugal visits. The prisoner and his spouse would repair to a small house trailer, known inevitably as the Fuck Truck, where they could enjoy a romantic interlude of no more than an hour.

At first Walbeck didn't want her to go, but he had to agree that her absence would make Jellin suspicious. So he took to going with her, and he would make an expedition out of it, inventing some pretext to explain his overnight absence to his wife, and switching shifts with other cops or, more often, getting me to sign him in and out.

The evening before a conjugal visit, Walbeck and Joanie Jellin would drive to the town where the prison was situated and check in at a motel with waterbeds and porn videos. ("This is where they ought to have the goddam visits," Joanie told him. "This beats the hell out of the fuck truck.") With a fifth of vodka and one or another illegal substance to keep the party lively, the two would screw themselves silly all night long.

Then, in the morning, Joanie would drive to the prison to meet her husband.

Walbeck tried to get her to skip her morning shower. "You gotta be crazy," she told him. "You want to get me killed? He smells you on me, he breaks my neck right there in the fuck truck. What's he care, they tack a few more years on his sentence?"

She won that argument. But she didn't argue when he wanted to take her straight to bed the minute she returned from the prison visit. While he embraced her, he would make her tell him in detail what she and her husband had just done.

"I don't know," she said. "Sometimes I get the feeling you're queer for Harv."

"I'm queer for you," he said. "I can't get enough of you. I could kill you, I could cook you and eat you, and I still couldn't get enough."

"Don't talk that way."

"I could suck the marrow out of your bones. Still wouldn't be enough."

The more time he spent with Joanie Jellin, the more certain he grew that Marie was having an affair. "He's nailing her," he told me, "and he's doing it right in my own house. I walk in there and I can feel it. The air's thick and heavy, like he's still there in spirit."

"You like getting Joanie right after Harv's done with her," I pointed out. "Maybe you should tell Marie to skip her shower after."

I was joking, but he didn't see the humor, and I thought he was going to lose it altogether. "She's my wife," he said. "Somebody touches my wife, I rip his fucking heart out. I cut his dick off, stuff it down her throat and let her fucking choke on it."

He became convinced not only that Marie had a lover, but that the man coordinated his visits to coincide with his own overnight stays with Joanie. He set a trap, telling Marie the same thing he told her whenever Jellin had a conjugal visit scheduled. He had to escort a prisoner who'd been extradited to another state, he told her, and he'd be gone overnight.

Then he staked out his own house, waiting. And of course he never saw a single suspicious car. Marie never left the house, and no one came to visit her.

The next morning, when he walked into his house, he was utterly certain someone had been with her. "Who was it?" he shouted at her. "Tell me who it was!"

"I've been here all night," she said, looking at him like he was crazy. "Alone, in a robe, watching tv. And then I went to bed. Michael, don't they have somebody you can see? Like a psychiatrist? Because I think you should seriously consider it."

"He must have seen my car," he told me. "Must have parked around the block, sneaked through the yards and went in the back door, then got out the same way."

"Maybe you're imagining things, Mike."

"I don't think so. Partner, you gotta help me out. Tuesday, when Harv has his next visit? What I want you to do is check my block. He won't recognize your car."

"I don't know what you've got planned for this guy," I said, "but I don't want to be a part of it."

"Believe me," he said, "I want him all for myself. All I want from you is a plate number. I can take it from there."

He drove off on Tuesday, and when I met him Wednesday afternoon he looked like he was running on empty. "Too much bed and not enough sleep," he said. "Remember the first time I laid eyes on Joanie? That was all it took for me to know what was waiting there for me. She's amazing."

"Maybe you could divorce Marie," I suggested. "Marry Joanie, have her all for yourself."

He looked at me as if I'd taken leave of my senses. "Number one," he said, "Marie's my wife. That makes her mine forever. Number two, why would I want to marry Joanie? There's the kind of women you marry and the kind you don't, and she's definitely one you don't." He shook his head at my naiveté. "If you were married yourself," he said, "you'd know what I was talking about. Listen, did you do what I asked you to do? Did you find out anything?"

I lowered my eyes. "Bad news," I said.

"I knew it!"

"She had a visitor."

"I fucking knew it. At the house?"

I nodded. "He was there for two hours. Then I had to leave, but he was still there when I checked back around dawn."

"The son of a bitch."

"I ran his plate," I said. "I got a name and address."

"You're a pal," he said. "You didn't have to do that."

"I wanted to," I told him. "Waiting out there, thinking about what was going on inside your house, I started getting mad at him myself. I don't know what you've got planned for him, and I don't want to horn in on it, but I think I ought to be there to watch your back."

"Let's go," he said, then stopped himself. "Maybe I should stop home first," he said. "Light her up a little, then drop in on lover boy."

"Of course, if you can tell her how you've already gone and cleaned his clock…"

"You're right," he said. "Cut off his dick, walk in and tell her I brought her a present. Maybe I'll put it in a box and giftwrap it so I can get a look at her face when she opens it. 'What's this, Michael? It looks familiar…'"

"Be something to see," I agreed.

I made a phone call and we got in the squad car. On our way he said, "You're a damn good friend, you know that? And you know what I'm gonna do? I'm gonna get her to fuck you."

For a second I thought he meant his wife.

"She'll do anything I tell her to do," he said. "Crazy bitch is wild. We'll team up on her, turn her every way but loose."

I didn't know what to say.

We drove across town to a dead-end street in the old Tannery district. It was a bad block, and the address I had wasn't the best house on it. It was a little square box of a house, with some of the window panes broken and weeds poking up through the litter on the front lawn. The paint job was so far gone it was hard to say what color it was.

"Better Homes and Gardens," Walbeck said. "I can see why he likes to spend the night at my place, the son of a bitch."

"That's his car," I said, pointing to a Chevrolet Monte Carlo with a crumpled fender and a busted taillight.

"He parked that piece of shit on my street? You'd think he would have been ashamed."

He led the way, marched right up to the front door. He put a hand on the butt of his service revolver and made a fist of the other. "Police!" be bellowed, as he pounded on the door. Then, before anyone could open it, he drew back his foot and kicked it in.

The shotgun blast picked him up and blew him back onto the front porch.

I was standing to the side when the gun went off, and I already had my own revolver drawn. The weasel-faced little guy in the broken-down armchair had triggered both barrels, and I didn't give him time to reload.

I put three slugs in his chest, and they told me later that two of them got the heart and the third didn't miss it by much. He was dead before the shots quit echoing.

I knelt down beside my partner. He was still breathing, but he'd taken a double load of buckshot and he was on his way out. But it was important to tell him this before he was gone.

"I'm the one," I said. "I've been dicking your wife for months, you dumb shit. It was fun, putting one over on you, but finally we both got sick of having you around."

I was looking at his eyes as I spoke, and he got it, he took it in. But he didn't hang on to it for long. A moment later his eyes glazed and he was gone.

FOR A long moment the room was silent, but for the crackling of the fire and an impressive rumbling from the bowels of the old man dozing over his book. "There's a metaphor," the doctor said. "Life is just one long dream, punctuated by the occasional fart."

"That's quite a story, Policeman," the soldier said. "Quite a story to tell on yourself."

"It happened a long time ago," the policeman said.

"And you set the whole thing up. Who was the man with the shotgun?"

"He was wanted in three states," the policeman said, "for robbery and murder, and he'd sworn he would never be taken alive. One of my snitches told me where he was holed up."

"And the rest of it was your doing," the priest said.

The policeman nodded. "Mea culpa, Priest. The call I made before we rolled was to the station, to let them know we were investigating a tip on a fugitive. I let the perp gun down Walbeck, and then I took him out before he could do the same for me."

"And made sure to tell your partner what had happened."

"I wanted him to know," the policeman said.

"And it was true, what you said? You'd been with his wife for months?"

"For a few months, yes. Not as long as he'd been suspicious of her. His suspicions were groundless at first, but I was intrigued, and filled with some sort of righteous indignation at the way he was treating her. I'd have been less outraged, I'm sure, if I hadn't deep down wanted to have her myself."

"And how long did you have her, Policeman?"

"When I set up her husband," he said, "I thought I'd wait a decent interval and marry the woman. But over the next several weeks I came to see why Walbeck cheated on her. It turned out the woman was a pain in the ass. The affair ran its course and ended, and she married someone else."

"And you didn't worry she would let slip how you'd arranged her husband's death?"

"She never knew," the policeman said. "As far as she was concerned, it was a death in the line of duty. He got a medal awarded posthumously and she got a generous widow's pension."

"Because she was such a generous widow," the doctor suggested. "Did the old fellow fart again?"

"I think that was the fire."

"I think it was the man himself," the doctor said. "And what did you get, Policeman? A citation for bravery?"

"A commendation," the policeman said, "and a promotion not long thereafter."

"Virtue rewarded. And the other lady? Joanie Jellin, the convict's wife?"

"I consoled her," the policeman admitted. "And once again came to appreciate my late partner's point of view. The woman did kindle the flames of lust. But I just spent a few afternoons with her and bowed out of the picture."

"No keeping her company on conjugal visits?"

"None of that, no."

"The flames of lust," the soldier said, echoing the phrase the policeman had used. "They cast a nasty yellow glow, don't they? Lust ruled your partner, ran his life and ran him out of it, but wasn't it lust that drove all the parties in your story? You, certainly, and both of the women."

"It was the story that came to mind," the policeman said, "when the conversation turned to lust."

"Lust," the soldier mused. "Is it always about the sexual impulse? What about the lust for power? The lust for gold?"

"Metaphor," the priest said. "If I am said to have a lust for gold, the man who so defines me is saying that my desire for gold has the urgency of a sexual urge, that I yearn for it and seek after it in a lustful manner.

"And what of blood lust?" The soldier cleaned the dottle from his pipe, filled the bowl from his calfskin pouch, struck a wooden match and lit his pipe. "Is that a metaphor, or is it indeed sexual? I can think of an incident that suggests the latter." He drew on his pipe. "I wonder if I should recount it. It's not my story, not even in the sense that the priest's story was his. That was told to him by one of the tale's principals. Mine came to me by a less direct route."

They considered this in silence, a silence broken at length by a low rumbling from the hearthside.

"Was that another fart?" the doctor wondered. "No, I believe it was a snore. The old man's a whole impolite orchestra, isn't he?" He sighed. "Tell your story, Soldier."

I BELIEVE it was Robert E. Lee (said the soldier) who expressed the thought that it was just as well war was so horrible, or else we would like it too much. But it seems to me that we already like it to a considerable degree. Who doesn't recall George Patton proclaiming his love for combat. "God help me, I love it!" he cried.

Or at least George C. Scott did, in his portrayal of Patton. Was that accurate, or do we owe some Hollywood screenwriter for the creation of this myth?

I'm not sure it matters. It's clear Patton loved it, whether he ever said so or not. And, while it's quite appropriate that he was played by Scott rather than, say, Alan Alda, I'm sure the man was not entirely lacking in sensitivity. He may have loved war, but he was very likely aware that he shouldn't.

But people do, don't they? Otherwise we wouldn't have so many wars. They seem to retain their popularity down through the centuries, and for all that they grow ever more horrible, we do go on having them. Old men make wars, we are occasionally told, and young men have to fight them. The implication is that older men, safely lodged behind desks, feel free to make decisions that cost the unwilling lives of the young.

But does anyone genuinely think there would be fewer wars fought if younger men were their nations' leaders? The reverse, I think, is far more likely. The young are more reckless, with others' lives as well as their own. And it is indeed they who fight the wars, and die in them, because they are often so eager to do so.

I am not wholly without experience here. I saw combat in one war, and ordered men about in others. War is awful, certainly, but it is also quite wonderful. The two words once had the same meaning, did you know that? Awful and wonderful. The former we reserve now for that which we regard as especially bad, the latter for what seems especially good, yet they both have the same root meaning. Full of awe, full of wonder.

War's all of that and more.

It is exciting, for one thing. Not always, as the monotony of it can be excruciating, but when it ceases to be boring it becomes very exciting indeed, and that excitement is heightened by the urgency of it all. One might be killed at any moment, so how can the body fail to be in a state of excitement? That, after all, is what adrenaline is for.

And there's the camaraderie. Men working together, fighting together, united not merely in a common cause but in a matter of life and death. To do so seems to satisfy a fundamental human urge.

On top of that, there's the freedom. Does that strike you as strange? I can see that it might, as there's no one less at liberty in many ways than a soldier. His every action is in response to an order, and to defy a direct order is to court severe punishment. Yet this apparent slavery is freedom of a sort. One is free of the obligation to make decisions, free too of the past and the future. One's family, one's career, what one is going to do with one's life—all of this disappears as one follows orders and gets through the day.

And, of course, there's the chance to kill.

I wonder how many soldiers ever kill anybody. Relatively few have the opportunity. In any war, only a fraction of enlisted troops ever see combat, and fewer still ever have the enemy in their sights. And only some of those men take aim and pull the trigger. Some, it would appear, are reluctant to take the life of someone they don't even know.

Others are not. And there are those who find they like it.

LUCAS HALLAM, if I may call him that, was to all appearances entirely normal prior to his service in the armed forces. He grew up in a small Midwestern town, with three brothers (two older than himself) and a younger sister. Aside from the usual childhood and adolescent stunts (throwing snowballs at cars, smoking in the lavatory) he was never in trouble, and in school he was an average student, in athletics an average participant. There are three childhood markers for profound antisocial behavior, as I understand it, and Luke, as far as anyone knew, had none of them. He did not wet the bed, he did not set fires, and he did not torture animals. (The pathological implications of the latter two are not hard to infer, but what has bedwetting to do with anything? Perhaps the doctor will enlighten me later.)

After graduating from high school, Luke looked at the vocational opportunities open to him, thought unenthusiastically of college, and joined the army. There was no war on when he enlisted, but there was by the time he finished basic training. He was a good soldier, and his eyesight was excellent and his hand-eye coordination superb. On the firing range he qualified as an Expert Rifleman, and he was assigned to a platoon of combat infantry and shipped overseas.

At the end of his hitch he was rotated back to the States, and eventually discharged. But by then he had been in combat any number of times, and had had enemy soldiers in his sights on innumerable occasions. He had no difficulty pulling the trigger, and his skills were such that he generally hit what he aimed at.

He liked it, liked the way it felt. It gave him an enormous feeling of satisfaction. He was doing his job, serving his country, and saving his own life and the lives of his buddies by killing men who were trying to kill him. Take aim, squeeze off a shot, and you canceled a threat, took off the board someone who otherwise might take you or someone you cared about off the board. That was what he was supposed to do, what they'd sent him over there to do, and he was doing it well, and he felt good about it.

The first time he did it, actually saw his shot strike home, saw the man on the other side of the clearing stumble and fall, he was too busy sighting and shooting and trying to stay behind cover to notice how he felt. The action in a full-blown firefight was too intense for you to feel much of anything. You were too busy staying alive.

Later, remembering, he felt a fullness in his chest, as if his heart was swelling. With pride, he supposed.

Another time, they were pinned down by a sniper. He advanced, and when someone else drew the sniper's fire, he was able to spot the man perched in a tree. He got him in his sights and felt an overall excitement, as if all his cells were more intensely alive than before. He fired, and the man fell from the tree, and a cheer went up from those of his buddies who had seen the man fall. Once again he felt that fullness in his chest, but this time it wasn't only his heart that swelled. He noted with some surprise that there was a delicious warmth in his groin, and that he had a powerful erection.

Well, he was nineteen years old, and it didn't take a great deal to give him an erection. He would get hard thinking about girls, or looking at sexy pictures, or thinking about looking at sexy pictures. A ride in a Jeep on a rough road could give him an erection. He thought it was interesting, getting an erection in combat, but he didn't make too much of it.

Later, when they got back to base, he went drinking and whoring with his buddies. The sex was sweeter and more intense than ever before, but he figured it was the girl. She was, he decided, more attractive than most of them, and hot.

From that point on, sexual excitement was a component of every firefight he was in. Killing the enemy didn't carry him to orgasm, although there was at least one occasion when it didn't miss by much. It did render him powerfully erect, however, and, when he was able to be with a girl afterward, the union was intensely satisfying. The girl didn't have to be spectacularly good-looking, he realized, or all that hot. She just had to be there when he was back from a mission on which he'd blown away one or more enemy troops.

As I said, his tour of duty concluded and he returned to the States. The war receded into memory. Back in his hometown, in the company of people who'd shared none of his military experiences, he let it all exist as a separate chapter of his life—or, perhaps more accurately, as another volume altogether, a closed book he didn't often take down from the shelf.

He found work, he dated a few local girls, and within a year or so he found one who suited him. In due course they were engaged, and then married. They bought a modest home and set about starting a family.

Now and then, when he was making love to his wife, wartime images would intrude. They came not as flashbacks of the sort common to victims of post-traumatic stress syndrome, but as simple memories that slipped unbidden into his consciousness. He recalled sex acts with the native prostitutes, and this made him guilty at first, as if he were cheating on his wife by having another woman's image in mind during their lovemaking.

He dismissed the guilt. After all, you couldn't hang a man for his thoughts, could you? And, if a memory of another woman enriched the sexual act for himself and his wife, where was the harm? He didn't seek to summon up such memories, but if they came he allowed himself to enjoy them.

There were other memories, though. Memories of drawing a bead on a sniper in a tree, holding his breath, squeezing off the shot. Seeing the man fall in delicious slow motion, seeing him fall never to rise again.

He didn't like that, and it bothered him a little. He found he could will such thoughts away, and did so as quickly as they came. Then he could surrender to the delight of the moment, untroubled by recollections of the past. That, after all, was over and done with. He didn't hang out at the Legion post, didn't pal around with other vets, didn't talk about what he'd seen and done. He barely thought about it, so why should he think of it now, at such an intimate moment?

Never mind. You couldn't help the thoughts that came to you, but you didn't have to entertain them. He blinked and they were gone.

After his second child was born, Luke's sex life slowed down considerably. The pregnancy had been a difficult one, and when he and his wife attempted to resume relations after the birth, they were not terribly successful. She was willing enough but not very receptive, and he had difficulty becoming aroused and further difficulty in bringing his arousal to fulfillment.

He'd never had this problem before.

It was normal, he told himself. Nothing to worry about. It would work itself out.

He tried mental tricks—thinking of other women, using memory or fantasy as an erotic aid. This worked some of the time, but not always, and never as well as he would have liked.

Then one day he used a fantasy about a woman at work to help him become erect, and, during the act, he tried to extend the fantasy to reach a climax. But instead it winked out like a spent lightbulb, and what replaced it was an involuntary memory of a firefight. This time he didn't blink it away, but let himself relive the fight, the aiming, the firing, the bodies falling in obedience to his will.

His orgasm was powerful.

If it troubled him at all to have used memories of killing, any disquiet he felt was offset by the height of his excitement and the depth of his satisfaction. Henceforth he employed memories and fantasies of killing as he had previously used memories and fantasies of other women, and to far greater advantage. His ardor had waned somewhat even before the second pregnancy, as is hardly uncommon after a few years of marriage; it now returned with a vengeance, and his wife caught a little of his own renewed enthusiasm. It was, she told him, like a second honeymoon.

That set his mind entirely to rest. It was good for both of them, he realized, and if what he did in the privacy of his own mind was a little kinky, even a little unpleasant, well, who was harmed?

Memories would take him only so far. You used them up when you replayed them over and over. Fantasies, though, were pretty good. He would think of someone he'd noticed at work or on television, and he would imagine the whole thing, stalking the person, making the kill. He would spend time with the fantasy, living it over and over in his mind each time he and his wife made love, refining it until it was just the way he wanted it.

And then, perhaps inevitably, there came a time when he found himself thinking about bringing one of his fantasies to life. Or, if you prefer, to death.

"HUNTING," THE policeman said. "Soldier, why the hell didn't the poor sonofabitch try hunting? No safer outlet for a man who wants to kill something. You get up early in the morning and go out in the woods and take it out on a deer or a squirrel."

"I wonder," said the priest. "Do you suppose that's why men hunt? I thought it was for the joy of walking in the woods, and the satisfaction of putting meat on one's table."

"Meat's cheaper in a store," the policeman said, "and you don't need to pick up a gun to take a walk in the woods. Oh, I'm sure there are other motives for hunting. It makes you feel resourceful and self-reliant and manly, fit to hang out with Daniel Boone and Natty Bumppo. But when all's said and done you're out there killing things, and if you don't like killing you'll find some other way to pass the time."

"He'd hunted as a boy," the soldier said. "You'd be hard put to avoid it if you grew up where he did. His brother took him out hunting rabbits, and he shot and killed one, and it made him sick."

"What did he get, tularemia?" the doctor wondered. "You can get it from handling infected rabbits."

"Sick to his stomach," the soldier said. "Sick inside. Killing an animal left him feeling awful."

"He was a boy then," the policeman said. "Now he was a man, and one who'd killed other men and was thinking about doing it again. You'd think he'd go out in the woods, if only for curiosity."

"And he did," said the soldier.

HE THOUGHT along the very lines you suggested (continued the soldier), and he went out and bought a rifle and shells, and one crisp autumn morning he shouldered his rifle and drove a half hour north, where there was supposed to be good hunting. The deer season wouldn't open for another month, but all that meant was that the woods wouldn't be swarming with hunters. And you didn't have to wait for deer season to shoot varmints and small game.

He walked around for an hour or so, stopped to eat his lunch and drink a cup of coffee from the Thermos jug, got up and hefted his gun and walked around some more. Early on he spotted a bird on a branch, greeting the dawn in song. He squinted through the scope and took aim at the creature, not intending to shoot. What kind of person would gun down a songbird? But he wondered what it would feel like to have the bird in his sights, and was not surprised to note that there was no sense of excitement whatsoever, just a queasy sensation in the pit of his stomach.

Later he took aim at a squirrel and had the same reaction, or non-reaction. Hunting, he could see, was not an answer for him. He was if anything somewhat relieved that he hadn't had to shoot an animal to establish this.

He unloaded his rifle and walked some more, enjoying the crunch of fallen leaves under his feet, the sweetness of the air in his lungs. And then he came to a clearing, and in an old orchard across the way he saw a woman on a ladder, picking apples.

His pulse quickened. Without thinking he slipped into the shadows where he'd be invisible. He stood there, watching her, and he was excited.

She was pretty, or at least he thought she was. It was hard to tell at this distance. He should have brought binoculars, he thought, so he could get a better look.

And he remembered that the gun's telescopic sight would work as well.

He spun around, walked back the way he'd come. He was not going to look at the woman through a rifle sight. That was not what he was going to do.

He walked around for another hour and wound up right back where he'd seen the woman. Probably gone by now, he told himself. But no, there she was, still in the orchard, still up on the ladder. She was working a different tree now, and he could get a better look at her now. Earlier her back had been toward him, but now he was presented with a frontal view, and he could see her face.

Not very well, though. Not from this far away.

He took the rifle from his shoulder, looked at her through the scope. Very pretty, he saw. Auburn hair—without the scope it had just looked dark—and a long oval face, and breasts that swelled the front of her plaid shirt.

He had never been so excited in his life. He unzipped his pants, freed himself from his underwear. His cock was huge, and fiercely erect.

He touched himself, then returned his hand to the rifle. His finger curled tentatively around the trigger.

He thought he must be trembling too much to take aim, but his excitement was all within him, and his stance was rock-solid, his hands sure and skilled. He aimed, and drew a breath, and held the breath.

And squeezed the trigger.

The bullet took her in the throat. She hung on the ladder for a moment, blood gouting from the wound. Then she fell.

He stared through the scope while his seed sprang forth from his body and fell upon the carpet of leaves.

He was shocked, appalled. And, of course, more than a little frightened. He had taken life before, but that involved killing the enemy in time of war. He had just struck down a fellow citizen engaged in lawful activity on her own property, and for no good reason whatsoever. His sharpshooting overseas had won him medals and promotions; this would earn him—what? Life in prison? A death sentence?

He left the woods, and on the way home he dropped his rifle in the river. No one would note its absence. He'd purchased it without mentioning it to his wife, and now it was gone, and as if he'd never owned it.

But he had in fact owned it, and as a result a woman was dead.

The story was in the papers for days, weeks. A woman had been struck down by a single shot from a high-powered rifle. The woman's estranged husband, who was questioned and released, had been arrested twice on drug charges, and police theorized that her death was some sort of warning or reprisal. Another theory held that mere bad luck was to blame; a hunter, somewhere in the woods, had fired at a squirrel and missed, and the bullet, still lethal at a considerable distance, had flown with unerring aim at an unintended and unseen target.

Luke waited for some shred of evidence to materialize and trip him up. When that didn't happen, he realized he was in the clear. He could do nothing for the woman, but he could put the incident out of his mind and make certain nothing like it ever happened again.

He could, as it turned out, do neither. The incident returned to his mind, its memory kindling a passion that heightened his relations with his wife a hundredfold. And he found, after his initial fear and shock had dissipated, that he felt no more remorse for the woman's death than he had for those enemy soldiers he'd gunned down. If anything, what he felt for her was a curious gratitude, gratitude for being an instrument of pleasure for him. Every time he thought of her, every time he relived the memory of her murder, she furnished pleasure anew.

You can probably imagine the rest. He went to a nearby city, and in a downtown motel room he mounted a hollow-eyed whore. While she toiled beneath him, he whipped out a silenced small-caliber pistol and held it to her temple. The horror in her eyes tore at him, but at the same time it thrilled him. He held off as long as he could, then squeezed the trigger and spurted into her even as the life flowed out of her.

He picked up a hitchhiker, raped her, then killed her with a knife. Two states away, he picked up another hitchhiker, a teenage boy. When he stopped the car and drew a gun, the boy, terrified, offered sex. Luke was aroused and accepted the offer, but his ardor wilted the moment the boy took him in his mouth. He pushed the youth away, then pressed the gun to his chest and fired two shots into his heart.

That excited him, but he walked away from the death scene with his passion unspent and found a prostitute. She did what the boy had attempted to do, and did it successfully as his mind filled with memories of the boy's death. Then, satisfied, he killed the woman almost as an afterthought, taking her from behind and snapping her neck like a twig.

He was clever, and it was several years before they caught him. Although the impulse to kill, once triggered, was uncontrollable, he could control its onset, and sometimes months would pass between episodes. His killing methods and choice of victims varied considerably, and he traveled widely when he hunted, so no pattern became evident. Nowadays there may be a national bank of DNA evidence, evidence that would have established that the semen in the vagina of a runaway teen in Minneapolis was identical to that left on the abdomen of a housewife in Oklahoma. But no such facility existed at the time, and his killings were seen as isolated incidents.

And in some cases, of course, the bodies he left behind were never found. Once he managed to get two girls at once, sisters. He killed one right away, raped the other, killed her, and withdrew from her body in order to have his climax within the first victim. He threw both bodies down a well, where they remained until his confession led to their discovery.

A stupid mistake led to his arrest. He'd made mistakes before, but this one was his undoing. And perhaps he was ready to be caught. Who can say?

In his jail cell, he wrote out a lengthy confession, listing all the murders he had committed—or at least as many as he remembered. And then he committed suicide. They had taken his belt and shoelaces, of course, and there was nothing on the ceiling from which one could hang oneself with a braided bedsheet, but he found a way. He unbolted a metal support strip from his cot, honed it on the concrete floor of his cell until he'd fashioned a half-sharp homemade knife. He used it to amputate his penis, and bled to death.

"WHAT A horrible story," the policeman said.

"Dreadful," the priest agreed, wringing his hands, and the doctor nodded his assent.

"I'm sorry," said the soldier. "I apologize to you all. As I said, it wasn't my own story, for which I must say I'm heartily grateful, nor was it a story I heard directly, and I daresay I'm grateful for that as well. It may have been embroidered along the way, before it was told to me, and I suspect I added something in the telling myself, inferring what went through the poor bastard's mind. If I were a better storyteller I might have made a better story of it. Perhaps I shouldn't have told it in the first place."

"No, no!" the doctor cried. "It wasn't a *bad* story. It was gripping and fascinating and superbly told, and whatever license you took for dramatic purposes was license well taken. It's a wonderful story."

"But you said—"

"That it was horrible," the priest said. "So Policeman said, and I added that it was terrible."

"You said dreadful," said the doctor.

"I stand corrected," the priest said. "Horrible, dreadful—both of those, to be sure, and terrible as well. And, as you said in your prefatory remarks, awful and wonderful. What do you make of young Luke, Soldier? Was he in fact a casualty of war?"

"We gave him a gun and taught him to kill," the soldier said. "When he did, we pinned medals on his chest. But we didn't make him like it. In fact, if his instructor had suspected he was likely to have that kind of a visceral response to firing at the enemy, he might never have been assigned to combat duty."

The doctor raised an eyebrow. "Oh? You find a lad who qualifies as Expert Rifleman and you shunt him aside for fear that he might enjoy doing what you've just taught him to do, and do so well? Is that any way to fight a war?"

"Well, perhaps we'd have taken a chance on him anyway," the soldier conceded. "Not so likely in a peacetime army, but with a war going on, yes, I suppose we might have applied a different standard."

"What passes for heroism on the battlefield," said the priest, "we might otherwise label psychosis."

"But the question," the soldier said doggedly, "is whether he'd have found the same end with or without his military service. The bullet that killed that first sniper put him on a path that led to the jail cell where he emasculated himself. But would he have gotten there anyway?"

"Your lot didn't program him," the policeman said. "You didn't have a surgeon implant a link between his trigger finger and his dick. The link was already in place and the first killing just activated it. Hunting hadn't activated it, though who's to say it wouldn't have if he got a cute little whitetail doe in his sights?"

The priest rolled his eyes.

"Sooner or later," the policeman said, "he'd have found out what turned him on. And I have to say I think he must have at least half-known all along. You say he didn't have sadistic sexual fantasies before the first killing, but how can any of us know that was the case? Did he state so unequivocally in this confession he wrote out? And can we take his word? Can we trust his memory?"

"Sooner or later," the doctor said, "his marital sex life would have slowed, for one reason or another."

"Or for no reason at all," the policeman said.

"Or for no reason at all, none beyond familiarity and entropy. And then he'd have found a fantasy that worked. And someone some day would have paid a terrible price."

"And the origin of it all?" the soldier wondered.

"Something deep and unknowable," the doctor said. "Something encoded in the genes or inscribed upon the psyche."

"Or the soul," the priest suggested.

"Or the soul," the doctor allowed.

There was a rumbling noise from the direction of the fireplace, and the doctor made a face. "There he goes again," he said. "I suppose I should be tolerant of the infirmities of age, eh? Flatulent senescence awaits us all."

"I think that was the fire," the policeman said.

"The fire?"

"An air pocket in a log."

"And the, ah, bouquet?"

"The soldier's pipe."

The doctor considered the matter. "Perhaps it is a foul pipe I smell," he allowed, "rather than an elderly gentleman's foul plumbing. No matter. We've rather covered the subject of lust, haven't we? And I'd say our stories have darkened as we've gone along. I've lost track of the hand. Shall we gather the cards and deal again?"

"We could," the priest said, "but have you nothing to offer on the subject, Doctor?"

"The subject of lust?"

The priest nodded. "One would think your calling would give you a useful perspective."

"Oh, I've seen many things," said the doctor, "and heard and read of many others. There's nothing quite so extraordinary as human behavior, but I guess we all know that, don't we?"

"Yes," said the priest and the policeman, and the soldier, busy lighting his pipe, managed a nod.

"As a matter of fact," the doctor said, "there was a story that came to mind. But I can't say it's the equal to what I've heard from the rest of you. Still, if you'd like to hear it…"

"Tell it," said the priest.

AS A medical man (said the doctor) I have been privy to a good deal of information about people's sex lives. When I entered the profession, I was immediately assumed to know more about human sexuality than the average layman. I don't know that I actually did. I didn't know much, but then it's highly probable my patients knew even less.

Still, one understands the presumption. A physician it taught a good deal about anatomy, and the average person knows precious little about his or her own anatomical apparatus, let alone that of the opposite sex. Thus, to the extent that sex is a physiological matter, a doctor might indeed be presumed to know something about it.

So much of it, though, is in the mind. In the psyche or in the soul, as we've just now agreed. There may well be a physical component that's at the root of it, a wayward chromosome, a gene that leans to the left or to the right, and a new generation of doctors is almost certain to know more than we did, but will they be revered as we were?

I doubt it. For years people gave us more respect than we could possibly deserve, and now they don't give us nearly enough. They see us as mercenary pill-pushers who do what the HMOs tell us to do, no less and no more. Lawyers sue us for malpractice, and we respond by ordering unneeded tests and procedures to forestall such lawsuits. Every time a fellow physician anesthetizes a pretty patient and gives her a free pelvic exam, why, the whole profession suffers, just as every cleric gets a black eye when one of the priest's colleagues is caught playing Hide the Host with an altar boy.

Lust. That's our subject, isn't it? And do you suppose there's a physiological explanation for one's tendency to natter on and on in one's senior years? Is there a gene that turns us into garrulous old farts?

My point, to the extent that I have one, is this: As a physician, as a trusted medical practitioner, as a putative authority on matters of the human anatomy, I was taken into the confidence of my patients and thus made more aware than most people of the infinite variety and remarkable vagaries of human sexuality. I saw more penises than Catherine the Great, more vaginas than Casanova. Saw them up close, too, with no fumbling around in the dark. Told husbands how to satisfy their wives, women how to get pregnant.

Why, I knew an older man who had a half dozen women, widows and spinsters, who came to him once a month on average to be masturbated. The old duffer didn't call it that, and I don't even know if he thought of it in those terms. He was treating them, he confided, for hysteria, and the treatment employed an artificial phallus hygienically hooded with a condom. He wore rubber gloves, did this doctor, and seemed genuinely offended at the hint that he might be getting more than a fee for his troubles. As to my suggestion that he might send them home with dildoes and a clue as to how best to employ them, he grimaced at the very idea. "These are decent women," he told me, as if that explained everything. And perhaps it did.

I have become inclined, through observation both personal and professional in nature, to grant considerable respect to the sex drive. The urgency of its imperative is undeniable, the variety of its manifestation apparently infinite. I will furnish but one example of the latter: One patient of mine, a lesbian, married another woman in a ceremony which, if unsanctioned by the state, was nevertheless as formal a rite as any I've attended. My patient wore a white gown, her spouse a tuxedo.

After a few years they parted company, without having to undergo the legal rigors of a divorce. My patient began living as a man, and eventually took hormone treatments and counseling and underwent sex-change surgery. And so, quite unbeknownst to her, did her former marriage partner. They are now pals, working out at the gym together, going to ball games together, and looking for nice feminine girls to hook up with and marry.

Infinite variety...

But, entertaining as their saga may be, I wouldn't call it lust. Lust is desire raised to a level that prompts unacceptable behavior—how's that for a definition? And I can think of no clearer example of that than a fellow I'll call Gregory Dekker.

Dekker was a serial rapist. That's spelled with an S, not a C, lest you imagine some lunatic having it off with a bowl of Cream of Wheat, or working his way one by one through a box of Cheerios. His sexual desire was strong, though probably not abnormally so, and he satisfied it in one of two ways—by rape or by masturbation. And, when he masturbated, the images in his mind were rape fantasies.

Rape, we are often assured, is not truly sexual in nature. Rape is a violent expression of hostility toward women, and has nothing at all to do with desire. The rapist is wielding his phallus as a weapon—a sword, a club, a gun that fires seminal bullets. He is getting even with his mother for real or imagined abuse.

What crap.

Oh, surely hostility may play a part in his makeup. And surely there are some rapists who are acting out their primal dramas. But, if the chief aim of the act is to inflict pain and damage, why choose such an uncertain weapon? Why reach for a gun so apt to jam or misfire?

Rape, you see, requires an erect penis. And a successful rape culminates in orgasm and ejaculation. And who would imagine that all of this takes place in the absence of sexual desire?

Rape, I submit, is often nothing more or less than the sexual activity of a sociopath, a man lacking conscience who, as he might tell you, quite sensibly seeks to satisfy himself sexually without having to resort to candy or flowers, sweet words and false promises. He doesn't have to take his chosen partner to dinner or a movie, doesn't have to feign interest in her conversation, doesn't even have to tell her she looks nice. Why, he *proves* she looks good to him, good enough to throw down and ravish. Isn't that compliment enough?

I've no clear idea what makes a person grow up sociopathic. Is it in the genes? The upbringing? I don't have the answer. Nor, in fact, do I know much about Gregory Dekker in particular. He was never a patient of mine.

Susan Trenholme was, however.

She was a remarkably ordinary young woman, neither beautiful nor plain. Her hair was light brown, not quite blond, and her figure was womanly, and fuller than she'd have preferred; she was always trying new diets and over-the-counter appetite suppressants, all in an effort to lose five pounds over and over again. She was, I suppose, no more neurotic in this area than most young women; if they were as obsessed about their height, they'd all put on weighted boots and suspend themselves from the ceiling.

Susan met a young man in college and lived with him for two years. They drifted apart, and she was twenty-six years old and living alone when Gregory Dekker caught up with her in the parking lot of her apartment complex, knocked her to the ground, fell on her, and told her not to struggle or make a sound or he'd kill her.

Looking into his eyes, she knew he was serious. And she became convinced that, whether she cried out or remained silent, whether she struggled or acquiesced, her fate was sealed. He would kill her anyway once he'd had his pleasure with her.

In fact she had grounds for this assessment, beyond what she was able to read in his eyes. A rapist whose description matched her assailant had committed a string of rapes in the area within the past several months, and had left his two most recent victims for dead; one recovered, one was dead on arrival at a nearby hospital. Unlike the monster in your story, Soldier, Gregory Dekker was not given to lust-murder; he killed only to avoid being caught.

And he would have been easy to pick out of a lineup. If Susan Trenholme looked ordinary, Gregory Dekker surely did not. Whatever the cause—a drunken obstetrician misusing his forceps, a mother who dropped him on his face in infancy—Dekker was an heroically ugly young man. His schoolmates, perhaps inevitably, called him Frankenstein, and they had reason. Extensive facial and dental surgery would have helped, no doubt, but his parents couldn't have afforded it, if they even thought of it.

Dekker probably assumed he could never have a woman other than by force. He was almost certainly wrong in that assessment. Some women find ugly men particularly attractive, and others respond to qualities other than appearance. I knew one woman, for example, who held that there was no such thing as an ugly millionaire.

Well, Dekker was no millionaire, nor did he have other attractive qualities, so perhaps rape was a sound choice for him. In any event, it worked. When he wanted a woman, he took her. Sometimes this happened in the course of his work, which was burglary; he broke into homes and offices, grabbed cash or something readily converted thereto, and fled. If there was a woman on the premises, and if he liked her looks, he would take her as automatically as he would take her jewelry.

In Susan's case, he saw her at a supermarket, followed her to her car, then tailed her in his car and assaulted her, as I've said, in her parking lot. And would very likely have left her there, dead or dying, if she hadn't taken action.

She didn't resist, didn't cry out. On the contrary, she did everything she could to make things easier for him, and, after he had entered her, she wriggled pleasurably beneath him and began uttering little moans and yelps of pleasure.

And she proceeded to do what countless of her sisters have done, not on the gritty pavement of a parking lot but in the sweet embrace of the marriage bed. To wit, she faked an orgasm.

It must have surprised the daylights out of her partner. I don't know what sort of fantasy life Gregory Dekker may have led, but he wouldn't have been the first rapist to persuade himself that a potential victim actually longed for his embrace, that a woman taken initially by force might be rendered passionate by his lovemaking, and might enjoy it as much as he did. None had shown any sign of enjoying his attentions in the past, but who was to say that his luck might not change?

If he'd entertained such fancies, he must have thought he'd died and gone to heaven. Because here was this creature, moaning and twisting in his arms, and ultimately wrapping her legs around him and crying out *Yes!* and telling him, as he lay exhausted in her arms, what a great lover he was and how she'd always dreamed of a man like him and a moment like this.

Did it enter his mind that she was putting on an act? Even if he believed her, wouldn't it be safer in the long run to bash her head in or break her neck?

He may have thought so, but she tried not to give him time for thought. She kept cooing at him, telling him how wonderful he was, talking about the extent of her excitement and satisfaction, running a loving hand over his distorted features, raising her head to kiss his misshapen mouth.

And then, as if unable to help herself, she fell upon him and behaved, well, like an impressionable White House interne.

By the time she was finished, she had effectively saved her life. Dekker believed what she wanted him to believe—that he'd excited and satisfied her and left her begging for more. And beg she did, wanting to know if she would see him again, if they could do this with some frequency. And wouldn't it be even more wonderful in a bedroom, with the lights lowered and soft music playing, and the comfort of a mattress and clean cotton sheets?

They made a date for the following night. He was to come to her apartment at nine. He got there at eight and rang her bell at ten, confident by then that she hadn't set up a police ambush. She met him with a drink in hand and soft music playing, telling him truthfully enough that she'd been worried he wasn't going to come.

He made an excuse, but later, at the evening's end, he told her how he'd staked out her building to see if any cops showed. "Just give me a minute," he told her, "and I'll hook your phone lines up again. I pulled them before I came in, in case you were planning to make a call."

"I wouldn't do that," she said.

"Well, I know that now," he said. "But I had to be sure."

Before he left she made him a cup of cocoa. After he left she stood at the sink, rinsing the cup, and pondering the curious situation she was in. Her rapist was her lover, and she was fixing cocoa for him.

He saw her the next night, and the night after that. When he came over the following day he had a sheepish expression on his face. She wanted to ask him what was the matter, but she waited, and he got around to it on his own.

"I may not be much good to you tonight," he said. "On account of what came up this afternoon."

"Oh?"

He was working, he said, prowling apartments, seeing what he could pick up, and this woman walked right in on him. "Last thing I wanted," he said, "but there she was, you know?" And he got this little-boy smirk on his face.

She let her excitement show in her face. "Tell me," she said.

"Well, I did her," he said.

"Tell me!"

"What, you want the gory details? You know something, Susie? You're as bad as I am. What I did, I was behind the bedroom door, you know, waiting for her, and she walks through and bingo, I got one hand over her mouth and the other grabbing her tits. Little tits, way smaller than yours, but they were nice."

The room was dark, the curtains drawn, and the woman never got a look at his face. "So I didn't have to, you know, do her."

"Kill her."

"Like you have to do if they get a good look at you. But it was dark, and I got some tape over her eyes before they got used to the dark. So she never saw my face and she never saw my dick, so what's she gonna tell them? What it felt like?" He laughed, and she laughed with him. "There's guys who get a kick out of, you know, finishing 'em off. Personally, I think that's sick. Waste of good pussy, you know?"

"But sometimes you don't have a choice," she said.

"That's it exactly. Sometimes you don't have a choice. And if I got to do it, well, it doesn't bother me. You do what you gotta do. Anyway, who told her to come home in the middle of the goddam afternoon? She's supposed to be working, so what's she doing at home?"

"She deserved it," she said.

"Probably half-wanted it," he said. "Like you the first time. Except this one wasn't like you, she was crying and making a fuss. Nice, though." He chucked her under the chin. "When I was done with her," he said, "I thought, oh shit, I'm not gonna be much good to Susie. She finds out, she's gonna be pissed."

"I'm not, though. It's exciting. Tell me what you did."

The report included anal intercourse, and she pouted when he told her. "We never tried that," she said.

"Well, most women don't like it."

"I'm not most women," she said. "Oh, what have we here? It looks as though you're going to be able to do something after all. My goodness!"

He left finally, after downing a cup of cocoa to soothe his stomach. His stomach had been bothering him lately, and he agreed that the cocoa would probably help.

Two nights later, she told him how it excited her to think of him raping another woman. "I only wish I could have been there," she said.

"You're some crazy dame," he said admiringly. "What would you do? Watch?"

She nodded, moistened her upper lip with the tip of her tongue. "Maybe help," she added.

"Help?"

"I could hold her hands," she said. "Or…"

"Or what?"

"I don't know. Maybe do stuff."

"Like fool around with her?"

"Maybe."

"Like how?"

"Oh, I don't know," she said. "Maybe, you know, touch her. Do things to her."

"You ever been with a woman?"

"No."

"But you've been thinking about it."

"Well," she said, "if she couldn't do anything, you know. Like if she was tied up? And I was in control?"

"You are one crazy bitch," he said.

"Well."

"Man," he said, "now you got me going. Maybe we could, you know, pick somebody out, follow her home. Or if I was working and I found somebody, like, I could call you. Or…"

She had a better idea. There was this woman she knew, a former co-worker. A honey blonde, creamy skin, good breasts.

"You're hot for her," he said.

The woman was attractive, she allowed. And she knew how they could decoy the woman to a motel, where he could have a room booked. And they'd be waiting for her, and when she came in…

He helped her plan it out. "One thing," he said. "This broad knows you. And she'll know who lured her to the place, and anyway she'll see you when we do her, she'll see both of us. Unless you're telling me she's gonna like it?"

"No," she said. "She's not going to like it."

"Well then," he said. "You got to realize what's gonna have to happen when we're done. When the party's over, she ain't gonna turn into a pumpkin."

"I know."

"What I mean, I'll have to do her."

"We'll both do her."

He shook his head. "I don't mean do her like have sex with her. I mean do her so she's done. Finish her, is what I'm saying."

"I know."

"And you're okay with that?"

"Maybe I'll help," she said.

A few days later they were driving around, and she pointed out the woman she had described. He was excited and wanted to take their victim immediately, decoy her into the car, take her out into the woods and leave her there when they were finished. "It's better if we let her come to us," she insisted. "We set a trap and she walks right into it. And we can take our time, and do everything we want."

"Right now's when I'm horny," he said.

She grinned. "I can take care of that," she said.

On the appointed evening, he was waiting at the motel room when she arrived. "We've got half an hour before she gets here," she said. "Did I tell you she's selling real estate now? She thinks we're a nice sweet couple, we want her to show us some houses. Well, we're not that sweet, and we'll be showing her more than she shows us. Honey, are you as excited as I am?"

"Take a look."

"Oh God," she said. "I can't wait to see that going in and out of her." They talked some about what they would do to the blond, and then she said, "Oh, before I forget," and took a small unlabeled bottle from her purse. "For your stomach," she said. "Is it still bothering you?"

"Off and on. It's worse at night."

"'Intermittent pain, worse in the evening,'" she said. "I have this herbal doctor, I started to tell him about it and he was finishing my sentences for me. If you drink this it should cure it completely."

"What is it?"

"A mixture of Chinese herbs, and it doesn't taste great. But if you can get it down your troubles are over."

He took the bottle from her. "How much are you supposed to take?"

"All of it, if you can."

He uncapped the bottle, shrugged, tipped it up and drained it. His face twisted. "Jesus, that's terrible," he said. "Anything tastes that bad, it must be great for you."

"He said it tasted pretty bad."

"Well, he got that right."

"And at first it may make you feel worse," she said. "That's a sign that it's working. But after fifteen minutes you should feel great, so by the time our little blond friend gets here…"

"She's not so little. Pretty big in the tits department."

"Well, you'll be ready for her."

"I'm ready for her right now," he said. "Oh, shit."

"What's the matter?"

"I think this shit is working, that's all." He clutched his middle. "Oh, shit, that's pretty bad. What'd you say it had in it? Chinese herbs?"

"That's what he said."

"Jesus, if chop suey tasted like this nobody'd eat it. I fucked a Chinese girl once, did I ever tell you about her? She was so scared I thought she was gonna have a heart attack. And it ain't sideways, in case you were wondering."

"What's not sideways?"

"Her pussy. That's what they say about Chinese women. You never heard that? Anyway, her pussy was the same as anybody else's. Oh, Jesus, that's bad." He sprawled on the bed, rolling from side to side, wracked with spasms. "Jesus, it's working. You sure I'm gonna be all right by the time the blond cunt gets here?"

"She's not coming."

"Huh? What do you mean?"

"She was just a woman I pointed out to you," she said. "I don't even know her name. She's not coming. It's just the two of us."

"What are you—"

"And that wasn't Chinese herbs in the bottle. It was the same thing you've been getting in your cocoa every night, and it came out of a bottle marked 'Rat Poison.'"

He stared at her. She forced herself to meet his gaze. "I was giving you small doses," she said, "but this is one big dose, enough to kill a hundred rats. But all it has to kill is one big rat, and you can puke your guts out but it's too late now. It's in your system. You'll be dead in fifteen minutes, half an hour tops."

"Where are you going?"

"I'm not going anywhere," she said. "I'm just getting comfortable. You can't even get off the bed, can you? So I don't have anything to worry about. You're dying, and I'm going to stick around and see the show."

"Susie…"

"Maybe I'll touch myself," she said. "Maybe I'll make myself come while you're busy dying. You want to watch me? Do you think you'd like that? Maybe it'll take your mind off what's happening to you. Maybe it'll get you hot."

THE POLICEMAN was the first to speak. "I suppose she got away with it," he said.

"She was never apprehended," said the doctor. "Never even questioned by the authorities. No one could connect her to Dekker, and the only risk she ran, aside from being discovered in the act, lay in the possibility that he'd left something incriminating among his effects. A diary, for instance, with entries detailing their relationship and their planned rendezvous at the motel. But that seemed unlikely, the man was functionally illiterate, and in the event nothing turned up to draw her into what investigation there was. And that was minimal, as you might suppose. Gregory Dekker's death was ruled a suicide."

"A suicide?"

"He checked in alone at a rundown motel and drank a bottle of rat poison. His prints were on the bottle, you know, and while it was unlabeled, one couldn't down it thinking it was a fine Cabernet just reaching its prime. The stuff tasted like poison. Dekker, of course, thought it tasted like medicine."

"She planned it," the soldier mused, "from the first cup of cocoa. It masked the taste of the non-lethal doses she fed him, which gave him the stomach aches."

"And probably accumulated in the soft tissues," the doctor said, "if the lethal ingredient was in fact arsenic, as I suspect it was. And the stomach aches made him quick to down a larger dose of the poison, in the hope of a cure. Oh, yes, I'd say she planned it. And got away with it, if in fact anybody ever gets away with anything. That would be more in your line, Priest."

The priest stroked his chin. "An undiscovered sin is a sin nevertheless," he said. "One is hardly absolved by the temporal authority's failure to uncover the sin and punish the sinner. Repentance is a prerequisite of absolution, and to repent is to acknowledge that one has not gotten away with it. So no, Doctor, I would hold that no one gets away with anything."

"A thoughtful answer, Priest."

"Long-winded, at least," the priest said. "But I find myself with a question of my own. Yours, like all our stories, is a story of lust, and the lust would seem to be that of the ill-favored young man, whom you call Gregory Dekker. And Susan Trenholme's sin, if we call her a sinner, would be a sin of wrath or anger. Blood lust, if you will. And yet…"

"Yes?"

"I wonder," he said. "When did she decide to kill her rapist?"

"When?"

"After the initial act, certainly," the priest said. "But would it have been before or after she arranged a second meeting? Did she at first plan to call the police and trap him, or did she know all along that she meant to kill him herself?"

The doctor smiled. "You have an interesting mind," he said. "But who can say exactly when the idea presented itself? Her first concern was self-preservation. She feigned a physical response to save her own life, then made a date with him to give him further reason to let her live. At first she must have thought she'd have policemen at hand when he came knocking on her door, but somewhere along the way she changed her mind. Why, if she reported the crime at all, she'd have no end of unwelcome attention, and there was even the chance the man would evade justice. And, as she planned her revenge, yes, we can say that blood lust came into it."

"And was that the only sort of lust she felt?" The priest put his palms together. "She faked one orgasm to save her life," he said, "but when she determined to punish the man herself, she drew up a scenario that called for her to engage in all manner of sex acts, and to simulate passion on several more occasions, and to fake a good number of orgasms. And was that passion simulated? Were those orgasms counterfeit?"

"What a subtle mind you have," said the doctor. "That's what bothered her, you know. That's what led her to tell me the story. In the parking lot, with his foul breath in her face and his body upon and within her, all she felt was revulsion. Her response was a triumph of an acting ability she had never dreamed she possessed, in or out of bed.

"He never doubted the sincerity of her response. He thought he had indeed turned her on. But he hadn't—she had turned herself on, and the experience, while profoundly disgusting to her on one level, was undeniably exciting on another."

"Awful and wonderful," murmured the policeman.

"Later, when she weighed her options, she knew that she would have to repeat her performance if she were to seek her own revenge. And the idea was at once distasteful and appealing. She had sex with him that second time, in her own apartment, in her own bed, and if anything she loathed him more than before. But it was not difficult to pretend to be aroused, and in fact she found she was genuinely aroused, though far more by her own performance and her own plans than by anything he was doing to her."

"And did she fake that orgasm, too?" the soldier wondered.

"I can't answer that," the doctor said, "because she didn't know herself. Where does performance leave off and reality begin? Perhaps she faked that orgasm, but faked it with her own being, so that he was not the only one taken in by her performance." The doctor shrugged. "From that point on, however, her response was unequivocal. She looked forward to his visits. She was excited by their lovemaking, if it's not too perverse to call it that. She was excited by him, and her excitement grew even as her hatred for him deepened. By the time she killed him, her sole regret was that she would no longer have him as a sexual partner."

"But that didn't stop her."

"No," the doctor said. "No, she wanted the pleasure of his death more than the pleasure of his embrace. But afterward she was appalled by what she'd done, and even more by what she'd become. Had she turned into a monster herself?"

"And had she?"

The doctor shook his head. "No, not at all. She did not find herself ruled by her passions, nor did an element of sadism become a lasting part of her sexual nature. It was not long before a boyfriend came into her life, and their relationship and others that were to follow were entirely normal."

"So she was unchanged by the experience?"

"Is one ever entirely unchanged by any experience? And could anyone remain unchanged by such an extraordinary experience? That said, no surface change was evident. Oh, sex was a little more satisfying than it had been in the past, and she was a bit less inhibited, and a bit more eager to try new acts and postures."

They fell silent, and the room grew very still indeed. The fire had burned down to coals, and had long since ceased to crackle. The silence stretched out.

And then it was broken by the fifth man in the room.

"THAT'S VERY interesting," said the old man from his chair by the fireside.

The four cardplayers exchanged glances. "You're awake," the priest said. "I hope we didn't disturb you."

"You didn't disturb me," said the old man, his voice like dry leaves in the wind, thin and wispy, yet oddly penetrating for all that. "I fear I may have disturbed you, by breaking wind from time to time."

The doctor colored. "I was impolite enough to remark upon it," he said, "and for that I apologize. We had no idea you were awake."

"When one has reached my considerable age," the old man said, "one is never entirely asleep, and never entirely awake, either. One dozes through the days. But is that state of being the exclusive property of the aged? All my long life, I sometimes think, I have never been entirely awake or entirely asleep. Consciousness is somewhere between the two, and so is unconsciousness."

"Food for thought," the soldier said.

"But thinner gruel than the food for thought you four have provided. Lust!"

"Our topic," the priest said, "and it did set the stories rolling."

"How I lusted," said the old man. "How I longed for women. Yearned for them, burned for them. Of course those days of longing are long gone now. Now I sit by the fire, warming my old bones, neither awake nor asleep. I don't long for women. I don't long for anything."

"Well," the policeman said.

"But I remember them," the old man said.

"The women."

"The women, and how I felt about them, and what I did with them. I remember the ones I had, and there's not one I regret having. And I remember the ones I wanted and didn't have, and I regret every one of those lost chances."

"We most regret what we've left undone," said the priest. "Even the sins we left uncommitted. It's a mystery."

"In high school," the old man said, "there was a girl named Peggy Singer. How I longed for her! How she starred in my schoolboy fantasies! She was my partner for a minute or two at a school dance, before another wretched boy cut in. I couldn't possibly remember the clean smell of her skin, or the way she felt in my arms. But it seems to me that I do."

The doctor nodded, at a memory of his own.

"After graduation," the old man said, "I lost track of her entirely. Never learned what became of her. Never forgot her, either. And now my life is nearing its end, and when I add up the plusses and minuses, they cancel each other out until I'm left with one irreconcilable fact. God help me, I never got to fuck Peggy Singer."

"Ah," the soldier said, and the policeman let out a sigh

"Women," the old man said. "I remember what I did with them, and what I wanted to do, and what I hardly dared to dream of doing. And I remember how it felt, and the urgency of my desire. I remember how important it all was to me. But do you know what I don't remember, what I can't understand?"

They waited.

"I can't understand what was so *important* about it," the old man said. "Why did it matter so? Why? I've never understood that."

He paused, and the silence stretched as they waited for him to say more. Then the sound of his breathing deepened, and a snore came from the chair beside the fireplace.

"He's sleeping," the priest said.

"Or not," said the doctor. "Neither asleep nor awake, even as you and I."

"Well," said the policeman.

"Does anyone remember who's deal it is?" the soldier wondered, gathering the cards.

No one did. "You go ahead, Soldier," said the doctor, and the soldier shuffled and dealt, and the game resumed.

And the old man went on dozing by the fire.

WELCOME TO THE REAL WORLD
A GOLF STORY

K RAMER LIKED ROUTINE.
Always had. He'd worked at Taggert & Leeds for thirty-five years, relieved to settle in there after spending his twenties hopping from one job to another. His duties from day to day were interesting enough to keep him engaged, but in a sense they were the same thing—or the same several things—over and over, and that was fine with him.

His wife made him the same breakfast every weekday morning for those thirty-five years. Breakfast, he had learned, was the one meal where most people preferred the same thing every time, and he was no exception. A small glass of orange juice, three scrambled eggs, two strips of bacon, one slice of buttered toast, a cup of coffee—that did him just fine.

These days, of course, he prepared it himself. He hadn't needed to learn how, he'd always made breakfast for both of them on Saturdays, and now the time he spent whisking eggs in a bowl and turning rashers with a fork was a time for him to think of her and regret her passing.

So sudden it had been. He'd retired, and she'd said, in mock consternation, "Now what am I going to do with you? Am I going to have you underfoot all day every day?" And he established a routine that got him out of the house five days a week, and they both settled gratefully into that routine, and then she felt a pain and complained of shortness of breath and went to the doctor, and a month later she was dead.

He had his routine, and it was clear to him that he owed his life to it. He got up each morning, he made his breakfast, he washed the dishes by hand, he read the paper along with a second cup of coffee, and he got out of the house. Whatever day it was, he had something to do, and his salvation lay in doing it.

If it was Monday, he walked to his gym. He changed from his street clothes to a pair of running shorts and a singlet, both of them a triumph of technology, made of some miracle fiber that wicked moisture away from the skin and sent it off somewhere to evaporate. He put his heavy street shoes in his locker and laced up his running shoes. Then he went out on the floor, where he warmed up for ten minutes on the elliptical trainer before moving to the treadmill. He set the pace at 12-minute miles, set the time at 60 minutes, and got to it.

Kramer, who'd always been physically active and never made a habit of overeating, had put on no more than five pounds in the course of his thirty-five years at Taggart & Leeds. He'd added another couple of pounds since then, but at the same time had lost an inch in the waistline. He had lost some fat and gained a little muscle, which was the point, or part of it. The other part, perhaps the greater part, was having something enjoyable and purposeful to do on Mondays.

On Tuesdays he turned in the other direction when he left his apartment, and walked three-quarters of a mile to the Bat Cave, which was not where you would find Batman and Robin, as the name might lead you to expect, but was instead a recreational facility for baseball enthusiasts. Each of two dozen batting cages sported a pitching machine the standard sixty feet from home plate, where the participant dug in and took his cuts for a predetermined period of time.

They supplied bats, of course, but Kramer brought his own, a Louisville Slugger he'd picked out of an extensive display at a sporting goods store on Broadway. It was a little heavier than average, and he liked the way it was balanced. It just felt right in his hands. Also, there was something to be said for having the same bat every time. You didn't have to adjust to a new piece of lumber.

He brought along cleated baseball shoes, too, which made it easier to establish his stance in the batter's box. The boat-necked shirt and sweatpants he wore didn't sport any team logo, which would have struck him as ridiculous, but they were otherwise not unlike what the pros wore, for the freedom of movement they afforded.

Kramer wore a baseball cap, too; he'd found it in the back of his closet, had no idea where it came from, and recognized the embroidered logo as that of an advertising agency that had gone out of business some fifteen years ago. It must have come into his possession as some sort of corporate party favor, and he must have tossed it in his closet instead of tossing it in the trash, and now it had turned out to be useful.

You could set the speed of the pitching machine, and Kramer set it at Slow at the beginning of each Tuesday session, turned it to Medium about halfway through, and finished with a few minutes of Fast pitching. He was, not surprisingly, better at getting his bat on the slower pitches. A fastball, even when you knew it was coming, was hard for a man his age to connect with. Still, he hit most of the medium-speed pitches— some solidly, some less so. And he always got some wood on some of the fastballs, and every once in a while he'd meet a high-speed pitch solidly, his body turning into the ball just right, and the satisfaction of seeing the horsehide sphere leap from his bat was enough to cast a warm glow over the entire morning's work. His best efforts, he realized, were soft line drives a major league centerfielder would gather in without breaking a sweat, but so what? He wasn't having fantasies of showing up in Sarasota during spring training, aiming for a tryout. He was a sixty-eight year old retired businessman keeping in shape and filling his hours, and when he got ahold of one, well, it felt damned good.

Walking home, carrying the bat and wearing the ball cap, with a pleasant ache in his lats and delts and triceps—well, that felt pretty good, too.

Wednesdays provided a very different sort of exercise. Physically, he probably got the most benefit from the walk there and back—a couple of miles from his door to the Murray Street premises of the Downtown Gun Club. The hour he devoted to rifle and pistol practice demanded no special wardrobe, and he wore whatever street clothes suited the season, along with a pair of ear protectors the club was happy to provide. As a member, he could also use one of the club's guns, but hardly anyone did; like his fellows, Kramer kept his guns at the club, thus obviating him of the need to obtain a carry permit for them. The license to own a weapon and maintain it at a recognized marksmanship facility was pretty much a formality, and Kramer had obtained it with no difficulty.

He owned three guns—a deer rifle, a .22-caliber target pistol, and a hefty .357-magnum revolver. Typically, he fired each gun for half an hour, pumping lead at (and, occasionally, into) a succession of paper targets. He could vary the distance of the targets, and naturally chose the greatest distance for the rifle, the least for the magnum. But he would sometimes bring the targets in closer, for the satisfaction of grouping his shots tighter, just as he would occasionally increase the distance, in order to give himself more of a challenge.

Except for basic training, some fifty years ago, he'd never had a gun in his hand, let alone fired one. He'd always thought it was something he might enjoy, and in retirement he'd proved the suspicion true. He liked squeezing off shots with the rifle, liked the balance and precision of the target pistol, and even liked the nasty kick of the big revolver, and the sense of power that came with it. His eye was better some days than others, his hand steadier, but all in all it seemed to him that he was improving. Every Wednesday, on the long walk home, he felt he'd accomplished something. And, curiously, he felt empowered and invulnerable, as if he were actually carrying the magnum on his hip.

Thursdays saw him returning to the gym, but he didn't warm up on the elliptical trainer, nor did he put in an hour on the treadmill. That was Monday. Thursday was for weights.

He did his circuit on the machines. Early on, he'd had a couple of sessions with a personal trainer, but only until he'd managed to establish a routine that he could perform without assistance. He kept a pocket notebook in his locker, jotting down the reps and poundages on each machine; when an exercise became too easy, he upped the weight accordingly. He was making slow but undeniable progress. He could see it in his notes, and, more graphically, he could see it in the mirror.

His gym gear made it easy to see, too. The shorts and singlet that served so well on Mondays were not right for Thursdays, when he donned instead a pair of black Spandex bicycle shorts and a matching tank top. It made him look the part, but that was the least of it. The close fit seemed to help enlist his muscles to put maximum effort into each lift. His weightlifting gloves, padded slightly in the palms for cushioning, and with the fingers ending at the first knuckle joint for a good grip, kept him from getting blisters or calluses, as well as telling the world that he was serious enough about what he was doing do get the right gear for it.

An hour with the weights left him with sore muscles, but ten minutes in the steam room and a cold shower set him right again, and he always felt good on the way home. And then, on Fridays, he got to play golf.

And that was always a pleasure. Until Bellerman, that interfering son of a bitch, came along and ruined the whole thing for him.

THE DRIVING range was at Chelsea Piers, and it was a remarkable facility. Kramer had made arrangements to keep a set of clubs there, and he picked them up along with his usual bucket of balls and headed for the tee. When he got there he put on a pair of golf shoes, arguably an unnecessary refinement on the range's mats, but he felt they grounded his stance. And, like the thin leather gloves he kept in the bag, they put him more in the mood, as did the billed Tam O'Shanter cap he'd put on his head before leaving the house.

He teed up a ball, took his Big Bertha driver from the bag, settled himself, and took a swing. He met the ball solidly, but perhaps he'd dropped his shoulder, or perhaps he'd let his hands get out in front; in any event, he sliced the shot. It wasn't awful, it had some distance on it and wouldn't have wound up all that deep in the rough, but he could do better. And did so on the next shot, again meeting the ball solidly and sending it out there straight as a die.

He hit a dozen balls with Big Bertha, then returned her to the bag and got out his spoon. He liked the 3-wood, liked the balance of it, and he had to remind himself to stop after a dozen balls or he might have run all the way through the bag with that club. It was, he'd found, a very satisfying club to hit.

Which was by no means the case with the 2-iron. It wasn't quite as difficult as the longest iron in his bag—there was a joke he'd heard, the punchline of which explained that not even God could hit the 1-iron—but it was difficult enough, and today his dozen attempts with the club yielded his usual share of hooks and slices and topped rollers. But among them he hit the ball solidly twice, resulting in shots that leapt from the tee, scoring high for distance and accuracy.

And therein lay the joy of the sport. One good shot invariably erased the memory of all the bad shots that preceded it, and even took the sting out of the bad shots yet to come.

Today was an even-irons day, so in turn he hit the 4-iron, the 6-iron, and the 8-iron. When he'd finished with the niblick (he liked the old names, called the 2-wood a brassie and the 3-wood a spoon, called the 5-iron a mashie, the 8 a niblick) he had four balls left of the 75 he'd started with. That suggested that he'd miscounted, which was certainly possible, but it was just as likely that they'd given him 76 instead of 75, since they gave you what the bucket held instead of delegating some minion to count them. He hit the four balls with his wedge, not the most exciting club to hit off a practice tee, but you had to play the whole game, and the short game was vital. (He had a sand wedge in his bag, but until they added a sand pit to the tee, there was no way he could practice with it. So be it, he'd decided; life was compromise.)

He left the tee and went to the putting green, where he put in his usual half-hour. His putter was an antique, an old wooden-shafted affair with some real collector value, his choice on even-iron Fridays. It seemed to him that his stroke was firmer and more accurate with the putter from his matched set, his odd-iron choice, but he just liked the feel of the old club, and something in him responded to the notion of using a putter that could have been used a century ago at St. Andrew's. He didn't think it had, but it could have been, and that seemed to mean something to him.

His putting was erratic, it generally was, but he sank a couple of long ones, and ended the half-hour with a seven-footer that lipped the cup, poised on the brink, and at last had the decency to drop. Perfect! He went to the desk for his second bucket of balls, and returned to the tee and his Big Bertha.

He'd worked his way down to the 6-iron when a voice said, "By God, you're good. Kramer, I had no idea."

He turned and recognized Bellerman. A co-worker at Taggart & Leeds, until some competing firm had made him a better offer. But now, it turned out, Bellerman was retired himself, and improving the idle hour at the driving range.

"And you're serious," Bellerman went on. "I've been watching you. Most guys come out here and all they do is practice with the driver. Which they then get to use one time only on the long holes and not at all on the par threes. But you work your way through the bag, don't you?"

Kramer found himself explaining about even- and odd-iron days.

"Remarkable. And you hit your share of good shots, I have to say that. Get some good distance with the long clubs, too. What's your handicap?"

"I don't have one."

Bellerman's eyes widened. "Jesus, you're a scratch golfer? Now I'm more impressed than ever."

"No," Kramer said. "I'm sure I would have a handicap, but I don't know what it would be. See, I don't actually play."

"What do you mean, you don't play?"

"I just come here," Kramer said. "Once a week."

"Even-numbered irons one week, odd ones the next."

"That's right."

"Every Friday."

"Yes."

"You're kidding me," Bellerman said. "Right?"

"No, I—"

"You practice more diligently than anybody I've ever seen. You even hit the fucking 1-iron every other Friday, and that's more than God does. You work on your short game, you use the wedge off the tee, and for what? So that you won't lose your edge for the following Friday? Kramer, when was the last time you actually got out on a course and played a real round of golf?"

"You have to understand my routine," Kramer said. "Golf is just one of my interests. Mondays I go to the gym and put in an hour on the treadmill. Tuesdays I go to the batting cage and work my way up to fastballs. Wednesdays..." He made his way through his week, trying not to be thrown offstride by the expression of incredulity on Bellerman's face.

"That's quite a system," Bellerman said. "And it sounds fine for the first four days, but golf...Man, you're practicing when you could be playing! Golf's an amazing game, Kramer, and there's more to it than swinging the club. You're out in the fresh air—"

"The air's good here."

"—feeling the sun on your skin and the wind in your hair. You're on a golf course, the kind of place that gives you an idea of what God would have done if he'd had the money. And every shot presents you with a different kind of challenge. You're not just trying to hit the ball straight and far. You're dealing with obstacles, you're pitting your ability against a particular aspect of terrain and course conditions. I asked you something earlier, and you never answered. When's the last time you played a round?"

"Well, as a matter of fact—"

"You never did, did you?"

"No, but—"

"Tomorrow morning," Bellerman said. "You'll be my guest, at my club on the Island. I've got tee time booked at 7:35. I'll pick you up at 6, that'll give us plenty of time."

"I can't."

"You're retired, for Chrissake. And tomorrow's Saturday, it won't keep you from your weekday schedule. You really can't? All right, then a week from tomorrow. Six o'clock sharp."

HE SPENT the week trying not to think about it, and then, when that didn't work, trying to think of a way out. He didn't hear from Bellerman, and found himself hoping the man would have forgotten the whole thing.

His routine worked, and he saw no reason to depart from it. Maybe he wasn't playing "real" golf, maybe he was missing something by not getting out on an actual golf course, but he got more than enough pleasure out of the game the way he played it. There were no water hazards, there were no balls lost in deep rough, and there was no score to keep. He got the exercise—he took more swings at the driving range than anyone would take in eighteen holes on a golf course—and he got the occasional satisfaction of a perfect shot, without the crushing dismay that could attend a horrible shot.

Maybe Bellerman would realize that the last thing he wanted to do was waste a morning playing with Kramer.

And yet, when he was back at the range that Friday, he felt vaguely sorry (if more than slightly relieved) that he hadn't heard from the man. He knew how much he'd improved in recent months, hitting every club reasonably well (including, this particular day, the notorious 1-iron) and of course it would be different on a golf course, but how different could it be? You had the same clubs to swing, and you tried to make the ball go where you wanted it.

And just suppose he turned out to be good at it. Suppose he was good enough to give Bellerman a game. Suppose, by God, he could beat the man?

Sort of a shame he wasn't going to get the chance…

"Good shot," said a familiar voice. "Hit a few like that tomorrow and you'll do just fine. Don't forget, I'm coming for you at six. So remember to take your clubs home when you're done here today. And make sure you've got enough golf balls. Kramer? I'll bet you don't have any golf balls, do you? Ha! Well, buy a dozen. They're accommodating at my club, but they won't hand you a bucketful."

ON THE way there, Bellerman told him he'd read about Japanese golfers who spent all their time on driving ranges and putting greens. "Practicing for a day that never comes," he said. "It's the cost of land there. It's scarce, so there aren't many golf courses, and club dues and greens fees are prohibitive unless you're in top management. Actually, the driving-range golfers do get to play when they're on vacation. They'll go to an all-inclusive resort in Hawaii or the Caribbean and manage to squeeze in thirty-six holes a day for a solid week, then go home and spend the rest of the year in a cage, hitting balls off a tee. Well, today's your vacation, Kramer, and you don't have to cross an ocean. All you have to do is tee up and hit the ball."

It was a nightmare.

And it began on the very first tee. Bellerman teed off first, hitting a shot that wouldn't get him in trouble, maybe a hundred fifty yards down the fairway with a little fade at the end that took some of the distance off it.

Then it was Kramer's turn, and he placed a brand-new Titlist on a brand-new yellow tee and drew his Big Bertha from his bag. He settled himself, rocking to get his cleated feet properly planted, and addressed the ball, telling himself not to kill it, just to meet it solidly. But he must have been too eager to see where the ball went, because he looked up prematurely, topping the ball. That happened occasionally at Chelsea Piers, and the result was generally a grounder. This time, however, he really topped the thing, and it caromed up into the air like a Baltimore chop in baseball, coming to earth perhaps a hundred feet away, right where a shortstop would have had an effortless time gathering it in.

Bellerman didn't laugh. And that was worse, somehow, than if he had.

BY THE third hole, he was just waiting for it to be over. He'd taken an eight on the first hole and a nine on the second, and at this rate he seemed likely to wind up with a score somewhere north of 150 for the eighteen holes Bellerman intended for them to play. That meant, he calculated, around 130 strokes to go, 130 more swings of one club or another. He could just go through it, a stroke at a time, and then it would be over, and he would never have to go through anything like this again.

"Good shot!" Bellerman said, when Kramer's fourth shot on Three, with his trusty niblick, actually hit the green and stayed there. "That's the thing about this game, Kramer. I can four-putt a green, then shank my drive and put my second shot in a bunker, but one good shot and everything feels right. Isn't it a good feeling?"

It was, sort of, but he knew it wouldn't last, and it had begun to fade by the time he reached the green, putter in hand. He was some thirty feet from the cup, and his first putt died halfway there, and he overcompensated with his second, and, well, never mind. He took a ten on the hole.

"Still," Bellerman said, as they approached the next tee, "that was a hell of an approach shot. That was a nine iron, right?"

"An eight."

"Oh? I'd probably have used a nine. Still, it worked out for you, didn't it?"

BY THE end of the seventh hole, he'd lost four of his new golf balls. Two were in the water hazard on Six, out of anybody's reach, and one was in the woods on Five, where it would take sharper eyes than his or Bellerman's to spot it. And another was somewhere in the rough on Seven; he saw it drop, saw it land, walked right to the goddam thing, and couldn't find it. It was as if the earth had swallowed it, and he only wished it would do the same for him.

On the eighth hole, the head of his Big Bertha driver dug a trench in the earth behind the teed-up golf ball, and the ball itself tumbled off the tee and managed to roll three feet before coming to rest. "I don't think we'll count that one," Bellerman was saying, but he stopped when Kramer lost it and, enraged, swung the club at a convenient tree. That was the end of the club, if not quite the end of the tree, and Kramer stood there looking at the ruined driver, embarrassed not only by what he'd done but by the unseemly feeling of satisfaction that stirred him.

"Probably not a bad idea to use the 2-wood off the tee," Bellerman said gently. "You gain in accuracy what you sacrifice in distance. Hey, you're not doing so bad, Kramer. This is real-world golf. Nobody said it was going to be easy."

NOR DID it get easier. The good shots, fewer and further between as the day wore on, were no longer even momentarily satisfying; he was all too aware that they were just a brief interruption to the parade of bad shots. He used his brassie off the tee, and every time he drew it from the bag it was a silent rebuke for what he'd done to his driver. At least he didn't get mad at his brassie. He hit the ball—never terribly well—and returned it to his bag, and went off to look for the ball, and, if he found it, hit it again with something else.

On the sixteenth hole, a 140-yard par-three on which he'd miraculously hit the well-protected green with his tee shot, his putter betrayed him. He'd brought both putters, of course, had in fact brought every club he owned, and he was using the antique wooden-shafted club, the one that might have been used at St. Andrew's.

He stood over the ball. The cup was eight feet away, and if he could sink this putt he'd have a birdie. A birdie! He'd been writing down sevens and eights and nines, he'd carded a hideous 14 on one endless hole, but if he could actually sink this putt—

It took him six putts to get the ball in the hole.

He couldn't believe what was happening. In his hands, the trusty putter turned into a length of rope, a strand of limp spaghetti, a snake. He poked the ball past the cup, wide of the cup, short of the cup, every damn where but into the cup. Bellerman tried to concede the fifth putt—"Close enough, man. Pick it up."—but Kramer stubbornly putted again, and missed again, and something snapped.

And not just within him. The graceful wooden shaft of the old putter snapped when he broke it over his knee.

• • •

THE LAST two holes were relatively uneventful. None of his shots were good, but neither were they disastrous. He drove with his brassie, and each time kept the ball on the fairway. He took four putts on 17 and three on 18, using the putter that matched his other irons. He didn't utter a word during the last two holes, just playing doggedly, and Bellerman didn't say anything, either.

They didn't talk much on the way back to the city, either. Bellerman tried a couple of times, but gave it up when Kramer failed to respond. Kramer closed his eyes, replaying a hole in his mind, and the next thing he knew they had reached his house.

"I know it was a rough day for you," Bellerman said. "What can I say? Welcome to the real world, Kramer. You can get that putter repaired, you know."

Kramer didn't say anything.

"There are craftsmen who fit old clubs with new wooden shafts. It's not cheap, but it's worth it. Look, you played real golf today. This was the genuine article. Next time it'll come a lot easier."

Next time?

"And before you know it you'll be hooked. You'll see." A hand on Kramer's shoulder. "I'll let you be, buddy. Lemme pop the trunk and you can get your clubs. Grab a shower, get yourself some rest. We'll do this again."

THAT WAS Saturday.

Sunday he stayed in and watched sports on TV. There was golf on one channel, tennis on another. Ordinarily he much preferred watching golf, but this day, understandably enough, it got on his nerves. He kept switching back and forth between the two channels, and was grateful when they were both done and he could watch *Sixty Minutes* instead.

Monday he went to the gym, warmed up on the elliptical trainer, then put in his time on the treadmill. There were runners, some of them men as old as he, some of them older, who entered the New York Road Runners races in Central Park, trying to beat others in their age group, trying to improve their times from one race to the next, trying to up their mileage and complete a marathon. That was fine for them, and he could applaud their efforts, but no one would fault a man who ran just for exercise, no one would argue that he wasn't doing it right if he never took it outside of the gym.

Tuesday he went to the batting cage and took his cuts. He hit some balls well and missed some of them entirely, but he wasn't so invested in results as to lose his temper with himself or his equipment. He never had the impulse to slam his bat against an unyielding metal post, or smash it over his knee. And he never for a moment saw his activity as a second-rate and laughable substitute for joining a team and playing baseball in the park.

Wednesday he went to the gun club, Thursday to the gym again, this time to lift weights. And Friday found him at the driving range at Chelsea Piers.

He hadn't yet replaced his Big Bertha. It would be easy enough to do, one Big Bertha was essentially indistinguishable from the next, but he hadn't yet had the heart for it. He hit his drives with his 2-wood, as he'd done on the course, hit a dozen balls with it, then continued to work his way through his bag of clubs and through two buckets of balls.

It wasn't the same.

Memories of the previous Saturday kept getting in the way. "The wonderful thing about golf," Bellerman had assured him, "is the way memory improves it. You remember the good shots and forget the bad. I suppose that's one of the things that keeps us coming back."

Wrong, dead wrong. He'd already forgotten the handful of good shots he'd managed to achieve, while the awful ones crowded his memory and got in the way of his practice today. He couldn't take a club from his bag without recalling just how horribly he'd topped or sliced or shanked a shot with it. His mashie, which he'd hit solidly on Twelve, only to send the ball thirty yards past the damned green. His 3-iron, which he'd used from the rough, visualizing a perfect shot to the green between a pair of towering trees. And of course the ball had struck one tree dead center, rebounding so that it left him further from the hole than he'd started, but with the same shot through the trees. Second time around, he'd hit the other tree...

"Want to go out tomorrow?"

Bellerman, damn him. He drew a breath, forced himself to be civil. "No," he said. "Thanks, but I can't make it tomorrow."

"You should, you know. Kid gets thrown from a horse, best thing he can do is get right back on him."

And get thrown again?

"You obviously love the game, Kramer. Otherwise you wouldn't be over here after a day like the one you had Saturday. But don't try to make this take the place of the real thing. You've had a taste of golf and you want to keep at it, you know? Say, did you find somebody to put a new shaft on that putter?"

"Not yet."

"Well, you will. Are you sure you can't make it tomorrow? Well then, maybe next week."

THE WEEKEND passed. Monday he ran on the treadmill, and afterward he went online and ordered a new Big Bertha driver. Tuesday he had a good session at the batting cage, and that afternoon he took his putter to an elderly German gentleman somewhere on the border of Brooklyn and Queens, who repaired old golf clubs and fishing rods in his basement workshop. The price was high, more than he'd originally paid for the club, but it was worth it and more if it could erase the evidence of his bad temper.

Wednesday he went to the gun club. He fired the deer rifle and the .22 at his usual targets, then took a break and sipped a cup of coffee. The weight machines tomorrow, he thought, and then the driving range on Friday, and Bellerman would show up, dammit, and what was he going to do about that, anyway?

The real world. There were, he supposed, fellow members of the gun club who hunted. Had country places in Jersey or Pennsylvania, say, and tried to get a buck in deer season, or a brace of pheasant at the appropriate time. But the majority of members, he was sure, just came to practice marksmanship. They didn't think of their activity as a pale substitute for the real thing, and neither did anybody else.

He went back to practice with the magnum, selected his usual paper target. Then something made him switch to a target he'd seen used by other members—law enforcement personnel, for the most part. The target was a male silhouette, gun in hand.

It was strange at first. He'd always aimed at a bull's-eye target, and now he was aiming at a human outline. It too had a series of concentric circles, centered upon the figure's heart, so you could see just how close you came. And it wasn't a person at all, it was just a piece of paper, but it still took a little getting used to.

And an odd thing happened. *Welcome to the real world*, said a voice in his head, and it was recognizable, that voice. It was Bellerman's voice, and he steadied the big handgun and squeezed off a shot, and the gun bucked satisfyingly in his hand, and the bullet found its mark in the silhouette.

He kept hearing Bellerman's voice in his head, and the two-dimensional generic silhouette began assuming three-dimensional form in his mind, and the face began wearing Bellerman's features.

He spent a longer time than usual at the range, and his hand and forearm ached by the time he was done. The real world, he thought. The real world indeed.

He returned the rifle and the target pistol to his locker. No one noticed that he walked out with the magnum tucked into the waistband of his trousers, and the remainder of a box of shells in his pocket.

Would Bellerman show up again at the driving range Friday?

Perhaps not. Perhaps the man would have gotten the message by then and would leave him alone, having done what he could to ruin Kramer's life.

But somehow Kramer doubted it. Bellerman was no quitter. He'd be there again, with the same abrasive drawl, the same smile that was never far from a sneer. The same invitation to a round of Saturday golf, which this time Kramer would accept.

Only this time there'd be something new in his bag. And, on one of the more remote holes at Bellerman's club, Kramer would bring out not his brassie or his mashie or his niblick, not his sand wedge, not his (and God's) 1-iron, but a .357 magnum revolver, cleaned and loaded and ready.

Welcome to the real world, Bellerman!

WHO KNOWS WHERE IT GOES

WHEN THE WAITRESS BROUGHT him his coffee, Colliard managed a nod and a smile. He added milk but no sugar, stirred, looked out the window at the entrance to the four-story commercial building across the street. He didn't really want the coffee, he'd had enough coffee today, and this cup wouldn't make him any more alert than he already was. Its only discernible effect would come hours from now, when he'd want to sleep and it wouldn't let him.

Of course that might be difficult anyway.

Maybe he should have ordered decaf. He never did, he never even thought of it until he already had a cup of regular coffee in front of him. He'd never been able to see the point of decaf. Why drink the stuff at all if not for the caffeine? It never tasted as good as you hoped it would. Sometimes, if it was particularly good coffee, the smell was wonderful. But then you took a sip, and all you got was disappointment. And caffeine.

He picked up the spoon, stirred the coffee some more, put the spoon down. And left the cup in its saucer. It wasn't as though he had to drink it. He'd had to order it, so that he could have this table by the window, but now that she'd brought it to him he could sit here until closing time. It wasn't as though they needed the table for another customer. The diner was mostly empty, and would likely remain that way, like every place else in town. Like every other town in the country.

Hard times. Sometimes it was tough not to take it personally, to see the entire break in the economy as having been aimed specifically at him. When he got that way he forced himself to take a good look around. And it was pretty easy to see that it wasn't just him. Everywhere he looked, businesses were failing and men and women were out of work. Corporations, absolute household names that had been around as long as he could remember, were going out of business. Banks were imploding. Retailers, from the big box chains to the hardware store on the corner, were turning off the lights and locking the doors. As an economy move, someone had quipped, the light at the end of the tunnel had been turned off.

A matter of months ago Colliard had been sitting on top of the world, and the perch was all the sweeter for the time and effort it had taken him to get there. He'd sweated it out to get the union card—an MBA from a top university. He'd lived off his savings and hit the books hard, and the degree got him his first corporate job. He worked hard, and when the headhunters came calling, he was ready to move up. He earned the promotions, he got the cash and prizes, and he bought the right house and married the right woman. He earned big bucks and lived within his income, and when the chance came along to start his own company, he jumped at it.

And made it work. And figured he had it made.

"WARM THAT up for you?"

It was the waitress, coffee pot in hand. He smiled, shook his head. "I've had too much coffee already," he said. "But thanks."

"Something to eat?"

He shook his head.

"That's okay," she said. "You sit there as long as you like. That way people look in the window, they see we're still open. You know Sacco's? On the next block?"

He didn't know the neighborhood at all, but the question didn't seem to require an answer.

"Thirty years they been there," she said. "Good times and bad. Friend of mine's worked there twelve years herself, and Friday afternoon the owner called them all together and told them it was the last day. Just like that. Twelve years, thirty years just like that. How can a business just disappear, here one day and gone the next?"

He said, "'Who knows where it goes when it's gone.'" She looked at him, and he told her it was a line from a song. She said she'd like to hear the rest of the song, and he said that was the only line he remembered.

"Well, it's a good one," she said, "'Who knows where it goes when it's gone.' Not me, that's for sure."

"I'D SEE your name in the papers," Sully had said earlier. "Morton H. Colliard. What's the H stand for?"

They'd met two days before in a diner not too different from the one he was in now, but a hundred miles away. They sat with cups of coffee in a rear booth. They knew Sully there, knew to bring him his coffee and then leave him alone.

"Henry."

"Never knew about the H, never mind the four letters after it. Just Mort Colliard, and I couldn't have said if it was Morton or Mortimer. Or just Mort. Means death in French, doesn't it?"

"I don't speak French."

"Didn't you have to learn it in school? Got my own hands full with English. Morton Henry Colliard. Gave me a turn the first time I saw it, and I can't say I ever got entirely used to it. Of course it was a good thing, a sign you were getting places, and I was happy for you."

Was he? Sully had cool grey eyes, hard to read. Colliard had learned to take what Sully said at face value, because trying to get any deeper was a waste of time.

"But all the years I knew you," Sully said, "the whole point was keeping your name out of the papers. So it was hard to get used to, that you were in the papers, and glad to be there. Was it a kick for you? Did you clip the stories, keep a scrapbook?"

"Not my style."

"No, I don't guess it would be. But people change, don't they?"

Did they?

"Saw the wedding announcement. Fine-looking woman. Never expected you to marry, though I can't say why not. Any kids yet?"

"One on the way."

"Boy or girl? Or don't you know?"

"We figured we'll find out soon enough."

"People need a little suspense in their lives, don't they? You care much one way or the other, boy or girl?"

"Just so it's a healthy baby."

Sully nodded his approval, and Colliard wondered at the lie he'd just told. The baby, due in four months, was a boy, and why had he kept that from Sully?

"I'll tell you," Sully said. "I swear I couldn't believe it when I picked up the phone and there you were on the other end of it. Never thought I'd hear your voice again, not in this world."

What should he say to that? He couldn't think of anything.

"Not that we parted on bad terms, but we parted, didn't we? You moved on to a different life, and you couldn't do that without leaving the old life behind. Be like a film I saw, young fellow from South-Central L.A., he's in a gang, Bloods or Crips, can't remember which. You see the film?"

"I don't think so."

"Well, he's bright, you know? Good in school. Studies hard, applies himself. And there's this teacher who believes in him, and she fixes it so he gets a scholarship to this Ivy League college. Couldn't tell you which one. And he goes there, and it's culture shock, you know? He's this street kid and his roommate is this typical preppy—you can see where this is going, can't you?"

Like he cared.

"He adjusts to campus life. And then he goes home because his mother is dying, and he gets sucked into the gang life again, because once you're a Jet you're a Jet all the way."

Wasn't it Bloods and Crips a minute ago? Oh, right, the song. He took a moment to hear it in his mind, and when he tuned in again Sully was telling him how the kid died in the streets after all.

"He could get away, see, but he couldn't stay away. Of course, all it was is a film. Didn't even claim it was based on a true story, which wouldn't make it true even if it did. Someone made it up, just to prove that a man can't get away from his true self. But what's a man's true self, can you tell me that?"

"All these questions," he said.

"Had your own company, didn't you?"

"Until it went bust."

"Well, this economy. No shame going broke in times like these. But you must have socked away a few bucks in the good years."

"At first it all went back into the business."

"How it's done, isn't it? And then?"

"Then it went into investments. There was this hedge fund, promised twelve percent on your money, good years and bad."

"That's not bad, twelve percent."

"That's what I thought. It's what everybody thought."

"This hedge fund, the player's the one who got his name in the papers a lot lately?"

"That's the one."

"And you got hurt pretty bad." It wasn't a question, and didn't require an answer. "You must have a nice home, though."

"If I can keep it away from the bank."

"They looking to foreclose?"

"Not tomorrow," he said, "and not the day after tomorrow."

"But the day after that? And you don't want to forget there's a baby on the way."

"No."

"The jobs in your new field—"

"The market's dried up. There's nothing out there for me."

Sully nodded. "Be different when the economy turns around, I suppose."

"I suppose."

"And you could wait it out, but that's not so easy since that hedge fund went south. That about sum it up?"

It was all he could do to nod.

Sully's fingers drummed the tabletop. "I have some investments myself," he said. "Different establishments where I'm what you'd call a silent partner. A man owes you money and can't pay, so he takes you in as a partner. You know how it works."

"Sure."

"Most of them, business is off. A lunch counter, a corner deli, you wouldn't think they'd be affected, would you? People still have to eat. Are they going to stop buying their newspaper in the morning, having a latte in the middle of the afternoon? They still have to have their beer and their cigarettes, don't they? Yet business is off all across the board."

"Hard times."

"And yet," Sully said, "the core business, *my* core business, remains untouched. I'm recession-proof, you might say."

"That's good."

"So there's work for you, my friend. If you really want it. If you think you can still do it."

IF HE really wanted it. If he thought he could still do it.

His coffee cup was empty. Lost in reverie, he'd drunk it without realizing it. He'd been looking out the window, but had he registered what had passed through his field of vision? Maybe the man he'd been waiting for—

No, speak of the devil. There he was now.

Colliard took a bill from his wallet, put it back. Ten dollars was too much, she'd remember him. Five was more than enough.

Besides, he didn't need to throw money around these days.

He put a five on the table top. Outside, the man he'd been waiting for was standing at the parking garage two doors down the street, waiting for them to bring his car down. He'd probably called ahead and wouldn't have long to wait. Colliard, parked at the curb, would have to get moving if he didn't want to lose him.

He stayed where he was. An attendant got out of a bright blue Subaru and held the door for Colliard's quarry. A bill changed hands—a dollar? A five? A ten? Colliard watched as the car pulled away and was gone.

He returned the five-dollar bill to his wallet, managed to catch the waitress's eye. He wasn't really hungry, but he decided to order something. You had to eat, didn't you?

IF HE really wanted it, if he thought he could still do it. Because, Sully had told him, people change. Even when they stay the same, they change.

"Like the film. He had to go back to South-Central, you know? The Ivy League clothes and the Ivy League friends suited him well enough, but he had the street in him, and he had to go back to it." An appraising glance. "But, see, it didn't work for him, did it? Harvard, Princeton, wherever it was, it changed him. Was it Dartmouth? Never mind, doesn't matter. Lost his edge, didn't he? Lost whatever it was that keeps you alive on the street. Lost it, and that's what got him killed. Not going back all by itself, but going back and not fitting in there anymore. *That's* what got him killed." A quick smile. "Of course, it's only a film, isn't it? Some story somebody made up. Wouldn't want to read too much into it, but it's something to think about, don't you think?"

COLLIARD HAD never been in a street gang. They hadn't had Bloods or Crips in the small city where he grew up, although he understood that they had them now. They'd had other gangs, ethnic in composition, raising a fair amount of hell, but Colliard had never gone near them. His family was lower middle class, just managing to hang on in a marginal suburb. Mortie Colliard was out of high school and bagging groceries at Safeway before he fell in with bad companions. The bad companions introduced him to Sully, and Sully found him things to do that paid better than bagging groceries.

"Paper or plastic, ma'am?" Life was simpler then, living in a room in his mother's house, getting by on minimum wage. He couldn't live like that now, but even if he could, who'd hire him? At his age?

At first what he did for Sully wasn't much more complex than putting boxes of Tide in grocery bags and loading them in the trunk of some lady's Toyota. But Sully was adept at finding the right person for the job, and when he got to know Colliard he spotted something—or the absence of something. And Sully sent him across town with a man everybody called Wheezy, though Colliard never knew why. Wheezy pointed out a man behind the counter in a hardware store, and the following afternoon Colliard returned on his own to the hardware store, examined power tools until another customer finished his business and left, and then approached the counter, took out the revolver Sully had provided, and shot the man twice in the chest and, after he'd fallen, once more in the head. He wiped his prints from the gun, dropped it beside the corpse, and went home. On the way he stopped for pizza, and had three slices with pepperoni and extra cheese. Drank a large Coke. Back home he watched TV for a while and then went to bed at his usual time. Slept fine, woke up refreshed.

Nothing to it.

BACK IN the day, before he'd improved himself and risen in the world, before the college courses and the first corporate job, Colliard would have timed things differently. He'd have been out of the diner before his quarry appeared, and would have been within a few feet of him when the attendant brought his car down. Even as the fellow was applying the brakes, Colliard would have put the brakes on the car's owner, drawing the .22 automatic, pulling the trigger twice, and quitting the scene before anyone knew quite what had happened.

Instead, all he did was sit there watching.

People change, don't they? Even when they stay the same, they change.

He'd ordered a grilled cheese and bacon sandwich. It came with french fries, and he asked the waitress to make them very well done. "Crisp and brown," she said, when she set the plate before him. "Some more coffee?"

He shook his head, told her to make it a Coke. She said they had Pepsi, and he assured her Pepsi was fine.

Like old times, he thought. Grilled cheese and bacon was close enough to pizza, and Pepsi was close enough to Coke. But shooting somebody and watching passively while he drove away, well, there was a fairly substantial difference there.

He had a fair appetite, and the food was good. The cheese had a toasty tang, the fries were the way he liked them, and if she'd simply passed off the Pepsi as Coke he'd never have known the difference.

So it was a good enough meal. And if it seemed to him that the long-ago pizza had pleased him more, well, maybe it had, but you couldn't blame the food for that. There were other factors.

IF HE'D followed the guy, if he'd set out after him, then what? Maybe he'd have aborted the mission somewhere along the way, turned left when the blue Subaru turned right. Maybe he'd have been able to tail him all the way into his driveway and gun him down before he got his front door unlocked. Or maybe he'd have stuck the gun in the man's face only to have his finger freeze on the trigger, or—

Endless scenarios. Too many ways it could go wrong, all of them possible because what was not possible was for him to know how much he had in fact changed, and whether he could still do this.

Go up to a stranger, some man who'd done Colliard no harm. Point a gun, pull a trigger, go home and wash your hands. Eat some pizza, watch TV.

He'd stayed in his seat just now because he couldn't go ahead and write the first chapter until he could see his way through to the ending.

Because if it turned out that he couldn't do it, that he was done with that stage in life and couldn't go back to it—well, that was not a discovery he wanted to make with a gun in his hand and his eyes locked with those of the man he was suddenly unable to kill.

All that could do was get him in trouble. With the law, if its minions showed up while he stood there, paralyzed, incapable even of fleeing the scene. Or, if he somehow got away clean, with Sully, for having put the quarry on notice, thus turning him from an easy to a hard target.

He finished his sandwich, finished his fries, finished his Pepsi. And left the waitress a very good tip, because he'd taken up a lot of her time, and because his failure wasn't her fault. And, finally, because it didn't matter anymore if she remembered him.

IT WAS past nine when he got home. He'd told his wife he wouldn't be home for dinner, but she'd made a casserole and offered to warm it up for him. They were eating out less since his business failed, and she'd surprised him by blossoming as a good cook. Nothing fancy, but good simple dishes.

She'd be a good mother, he was confident of that. That hadn't been on his mind when he married her. He chose her because she'd be a good companion, an attractive and personable partner in social situations. And now they were going to have a baby, and she was going to be a good mother.

"We can live in a trailer," she'd said, when the hedge fund turned out to be a Ponzi scam, when it was clear that the money was irretrievably gone. "I don't care where we live, or how we live. We're two people who love each other. We'll get by."

But of course she cared, and of course he cared, and they couldn't swap this house for a double-wide, surrounded by the kind of neighbors who wound up flunking sobriety tests on *Cops*. They loved each other, but how long would they go on loving each other in a trailer park?

He said he'd have the casserole for tomorrow's lunch. He'd had an interview, he told her, and it was promising, with a decent prospect of some case-by-case consulting work. The hours would be irregular and the work off the books, but he'd be well paid. If he got the work.

She said she'd keep her fingers crossed.

• • •

HE SLEPT late, and when he did get up she'd already left for a doctor's appointment. He found the casserole in the refrigerator and nuked a helping in the microwave. It was spicy, and not his usual breakfast fare, but he ate it with good appetite. The coffee she'd made was still hot, and he drank two cups.

He'd slept soundly, and any dreams he'd had were gone and forgotten when he opened his eyes. But he'd gone to sleep with a question, and now the answer was miraculously there.

He got in his car, drove for an hour and a half.

THE TOWN he'd picked was one he'd been to only a handful of times, and not at all in at least ten years. At first glance it looked the same, but then it hadn't changed much since before he was born. It had been a mill town, and the industry moved south after the Second World War, and the local economy had settled into a permanent state of depression. There were changes over the years—strip malls thrown up, a drive-in theater torn down—but the town went on, always a decade or two behind the curve.

There was still a Main Street, and there were still shops on it, but it seemed to Colliard that there were more vacant storefronts than he remembered. A sign of the times? Or just the next phase in the continuing decline of the place?

But what did it matter? He wasn't looking to start a business, and if he did he wouldn't start it here. He hadn't been here in years, and in an hour he'd be gone, and it would be more years before he returned. If he ever came back at all.

Oddly, there were places he recognized. The drugstore on the corner of Main and Edward. The sporting goods store diagonally across the street. The little shop halfway up the block—Mulleavy's, the sign announced. He remembered the name, but had long since forgotten what it was Mulleavy sold, if he'd ever known in the first place.

Two doors down from Mulleavy's was a hardware store. He noted it, unable to recall it from a previous visit, and he thought of another hardware store, and that made the decision for him. He circled the block, parked right in front of the hardware store. There were plenty of empty parking spaces, right there on Main Street, and that told you pretty much all you needed to know about the town, and what it was like to be in business there.

Be doing the man a favor.

He stood out front for a moment, checked out the fly-specked merchandise in the front window. The shops on either side were vacant, and the For Rent signs in their windows looked as though they'd been there forever. Colliard drew a breath, let it out, opened the door.

No customers, and no one else either, not for the moment. Then a man in his sixties, balding, round-shouldered, emerged from the back in response to the little bell that had announced Colliard's entrance.

"Hello there," he said brightly. "We get that rain yet?"

Were they going to talk about the weather? No, the hell with that.

Colliard drew the gun, watched the man's eyes widen behind his glasses. He shot him three times in the chest and once behind the ear.

Wipe the gun and drop it? What, and then go looking for another one?

He put it in his pocket and left.

THE FIRST thing he did was get out of town. There'd been no one around to hear the shots, and it might be an hour before anyone entered the store. The dead man was on the floor behind the counter, where he couldn't be seen from the street. So there was no rush to quit the scene, but Colliard wanted to be away from there all the same.

He drove well within the speed limit, knowing that a routine traffic stop was more to be feared than that someone would actually come looking for him. He had the murder weapon in his pocket, and a paraffin test would establish that he'd fired a gun recently. But they wouldn't know that unless he found a way to call attention to himself, and this was something he'd long ago learned to avoid.

He drove for a while, and when he stopped for a cup of coffee he picked a diner quite like the one with the nice waitress and the tasty sandwich and fries. All he had was coffee, and he took his time drinking it, letting himself sink into the reality of the present moment.

He went over it all in his mind. And he tried to take his own emotional temperature, tried to determine how he felt.

As far as he could tell, he didn't feel a thing.

No, that wasn't entirely true. There was something he felt, something hovering on the edge of thought, visible only out of the corner of his eyes. And what was it?

Took him a moment, but he figured out what it was. It was relief.

He took out his cell phone, thought for a moment, put it back in his pocket. The diner had a pay phone, and he spent a couple of quarters and placed a call. The girl who answered put Sully on the phone, and Colliard said, "That order you placed the other day, I wanted to tell you I'll be able to fill it tomorrow."

"You sure of that, are you?"

"It might take an extra day."

"A day one way or the other doesn't matter. The question is do you have the goods for the transaction."

"I do."

"It seems to me," Sully said, "that it's a hard question to answer ahead of the event, if you take my meaning."

"I know it for a fact," Colliard said. "What I did, I went and took inventory."

"You took inventory."

"Checked the shelves myself."

HE FINISHED his coffee, and stayed at the table long enough to make another phone call. He used his cell phone for this one, there was no reason not to, and called his own home. The first three rings went unanswered. Then his wife picked up just before the phone went to Voice Mail.

He asked how it went at the doctor's office, and was pleased to learn that everything went well, that the baby's heartbeat was strong and distinct, that all systems were go. "He said I'm going to be a perfectly wonderful mother," she reported.

"Well, I could have told you that."

"You sound—"

"What?"

"Better," she said. "Stronger. More upbeat."

"I'm going to be a perfectly wonderful father."

"Oh, you are, you are. I'm just happy you're in such good spirits."

"It must have been the casserole. I had some for breakfast."

"Not cold?"

"No, I microwaved it."

"And it was good?"

"Better than good."

"Not too spicy? So early in the day?"

"It got me off to a good start."

"And it's been a good day," she said. "That much I can hear in your voice. Did you—"

"I got the job. Well, case by case, the way I said, but they're going to be giving me work."

"That's wonderful, honey."

"It may take a while to get back where we were, but we're finally pointed in the right direction again, you know?"

"We'll be fine."

"Damn right we will. And we'll be able to keep the house. I know you had your heart set on a trailer, but—"

"I'll get over it. What time will you be home? I should really get dinner started."

"Let's go out."

"Really?"

"Nothing fancy," he said. "I was thinking along the lines of pizza and a Coke."

WITHOUT A BODY

WHAT'S GOING ON?
I'm in my own house minding my own business, and he motions me over. That Manny, whatever his name is, but one thing I'm sure of is it's not Manny. And that Eva of his, her name's not Eva.

Is she even his mother? She's old enough to be his mother, but the way they act, the way they look at each other, you'd think they were something else. Let me put it this way, it's not something I want to say.

He calls me over, this Manny, like you'd signal for a waitress. In here, he says. Something you should see, he says. Stand here, he says. And there's this plastic sheet spread on the carpet, like the painters put down.

I ask him what's this, what's it doing here. Just wait a minute, he says, and he takes this thing out of his pocket, and I'm starting to ask him what it is, and he's saying something, who knows what, and he reaches out with the thing and before I can move he touches my neck with it, and the next thing I know I'm up in the air.

Will somebody please tell me what is going on?

I am up in the air. I am floating. One minute I've got both feet on the floor and the next minute I'm up at the ceiling, and...

Oh.

I'm both places. I'm up here, but I'm down there, too. Lying down, on this plastic sheet on the floor. That's my body down there, but up here is—what?

Me. Me, myself. Irene Silverman, the same person, no different, but without a body. It's down there. I'm up here.

It. I.

What am I, dead?

I must be dead. I don't know what he touched me with, but it was like sticking your finger in a light socket. It gave me such a shock that it shocked me right out of my body. Like being struck by lightning, and I'm dead, and there's my body down there.

No, wait a minute. I'm not dead. I'm out of my body, I'm here and it's there, but it's still alive. I could go back into my body and sit up and walk and talk.

When I'm ready.

"What are you waiting for?"

It's her, the mother.

"Go ahead, honey. Finish what you started."

He kneels down next to me.

"The gloves, honey."

He puts on a pair of clear plastic gloves. Everybody wears them lately. Nurses, doctors. The girl who cleans your teeth. The clerk in the food market. In the market it's a sanitary thing, but the others are afraid of AIDS.

So what's with the gloves? I'm an eighty-two year old woman, does he think I've got AIDS?

Oh.

His hands are on my throat.

IT LOOKS so small, my body.

I was always short, but a person shrinks. You get used to being short, and then you get shorter.

Some system. What genius thought it up?

I guess I'm dead now. I feel the same way, floating up above everything, as I did before he strangled me. But my body was alive then, and he choked me, and the life went out of me like a cork coming out of a bottle. But not champagne, it didn't pop. It just came out.

So where's the white light? Where's the long tunnel with the white light at the end of it? Isn't that what's supposed to happen?

You die and there's this tunnel and this white light, and every dead person who ever loved you is waiting to welcome you. And so on. People come back and tell about it. It was beautiful, they say, and I wanted to stay, they say, but it wasn't my time.

Very nice, I used to think, but personally I'd rather go to Paris.

But did somebody just make that up? If I'm dead, what happened to the tunnel? Where the hell is the light?

Maybe that only happens if you die and come back. Maybe when you die for keeps, that's it. Lights out, end of story.

So what am I doing here?

ALL WRAPPED up.

They wrap me in the plastic sheet, stuff me in garbage bags, seal me in with duct tape. What am I, meat for the freezer?

"No body," she's saying. "No DNA, nothing. No trace evidence. She'll disappear and they'll never even know what happened to her. And if they suspect, so what?"

I'm watching while they put me in a big duffel bag and carry me out to their car. There's another sheet of clear plastic lining the trunk, and they lay the duffel bag on top of it. The trunk lid's electric, you don't have to slam it. You close it gently and it shuts itself the rest of the way automatically.

They get in the car, and it pulls away, and I'm floating in the air watching them drive off with my body. And the next thing I know they're getting out of the car at the edge of a field. The trunk's open and he's carrying the duffel bag.

There's a hole in the earth. They dug the grave ahead of time. I was walking around, having my breakfast, reading the paper, and all along there was a hole in the earth, waiting for me.

The duffle bag goes in the hole. And the plastic sheet from the trunk of the car. And the gloves he wore.

The grave's filled in now. "She's gone forever," she says. "They'll never find her."

They never do.

TIME IS different when you're dead. You're someplace and then you're not.

I'm around when they get arrested. And then I'm all over the place. People are talking about me—my friends, people from the neighborhood—and I'm there.

But I don't really care what they say. I stop listening, and I'm somewhere else.

283

I'm at the trial. Powerful circumstantial evidence, the prosecutor says. He reads her notebook, and it's all there. Everything they did, so they could steal my house.

Who kills a person so they can steal her house?

Nothing but circumstantial evidence, the defense says. How can you convict without a body? How can you know for certain that a crime has been committed?

But I have a body. Listen to me. If I could talk to you I could tell you where to look. If I could take your hand I could lead you there.

GUILTY, THE verdict comes, guilty of everything. Oh, she can't believe it. How could they convict her? There's no body, there's no DNA, so how on earth could they convict her?

Over a hundred years for each of them. I'm here, floating, seeing, hearing, and the sentence comes and the gavel comes down and they take them away in handcuffs.

It feels like I've been holding my breath all this time. That's ridiculous, I don't have lungs to hold a breath with, but that's how it feels. And now I let it out, this breath that I haven't been holding.

And now? They're done, they'll be in prison as long as they live, but what about me? Am I stuck with these two forever?

Oh.

Oh, there's the tunnel. It's like a whirlpool, an eddy, but not down. Through, it goes through. And there's the white light they all talked about, and it's so bright. I never saw anything so bright. It should hurt your eyes, but it doesn't.

It's beautiful. And, oh my God, look who's here...

I have to say it was worth the wait.

STORY NOTES

WRITING THE STORIES IS, if not necessarily easy, at least relatively simple and straightforward. The tricky part is putting them in sequence.

Well, not always. My most recent collection prior to this volume was *The Night and the Music*, comprising all the Matthew Scudder short fiction, eleven pieces in all, and it seemed obvious that they ought to appear chronologically.

But here we're dealing with a great variety of material, including not only traditional fiction but also a one-act play and a newspaper op-ed piece. For a while I struggled to find a way to make one work lead into the next, and then I remembered the sterling example of a favorite author, John O'Hara, in one of his later collections of short stories. (*Waiting for Winter*, I think it was, but maybe not.) I bought the book as soon as it came out, opened it to the table of contents, and was struck by the fact that O'Hara had let alphabetical order determine the sequence of the stories.

At the time I couldn't decide whether I was looking at a brilliant solution or an abdication of responsibility. I've since decided that the two are not mutually exclusive, and that what was good enough for the Bard of Gibbsville is good enough for me. And I have to say the sequence serves the stories well.

A Burglar's-Eye View of Greed appeared in the newspaper *Newsday* in July 2002. I believe there was some news event that prompted an editor to commission the piece, which takes the form of my interviewing Bernie Rhodenbarr, my favorite burglar. Five years later, Mark Lavendier used the text in a limited-edition broadside.

A Chance to Get Even was written after Otto Penzler requested a story for a poker anthology. He liked it but requested some changes which I didn't want to make, and for some reason we were both uncharacteristically stubborn. I took the story back, and it was published in *Ellery Queen's Mystery Magazine* in 2007.

A Vision in White is another Otto-inspired story, and another which he didn't publish. I'd written a story (*Terrible Tommy Terhune*) for his anthology, *Murder is My Racquet*, but included it in my omnibus collection, *Enough Rope*. Otto pointed out that stories for his anthology had to be previously unpublished, and so I wrote *A Vision in White*; I sent it to Otto, and he thanked me for it, but then the whole thing slipped his mind and he wound up using *Terrible Tommy Terhune* in the book after all. When I realize this, I dusted off *A Vision in White* and sent it to Janet Hutchings, who published it in *EQMM* in 2008.

Catch and Release was also written for an anthology, in this case the cross-genre *Stories*, edited by Neil Gaiman and Al Sarrantonio, published in 2010. A number of reviewers singled out the story, several praising it, and one objecting to it because she found it too troubling. Unless there's another that I'm forgetting, it's one of two stories I've written about fishing, and it's interesting (well, to me, anyway) that they've both wound up as the title stories of collections. (The other is *Sometimes They Bite*.)

Clean Slate first appeared in *Warriors*, the cross-genre anthology edited by Gardner Dozois and George R. R. Martin and published in 2010. And thereby hangs a tale.

Earlier, I'd written three stories about a then-unnamed young woman for whom the pursuit of happiness consists of picking up men, going home with them, enjoying sex with them, and then killing them. When Gardner and George requested a story about a warrior, I thought of my girl, and by the time I'd written the story I knew far more about her than I'd previously known, and realized that I was, not for the first time, writing a novel on the installment plan. The book, of course, is *Getting Off*, published in 2011 by Hard Case Crime, "by Lawrence Block writing as

Jill Emerson." *Clean Slate* is a pivotal chapter, and got further recognition as a short story in its own right when Harlan Coben selecterd it for *Best American Mystery Stories of 2011.*

Dolly's Trash and Treasures, inspired by the reality shows about hoarders, was an interesting tour de force, in that it was commissioned for a 2010 UK audiobook anthology edited by my friend Maxim Jakubowski; thus it was written specifically to be read aloud. (I'd done something like this once before; *In For a Penny* was commissioned by the BBC to be read over the radio.) *EQMM* subsequently published it in 2011.

In 1997, *EQMM* published my short story, *How Far It Could Go.* A while later a theatrical producer in Los Angeles inquired about adapting it for the stage, and I looked at it and realized it was already a stage play in prose form. I offered to adapt it myself, and did so, and nothing happened. (That's mostly what happens in the theater.) It's since been performed by an amateur company in Australia, and may be included in an evening of off-off-Broadway one-act plays, but I'm not holding my breath. I rather like *How Far* as a play, and it certainly lends itself to low-budget production— two principal characters, one simple set. I've made it eVailable for $2.99, more in the hope that someone will want to stage it than in the hope my share of the $2.99 will make me rich, and I'm pleased to include it here for whatever enjoyment it might bring you.

Mick Ballou Looks at the Blank Screen was written as the text for a 2007 Mark Lavendier broadside; in 2011 I included it in *The Night and the Music.* And you'll note that, as a happy alphabetical accident, it's followed immediately by *One Last Night at Grogan's*, which was written for *The Night and the Music* and has appeared nowhere else.

And now for something completely different. *Part of the Job* is a lost story, written in 1963-4, published (though I never knew about it) in 1967, and discovered over four decades later by the indispensable Lynn Munroe. The story that goes with it is better than the story itself, and you'll find both included here.

287

Scenarios was written for *The Dark End of the Street*, a 2010 anthology edited by S. J. Rozan and Jonathan Santlofer and featuring a mix of writers of crime and literary fiction. I suppose my story has postmodern elements to it; I had in mind all the people (you know who you are) who commit no end of crimes in the privacy of their own minds.

L. A. Noire was a commissioned anthology designed to publicize a videogame of the same name. I was dubious when John Schoenfelder proposed that I write a story for it, and then surprised myself by coming up with an idea that engaged me within two hours of our phone conversation. *See the Woman* is the resultant story.

Speaking of Greed and *Speaking of Lust* were both written to be the title novellas of a pair of Cumberland Press anthologies, which I edited in partnership with the late and much lamented Marty Greenberg; the rest of the contents consisted of reprinted stories by other writers. Both books were published in 2001. Plans called for a series of seven books in all, with an original novella for each, but we stopped at two. I had a wonderful time writing the pair, greatly enjoying the old-fashioned frame device, but when it came time to try a third one (*Speaking of Wrath*, it would have been) I discovered the tank was bone-dry.

Welcome to the Real World is another story commissioned by Otto Penzler, this one for a golf anthology called *Murder in the Rough*. Once again, it was the second story I wrote for the book; I'd included the first (*Hit the Ball, Drag Fred*) in *Enough Rope*, and wrote this as a replacement. And this time around Otto remembered to replace *Fred*, and *Welcome* wound up in the book, published in 2006.

Who Knows Where It Goes was inspired by the economic downturn. I wrote it without a destination in mind, rather a rarity in recent years, and sent it straight to Janet Hutchings at *EQMM*. The title is from the haunting song by my friend Junior Burke.

Without a Body is more a vignette than a story. It was commissioned a good ten years ago by *Esquire*; I was one of five or six writers asked to write something inspired by the Sante and Kenny Kimes murder case. (You could look it up.) A private investigator friend of mine was doing some investigative work for the defense, so I talked to her and spent a day at the trial and wrote an impressionistic piece from the victim's point of view. *Esquire* meanwhile had second thoughts, paid everybody, and returned all the stories. I quite forgot about it until it turned up on my hard drive— whereupon I sent it to *EQMM*, where I'm pleased to say it found a home in 2010.